No one keeps secrets like the dead.

He moved to kiss her again.

A part of her wanted to let him, really wanted to, but she was still offended by his thinking she'd be so willing to have a tryst with him and then marry Luca as if no one would ever be the wiser. "Don't," she said, leaning against the side of the boat. She stared into the night, seeing nothing. No movement. No lanterns. It was as if Cass and Falco were the only two people in the world.

Now it was his turn to look offended. "It can't be wrong if we both feel the same way."

Cass didn't know how she felt; that was the problem. She could feel Falco's eyes burning into the back of her neck, and resisted the desire to turn and meet his gaze. She skimmed her fingers over the water. She wondered exactly how she had found herself in this place. They passed a palazzo where yellow fire from a pair of cressets still lingered, long after a party had broken up. Cass saw her reflection ripple across the water. She hardly recognized the girl that looked up at her. Her face was thinner, paler, almost a stranger.

Then the flames flickered and the reflection shifted slightly. Cass realized she *was* staring down at a stranger. The girl's head floated to the surface of the canal, ringlets of dark hair writhing like serpents, vacant eyes staring up at Cass almost accusingly. Cass screamed as the girl's swollen torso surfaced, her neck encircled with bruises, her chest marred by a bloody X.

OTHER BOOKS YOU MAY ENJOY

Belladonna   Fiona Paul

Bloodrose   Andrea Cremer

Born Wicked   Jessica Spotswood

Crossed   Ally Condie

Gilt   Katherine Longshore

Imaginary Girls   Nova Ren Suma

The Madness Underneath   Maureen Johnson

Matched   Ally Condie

The Name of the Star   Maureen Johnson

Nightshade   Andrea Cremer

Reached   Ally Condie

The Reluctant Heiress   Eva Ibbotson

Tarnish   Katherine Longshore

Wolfsbane   Andrea Cremer

THE SECRETS OF THE ETERNAL ROSE

Venom

FIONA PAUL

speak
An Imprint of Penguin Group (USA) Inc.

In memory of **MY FATHER**

SPEAK

Published by the Penguin Group

Penguin Group (USA) Inc.

375 Hudson Street

New York, New York 10014, U.S.A.

USA / Canada / UK / Ireland / Australia / New Zealand / India / South Africa / China

Penguin Books Ltd, Registered Offices: 80 Strand, London WC2R 0RL, England

For more information about the Penguin Group visit www.penguin.com

First published in the United States of America by Philomel Books,
an imprint of Penguin Young Readers Group, 2012
Published by Speak, an imprint of Penguin Group (USA) Inc., 2013

Copyright © Paper Lantern Lit LLC, 2012

THE LIBRARY OF CONGRESS HAS CATALOGED THE PHILOMEL BOOKS EDITION AS FOLLOWS:

Paul, Fiona

Venom / Fiona Paul. p. cm. — (The secrets of the eternal rose ; bk. 1)

Summary: In Renaissance Venice, orphaned Cassandra Caravello is one of the elite but feels trapped in the city of water until she stumbles upon a murdered woman and is drawn into a dangerous world of courtesans, graverobbers, and secret societies, guided by Falco, a mysterious and alluring artist.

[1. Mystery and detective stories. 2. Social classes—Fiction. 3. Artists—Fiction. 4. Orphans—Fiction. 5. Love—Fiction. 6. Venice (Italy)—History—1508–1797—Fiction. 7. Italy—History—1559–1789—Fiction.] I. Title.

PZ7.P278345Ven2012 [Fic] —dc23   2011047154

ISBN 978-0-399-25725-4

Speak ISBN 978-0-14-242632-6

Printed in the United States of America

Edited by Jill Santopolo. Design by Amy Wu.

1 3 5 7 9 10 8 6 4 2

The publisher does not have any control over and does not assume any responsibility for author or third-party websites or their content.

ALWAYS LEARNING   PEARSON

THE SECRETS OF THE ETERNAL ROSE

Venom

"It is human nature

to fear the dead,

but it is the living

who are capable of malice,

evil, and utter destruction."

—THE BOOK OF THE ETERNAL ROSE

one

M
an falls down before the Angel of Death like a beast before the slaughterer." The priest's low voice echoed across the cavernous church. Thin shafts of sunlight cut paths through the stained-glass windows high above the altar.

Cass tugged at the neckline of her deep purple dress, wishing Siena hadn't laced her stays so tightly. The stiff undergarments pressed down on her chest; she could hardly breathe. She looked over at Madalena. Mada's expression was partially hidden beneath layers of black silk. Cass wondered if her friend was thinking the same thing she was: that the priest made it sound like this was an *execution*, not the funeral of a fourteen-year-old contessa from one of Venice's most prominent families. Madalena dabbed at her kohl-lined eyes with a handkerchief.

Cass turned her gaze back to the priest. His robes were cinched with a belt of fraying rope, and his eyes were as sharp and dark as volcanic glass. He gestured expansively with his arms as he spoke, making his cloak billow from his shoulders like a pair of wings.

In front of the priest, a flimsily wrapped bundle lay on a stone pedestal. Liviana. The young girl had spent her last few weeks in bed, coughing up blood, growing weaker and weaker. Gradually, her thin, pale figure had disappeared into her silken sheets.

Now her body—for that's all it was, Cass had to keep reminding herself—lay shrouded in white burial wrappings and covered in flower petals.

After the service, Liviana would be carried out of the church, rowed through the canals of Venice, and then transported across the lagoon to tiny San Domenico Island. There, she would be entombed in the old family crypt within the church graveyard just next to where Cass lived.

Cass had caught a glimpse as the body was being wrapped and prepared for this final journey. Dressed in a pale pink gown that emphasized Livi's porcelain skin and gaunt figure, the young blonde girl had looked more ghost than human. Livi's mother had hung a loop of amethyst stones around her neck. The color would have perfectly highlighted the contessa's light blue eyes.

Only now those eyes were closed. Forever.

Cass swallowed back a lump that rose suddenly and painfully in her throat. She had known Liviana for years—had spent many days playing in Livi's family palazzo. And yet, she'd never felt close to her, never felt they could share secrets. Liviana had been angelic, and not just in her looks. She always behaved according to expectations, always spoke in a quiet murmur, was always docile and agreeable.

And that was precisely why Cass had never understood her.

Cass tried to behave; she really did. But sometimes the urge to *do* something completely overrode her education and upbringing. She didn't *want* to break rules, but saw nothing wrong with climbing up the side of a building to get a better view of the busy Grand Canal, or running her hand across the velvety forehead of one of the Doge's horses as they paraded through the narrow streets during a festival. Impulsive, her aunt, Agnese, called her. Cass preferred to think of it as *living*.

A loud sniffling attracted Cass's attention. She looked around. Many of her friends were in attendance, clothed in mourning garb: girls in dresses dark as thunderclouds, boys in their finest velvet cloaks.

Madalena was now covering her mouth with her handkerchief. She let out another dainty sob. Mada was a year older than Cass and almost three years older than Liviana. She hadn't even really been friends with Livi, but that didn't matter. Mada felt everything intensely, and it made her all the more striking. It was as though the depth of her emotions had been written in the curve of her cheekbones and the darkness of her eyes.

Madalena's fiancé, Marco, stood to Mada's left, tracing soft circles on the small of her back with his fingertips. The tender gesture made Cass's chest tighten. She couldn't help but think of her own fiancé, Luca da Peraga—a boy she hadn't even laid eyes on in the last three years, and had never liked much as a child. She wondered if Luca would ever touch her like that. Probably not.

She gave Madalena's gloved hand a squeeze.

Mada squeezed back and whispered, "It's just . . . she's so *good*. So sweet. *Was*, I mean. I can't believe she's—"

"I know," Cass murmured. "It doesn't feel real."

Her friend was dead and she was just beginning to live. If you could call it that.

Cass knew that the grief she was feeling—the hard, sharp pain behind her breastbone—was not only for Livi's death, but for herself as well. With Liviana gone, Cass was more alone than ever. She might as well be dead; her life was spread in front of her, a series of high walls and predetermined paths, rules, and expectations, all as narrow as the canals, as stifling as a coffin.

She glanced over at her aunt, Agnese, who stood stiffly to her right. Cass had moved into Agnese's crumbling old villa five years ago, after her parents died. Her aunt had the money to maintain the estate properly, but seemed to relish the fact that the place was mimicking her own physical deterioration. Even some of the servants seemed just a tumble down the stairs away from disintegrating into dust. Plenty of people floated in and out of the villa—tutors and washerwomen, a near-constant flow of doctors and apothecaries—but no one that Cass could really *talk* to. Her lady's maid, Siena, did her best, but she was so shy and obedient that Cass felt awkward speaking to her about anything but the most superficial subjects.

Her aunt swayed dangerously, and Cass grabbed Agnese's elbow to keep her from toppling over. *No one is falling down before any angels today.* The old lady regained her balance, but Cass thought she detected a soft snuffling sound coming from beneath Agnese's veil. She leaned in toward her aunt. Agnese was snoring. She'd fallen asleep standing up! Cass bit back the wild and inappropriate urge to laugh. Good thing the maids were generous with the starch in their dresses. It was likely the only thing keeping her aunt from tumbling to the floor in a heap.

"Aunt Agnese," Cass whispered sharply.

The old woman awoke with a grunt and refocused on the service, where the priest was now talking about how death was the great equalizer of men.

As the priest droned on, Agnese's eyelids drooped again. The stiff lace collar of the old woman's dress kept her head from bobbing back on her neck, but her legs started to wobble. This time it was Siena, on Agnese's other side, who steadied her. The lady's maid flashed Cass a small smile before turning back to the ceremony.

The priest waved his wooden crucifix in front of him. "It is not only the wicked that the serpent chooses to tempt. Like Eve, the righteous may also fall victim to his trickery." His voice was reaching a crescendo. He slashed the air with the crucifix again, as if it were a weapon and he thought the devil himself might be present at the funeral. "You must *always* be mindful. Even in the waters of this city—no, *especially* in the waters of this city!—evil flows silently among us like venom. We are at its mercy."

Cass swore the priest's eyes lingered on her for a moment. She suddenly felt unsteady, as if she were standing on water instead of solid ground. Recoiling slightly, she stepped backward to maintain her balance. She was grateful when the priest motioned for the mourners to be seated.

As she gathered her skirts and settled into the wooden pew, Cass's eyes flicked around the inside of the church. Everything looked slightly off, the way it did in dreams. Darkness merged with light. Liviana's family and friends sat in orderly rows, black hats and veils obscuring their pale faces. Sunbeams ignited the brightly colored panes of stained glass, bathing the deep mahogany altar in hues of gold and green.

The first days of spring had been wet and gray as always, but today had brought a brief reprieve: outside the church, songbirds warbled and tree limbs bowed toward the ground, heavy with white blossoms. The sun filtered through a new layer of haze that had just begun to settle over the city, and the wet surfaces of walls and cobblestones almost seemed to sparkle.

It would rain again, and soon. But for now, it was like God was watching down on Liviana's service, waiting for her to ascend. It gave Cass a strange feeling of hope intermingled with a restlessness to be out, away from the ceremony, away from all the death. Her heavy dress was too hot, too tight. It was suffocating her. The funeral was suffocating her.

The idea of her whole life already decided, that was even worse— strangling.

Beads of sweat formed on the back of her neck. She needed to get out.

She blotted her eyes and scooted away from her still-dozing aunt. Sliding past Madalena, Cass tiptoed down the side aisle of the church. She made her way to the narthex and slipped quietly through one of the heavy wooden doors. Outside, a few men from Liviana's family stood stiffly in their mourning attire; they would be in charge of moving the body from the church to a gondola for the ride out to San Domenico Island.

Cass headed past them, to the corner of the cobblestone street that ran along the Grand Canal. If only she had her journal with her. She could jot down some thoughts, calm herself, see things as they really were. Cass's journal had become a necessity; she wrote in it daily, and even when she had nothing to write about, the mere feel of her quill scratching across the paper soothed her. Agnese had forbidden her to bring it today, and Cass felt almost as if she were missing a limb.

She paused in the shadow of a stately palazzo, leaning against the smooth marble wall, breathing in the familiar smells of Venice: moss and salt, the faint tinge of rotting garbage. Cass often took walks around her aunt's estate at night; being unaccompanied in the light of day felt strange and a little bit frightening—but also freeing. She probably had only a few minutes to herself before Agnese woke up and sent Siena after her.

Thick clouds were rolling in, but the spring day was still humid and hot. Cass pulled a black lacquer fan embellished with amethyst and gold leaf from the pocket of her cloak and waved it in front of her face. A piece of auburn hair fell across her eyes. She tucked the wayward strand back into her bun as she watched the people bustling past her—merchants carrying baskets of fish and vegetables, a pair of soldiers walking stiffly, the hilts of their swords clanking against their armor, a man with a long gray beard wearing a bright red cap that marked him as a Jew.

This was more of Venice than Cass usually saw. Agnese rarely permitted her to leave San Domenico anymore. Even when she had lived on the Rialto, the commercial center of Venice proper, Cass's parents had always given the gondoliers extra gold to take Cass and her lady's maid straight from doorstep to doorstep. She had never been allowed to walk along the canals or loiter in the street as she was doing now. It wasn't safe, her parents said, and of course, it wasn't proper.

Down the street, two men were shouting at each other in the alley outside a butcher shop. The argument seemed to be about a small white goat that the larger of the two men was holding. The other man kept trying to grab the goat. The poor animal bleated in fear as the men threatened to tear it in two. *Venice . . . la Serenissima. The most serene republic.* Cass knew Venice had gotten the nickname because the government preferred trade to war, but that didn't mean the place was always peaceful.

Just beyond them, a circle of boys were waving and hollering at her. They pushed and shoved one another and laughed as they beckoned. She scanned the group, looking for someone she recognized. There were four of them: unkempt hair and plain clothing marked them as commoners. One had an old fraying hat tipped at a crooked angle. The tallest of the group wore a brown suede doublet, covered in splotches of blue and green paint.

Cass felt her heartbeat quicken. *Artists.* She had always been fascinated by art, but she'd never met a real artist. So why were they acting like they knew her? The tall boy paused to take a long drink from a leather canteen. He tossed the container to one of his friends, who caught it just before it would have bounced off the damp cobblestones. A couple of peasant children hanging out of a doorway cheered and applauded. Maybe the boys were drunk and had confused her with someone else? Still, Cass raised her gloved hand in a hesitant half wave.

Too late she realized the boys weren't motioning to her at all. They were looking past her, shouting at someone behind her. She had just started to turn around when a boy slammed into her with the force of a bull.

"Accidempoli!" Cass hit the cobbled ground hard, her back landing in a dirty puddle, the palm of her left glove ripping on the rough stone street. Miraculously, she had not hit her head.

Cass felt warm breath against her chin. She had clenched her eyes shut, but opened them now to find herself pinned underneath a boy a couple of years older than she was. She could feel his body radiating heat into hers. The boy wore a thin smock spattered with paint.

Dots of blood red and bright yellow swam before Cass's eyes. She struggled to focus.

He had dark brown hair that curled under at the ends and eyes as blue as the Adriatic. His smile tilted a little to the right. It was the smile of someone who loved getting into trouble.

"*Molte scuse!*" He hopped back onto his feet. "I didn't see you at all, *bella signorina*." He bowed, then reached out a hand and yanked Cass off the ground unceremoniously. She felt a little dizzy as she stood. "Though I can't say it wasn't a pleasure running into you." Letting go of her hand, he brushed a droplet of dirty water from the side of her face. He leaned in close to murmur in her ear. "You should be more careful, you know."

Cass opened her mouth but no words came out. Again, she felt her stays crushing down on her chest. "Careful?" she managed to croak. "You're the one who knocked me over."

"I couldn't resist," he said, and he actually had the nerve to wink at her. "It's not often I get the chance to put my hands on such a beautiful woman."

Cass stared at him, speechless. Without another word, he turned away and followed the group of laughing artists into a crowded *campo*, his muscular form disappearing among merchants' sacks of cabbages and potatoes. The scene blurred a little, like a painting, and for a second Cass wondered if maybe she *had* hit her head and had imagined the whole exchange.

Liviana's uncle Pietro materialized suddenly by her side, followed by Madalena. "What were you thinking, running off by yourself?" Pietro frowned severely. "And that common street thug put his hands on you! Do you want me to go after him?"

"No, no," Cass said quickly. "It was just an accident." Still, the nerve of the boy to tell *her* to be careful. He, clearly, was the one who needed to watch where he was going.

"Your dress!" Madalena reached toward Cass, but stopped short of touching the soiled fabric. "You must be furious."

Cass looked down at her soggy gown. Even the rosary hanging from her belt had gotten dirty. Cass wiped the coral and rosewood crucifix clean in the folds of her skirt. The dress was obviously ruined, but she had always found it a bit uncomfortable, and she had plenty of others.

"You're lucky you weren't hurt," Liviana's uncle said sternly. "I hope that teaches you not to wander the streets unaccompanied again."

"Who was he?" Madalena asked in a whisper as Cass allowed her to take her arm and lead her back to the church.

"No idea." Cass realized she was trembling. Her heart thudded against the walls of her rib cage. The sting in her palm was already fading to a dull throb, but she couldn't stop thinking about the boy's devilish smile, or the feeling of his hands on her. Mostly, she couldn't shake the image of those bright blue eyes that just for a second had gazed at her so intensely, in a way no one had ever looked at her before.

"At the instant of death,

the workings of the body

grind to a halt.

The gates of the vessels fall open,

flooding the tissues with

bile and other humors.

The eyes glaze.

The flesh turns a ghastly hue."

—THE BOOK OF THE ETERNAL ROSE

The gondola moved slowly through the murky water of the canal. A warm rain began to fall, clouding the air with a pale white fog. Cass, Siena, and Agnese huddled together in the *felze*, the three-sided enclosure in the middle of the boat. With a vigorous tug, Cass flipped open the slats on the felze and peered out across the canal. She followed the path of the rain, watching the drops form tiny circles on the surface of the water. A cluster of grand reddish-brown stone buildings floated by, their black shutters pulled tight like closed eyes. Agnese leaned over and snapped the blinds closed.

Cass sighed. "I still don't see why we had to disturb everyone by leaving in the middle of the service." Her face burned as she remembered the way her aunt had grabbed hold of her and Siena and dragged them through the group of mourners, coasting from the church on a wave of concerned whispers.

"You should have thought about that before you went tramping through mud puddles." Agnese clucked her tongue. "At a funeral one must always respect the dead and one's attire. Today you showed respect for neither."

Cass frowned at the way Agnese emphasized the word *tramping*, as though it were her fault, but she kept her mouth shut. Her aunt had spent the first half of the canal ride huffing about the ruined dress, and Cass knew that further misbehavior would earn her a punishment. Maybe Agnese would force her to spend hours embroidering pillowcases for the divans or sewing shirts for the poor. Cass hated to sew, but the skill was expected—no, demanded—of her. Her aunt had also been fond of assigning extra hours with the tutors when Cass misbehaved, but since Cass had turned fifteen, her lessons had dwindled to just a couple of sessions per month. The subject matter seemed to be increasingly geared toward the skills required to run a household—more about basic math and inventory, less about the more interesting subjects like architecture and literature.

Aunt Agnese reached over and fingered a bit of the torn lace on Cass's dress before releasing it with an expression of disgust. "Really, Cass. What would Matteo think?"

Cass knew better than to answer this question. Matteo was Agnese's nephew by marriage, whom Cass had never met. When he came of age, he would inherit her aunt's estate. Agnese fretted constantly about what Matteo would think about this or that, even though the boy lived on the mainland nearly a hundred miles away. Privately, Cass believed he probably didn't think much about *anything* besides women and wine, just like every other boy his age.

Agnese grimaced as she adjusted her body on the cushioned seat, and Cass thought, as she often did, of how fragile her aunt was becoming. Agnese's face softened. "Perhaps I should cancel my trip to Abano. Maybe now isn't the best time to leave you alone. You're obviously distressed about poor, dear Liviana. And when you're distressed, you're simply impossible."

"No," Cass said quickly. Twice a year her aunt traveled to the mainland to the therapeutic salt baths at Abano. She always came back refreshed, talking about how the warm water healed her aching bones. Cass didn't want to deny her this. Plus, she always looked forward to a little time away from her aunt's watchful eye. "I won't get into any trouble. I promise."

Agnese snorted, as if everyone in the gondola knew this was highly unlikely, but she didn't argue.

Across from Agnese, Siena studied her palms, trying to appear as if she hadn't been eavesdropping, though there was really no way for her to avoid it. Her fingers were tiny, half the size of Cass's. Doll-like. Cass felt gigantic next to her. She couldn't help wishing Siena's older sister, Feliciana, was still working for her aunt. The girl had recently accepted a position with a wealthy foreigner living in the most glamorous district on the Rialto, not far from where Madalena lived. Siena was then promoted from kitchen servant to lady's maid, but Feliciana was everything Siena was not: vibrant, funny, curious. She had kept Cass entertained during endless lonely dinners and always brought in gossip from the Rialto.

Cass leaned forward. "You should have seen the boy who ran into me, Siena," she whispered. "He had eyes like yours. So blue!"

Siena nibbled on one of her impossibly tiny fingernails. "I'm just relieved that only your dress was harmed."

Cass shot a glance in her aunt's direction. "And my social standing, apparently," she whispered, just loud enough for Siena to hear.

Her lady's maid smothered a smile. Cass pressed her eyes to the slats of the felze, watching the outskirts of the city pass her by. The canals ran like veins through the body of the Rialto and then bled into a vast lagoon that separated the city from the southern islands of the republic.

Cass and her parents had lived in a popular district of the Rialto, and moving in with her aunt after her parents' death had meant relocating to San Domenico, an islet just south of the sandbar island of the Giudecca. On the Rialto, Cass had always been in the thick of things, with the glitz and glamour of Venice proper right outside her door. On San Domenico, the "town" was more a wide spot in the road, and the only things right outside her door were corpses.

Even though Cass longed for the excitement of the city, she had actually grown fond of the church graveyard that flanked Agnese's villa. It served as a refuge from her aunt's watchful eye. The place was rarely used, and the tall iron gates were shut tight most of the time. That would change today when men laid the contessa's body inside her ancient family crypt. She and Livi would be neighbors now.

Once again the lump appeared in Cass's throat, unmovable. She blinked, trying not to think of how her life would be different now that Liviana was gone. At least Cass still had Mada and her wedding to distract her. Once that was over, the only thing to occupy Cass's time would be preparations for her own wedding. And that was one thing she didn't want to think about.

Aunt Agnese's aging gardener, Giuseppe, steered the gondola around the coast of the Giudecca. The old man hummed to himself as he rowed the boat through the bluish waters of the lagoon. He seemed to thoroughly enjoy shucking off his gardening clothes and donning the blue and silver livery of the estate to play gondolier.

The Isle of Giudecca rose out of the lagoon like a sea monster that protected the southern border of Venice. Giuseppe followed the shoreline, steering the boat between the Giudecca and the island of San Giorgio Maggiore. San Giorgio's giant church had been under construction since before Cass was born. Clusters of stonemasons huddled together on wooden scaffolding, chiseling away at the façade, the only aspect that was not yet completed.

Southwest of San Giorgio Maggiore, San Domenico peeped out of the lagoon waters like a green teardrop. Only about twenty families lived on the tiny island that was named for the church that abutted her aunt's property. A thin strip of golden sand ringed the island's northern side. The rest of the place was overgrown with moss and wild grass.

As Giuseppe approached the mold-slicked dock in front of Agnese's villa, Cass stood up, mindless of the rain, and prepared to exit the gondola. She wobbled slightly in her tall chopines. After carefully lifting her soiled skirts over the side of the boat, Cass turned to wait for Siena to assist her aunt from the gondola. Once the old woman was safely on the ground, Siena unfastened a leather umbrella and lifted it above Agnese's head to help protect her from the weather.

Agnese shooed the umbrella away. "Look at me, girl. Do you really think a few drops of spring rain are going to make much of a difference?"

"*Mi dispiace*, Signora." Siena meekly tucked the umbrella under her arm.

It was Cass's turn to hide a smile as she took one of her aunt's swollen arms. She found the old woman's sharp tongue hilarious—when it wasn't directed at her. Siena moved to Agnese's other side. Agnese often required assistance walking. The trip to the Rialto had been taxing. She wheezed as she hobbled up the steps, and Cass wondered at the deep bluish circles under her eyes. The skin on her face was practically translucent.

The doctors said her aunt suffered from an imbalance of the four humors. Her body was overloaded with both blood and black bile, so they came often to the villa to perform leeching. Agnese had undergone the procedure just two nights ago, and even though it always helped her condition temporarily, Cass detested it. Seeing those slimy black sluglike monsters attached to her aunt's skin made her nauseated.

Sometimes a doctor would sniff a chamber pot full of her aunt's urine and administer foul-smelling syrupy medicines that made Agnese vomit. Cass didn't know how her aunt could stand being so ill, but she didn't want to think about what would happen if Agnese didn't make it through one of her episodes. Aunt Agnese was the only family Cass had left. If something happened to her, Cass would have to choose between joining her fiancé, Luca, in France and asking Matteo's permission to remain in the villa on San Domenico. Neither seemed an ideal option.

The villa's façade was a mix of white marble and gray stone. A wide staircase, cracked and chipping in places, led directly up to the *piano nobile*, the main living floor. Cass, Siena, and Agnese picked their way around the dusting of red clay shards that littered the bottom of the steps. The last storm had blown more tiles off the roof. Cass hoped the old place hadn't sprung any leaks.

At the top of the stairs was the *portego*, the long gala salon that ran the full length of the villa. Portegos were often used for parties and receiving rooms, though Agnese's hadn't seen much action in years. Currently the room was devoid of furniture except for two white satin divans and a small table sitting in front of a wall-sized mosaic of *The Last Supper*. A brick fireplace was built into the north wall. Cass couldn't remember the last time Agnese had ordered it to be lit.

Her aunt's harp stood in the far corner of the room, flanked by a pair of angel statues. Both angels had their marble arms outstretched, reaching toward the instrument as if they were fighting over who would get to play first. Cass had never seen her aunt go near the harp. She had asked about it once, and the old woman had muttered something about her fingers being too swollen. The look on her face had been heartbreaking, as if Cass had brought up a lost love. Neither Cass nor her aunt had ever mentioned the instrument again.

Bortolo, Agnese's butler, was seated upright, fast asleep on one of the divans. Cass wondered what aspect of old age made it possible to fall asleep in such strange positions.

The man awoke with a snuffling sound. His fingers explored the fraying cuff of his bright blue cotton doublet. "Signora Querini. Is that you?" According to some of the other servants, Bortolo had been a hardworking employee until he was struck blind by smallpox a few years ago. Now he mostly sat around the house and slept. Cass couldn't understand why her aunt kept him on. Then again, she seemed to enjoy surrounding herself with broken-down things.

"Good day, Bortolo," Agnese said crisply. The butler managed to bow without getting up from his seat. Siena and Cass assisted Agnese, a half step at a time, through the portego to her bedchamber at the back of the villa.

Cass had just entered her own room a bit later and flopped down on her velvet canopy bed when Siena knocked timidly. "Signorina, would you like to wash up? Narissa has drawn and heated a basin of water already."

Cass did feel a bit grimy from her tumble on the soggy streets. "Yes, thank you," she said.

Siena helped Cass disrobe in the small square bathroom next to her prayer alcove and then left Cass alone so that she could wash herself in private. The bathroom floor had been beautiful once, white and pink ceramic tiles laid out in the shape of a rose. Now many of the tiles were chipped or broken, becoming gravelly under Cass's bare feet.

Time and moisture had warped the long mirror in places so that parts of Cass's reflection bubbled and curled. Cass made a face when she saw the smattering of tiny brown specks across her nose and cheeks. It wasn't even summer yet, and already her freckles were beginning to emerge with a vengeance. She would have to remind Siena to carry a parasol with her at all times.

Cass dunked a soft cloth in the basin of warm water, then ran it over her arms and legs. As she wrung out the dripping cloth, she tried to clear her mind of everything. The priest's dark words. Livi's body, wrapped in white.

Funerals always made her think of her parents. They had died five years ago while away on a journey. Though her father had been a nobleman, he'd become obsessed with the trade of medicine, venturing far from the comfortable role of Venetian politics in the name of research. He'd been off "investigating" an outbreak of plague, and her mother had accompanied him.

They had planned to stay away until the spring. But something—maybe Cass's letters, begging them to return in time for Christmas—made them change their plans. They'd been on the perilous journey back to Venice, during a fiercely cold December, when they died. Cass never understood exactly what had occurred—whether her parents had contracted the illness they were studying, or something even worse. Aunt Agnese refused to discuss the details. All Cass knew was that their bodies were considered "unfit" to be returned to Venice.

Cass felt the hard pressure of tears at the backs of her eyes. She held her breath for a moment, willing away the pain in her chest. Willing the memories back.

Later that night, lying in her silk sheets, Cass tossed and turned—even with her cat's furry body nestled against her arm, which usually gave her comfort. She had found Slipper as a tiny kitten, curled up on the family tomb. After receiving word of her parents' death, Cass had made her way through the overgrown grass to the old stone crypt at the far corner of the cemetery on a regular basis for a while. She had brought roses from Agnese's garden and clipped the ivy that threatened to overtake the tomb. Even though their bodies weren't inside, Cass swore she'd been able to sense her mother's presence nearby.

After she'd discovered Slipper, the feeling faded somewhat. Cass sometimes wondered if her mother had lingered to watch over her, and then left her one final present before moving on. Cass hadn't gone out to the family tomb much since then. Now weeds blocked the crypt door and vines crawled like serpents over the roof. Cass had become a little afraid of the place.

She watched the cat's soft white belly rise and fall. Her head was still spinning with visions of Liviana's pale, wasted body, with memories of her parents. She heard the priest's ominous words, felt his gaze searing into her like hot metal.

Just then, a clanking noise from outside made Slipper perk his head up with a start. Cass turned toward the bedroom window, through which she could see the outskirts of the churchyard adjacent to Agnese's estate.

The clanking sounded again, followed by a long scratching noise, like a knife being dragged across stone. Cass slid out of bed and went to the window. Slipper bounded to the floor beside her.

The rain had let up. The full moon was enshrouded by low clouds, but in its dim light she could see the wrought-iron fence surrounding the graveyard. Behind it, the boxy outlines of crypts protruded from the high grass like crooked teeth.

Cass shivered. The graveyard looked the same as it always did, so why did it give her the chills tonight?

Liviana was there now. That had to be why.

She heard the scraping noise again, like someone trying to push back the lid of a heavy stone coffin. She couldn't help but imagine tiny Livi writhing inside the marble box that held her, struggling to break free of the burial shrouds.

Cass turned from the window. She'd heard plenty of stories about people being buried alive, of ghosts and vampires rising from graves. But she had lived beside a graveyard for years now and had never seen anything like that. More likely, the noise was caused by stray cats. San Domenico was crawling with them.

Still, her heart was hammering, and she knew she wasn't going to sleep anytime soon. Maybe she should just go down there. She often wandered the graveyard or her aunt's property at night when she was having trouble sleeping. And it would give her the chance to say good-bye.

Opening her bedroom door just a crack, Cass paused and listened for sounds within the dark villa. As usual, everything was silent. She fastened a long velvet cloak with a fur-lined collar around her shoulders, gathering it at her waist to cover her nightgown. Behind her, Slipper opened his mouth wide in a yawn before curling his tail around himself and going back to sleep, his head resting on top of one of her shoes.

Cass grabbed her leather-bound journal, a jar of ink, and her favorite quill. She often found she could do her best writing at night. Tucking the materials into the pocket of her cloak, she stole through the house, careful to skip the creaky third step as she made her way downstairs. A small steel lantern and tinderbox sat on the side table just inside the main entrance. Cass took them, and then headed outside. Shutting the massive wooden door behind her, she lit the lantern and cut across the lawn toward the graveyard.

The night wind was brisk and Cass's hair whipped around her face, stinging her eyes and cheeks. As she made her way across the wet grass, blood pounded through her veins like ocean waves beating against the shore. Cass normally liked the graveyard—it was both peaceful and a little exciting. Ironically, it made her feel alive. Funny, she thought, that it took an army of corpses to make her feel like one of the living. Agnese had once found out that Cass enjoyed writing there and declared the place improper for a lady, even during daylight hours. And somehow that made the graveyard all the more appealing.

Usually.

But tonight, Cass's head was full of ghosts. She lingered outside the fence for a moment, casting a long glance back toward the sanctuary of the villa. No, she had to see this through. It was just the funeral, the idea of Livi's wrapped body so nearby. That had to be why the whole night seemed tinged with foreboding.

The metal gate tilted on one hinge and groaned as the breeze pushed it back and forth, occasionally slamming it against the fence. No doubt this was the clanking noise she had heard from her bedroom. Cass passed through the gate and headed off to her left, where Liviana's family crypt had stood for more than a century. She picked her way across the uneven ground, moving swiftly through the tufts of tall grass, some bleached a ghostly white by the salty air.

Something snapped. A foot, crushing a dead branch. Cass spun around, her eyes picking up movement among the uneven rows of gravestones. A flapping cloak melted into the low shrubbery.

Or had she imagined it? Cass couldn't be certain. There was no reason for anyone else to be in the graveyard at this hour. Slowly, she scanned the area all around her. Headstones seemed to be tilted at strange angles. A carved angel sculpture on the top of a nearby crypt looked more like a bird of prey than a heavenly being. Bats passed over her head, fluid forms against the static blackness, coasting silently on leathery wings.

Cass shivered—she *hated* bats. The creatures overhead melted once again into the darkness, but she couldn't shake the idea that they were toying with her. Stalking her, like vampires would . . .

As soon as the thought came to her, Cass dismissed it. Madalena liked to tell tales about vampires gliding over the Grand Canal late at night, but Cass had always laughed off her friend's stories.

Now, however, they didn't seem so funny.

The light from the lantern wavered, and Cass realized her fingers were shaking. She took a deep breath to steady her hands and her heart. The exit gate seemed miles away. Cass backtracked a few steps and nearly stumbled upon a patch of dead grass, glowing white against the darkness of the night. She stopped. Turned back. She was being ridiculous. She had never been scared of the graveyard before.

Insects hummed in the shrubbery, and leaves brushed against one another, filling the air with a constant whispering sound. Cass ran her fingers across the walls of each tomb as she made her way to Liviana's crypt. The rough stone against her skin was comforting.

And then she froze. From yards away, Cass could make out the huge gray stone angel perched at the top of the monument, wings wide. But that wasn't what made her stop. Her eyes were riveted to the front of the crypt, to the thin rectangle of blackness that made it look as though the door was open.

Impossible. The tombs were always locked up tight. It was the moonlight playing tricks on her. It had to be. Cass navigated her way around a pair of underground graves. She focused her eyes on the door to Livi's tomb, expecting what she saw to be just an illusion, expecting any minute to see that the large iron door was shut and locked as it should be.

But no. There was definitely a tiny slice of darkness there. And on the ground lay a broken padlock, partly obscured in a tuft of grass. Cass paused a few feet from the tomb, torn between the desire to shut the door and flee, and sneaking inside to make sure everything was okay.

She had never been inside a crypt.

A sharp scrabbling noise made the decision for her. She backed away, nearly dropping her lantern. Suddenly, she was certain that if she dared go near, even just to close the door, a ghost would pull her inside and trap her there.

The scratching sounds continued, like fingernails on stone. Cass realized her own nails were digging deep crescent moon impressions into her palm. More scratching. Grating. Frantic. Like someone or something trying to escape.

What if Liviana really *had* been buried alive? Siena's sister, Feliciana, had once told Cass a story about a woman who was buried alive in Florence. The greedy graveyard caretaker had broken into her crypt to steal her diamond rings from her cold, dead fingers. But the rings were stuck, and when the caretaker sliced through the first finger with a rusty old machete, the woman had awakened with a shriek as if never dead.

Maybe Livi wasn't dead. Maybe the doctors had made a mistake. What if the poor girl was in there, terrified, clawing at the stone lid above her head? Those lids weighed as much as she did. There was no way she would be able to escape without help.

Holding her lantern out in front of her, and trying to control the frantic drumming of her heart, Cass shoved the crypt door open all the way to let in as much light as possible. The contessa's coffin lay at floor level, below the shelves that supported the coffins of her grandparents and ancestors. Carvings of angels and doves decorated the outside of the stone box that held Livi's body. Someone or something had disturbed the lid, just slightly. Shaking, Cass maneuvered her lantern so she could see more clearly . . . just as a huge brown rat skittered past her.

Cass squealed and jumped back. The rat disappeared into a dark corner, its naked tail leaving a serpentine trail in the dust. She leaned against the wall of the tomb, taking deep breaths, grateful that no one was around to witness her stupidity.

Ghosts. Buried alive. What a bunch of nonsense. Luca had always teased Cass about reading too many scary stories. Maybe he was right.

She turned to leave, then stopped. The least she could do was try to slide the coffin's stone cover back in place so her friend could rest without being invaded by vermin.

Cass placed her lantern on the floor and took hold of the stone lid in both hands. But as she started to pull, morbid curiosity got the best of her and she slid the heavy cover down just enough so she could peek at Liviana. Right then, the moon shucked off its veil of clouds and the light in the crypt brightened momentarily. Cass leaned in for one last look at her friend's golden hair and pale skin.

Her breath turned to ice inside her chest. The hair flowing across the satin pillow wasn't blonde—it was raven black. And the corpse— it wasn't Liviana.

Cass squeezed her eyes shut and then opened them for a second look. The girl looked a few years older than Livi and wore red makeup on her cheeks and lips. Clouded-over eyes lined in black stared vacantly up out of a face swollen from death. A circle of purple-black bruises ringed the girl's slender neck. Cass reached out with one finger to touch a heart-shaped birthmark on the girl's left temple. Her skin was firm and cold.

Cass knew she should turn around and run, but she couldn't look away from the bloated corpse. Her eyes trailed downward. The girl's satin underdress, fit to scoop low over her breasts and peek out over her stays, had been slashed to ribbons.

And there was an X carved over her heart.

Cass's stomach twisted violently and bile flooded her throat. She stumbled back from the casket and out of the crypt, whimpering. She ran on the uneven ground, grass whipping her legs and branches snatching at her cloak like tiny hands trying to pull her backward.

She wasn't alone. She could almost feel breath on the back of her neck, the heat of a murderer tracking her through the graveyard.

She ran so fast, she could barely breathe. Her heart and lungs felt like they had lodged in her throat. The narrow spikes of the wrought-iron gate appeared in front of her. Safety was just a few seconds away.

Then a shadowy figure unfolded from behind a tall obelisk and Cass tripped. Her toes slammed against a half-buried headstone and she started to fall. Hands reached out for her. The moon illuminated a pair of glowering eyes and a face streaked with blood.

Tumbling straight into the figure's arms, Cass screamed.

"Certain living things prefer the dark,

thriving in the shadows of

tombstones and crypts,

flowering amidst the dead.

Others tend toward the sun,

blooming in the light,

embracing its warmth."

—THE BOOK OF THE ETERNAL ROSE

three

No need to split my eardrums. I'm not going to hurt you."

Something familiar about the boy's lilting tone made Cass stop screaming and flailing in his grip. She looked up just slightly, into his face. Even by the dim light of the moon, she recognized his dazzling blue eyes. "You," she breathed.

"Mourning girl?" The boy laughed, and steadied her on her feet. "So nice to run into you again."

She wrenched away from his grasp, pulling her cloak tight around her body. "What are you doing here?"

The boy shrugged his broad shoulders. "I was just standing here enjoying the view when you almost ran me over."

"The view?" Her voice rang out shrilly. "In a graveyard? At this hour?" Her fear began to give way to irritation. He was clearly lying to her.

The boy gestured around him. In the dark, a group of flowering weeds looked like a giant hairy spider crouched against the side of a crypt. "These flowers actually grow best in cemeteries. Did you know that? Something about the mix of soil and shade. Death and life, intertwined. One feeding off the other. It's kind of magical, don't you think?" He seemed distracted for a moment, like he really was fascinated by their surroundings. Just as Cass was about to respond, he turned to her again. "Plus the company here is much more agreeable than at *la taverna*. And much less likely to talk my ear off."

Cass felt dizzy. She took one more step back. "What's on your face?" she demanded, pointing at his right cheekbone.

"What?" He licked a finger and wiped haphazardly at the area Cass had indicated. His hand came away smudged with red. "Oh. Paint, probably. It gets all over everything." His lips twitched as if he were trying not to smile. "It's a wonder you aren't the one being mourned, as accident prone as you seem to be."

"I hardly think you jumping on me earlier qualifies me as accident prone." She was surprised by how quickly the response came to her.

"Oh, if I had jumped on you, you'd know it," he said with a wink. He reached toward Cass to dislodge a twig from her hair. "I'm Falco, by the way."

Cass narrowed her eyes. Now, since he was obviously laughing at her, she found his mischievous grin annoying. Still, it didn't seem to be the deranged smile of a murderer. But her heart wouldn't stop pounding, and when she thought about the mutilated body just steps away from them, inside Liviana's crypt, her stomach surged. Cass glanced around. She couldn't shake the feeling that they weren't alone.

"What are *you* doing here, Signorina . . . ?" He trailed off, waiting for her to provide her name.

"Caravello. Cassandra," she said distractedly, her mind consumed by shadows, by faceless corpses and killers hiding in the dark.

"Cassandra," he repeated, as though her name pleased him. "So. Did I interrupt something? A sordid little tryst, perhaps?"

"You must be joking." Cass was in no mood for humor. Besides, the closest she'd ever been to a tryst was when he'd fallen on top of her in the street earlier that day.

"Always. Sadly, you don't seem like the type of girl who would be up for a midnight . . . encounter." Falco's eyes drifted downward. "Too bad."

Cass realized her cloak had fallen open, exposing the white nightgown she wore underneath. She pulled the velvet fabric tight around her body. Then the shrubbery rippled once more with unfamiliar movement. Cass's heart froze.

"We should get out of here," she said. "It's not safe."

"Not safe?" Falco raised an eyebrow. "Why? Because it's dark and you might accidentally trip over your own two feet? I feel quite safe. In fact, I was just settling in to do some reading."

Cass furrowed her brow. "Reading?"

Falco wagged her journal in front of her. "This is yours, I presume." A slow smile spread across his face. "Let's find out exactly what you've been doing, shall we?"

"Give it back!" Cass reached for the journal, but Falco easily dodged her. He opened the leather-bound book to a random page and cleared his throat. Clutching a hand to his chest, he pretended to read aloud in a high-pitched voice. "Oh, how I love the way his fingers explore my soft flesh. The way his eyes see into my very soul."

This time, Cass managed to snatch the book out of his hands. "That is *not* what it says."

"I guess that means you won't be keeping me warm tonight?"

Falco quirked an eyebrow. Before she could muster up a response, he laughed. "Then again, the accommodations probably wouldn't meet your standards. You've probably never slept on anything but the finest satins, have you?"

Cass hoped the darkness camouflaged her scarlet cheeks. Who was this boy to talk to her the way he did? "Is that why you're here? Looking for a date?" Cass gestured toward a row of pointed headstones. "I do believe you're in luck. I see some ladies who won't be able to refuse you." The words flew out of her mouth before she could rethink them.

"Funny. And correct. Sort of. I was actually just looking for a place to get a little rest." For a second, the smile dropped from his face, and an expression passed across it that Cass couldn't identify.

"Sleep in a graveyard?" Cass frowned. "You can't be serious." Again Cass felt certain he was lying to her. Could he have had something to do with the body stashed in the contessa's family tomb? Cass didn't think so. He was a bit too relaxed for having just killed a woman. Behind him, in the darkness, Cass again thought she saw movement. Her breath caught in her throat, but it was just one of the stray cats, darting out in front of a crypt.

If Falco noticed her look of alarm, he didn't comment on it. "Why not? Normally it's quiet," he said, grinning at Cass. "No wild women running about. My roommate and I were drinking at Il Mar e la Spada and got into a fight as usual. Tonight I decided to avoid the inevitable thrashing." He coughed. "His, not mine."

Il Mar e la Spada. San Domenico's finest—and only—taverna. Cass had never been inside the decrepit old place.

"Come on," Falco said. "I'll see you safely home to your fancy sheets. I'd say you need your beauty sleep, but it looks like you've been getting plenty." He took Cass's hand in one of his own, his warm touch like a bolt of lightning, causing her to jump.

Cass wrenched her hand out of his. "I'm not going home. I'm going to the town guard."

Falco's blue eyes went cold at the mention of soldiers. "Why would you waste your time talking to those degenerates? They're worse than the criminals themselves."

"I've discovered a dead body." Hearing the words brought back the true gravity of the situation, and panic shot through her all over again. She hugged her arms across her body to keep from trembling.

Falco laughed tersely. He made a sweeping motion with his hand. "Of course you have, my dear. We are literally surrounded by the dead."

Cass tossed her hair back from her face. "Don't treat me like I'm stupid," she said coldly. "When you knocked me down today, I had come from a funeral. My *friend's* funeral. I just went to her tomb and her body is gone, replaced by another, a girl I've never seen before." Again, the confidence in her tone surprised her. It was the kind of thing she might have thought in her head or written in her journal, but would never have spoken aloud.

"That makes no sense," Falco said gently.

Cass bristled at his tone of voice. "Exactly. That's why I'm going to the guard."

"Perhaps you imagined her to be someone else? Grief does strange things . . ." For a second, Falco's eyes softened, as though he were looking at something far away. Then he shook his head. "Or maybe she just looks different to you now. My master often paints the dead as they're being prepared for burial. You know, the body changes as it cools."

Was he accusing her of hallucinating? Of being crazy? Her mouth tightened into a thin line. "Does it go from blonde to brunette?" she asked. Her voice still had an unfamiliar, sharp edge to it.

"Maybe the light played a trick on you. Maybe you were in the wrong crypt?" he persisted.

Cass hesitated. Could it be? Could the light have made Liviana's hair look dark? No. Why would Livi have an X carved over her heart? But could Cass have wandered into the wrong crypt? Many of the tombs were decorated with stone angels.

"I'll show you," she said, unsure of whether she was hoping to prove him wrong or to be proven wrong by him. The graveyard had been her haven ever since moving to San Domenico. She couldn't imagine having to relinquish it to a corpse-mutilating monster.

Falco consented silently, and gestured for her to lead the way. Cass led Falco back to Liviana's family crypt, where the door still stood partially ajar. She pointed at the raised letters that formed a semicircle over the door. "Greco—her family name. This *is* the right crypt."

"You stand watch," he said. "I'll make sure no walking dead girls have invaded your little friend's tomb." Falco moved through the open doorway, humming to himself. His cheerful mood had returned. "Look, someone even left me a lantern. I might have to avail myself of these lodgings the next time I need a place to stay. Oh, and even a trinket. I think propriety dictates that it is I who should be buying gifts for you at this stage in our—"

Then his voice cut off.

A second later, Falco practically exploded out of the tomb, blue eyes burning in the moonlight. "Tell me what you saw tonight," he demanded. "Tell me everything."

Cass's heart once again began to batter itself against her rib cage as she looked at Falco's pale face. He was breathing hard. Something was very, very wrong.

"Nothing really," she insisted, and all the fear came rushing back. "I thought I saw a cloak flapping in the bushes. But the moon was dim and it may have been a raven, or nothing." Cass swallowed past the sawdust that seemed to be coating her throat. "Do—do you know her?"

Falco shook his head. "She looks like a courtesan. Young. New to the trade, probably."

A courtesan. Of course. As a child growing up on the Rialto, Cass had been fascinated by the city's glamorous women who gave favors to men in exchange for clothes and jewels and other payment. She had often seen them hanging out of windows along the main canals, waving coyly and flashing just the slightest hint of nipple to attract wealthy patrons, but she had never actually known one. They had always seemed both perfectly normal and strangely exotic, like vividly colored birds.

Falco's eyes flitted quickly between the crypts and the bushes and the path back to the gate. "We need to get moving. I wish you'd never shown me this. Whoever killed her might have seen us go in here. He might be looking for us. He might be looking *at* us, right this second."

He might be looking at me, Cass thought. But no, Falco couldn't be a murderer. Not with that smile. Besides, if he were the murderer, Cass would already be dead. Right? She thought back to the flapping cloak, the movement she had sensed in the shrubbery. She glanced out into the dark. There were a million places for a killer to hide, and there was only one way out.

"Let's go," she said.

Falco grabbed her hand, and this time she allowed it. The rounded gravestones blurred like gray ghosts against the black night as they ran. Cass and Falco paused outside the gate, gasping for breath.

"So you'll come with me?" Cass asked. "To see the guard?"

Falco shook his head violently, his longish brown hair flapping from side to side, as he continued toward Agnese's estate. "No, we can't tell the guard about this. Go home. Forget what you saw."

"What?" Cass stopped walking. "But that's outrageous. A girl's been murdered. And a body's gone missing. A contessa's body." Cass wasn't sure if she was more disturbed by the body she'd found, or the fact that Livi's seemed to have completely disappeared. "The guard can go to the Rialto and tell the *rettori*. The councilmen look into crimes such as this. They could send an *avogadore* to investigate."

Falco spun around to face her again. "Who is she? You don't know. Who killed her? You don't know. Even if the guard stopped drinking and playing dice long enough to row over to tell the rettori, I doubt the magistrate will be concerned. They only care about crimes that upset the merchants or that scare away tourists. They won't care about a robbed tomb out here on San Domenico, or about the murder of an unknown courtesan."

"Maybe you're afraid they'll think *you* killed her." Cass lifted her chin, forcing herself to meet Falco's eyes, searching them for signs of evil. She saw none. And yet, there had to be a reason he was so opposed to reporting a murder.

Falco folded his arms. "And what will they think about you, trolling the graveyard, unchaperoned, with a stranger? A commoner, no less. What will your parents say when the soldiers drag you home? Won't they be shocked to find out what late-night company their lovely daughter has been keeping?"

"My parents are dead," Cass said simply. She didn't say it to make him feel guilty. It just came out of her mouth instinctively. She'd probably said it a hundred times, so often that the words themselves felt dead to her, meaningless.

Falco softened. "Your guardians, then. They won't believe that we weren't . . ." He trailed off. "It'll be the talk of the city by daybreak." He reached out and stroked her hair. "Fun thought, though, eh? A girl like you with me?"

His soft touch made Cass warm and cold at the same time. He was right. Aunt Agnese would lock Cass inside the villa if she found out where Cass had spent the evening. And if she found out Cass was consorting with a commoner? Well, that would be very bad, possibly exiled-to-a-nunnery-in-Spain bad. If Cass did anything to mess up her engagement to Luca, it would bring shame on her family name. Agnese's nephew Matteo would probably toss Cass and her aunt out on the street as soon as he came of age. Agnese would never forgive her.

Falco's hand dropped from her hair to her shoulder, and Cass instinctively stepped away from him.

"You're right," she admitted. She cast a glance through the tangled branches at the old villa beyond. "My aunt would kill me, or worse, never let me leave the house again."

"And the guard would use this as one more reason to harass my friends and me," Falco said. "They'd like nothing better than to run us all out of town." His voice was soothing, coaxing. "It's terrible, what happened, but there's nothing we can do."

Cass looked back toward the graveyard, biting her lip. She wondered how Falco knew so much about courtesans and murderers and the town guard.

"Come on." Falco reached out for her hand again. "You shouldn't be out at this hour, and dressed in so little." This time, he did not appear to be teasing her. He kept his fingers twined through hers until they crossed the wet grass to where her aunt's property started. "I assume this is you?" He pointed at Agnese's crumbling villa, so old that in the night it almost looked like an extension of the ancient church that sat adjacent to it.

"My aunt's, yes," Cass said.

Just then, two earth-rattling gongs split the sky. The noise came from nearby San Giorgio Maggiore, from the bell tower of the giant church. It was ringing to call the nuns and monks to matins, their early morning prayers. Cass put a hand to her chest again. Her heart felt ready to pound its way right through her ribs.

Falco turned in the direction of San Giorgio, even though the larger island was cloaked in fog and darkness. He rubbed at a spot beneath his right eye. "That late already? I'm sorry, Cass. I've got to go."

"Where could you possibly have to go at two o'clock in the morning?" she asked.

"Business." His tone was light.

"Urgent middle-of-the-night artist business?" She arched one of her eyebrows.

Falco grinned. "What can I say? My life is never dull."

The breeze blew his dark hair back from his face, and Cass found herself once again staring into his brilliant blue eyes. She hadn't realized they were almost the same height. "Will I see you again?"

Falco's lopsided smile lit up the dark. "Perhaps," he said. And then he was gone, loping off in the direction of the shoreline, and then fading into the stillness and darkness of the night.

Cass crept quietly back into the house, thankful that at least she hadn't awakened any of the servants. There were some benefits, at least, to the fact that most of Aunt Agnese's staff were ancient, blind, deaf, or some combination of the three.

She crawled beneath her covers, curling around Slipper, who was fast asleep in the exact center of the bed. The night seemed like a dream. Had she really found a mysterious dead body? And Falco: he could not be any more infuriating. And offensive.

And exciting.

Cass's eyelids fluttered shut and she was with Falco again, walking across a field of flowers. The boy plucked one and tucked it behind her left ear. A white lily. Cass breathed in the aromatic scent. Almost overpowering. Intoxicating. His lips fell on her's, soft, then harder. So hard she was having trouble finding her breath. Falco laid her on the ground, and Cass realized that all the flowers were white lilies. White lilies piled on top of a coffin.

Drops of red splashed on the petals. Cass gasped, but then saw it was paint, not blood. Scarlet teardrops falling from a brush Falco held poised above her. Two quick brushstrokes left a red X, emblazoned across her chest. And then Cass couldn't breathe at all.

She sat up so quickly that Slipper tumbled off the bed with a mew of surprise. Cass was almost afraid to look down at her chest. She felt the fabric of her nightgown with her hands, relieved to find it clean, unviolated. Under her fingers, her heart pounded in double time. She lay back in her bed, listening to the frantic drumbeats coming from within. Beneath the slickness of her sheets, her body burned, almost feverish, filled with a longing that she didn't understand.

"The sensation of drowning
may be likened to that
of swallowing acid.
As fluid fills the lungs,
displacing the last pockets of air,
the whole chest burns as if
suffused with scorching fire."

—THE BOOK OF THE ETERNAL ROSE

four

"Signorina Cassandra! *Sveglia!* Wake up!"

Cass opened her eyes and yawned. Siena was patting her on the shoulder. The maid looked frantic. "What is it, Siena?" Cass asked. "Why on earth are you hitting me?"

Siena's normally perfect porcelain skin was blotchy. "You have to hurry."

Cass noticed a spot of dirt on the sleeve of her nightgown, no doubt a souvenir from the previous night's misadventures. She pulled her covers up to hide it. "Is it Aunt Agnese? Has she fallen ill?"

"No. It's Madalena. You were supposed to be at her palazzo an hour ago." Siena paced back and forth in front of Cass's canopy bed. "I was sewing. I thought you were awake. I should have—"

Cass glanced at the red lacquer wall clock. The gold-leaf hands both pointed upward. "*Mannaggia.*" She slid out of bed, wincing at the coldness of the hardwood floor beneath her bare feet. She examined her reflection in the mirror. Tangled hair, bluish circles under her eyes. Her hand went to her chest as she remembered the weird dream.

"You look feverish," Siena said. "Are you feeling well?"

"I feel fine," Cass said, a little too loudly. She began struggling out of her nightgown. "Please get me a dress and shoes."

"Which dress would you—"

"*Any* dress." Cass regretted her tone immediately. Sometimes she couldn't stand the way Siena stared at her, like a wounded dog. She missed Feliciana, who would have retorted back, at least.

Siena scampered off to the giant oaken armoire and returned with a burgundy dress, suede slippers, and a pair of wooden platform shoes embellished with red leather flowers. Cass hated her chopines—all five pairs. Platform shoes were useful when it came to protecting her slippers and hemlines, but she was already taller than many of the boys her age, and the extra height made her feel like a giraffe. Still, Agnese insisted she wear them.

"Does my aunt know I'm late?" Cass asked, sliding into the dress and hurriedly trying to work the laces despite Siena's already flying fingers.

Siena shook her head, her tight blonde braid swinging from side to side. "No, Signorina. She's in her room, resting."

"Well then, let's go before she finds out." Cass grabbed her belt and a hat from the edge of her washing table. There was no time to put up her hair today, a process that sometimes took more than an hour. With her chopines dangling from one hand, she thundered down the spiral staircase, taking the last three steps in an unladylike jump.

Siena followed behind her at a more appropriate pace. "One second, Signorina." Siena disappeared back into the butler's pantry and returned with Cass's *cadena*, a carved rosewood box embossed with gold corners. Inside was Cass's personal silverware, though Cass suspected she might arrive too late to use it.

Cass saw Siena's eyes linger on a long ivory envelope placed on a side table just inside the arched door. Cass recognized the slanted, impeccably neat handwriting. It was a letter from Luca. Cass hadn't seen her fiancé since his father's funeral three years ago, just before he left Venice to study law at the renowned Université Montpellier in the South of France, but it didn't seem like the time away had done much to change him from the dull, conventional boy she remembered from her youth.

"Shall I bring it . . . ?" Siena reached for the letter.

"It can wait," Cass said. No doubt it was some boring missive about his latest lessons.

The two girls headed outside and down the crumbling villa steps. Cass slipped into her chopines before heading across the wet front lawn. The air was less hazy around San Domenico, and Siena handed Cass a white parasol to protect her from the sun. Several young boys dressed in gray chemises and wide-brimmed hats were kneeling on the front lawn, cutting back the grass with rusty shears. Cass looked around for the gardener. She had expected Giuseppe to be waiting in the gondola for them, but no boat bobbed at the edge of the moldy old dock. "Where's the gondola?" she asked.

"Giuseppe must have taken it to the city for supplies," Siena said, frowning as if *she* were the one late for an engagement. "He probably thought one of the other servants had taken you to the Rialto earlier. We'll have to find a ride in town."

They started along the narrow path that skirted the thin strip of sand and led to San Domenico village. Halfway there, a dead fish, its eyes swollen and milky, washed up in the surf at Cass's feet. She yelped, immediately recalling the courtesan's discolored body from last night. She swallowed hard, willing the image away. But she could not stop herself from nervously scanning the road.

Behind them, a lone man in a black cloak was walking. He turned away when Cass looked at him, pulling his wide-brimmed hat low to hide his face.

"Signorina Cass?" Siena, a few steps ahead, turned back to look at her questioningly.

"A dead fish," Cass croaked. She cleared her throat. "I almost stepped on it."

Siena switched sides with Cass to put her farther away from the lapping waves. The maid nodded delicately. "So, how is Signor da Peraga?" she asked. "Will he be returning for a visit anytime soon?"

"I don't think so," Cass said, trying to ignore the feel of the strange man's eyes on her back. "Luca's very busy with his studies. That's practically all he ever writes about."

"It must be years since you've seen him," Siena ventured timidly. She waved her hand in front of her face to dissipate a cloud of gnats that had appeared from nowhere. "How lonely you must get. That's a very long time."

"I haven't been keeping track," Cass said shortly. She wished that Siena would walk faster. She was certain the strange man would catch up to them any second. She swore she could hear his footsteps in the sand, two for every one of her own. She resisted the urge to turn around again. When she reached the edge of town and glanced casually over her shoulder, she was surprised to see that the path was deserted. The man in the cloak was gone.

In Cass's opinion, the center of San Domenico didn't even qualify as a village—just a small, sad collection of shops and the single taverna. The servants went there occasionally to shop, though Agnese preferred that they cross the lagoon to Venice proper, where the selection and quality of everything was much greater. As Siena guided Cass past Il Mar e la Spada, Cass's eyes were drawn to the wooden emblem of a sword slicing an ocean wave that hung crookedly over the door. A sour odor emanated from the place; she couldn't imagine spending any time there.

The girls made their way around to the back of a bakery, to a small dock where one could usually find a boat or two for hire.

They were in luck. Though none of the usual fishermen's sons were waiting for a fare, a gondolier sat idle in his long black boat. He must have just brought someone over from the city.

"*Bellas signorinas,*" he greeted them, reaching out a hand to help Cass and then Siena into the craft.

As she stepped carefully inside the gondola's stamped leather interior, Cass felt a little guilty about leaving Luca's letter behind. She could have at least taken it to read. Madalena was always telling Cass she should count herself lucky to have an intelligent and reliable fiancé like Luca. Cass's dowry, consisting mainly of gold Agnese had squirreled away for the occasion, was acceptable, but it wasn't exactly anything to brag about. Despite being of the artisan class, Mada's father had been able to offer Marco much more. Maybe Madalena was right. Maybe Cass should be happy she wasn't being married off to a toothless old shopkeeper.

The day was brilliant, with a blue sky—for the moment. Spring in Venice was volatile, unpredictable. Cass and Siena closed their parasols and tucked themselves inside the privacy of the felze, away from the bright sun. Cass leaned back in her seat and breathed deeply.

Siena handed her a fan made of ivory and ostrich feathers. Cass waved it in front of her face. Her stays felt extra tight as usual.

Siena looked concerned. "Are you sure you're all right?"

Cass didn't answer immediately. *Was* she all right? Last night seemed like a dream. The graveyard. The mysterious mutilated body in Liviana's place. Falco. Could it all have been real? She rubbed her eyes as questions spun through her mind, making her dizzy. What had the murderer done with her friend's body—why move one to hide another? Why the gruesome X carved across the girl's heart? Where was Livi now?

It wasn't a dream; it was a nightmare. For a moment, Cass imagined the red gashes carved into her own skin. Her chest started to hurt.

"Signorina?" Siena was staring at her now.

"I'm fine," Cass said sharply. And then, with a tight smile: "A bad night's sleep. That's all." She had to hold herself together until she had a chance to consider everything rationally. Again, she wished she had her journal. If she could list out everything that had happened, examine the facts coolly, then maybe the previous night's events would make more sense. Maybe she'd see something that she had missed in the moment. If she blurted everything out to Siena, the maid would no doubt run to tell Agnese that she'd been gallivanting around the graveyard. No, Cass had to keep this a secret, at least until she knew more. She'd return to the graveyard tonight, she decided. She'd look for more clues. She'd look everywhere for signs of Livi's stolen body.

But for now, she had to forget about it, as Falco had counseled her to do. Desperate for any type of distraction, she raised the shade on the felze so that she and Siena could observe as the gondolier passed between the Giudecca and San Giorgio Maggiore Island.

"Cass," Siena protested, "you know how your aunt dislikes the whole world staring at you."

Cass pulled her hat off just long enough to shake out her thick wavy hair and then tuck it back under her bonnet. "They're not staring at me, Siena. They're too busy living."

Siena shook her head but didn't say more. The two girls watched as the gondola neared the main island of Venice. As usual, and despite the sunshine, the Rialto was encased in mist; moisture clung to its buildings like a fine lacy veil. They passed by the docks that ran along the back of the Palazzo Ducale, home to the Doge of Venice. A pair of flat-bottomed *peàtas* were tied up here, and coarse-looking men walked up and down gangplanks, unloading crates and barrels. Cass blushed at the language they were using. She rarely heard such foul words, but then she had never paid much attention to commoners before. Maybe everyone in the working class spoke crudely. Falco had practically invited her to spend the night with him.

She remembered the way his eyes had worked their way over her whole body, like he could see straight through her clothing. She felt her face growing hotter and turned quickly away from Siena. Cass was going to throw herself into the Grand Canal if the girl inquired about her health one more time.

The brackish water below their gondola rolled back and forth, a yellow froth floating on the surface. She had almost jumped in the canals once, when she was nine. She and Liviana had been running through the streets ahead of their maidservants. Cass had crossed a rickety stone bridge by balancing on one of the handrails. She'd dared Liviana to do the same. The younger girl had gamely clambered up onto the railing with Cass's help, but just then the servants looked up and started yelling. Poor Livi had toppled off the edge, right into the canal. When her head emerged from the water, she'd looked so distraught that Cass decided to jump in next to her as a show of solidarity. But Cass's maidservant had seized her as she was slipping out of her shoes, leaving Liviana to bob in the muddy water by herself.

Cass had never forgotten the lecture they had received. The canal water was dirty, filthy, foul, disgusting, filled with God knows what kind of sicknesses. Livi didn't become ill until years later, but Cass still wondered sometimes if she was partially at fault for her friend's failing health.

She missed her.

The gondolier hummed as he navigated the gondola into the Grand Canal. Cass focused on the commotion along the banks. Children ran in circles at the edges of the canal while peasant women in plain brown dresses scurried along alleyways, shouting to their neighbors or emptying chamber pots into the water. Cass wished she had thought to bring along a sachet of herbs. Though the sun was less intense here, the dense blocks of buildings trapped in the heat and magnified the stench of the canals.

They drifted by palazzo after palazzo, each more magnificent than the one before. Cass admired the grand marble balconies and the gleaming golden façades of the Ca' d'Oro, one of Venice's most ornate palazzos, owned by the famous Contarini family. Several Venetian Doges had come from the Contarini bloodline. Down a side canal, Cass saw a group of boys clustered on the banks, feet dangling over the walls. Their heads were bowed over scraps of parchment. They had to be artists. Cass squinted but didn't see Falco among them. He was probably still asleep after his late-night "business."

The gondolier slowed to a stop in front of Madalena's home, bumping against the stone shoreline. He tossed a loop of rope over a green and gold mooring post. Madalena lived in one of the bigger palazzos on the Rialto, right on the Grand Canal and within walking distance of the famous Piazza San Marco. The palazzo's façade was made of intricately carved white marble. A series of crosses decorated the top of the building and a bas-relief of roses encircled each arched window. Giant yellow banners with the Rambaldo family crest—a black bear holding the leash of a green dragon—flanked both sides of the main entrance.

Cass paid the man and let him help her and Siena from the boat. Then Cass knocked on the arched door. She was surprised when Madalena answered it herself.

People often told Cass that she and Mada looked like sisters. They did have the same long dark hair and heart-shaped faces, though Cass's hair was redder than Mada's. Sometimes Cass could see the resemblance, but not today. Madalena wore a beautiful red silk dress with fine gray lace at the edges of the neck and sleeves. Her skin was luminous, hazel eyes shining; her smile radiated heat. Cass felt drab, like a shadow, next to her glowing friend.

"Cass!" Madalena threw her arms around Cass's neck as though it had been months since they'd seen each other instead of just a day. Cass breathed in the scent of Mada's lilac perfume and instantly felt better. All of the dark thoughts and fantasies that had troubled her since last night seemed to dissipate.

"Have you taken to answering your own door?" Cass teased. "Or have you given all your servants leave for the day?" She couldn't help but stare at her friend's scarlet gown. The fabric was a stunning contrast to her ivory skin and dark hair. Dye that red could have come only from the belly of the kermes beetle, which made it some of the most expensive fabric Venice had to offer.

"I was looking for the butler to ask if you had sent a message saying you weren't coming. But then I saw you through the window and just couldn't wait another second," Madalena announced with a laugh. "You're so late! We've already eaten and everything."

"Sorry, I—I lost track of time," Cass said, leaning against the grand marble entryway. If Cass confessed to sleeping this late, her friend would demand an explanation, and Cass wasn't ready to tell her about Falco or the body they had found. Mada would worry, and a worried Mada was a talkative Mada.

Madalena waved off the apology with a slender hand. Her fingernails were long and perfectly rounded at the tips. "I'll forgive you *only* if you help me make my wedding absolutely perfect."

"Just the fact that you and Marco will be there practically attached lip to lip will make it perfect," Cass teased. As Mada laughed, the remaining tension ebbed out of Cass. The whole day seemed brighter, the haze thinner, with Madalena around—or maybe lack of sleep had made Cass giddy.

"Signorina," Siena suddenly interrupted, "I'll be heading to the market to get some things for your aunt. I'll come back for you later?"

"Sure, Siena." Cass waved at her maid, more than a little relieved to see her go, and turned to follow Madalena up the stairs from the canal into the gorgeous house. Bowls of cut flowers sat on pedestals at the top of the stairs, perfuming the whole palazzo with the smell of lavender and roses.

Cass loved coming to Mada's house. The layout was almost exactly the same as the home where she'd grown up. She couldn't resist running a hand across the back of a green velvet divan as they cut through the cavernous portego. She could almost see her mother sitting there, a medical book tucked between her hands, while her father paced back and forth in front of the fireplace, deep in thought. Cass trailed behind Madalena, gazing at the vaulted ceilings, the intricately carved furniture, the oil paintings and enormous tapestries that covered each wall. She'd been in her friend's palazzo probably a hundred times, and she always felt more at home here than she did at Agnese's.

A tall man with shoulder-length blond hair stood at the far side of the portego, just in front of a framed military uniform worn by one of Madalena's ancestors. He swung a green and black velvet cloak with brilliant gold embroidery over his shoulders. "I'll be back later, Signorina Rambaldo," he said with a slight bow. His voice had a touch of an accent. Cass couldn't quite place it.

Madalena smiled sunnily. "Have a wonderful day, Cristian." Almost as an afterthought she touched the man's arm as he turned to leave. "This is my friend Cassandra Caravello. Cass, this is Cristian de Lambert. He's been doing some work for my father. And he's been a great help to me, as well. You know this wedding has been making me crazy."

Cristian's dark brown eyes met Cass's briefly. "Pleased to meet you," he said, dipping into another bow. He seemed to linger for a moment, staring at Cass, as if wanting to say more.

"Be careful," Cass said with a smile. "Assisting Mada with her wedding might turn into a full-time job."

Cristian smiled slightly. "Yes. Well, it's the least I can do, given her father's generosity toward me." He fiddled with one of the gold braided tassels that adorned his cloak. His face and arms were tan. Cass wondered what sort of work he did that required him to spend so much time outside. "I hope you two have a nice visit," he said, crossing the long portego in what seemed like just a few strides. The tail of his cloak billowed behind him as he headed down the stairs to the street level.

"So he works for your father? I'm surprised I've never met him before," Cass said.

"Cristian worked for one of Father's friends, but he was injured and lost his position while he was convalescing," Madalena said. "My father has given him some work to do here at the estate. Helping get the invoices for the business reconciled or some such." She paused for a moment. "I believe he also does some work for Signor Dubois."

Signor Dubois was the Frenchman who had spirited away Cass's former lady's maid. Cass wondered if Cristian had ever met Feliciana. As a member of the merchant class, he was still well above interacting with servants, but if anyone could get a man's attention, it was Siena's beautiful older sister.

Cass and Mada exited down a set of stairs and descended into a lush courtyard garden—open to the air, but surrounded by walls on all sides—and headed to a small table, protected from the sun by an overhanging marble ledge adorned with carved cherubs. Someone had draped the tabletop with a green and gold cloth. A leather-bound book sat open; the feathered edge of a quill protruded from a small pot of ink.

Madalena gathered her dress around her before sitting down.

Cass's eyes lingered on the tight bodice and the wide farthingale Mada wore to support her skirts. They made her friend look slim and curvy at the same time.

A servant dressed in the green and gold livery that designated Madalena's estate brought goblets of red wine and a plate of bits of meat and bread left from dinner. She returned with a second platter containing flaky pastries drizzled with honey.

Cass twirled the stem of her beautiful blown-glass goblet. Swirling mermaids twisted their way up the delicate stem. No doubt the piece was from nearby Murano, the glassblowing capital of the world. She felt a small pang of envy. Her friend was surrounded by glamour, by beauty. Life was so different here from how it was out on San Domenico.

As Mada began prattling happily about her upcoming marriage to Marco, Cass couldn't help thinking of her own wedding, which Aunt Agnese had already begun to speak of whenever she and Cass had a moment alone. If the old woman had her way, the ceremony would no doubt be as grim and proper as the funeral yesterday.

"I meant what I said before, you know," Cass said. "All you need is you and Marco."

Madalena laughed. "Me. Marco. Hundreds of guests. An unforgettable dress. A fantastic cake. Music. Flowers. Stunning jewelry." She drummed her manicured nails on the table. "Speaking of which, I notice your neck is conspicuously bare today."

Cass thought back to the rush in which Siena had dressed her. Leave it to Madalena to notice everyone's jewelry, or lack thereof. "Nothing caught my eye."

Mada nodded. "You should ask Agnese for some new pendants. Yours are all years old, aren't they?" Without waiting for a response, she pulled the quill from the pot of ink and began adding to the list of things written in the book. "Let's see. There's the crystal wineglasses, and the water clock in the entrance hall. Oh, and I want the napkin set embroidered with dolphins. Mother made those."

"What are you doing?" Cass asked, her eyes following Madalena's quill as it scratched its way across the page.

"Selecting my trousseau. Father said I could take anything I wanted to Marco's villa."

Madalena's mother had passed away giving birth to Mada's younger brother, who died weeks later from a series of fevers. Mada had been only around ten years old at the time. Ever since then, her father had prided himself on spoiling his only child.

"I can't believe you're getting married in only a couple of weeks," Cass said. She felt a quick flash of sorrow—now that Livi was gone, once Mada was busy tending to Marco, Cass really would be alone. But she managed to smile.

Madalena pouted. "If it weren't for Father's business dealings, we'd have been married months ago. It took him forever to recoup his losses from the wars."

Cass didn't know much about the seemingly never-ending wars with the Ottomans. It was all over land much farther down the coast, mostly out in the Mediterranean Sea. Maybe it wasn't so bad to live on insignificant San Domenico, a little piece of property no other country seemed intent on taking over. Why would they?

Madalena's mouth quirked into a half smile. "Did I tell you about what happened last week with Marco?"

Cass shook her head.

"Well," Mada began coyly, leaning in close to Cass and speaking quietly, "Father was out of town, you know, on business. But still, I can't just have Marco over to the house, because one of the servants will tattle on me, guaranteed."

"So what did you do?" Cass played with a strand of hair that had escaped from her bonnet.

Madalena lowered her voice even more. "I didn't do anything. It was all Marco. He climbed the ivy vines from the canal to my window. I'm lucky he didn't fall and drown." She smiled dreamily. "I woke up in the middle of the night. I don't know why. I just did. And Marco was sitting next to my bed, watching me sleep." Madalena giggled. "At first I was mad at him for scaring me."

Cass couldn't keep her jaw from dropping a little. She tried to imagine a boy sneaking into her own room to watch her sleep. Immediately, it was the face of the artist Falco she saw. Bright blue eyes. Crooked smile. She struggled to push his image from her mind. "And then?"

Mada paused just long enough to allow the suspense to build. "And then he sat down next to me and took me in his arms. And we kissed until sunrise."

"Madalena Rambaldo! In your father's house?" Cass made a pretend-scandalized face.

Madalena giggled again. "Marco snuck back out—through the house, thankfully—just before first light, when the servants begin to go about their chores. A few minutes later and he might have gotten caught."

At that moment, the gardener, a stern-faced old man, appeared around a column in the courtyard with a large pot of water in his arms. Ignoring the girls, he began to water the rosebushes, which were still awaiting their first buds. Madalena and Cass bent their heads close together and laughed.

"Let's just say last week's confession was interesting," Madalena finished. "I think I made the priest blush."

Cass took a sip of her wine, savoring its sweetness. She wondered what it would feel like to kiss someone all night. Falco's face materialized in her head again and she felt her cheeks redden.

Cass had the sudden urge to tell Madalena everything, right now—the body, the artist, the killer lurking somewhere in the darkness. How the fear, and the thrill of it, and the something-else-she-couldn't-quite-say all jumbled together in her chest. The secret was too big. She was going to burst if she didn't share it with someone.

But just then Madalena said, "On my wedding day . . . you'll be there all day, to make sure everything goes as planned, won't you?"

If Cass hadn't known better, she would've sworn her friend was nervous. "Of course. Anything you need."

Madalena leapt up and kissed Cass on the cheek. "You're the best. Of all my friends, you're the most reliable, you know? It's no wonder your parents paired you up with Luca da Peraga. You two are perfect for each other."

"You mean because we're both boring?" Cass asked, getting up from her chair and wandering over to the Venus fountain in the center of the garden. As Cass dipped her hand beneath the cool spray, her eyes were drawn toward the goddess's full breasts, covered only by locks of long, flowing hair. Around the edge of the fountain, other Greek figures were depicted, frolicking in various state of undress.

Madalena followed her. She ran one of her hands along the fountain's edge. Then she laughed and splashed a handful of water at Cass. "Because you both always do the right thing."

Cass dodged the flying droplets and looked away from her friend.

She didn't know why the words made her defensive, like a child being humored by a parent. If only Madalena knew what Cass had been doing. Running around the graveyard with a peasant. Not reporting a dead body. Not reporting the disappearance of their friend's body! Oblivious to the tension in Cass's face, Madalena grabbed Cass's hand. "You seem even quieter than usual today," she commented. "Are you upset about Livi?"

Cass imagined the whole story spilling out of her while Mada's eyes grew wider and wider, her mouth dropping open in surprise. *Because you both always do the right thing.*

But no. She couldn't say a word. Madalena would panic. She'd think Cass was ill or insane or possessed by demons. Even if Cass swore her to secrecy, Mada would end up telling her father. And Madalena's father would tell Agnese. Cass struggled to come up with an answer. "I'm not sure what's wrong with me," she said. "I guess I am feeling a little . . . sad."

Madalena patted her hand. "I know what you need. And he's blond and sort of bookish, with kissable lips. How long until Luca is back in town?"

Cass thought again of her fiancé's letter, sealed up tight. "Not sure," she said, returning to the table. Once again, Mada followed. Cass traced the fleur-de-lis pattern in the tablecloth to avoid having to look at her friend. She had never vocalized to anyone her doubts about the planned marriage, and she certainly had never confessed to wanting out. "It's different with us than it is with you and Marco."

"Why do you say that?" Madalena tilted her head to the side and stared at Cass with her wide-set eyes.

Cass thought again of Falco. "It just is. We don't know each other very well." She again looked down at the tablecloth. The repeating pattern soothed her for some reason. "How did you know that Marco loved you?" She bit her lip as soon as the words left her mouth, afraid that Madalena would tease her for being hopelessly immature.

"I could tell by the way he looked at me, by the way he found little reasons to touch me." Mada blushed a little. "You know what Mother used to tell me? She used to tell me that if you want to know how a boy feels, you should drop your handkerchief in front of him. If he gives it back to you right away, he's just being polite, but if he keeps it for a little while, then he's yours."

"Drop it on purpose?" Cass watched a pair of songbirds chase each other around the naked rosebushes. They sparred with sharp beaks, releasing a trail of brown feathers into the wind. One of the birds escaped, fluttered off a few feet, and then landed again, almost as if it wanted to be chased.

"What's this about, Cass?" Madalena watched her narrowly. "Are you having doubts about Luca?"

Yes. Cass's eyes followed the antics of the birds.

"Quit worrying," Mada said. "He's as steady as a rock, your Luca."

Thoughts, as heavy and turbulent as ocean waves, coursed through Cass's head. Madalena was right. Luca *was* a rock. And he wasn't the only one. Aunt Agnese was a rock. Life on San Domenico Island was a rock. Sometimes Cass wished she could throw herself into the lagoon, feel the cool water on her skin as she swam away to freedom. But she couldn't swim. She was weighted down, drowning; her whole life was pulling her under.

"Fire is a Janus, both harmful
and healing. It obliterates buildings and
incinerates flesh but also cleanses
implements and cauterizes wounds."

—THE BOOK OF THE ETERNAL ROSE

When Cass was ready to leave, she fetched Siena from the kitchen, where the girl was chatting with Mada's lady's maid, Eva, and some of her other friends who worked for the Rambaldo estate. Laden down with paper-wrapped packages, Siena headed out to the canal to find passage back to San Domenico. Getting from the little island to the city was never a problem; the boats there were happy for the fare, but sometimes a way back was more difficult to negotiate. Thankfully, Siena located a young gondolier who was willing to make the journey. His rough hand squeezed Cass's tightly as he helped her into the boat. Siena stacked her purchases carefully in the front of the gondola and then settled into the felze with Cass.

"Did you buy the whole market?" Cass teased her.

Siena smiled brightly. "Just some herbs and potions for your aunt, a bolt of cloth to make new aprons, and some spices for Cook." She lowered her voice. "Oh, and a sample of that drink the Spanish are so fond of. Coffee." Siena sniffed one of the wrapped parcels. "Cook thought maybe now that the Pope has decreed it an acceptable beverage, your aunt might like to try it."

Cass didn't understand how Siena could get so excited about doing Agnese's shopping. She reclined on a plush velvet-covered pillow and listened to the gentle lapping of the canal water as it rolled up against the walls of some of Venice's biggest palazzos. Tiny waves sloshed back and forth, exposing semicircle patterns of mold on sand-colored stones. Through the haze, Cass could see the sun hanging low in the sky, staining the horizon a bronze color.

The gondola floated toward the Rialto Bridge. A group of peasant children with dirty faces and ragged clothing hung over the side, watching the boats float by. Some of the older kids lay on their stomachs, dangling low over the edge of the bridge between the railing posts, stretching out their hands in attempts to shake hands with the fishermen and gondoliers. Most of the men ignored them. Cass's gondolier reached up high to slap the hands of a few of the tallest kids. They grinned and shouted.

As Cass watched the kids, a plump brown and white chicken scampered past the gondola, half flying, half skimming across the surface of the Grand Canal. The gondolier swore loudly. Cass poked her head completely out of the felze and let out a cry of surprise. About twenty yards past the Rialto Bridge, a giant flat-bottomed boat that had once held produce and live chickens was floating on its side. Behind it, a line of gondolas and fishing boats were trapped, with no way to navigate around the capsized craft.

Peasants gathered at the bank of the canal to watch the show, a few of them venturing carefully down the access ramps into the water to steal a runaway chicken or a floating sack of cabbage and potatoes.

Cass watched as a pair of lanky boys corralled a chicken and pinned it down in front of a round-faced woman holding an ax. Cass tensed as the ax whistled down in an arc and landed on the bird's neck. A fine river of blood flowed down onto the stone.

The evening air was now a crescendo of shouting and swearing. Cass turned around. The Grand Canal was jammed up with boats all the way back to Madalena's palazzo. Cass saw a messenger boy with a canvas sack of letters making his way down the canal, hopping from gondola to gondola. Passengers cursed at him and gondoliers threatened him with their oars, but he was undeterred. Cass was shocked when he stopped at their gondola, balancing on its prow, dodging the gondolier nimbly.

"What are you—?" Cass cried out, but he interrupted her.

"For you," he said, pressing a folded piece of parchment into her hand. Then he darted off, leaving Cass openmouthed with surprise.

She peeked into the folded note and her hands began to shake. The short message was scrawled in crooked letters.

Soon, bella, it will be your turn.

Her breath caught in her throat. The Grand Canal blurred in front of her for a second, and she feared she might faint right into the water. She saw the messenger make his way across the stalled gondolas and over to the south bank of the canal. "Wait," she called after him, but he melted into a throng of street vendors without looking back.

"Is it news of Luca?" Siena asked.

Blood pounded in Cass's head. "No," she said. She looked down at the parchment again. The note was signed with only a bloody X. Cass touched her finger to the X, half expecting the red lines to cut into her like a blade.

"You look like you've seen a ghost." Siena was still looking at Cass searchingly.

"I'm fine," Cass insisted. She folded the note into smaller and smaller squares until it disappeared into her right palm. She clenched her hand tightly around the folded paper.

Could the murderer have seen her last night? He must have. That was the only explanation. And if he had seen her, he had seen Falco too. They were both in danger.

Unless Falco . . . But no. Impossible. If *he* was dangerous, if he was the murderer, he could have easily killed her last night.

"Was—was the note from a man?" Siena asked. "Someone you know well . . . ?" She trailed off, her lily-white skin reddening at the unspoken implication.

"No," Cass said sharply. "Whatever would give you that idea?"

"Well, you do go out late at night sometimes." The maid fumbled over her words.

Cass sighed. Everyone thought she was off trysting in the grave-yard. "I go out to write in my journal, Siena."

"I'm sorry, Signorina. I meant no disrespect. I just know it must be hard to have Signor da Peraga so far away."

Cass didn't answer. She scanned the crowded canal, looking for anyone or anything unusual. Next to her, three young women were dangling their bare feet over the side of their gondola. They wore their hair in braids twisted up on the top of their heads like horns, and their swanlike necks were ringed with pendants and chokers. Each of the girls held large fans made of peacock feathers and embellished with gilded edges. Courtesans, perhaps? The women laughed and waved to passersby. So vibrant, so alive. So different from the broken, lifeless body Cass had found the night before.

On the bank, a tall man in a black cloak weaved in and out of the crowds that had gathered alongside the canal to watch the chaos. Cass tensed up. Was it the same man from San Domenico? She wasn't sure. The sun had set and Cass couldn't make out his face. He turned away as her gondola floated by, melting into the darkness like fading smoke. Cass felt her breathing accelerate. Usually, she found the frantic activity of Venice magical, but suddenly everything felt ominous and evil, as if God had abandoned the city to the forces of chaos. She snapped the blinds closed and sat back in the felze with her arms wrapped tightly around herself.

But even hidden inside the little cabin, Cass suddenly felt dangerously exposed, as though strangers' eyes were burning through the slats of the felze and into her skin. Hot breath swirled around her like mist off the canals. Oars hissed their way through the water. The greenish waves of the lagoon writhed as though filled with venomous snakes. Even the wood of the boat looked malevolent—warped and rickety, as if they might capsize before they made it home.

Later on, in her room, Cass still found it impossible to relax. Her shutters rattled against her window, making her think strangers were knocking at the door. Each time the house creaked, she searched her room again, positive the murderer was under her bed or in her armoire or crouched below her washing table, waiting for her to go to sleep.

Cass grabbed her journal and sprawled out across her bed. Writing usually calmed her. Not tonight. She stared at the blank page, her knuckles whitening as her hand gripped the quill tighter and tighter. She squeezed her eyes shut. She was frozen. Locked up. Imprisoned. When she opened her eyes, she saw that she had managed to scrawl something on the ivory parchment—a repeating series of Xs slashed across the page. She slammed the book closed in disgust.

It was hopeless. She couldn't stop thinking about the note, and Livi's missing corpse. She couldn't just sit there. She had to go back to the graveyard. Maybe she could find a clue, some hint of what had happened to Liviana's body.

Cass twisted her hair back and pinned it up with a tortoiseshell hair clip. She grabbed the note from the top drawer of her dressing table—where she had been keeping it locked up, as though it might fly out and bite her—and stole quietly down the stairs. She went to grab the lantern off the side table and then remembered she'd left it in Liviana's tomb. She headed into the kitchen to get another lantern and saw Siena's cloak hanging on a polished brass hook beside the pantry. She wrapped the rough woolen garment around her nightgown. She'd draw less attention in a servant's cloak than her own. Now that there might be a murderer lurking, she would take no chances.

As she passed back through the room, she noticed a small knife on the far counter. The cook must have forgotten to put it away. She tucked the knife into the pocket of Siena's cloak.

Moving quietly through the house, Cass stepped out into the night without even glancing at Luca's still-sealed letter. Once outside, she lit the lantern and headed straight for the graveyard.

The wind off the water was brisk, and the smell of salt stung the inside of Cass's nose. Passing over the rough, uneven ground, Cass slipped through the creaky gate and gazed around, wondering where to start investigating. There had to be some clue about what had happened to Livi's body, if she just knew where to look. She headed back toward the Greco family tomb, but stopped halfway there. She wasn't moving toward Liviana anymore. No, that crypt now belonged to another, to a stranger. Cass felt herself pulled away, drawn toward the section of the graveyard closest to the old chapel, where there were more underground graves than tombs.

She let her intuition guide her. The combination of the warm day and cool night wind had brought on a thick mist, and she couldn't see more than a few feet in front of her. The gravestones disappeared and reappeared in her line of vision like faceless ghosts.

Someone or something disturbed the haze close to her. Cass froze. She squinted through the swirling fog. "Who is it?" she cried out. No answer. "Is someone there?" Her voice sounded thin and terrified. "Show yourself!"

A sleek black cat materialized from the mist. It glowered at Cass with yellow eyes, and then crossed in front of her before dissolving back into the fog. Cass took a couple of deep breaths. Her eyes began adjusting to the gloom as she crept past rows of headstones, pausing at one that lay flat on the ground, cracked in half. Cass felt a chill run through her. Anyone, or anything, could be hiding nearby.

Anyone, or anything, could be hunting her.

Cass swept a hand out in front of her, trying to clear the haze. She held her lantern high. A branch snapped. She spun around, her heart thudding in her ears. The path behind her seemed less foggy than what lay in front. She could almost make out the jagged tips of the iron fence that separated Agnese's property from the land of the dead. Just as she decided to turn back and give up, the mist parted, and she saw him.

Falco. He sat cross-legged on the damp ground, his hair blowing in the breeze. He was facing away from her, focused on the gravestone in front of him, a beautiful piece of gray marble carved into the shape of a cross with a pair of doves perched on the top. A dim lantern flickered next to him on the ground.

Cass moved as close to him as she dared, stepping as quietly as she could. She couldn't make out the picture taking shape on his parchment. Falco's hand moved swiftly, laying down a series of sharp strokes on the paper. Fascinated, Cass took another step closer. Her left foot snapped a dry twig.

Falco's head whirled around so quickly that Cass stepped back, startled, as the boy sprang to his feet. His blue eyes looked almost black in the moonlight. *Hot. Angry. Violent.* The words flared up in Cass's mind.

"Oh, it's you." Immediately his eyes returned to normal. He smiled his lopsided grin. "I'm beginning to wonder if you're following me." The way he said it suggested it wouldn't necessarily be a bad thing.

Cass pulled the crumpled note out of her pocket. Wordlessly, she handed it to Falco.

She watched him read it over several times, his mouth settling into a fine white line.

"Where did you get this?" he asked, rubbing at a spot beneath his right eye.

"A messenger delivered it to me in the canals."

"He followed you into the city?" Falco studied the note again and then, without warning, he leaned down and thrust it into his lantern's flame.

"What are you doing?" Cass tried to pull the smoldering

parchment from the flame, but her thumb landed on a hot ember and she jerked away. The paper fell to the ground, where it continued to burn until it was nothing but ashes. "That might have been a clue!"

"For whom? We already determined there's nobody to tell," Falco said, his voice low and harsh.

"But it's obvious he's coming for me." Cass felt her lip trembling and bit back the tears. She refused to cry in front of this boy. "And I still don't know what happened to Liviana's body. Her family would be devastated to know it's disappeared."

"Forget the body," Falco said. "She's dead. You're alive. If you want to stay that way, I suggest pretending none of this ever happened. Whatever the murderer's motives, he'll have no need to kill you unless you give him cause." Falco's voice was light, but it still sounded like a threat.

Cass shivered as she looked around at the gravestones and the monuments. So many dark shadows a murderer could fit inside. "I will not just *forget* the body of a friend—a contessa, I might point out—that vanished into the night. And it's easy for you to say he won't hurt us. No one's left *you* any deranged love notes." She turned to head back to the villa.

Falco grabbed her shoulder. "Hold on," he said.

His strength surprised Cass. She tucked her right hand inside her cloak pocket, and her fingers closed around the handle of the small knife. "Let me go," she said, "or I'll scream."

Falco released her. "Please, not that again. My head still hurts from last time." He flashed a half smile. "Look, I understand why you're scared. And I understand why you think you'll feel better if you go to the guard, but they won't help you."

"So your plan is just for me to stay here with my aunt and wait to be murdered? You do realize you'll probably be next on the list, don't you?"

"Yes, yes," Falco said wryly. "I'm not thrilled about the idea of being stalked by a killer, either."

"We could go to Piazza San Marco," Cass said slowly, "and put a letter in the *bocca di lione*." The lion sculpture stood just outside the Palazzo Ducale, its mouth open wide to accept anonymous tips and accusations.

"We could." Falco nodded. "But I've always thought that box was watched, if not by rettori, then by prying eyes." Falco tucked the drawing he'd been working on into the pocket of his cloak and leaned back against a tall grave marker topped with a cross. His dark brown hair curled around his face, making him look like an angel in a painting. Cass stood directly in front of him, acutely aware of the fact that they were almost eye to eye. And lip to lip, she realized, tilting her body slightly backward at the thought.

"What if," Falco continued slowly, as though he were only just piecing together the idea, "you and I do a bit of investigating on our own?" His eyes lit up as he spoke.

Cass took a step back. She felt her breathing slow and her head clear a little. Even the mist seemed to thin. "The two of us? Together?" Cass tucked an unruly strand of hair back into her bun.

Falco reached up and yanked the tortoiseshell clip out of her hair, letting the tangled waves fall around her face. "Could be fun, don't you think?"

A hot flame coursed through Cass's blood. She looked away from Falco, hurriedly retwisting her hair up on top of her head. She turned back just in time to see his sketch fall from his pocket and, picked up by the wind, go tumbling end over end across the grass. "Your drawing!" Her lantern fell to the ground, the candle flame blowing out as she ran after the flying parchment and tackled it.

"So fierce," Falco murmured, holding out a hand to help Cass to her feet. "I'm beginning to enjoy picking you up off the ground."

Cass looked down at the paper in her hand, which had unrolled during its journey across the grass. The moonlight illuminated what he had drawn: a gorgeous reproduction of the gravestone with the doves on top. Cass flipped the parchment over. On the other side, Falco had sketched the rough outline of a woman's body.

Cass's breath caught; she couldn't tear her eyes away from the figure. She marveled at the sharpness of the knees and elbows, at the soft roundness of the figure's breasts. The face was still a heart-shaped blank, but the hair looked familiar: it fell in thick, lustrous waves like Cass's own.

Falco laughed, leaning in close to Cass. "It almost looks like you're blushing. Why? It's not like you've never seen a woman's body before."

"You've obviously seen more than I have," Cass said sharply. Her fingers trembled as she handed the parchment back to Falco, trying to look everywhere but at the drawing, wishing he hadn't seen her staring at it. *Who is she?* She wanted to ask, but the words held fast to her lips.

"If I have, it's a shame." Even in the dark, his eyes were flashing. "If I had your body, I'd stare at it for hours. Days, maybe."

Cass sucked in a sharp breath. "You can't just say things like that. It's not, it's not—"

"Proper?" Falco finished. "Perhaps. I didn't mean it to be

offensive. A woman's body is a beautiful thing." He took ahold of Cass's hand and twisted it from side to side, opening and closing her fingers. "The human form, it's a symphony. Tiny interlocking movements that join together in song." He slid his hands down over her knuckles until he was gripping the very tips of her fingers. "You play a more delicate tune than I do. Have you never noticed?"

Cass stared at her own hand. She tried to visualize the structures beneath her skin—the bones and muscles, the strange ropelike things connecting the two. It was hard to focus. Falco's touch was so warm. "I'm not in the habit of staring at myself," she said, pulling away. "It's vain."

Falco shook his head. "How terrible it must be to be a member of the noble class. So many rules. Such restraint. You must feel like a caged bird, battering its wings against the sides of its golden prison."

Cass didn't say anything for a second. That was exactly how she felt, and he had put it into words better than she had ever been able to do. She repeated the sentence in her mind, intending to write it in her journal when she returned home. But even though it was true, she didn't want to admit to Falco that he was right. "I'm no one's pet," she insisted.

"You're not?" Falco raised an eyebrow. The way he was looking at her made Cass feel out of breath. He tucked the bit of parchment into the pocket of her cloak. "Keep it," he said. "You can hang it in your cage." Then he turned as if to go.

"I mean it!" Cass cried out. "I'm not like all the others." She realized she was squeezing her hands into fists.

"Is that so?" Falco turned back toward her, and all of the air went out of Cass's chest. They were separated by half an inch of space. She was hot all over, as though someone had lit a fire under her skin. Falco stared at her so intensely, she felt she could fall into his eyes, into the swirling mists she saw reflected there.

"Yes," she whispered.

His lips quirked into a small smile. "Prove it," he said.

"Religion would have us believe that immortality is reserved for the gods. We remain skeptical."

—THE BOOK OF THE ETERNAL ROSE

Cass studied Falco's face in the darkness as he pulled away from her again. Breeze whipped through his hair and he looked completely wild.

"Prove it? How?" Cass asked, suddenly feeling wild too.

"Come with me to look for clues," Falco said.

Cass searched his face for signs that he was joking, but found none. "N-now?" she stuttered. "Isn't this your general business hour?"

Falco did not reply. Instead, he headed toward the graveyard gate. He paused to allow her to catch up. "Are you with me or not?"

So many thoughts flew through Cass's brain at once that she couldn't latch on to a single one of them. "But—but we don't have any idea where to begin," she said.

Falco pulled something from the pocket of his cloak. "Wrong. We have this." A strange ring sat on his palm, a smooth red stone set in sturdy silver. "I found it in your friend's tomb."

So that was what Falco had meant when he mentioned a trinket the previous night. She had forgotten all about it in her haste to escape the graveyard. Cass lifted the ring from his hand. A strange symbol was engraved in the center of the red stone: A six-petaled flower, inscribed in a circle. She had never seen Liviana wear anything like it. "Why didn't you mention this before?" she asked sharply.

Falco's eyes glinted in the dark. "*Mi dispiace*, Signorina. I got a bit distracted by the body of a murdered woman."

"This isn't Liviana's. It's far too big, and it isn't her style." Cass handed the ring back to Falco. "So maybe it belongs to the dead girl. Maybe it belongs to the murderer. How does that help us?"

Falco slipped the ring back into his pocket. "I've seen this symbol before. Traced in charcoal on a building, abandoned as far as I can tell. Maybe it's a hideout for a murderer."

Before Cass could respond, Falco started walking again, passing through the rusted iron gate and skirting the edge of her aunt's property. Cass hurried to catch up with him. Though he was only a few paces in front of her, the thick folds of mist nearly obscured his form.

"Where are you taking me?" she asked, then realized she had just given him tacit permission *to* take her somewhere. She pulled Siena's cloak tighter around her thin nightgown and added quickly, "I haven't even agreed to go anywhere with you."

"And yet here you are, stumbling alongside me like we're in a race." Falco's voice had a lilting, laughing quality to it, despite the fact that they were surrounded by ghostly white clouds, in the middle of a pitch-dark night. Then he said, "The city. The building is in a run-down block of the Castello district."

"The city?" Cass repeated. She realized they were nearing her aunt's moldy old dock. Her shoes sank slightly into the damp ground.

She could hear the whispering of gentle waves as they coursed up against the rotting wood. Cass looked north, across the lagoon, toward where she knew Venice proper lay. Madalena had talked of stabbings and brawls that occurred in the streets at night. Cass could only imagine what sort of creatures prowled the dark. Thieves, murderers . . . vampires. Could Falco protect her? *Would* Falco protect her?

She remembered the way his eyes had blazed when she found him in the cemetery. Violent one moment, joking the next. The wind blew her cloak against her hip, and she felt the weight of the small knife in her right pocket. She was glad to have it.

"Well, it's too late to go anywhere now," she said, trying to keep the relief from her voice.

"No it isn't," Falco said, gesturing toward Agnese's gondola, bobbing in the shallow water. "Come on."

"But I'm not even dressed!" Cass protested.

Falco snickered. "You're dressed enough. What? Do you need to run home and have your servant lace you into a proper gown before you can go sneaking around in the night?" He crossed his arms in front of his chest. "Or are you just scared?"

"You're not afraid at all?" she asked, lifting her chin and deliberately avoiding his question. "My friend swears the city is crawling with evil spirits at night."

"I don't believe in that superstitious nonsense," Falco said.

Cass looked around them at the hanging mist. If she squinted, she swore she could see faces swirling in it. When she was younger, she had often walked along the shore and imagined the mist was full of the spirits of people who had died at sea and now floated the shores to greet other souls who suffered their same fate.

"You don't believe there are evil spirits lingering here on earth? Forbidden to enter the kingdom of heaven?" Cass asked.

Falco shrugged. "Heaven. Hell. Just more superstitions. Superstitions that cause people to behave with ignorance and stupidity."

Cass stared at him, certain he was joking, but his expression remained neutral. "But . . . but then where do you think spirits go?"

"I don't know where spirits go, but I know what happens to bodies. They rot. It's that simple. It almost seems ludicrous to lock them up or bury them in dirt." Falco began to fade away into the fog as he headed for the edge of the dock.

Cass reached out for him. Her hand landed on the center of his back. She could feel ridges beneath her palm. Muscle and bone. "What would you have us do?" she asked. "Burn them?"

The ridges moved beneath Cass's palm as Falco shrugged again. "There's got to be a better answer," he said, turning back to face her. "Maybe we should be studying them. Learning. After all, death and life are just two phases of the natural order of things. It seems silly to embrace birth and fear death."

Cass was so surprised, she could hardly speak. "Studying? As in . . . *dissecting*? Mutilating? That's sacrilegious."

"Science is my religion," Falco said. "I care about facts, not fleeting beliefs with no grounding in the real world. Everything can be answered through science." He stretched his arms over his head and yawned. "Your problem is that you do believe in all of that nonsense. And that's why you're scared."

"I'm not scared," she insisted, but even she wasn't convinced by the thin protestation.

"Yes, you are, or you wouldn't be asking all these questions. You're stalling."

Falco bent down and started untying the gondola's rigging. His hands worked through the ropes easily, as if this were a trick he'd performed many times before. "Hop aboard before I let it go completely loose."

Cass swore she saw him wink at her through the gloom. "My aunt will positively murder me if she finds out I took her gondola without asking." *In the middle of the night. With a strange boy.*

"Oh, don't get your laces all in a knot. We're just going to borrow it. We can have it back before your precious auntie realizes it's missing."

Cass stood by the dock, staring at the sleek gondola. The early morning was cool, but the blood racing through her veins kept her warm. As long as Falco was certain they could return before anyone found out . . .

Falco knelt in the middle of the boat, one hand held out in Cass's direction, the other poised to release the gondola from the dock with a quick tug of the rope.

"I understand if you don't want to come. So many rules to break." Falco's voice still had that lilting quality to it, but his eyes were serious. "It is safer in the cage, isn't it?"

It *was* safer. If her parents had stayed in Venice instead of plunging themselves into plague-afflicted foreign cities, they might still be alive. They had wandered outside the little circle of safety and expectations, and had paid the ultimate price.

But Cass didn't want to stay in the circle. She wanted to *live*.

Besides, if there really *was* a murderer out there, and he had his eye on Cass, what was the point in sitting around waiting for him to come to her?

Cass glanced back over her shoulder. The hanging mist reminded her of Liviana's burial wrappings. It beckoned like a white death. Suddenly, Cass felt certain that if she turned back toward Agnese's villa by herself, the haze would devour her and her body would be torn to shreds.

She took a step toward the gondola. "I want to go."

Falco grinned. "I knew you would."

Cass paused, her hand on the side of the boat. She looked up at Falco. "Why is that?"

This time, he definitely winked. "Not every girl likes to wander through graveyards in the middle of the night."

"I guess I'm not every girl," Cass said, allowing him to take her hand and gently assist her into the gondola.

An indecipherable look flashed across Falco's tan face for just a second. Then he smiled. "No, Signorina," he said. "You are definitely not. You're different, and I like it."

Cass couldn't help but think that Falco, with his teasing manner and bizarre beliefs about life and death, was also quite different.

And she, too, liked it.

"In dissection, the body is
cut open and studied after death,
whereas vivisection is performed
upon the still-living subject.
Each can provide useful knowledge."

—THE BOOK OF THE ETERNAL ROSE

Falco loosened the final rope with a flourish and the gondola floated free of the dock. He laughed when Cass instinctively took her usual spot, tucked back inside the felze. Then he went to the rear of the boat and began to use the long flexible oar to steer toward the Giudecca, the sandbar island that separated San Domenico from the more populated islands of Venice.

Cass felt a bit foolish. She slid out of the felze and went to stand beside Falco as he moved the boat through the water. Fog swirled around the gondola.

"Don't expose yourself to the elements on my account," Falco said with a crooked smile. "I don't mind playing gondolier for you."

"Is it difficult?" Cass asked. "To steer the boat?" Though she'd ridden in a boat almost every single day since her birth, she had never paid any attention to the mechanics of it.

"It's not so bad," he said. The wind blew a shock of dark hair into his eyes and Cass had the sudden urge to reach out and rearrange it. "Takes a little strength. Want to try?"

Cass was surprised to hear herself saying yes. She secured the cloak tightly around her waist and pushed her hair back from her face. The boat wobbled as she stepped onto the tiny platform beside Falco, and she gasped.

"You have to move with the rhythm of the water," he explained.

The platform was tiny, really only enough space for one person, so Falco had to press his body against Cass's back. His forearms fit neatly across her hip bones; she could feel his soft hair brushing against her cheek. He exhaled, a warm breath that tickled her neck and sent a shiver through her. She stiffened and nearly lost her balance. Falco tightened his grip on her momentarily until she regained her footing. His body radiated heat through her cloak.

Falco gave her the oar and put his hands on her waist to steady her. Cass awkwardly thrust the oar through the murky water and the boat skewed off at a funny angle. She felt herself wobbling, but Falco moved one hand from her waist to the oar and helped her guide it through the water. Cass began to relax her body against Falco's.

She laughed, in spite of the mist and the night and their destination. Steering the boat was fun, and she was doing something that probably no other woman in all of Venice had ever done. After a few minutes, she got the hang of steering and the long wooden gondola started to move swiftly through the water. Falco offered to take over, but she persisted, despite the aching in her arms and shoulders.

"I'm impressed," Falco said. "You're a natural."

Cass was grateful that he was standing behind her, so he couldn't see her smile. She didn't want him to know how much the comment pleased her. She lengthened her stroke and the boat coursed over the frothy water. A sleek form rose out of the mist like a sea snake. Cass teetered on the tiny platform, holding her oar in front of her to keep from falling into the lagoon. A man swore loudly as his small fishing vessel glided by.

"Forgot to tell you to watch out for other watercraft," Falco said, leaning in to help support her. "Not everyone has a lantern."

Cass glanced around for other boats, but didn't see any. "What do you make of the X carved in the girl's chest?" she asked, trying to distract herself from the feel of Falco pressing up behind her. The strange slash marks haunted her. She shivered even now, just talking about them.

Cass felt Falco shrug. "Judging from the bruises on her neck, I'd say she died of strangulation." His breath was warm on her jawbone. "Those cuts were made by someone who was angry. Someone who dislikes women, or at least women-for-hire."

Cass could almost feel fingers squeezing her own throat, a blade slicing into her skin. How terrified the girl must have been. Cass attempted to change the subject. "Do you really think we'll find something in the city? I want to know what happened to Livi's body."

"I wouldn't get your hopes up." Falco's voice was soft in her ear, but it had a slight edge to it. "The murderer probably dumped it in the lagoon."

Cass swallowed hard as she imagined Liviana's decomposing corpse floating to the surface by the dock outside Agnese's villa. "Maybe not," she insisted, forcing the gruesome image from her mind. "Why dump one body to hide another?"

The Giudecca was coming into focus, its southern coast barely visible through the low-hanging haze. Cass steered the boat toward the dark finger of land.

"Your friend is already dead. It doesn't really matter where her body is now, does it?" Falco said curtly. Before Cass could protest that it did matter—of course it did—he pointed toward the eastern side of the island. "The water is calmer if you hug the shoreline." There was silence for a moment before he added, more softly, "Anyway, what matters is finding out who sent you that threatening note, so we can stop him from whatever he's planning next."

Cass let the argument go. He was right, of course—what mattered most was making sure the murderer was caught and put away, before he could do more harm. They needed evidence of some kind. They needed a suspect.

As they neared the Grand Canal, Cass began to feel the weight of fear pressing down on her once again. The Chiesa delle Zitelle loomed like a stone guardian southwest of the entrance to the canal. Lanterns burned in the church's twin bell towers, illuminating the structure's gleaming cupola. It was like God was watching over the city. Cass steered the boat into the large backward-S-shaped canal that wound its way through the main areas of Venice proper.

The air was warmer inside the city, tall palazzos sheltering the small boat from the night wind. Cass leaned forward to put space between herself and Falco. The darkness swallowed up all but a faint halo of light from their lantern.

As Falco directed Cass down a side canal, the two maneuvered the gondola by the light of the moon reflecting off the water. Cass held her breath, hoping she wouldn't awaken anyone by running the boat into the canal wall.

Falco seemed to sense her discomfort. He took the oar from her and navigated toward the Castello district, toward a seedy block where the buildings looked as though they'd been under siege. Even in the darkness she could see that their roofs were full of broken red clay shingles; shutters hung open and tilted at funny angles.

As Falco steered the gondola along the edge of the canal, Cass saw a man slink across a bridge and head down an alleyway.

Cass pointed out the retreating figure. She and Falco watched the man vanish into a broken-down shack. "Probably just a thief, or a Jew hiding from the soldiers," Falco said. "Ah, there it is." Falco pointed to a square brick building with a pair of cracked marble lions flanking the front door. He steered the boat over to a dock. Sliding his body nimbly over the side of the gondola, Falco looped the rope over a mooring post. The gondola swayed back and forth. "Leave the lantern," Falco said. "I'll guide you."

Cass reached out for Falco's hand as she exited the boat, thankful that she was moving without the constraints of her heavy skirts and chopines. She had never been out in the streets like this before—unfettered, nearly undressed—and it gave her a quick thrill.

Falco led her quickly into a narrow alley and pressed their bodies up against the side of a private residence. The alley was completely dark. Cass again felt the weight of the knife in her pocket. She realized she was holding her breath. She exhaled slowly. The night was so quiet, she swore she could hear her eyelashes feather together each time she blinked.

From where they stood, they could see the front of the abandoned building. The whole street was deserted.

"Come on." Falco took Cass's arm and pulled her past the front of the building around to the back. Another alley. This one was home to a butcher shop and an apothecary.

The two of them maneuvered around a large pile of trash. Cass's insides churned from the smell of spoiled meat, and she brought the sleeve of her cloak to her face, inhaling through it. Falco pointed; Cass could just barely make out a small six-petaled flower inscribed in a circle beneath one of the windows. Though mist or rain had faded part of the symbol, she could tell each petal was exactly the same size and shape, meeting at a point in the center of the circle. There was something almost mathematical about the design.

"What now?" she whispered.

Falco didn't answer. He stood on tiptoe, his face pressed against a pair of grimy shutters. Cass leaned in next to him, but the crack between the shutters was too small and the room beyond too dark to make out anything.

"Do you hear something?" he asked her.

She stretched up and tried to press her ear to the warped wood, but her face only reached the stucco. For once, she would have welcomed her chopines. "Nothing."

Cass's stomach flipped over as Falco reached into the stinking heap of garbage. He closed his hands around a tangled chunk of blackened metal.

"What is that?" she asked.

"Blacksmith's error, most likely," he said, reaching up and slamming the metal into the shutters. The wood splintered.

Cass jumped back and covered her face with her hands as a cloud of dirt sprayed outward. "Are you insane?"

"Only occasionally." Falco brushed the dust from Cass's cloak. He reached his arm through the jagged hole and winced as he felt around for the latch. The shutters opened with a groan, unveiling an inky rectangle of open space that reminded Cass of a coffin.

Falco hoisted his body up through the opening and into darkness.

"We can't just break into the place," she whispered loudly.

"And yet, it appears that we can," Falco said, perching like a cat on the narrow windowsill. "Were you hoping a servant might admit us through the front door?"

"No, but . . ." Cass glanced around the dark alley, half expecting a battalion of soldiers to come running with their swords drawn. All she saw were the lurking outlines of dilapidated buildings. All she heard was her own breath and the lapping of the canal water against wet rock.

"Do you want to find out about the murder or do you want to go home to your satin sheets?" Falco asked, extending his hand in Cass's direction.

She felt heat rising to her cheeks. He had no right to speak to her like that, so scornfully. She glanced around the alley again. A pair of beady eyes stared back at her from the trash heap. The rat chittered and then let out a high-pitched squeal. Cass bit back a scream.

"I'm coming," she said hurriedly. She reached up to let Falco help her through the window.

He pulled her up under her arms, grabbing her waist and easing her through the opening. Cass felt her body tighten momentarily. She wondered if Falco had felt the jolt of tension pass through her.

She landed in a cold, shadowy space. The air smelled acrid. A glimmer of moonlight through the broken shutter illuminated the room's basic features. Along one wall, a group of glass cabinets held rows of silver instruments. Most of them looked like scissors. Or knives. Some of the tips were crusted over with a reddish-brown substance Cass hoped was rust. She jiggled the handle of the nearest cabinet. Locked.

"Look at this." Falco stood at the edge of a square table in the center of the room. A thin white sheet covered a mounded form beneath it. He yanked the corner of the sheet, pulling it back to expose the corpse of a dog. Cass drew in a sharp breath and stepped back, bumping against a cabinet. The animal's four legs were tied out at its sides. Someone had sliced a Y-shaped incision down its middle, pinning back flaps of skin so that even in the darkness, Cass could see the sinewy red muscle beneath.

"What *is* this place?" Cass whispered, past the lump that had grown huge in her throat.

Falco's mouth was set in a grim line. "I don't know," he said. "It's set up like some sort of workshop." He drew the sheet back over the dog's corpse and crept across the stone floor to the doorway.

Cass followed him, pressing one hand to his back as she peered over his shoulder and into the hallway: darkness, in both directions.

"Come on." Falco grabbed Cass's hand and pulled her out into the hall before she could even protest.

The blackness thickened with each step they took away from the room with the broken shutter. Cass gripped Falco's fingers with all her strength, positive that the hallway would swallow her up if he released her, blinking rapidly in a futile attempt to adjust her eyes to this new level of darkness.

Something sticky slapped across her cheek and she fought to keep from screaming. She flailed her free hand out in front of her face.

"Spiderweb," Falco said. "It got me too." His voice was calm, reassuring.

They crept farther down the corridor. The hair on the back of Cass's neck pricked up. She could swear they weren't alone, that someone else was walking alongside them, toying with them. "Do you hear that?" she whispered. "I hear someone breathing."

"All I hear is you huffing and puffing," he answered.

Cass paused and held her breath. Sure enough, the hallway was silent except for Falco's smooth, even exhalations. How could he be so calm when she was panting like a dying animal? *Dying animal.* She touched her rib cage, imagining thick bands of red muscle like there had been on the dog. Who would do something like that? Why would anyone be so violent and cruel? What *was* this place?

A faint glow lit up an arched doorway in front of them. Grateful for the reprieve from total blindness, Cass moved toward the light.

This room was spacious, with a high, vaulted ceiling, but it had no window and no real furniture. Instead, the floor was lined with rows of oval-shaped tin basins. Six rows of eight. Cass did the math in her head. Forty-eight. The ones nearest to them were small, just big enough to bathe an infant. Along the far wall stood three larger basins. A thick white candle sat in a far corner of the room, its weak flame flickering. Someone had been here recently. Cass stared at the dim flame. Whoever it was, he or she was planning on coming back.

Cass knelt down by the nearest basin. A shapeless blob was submerged in some kind of liquid. It looked soft and squishy and *fleshy*, like something that had come from a body . . .

But no, she was likely letting her imagination run wild again. Still, she wanted to get up and run. The faint, flickering light no longer comforted her—it made everything more uncertain, more terrifying.

But she couldn't run. Instead, she found herself bending closer, her head just inches above the fluid. A familiar odor, crisp and cold, wafted up into the air. Where had she smelled it before? Falco drew his index finger across the surface of the liquid.

"Are you crazy?" Cass hissed. "That could be poison."

He held his hand up to his nose and sniffed. "I didn't plan on tasting it," he responded.

A series of soft thuds drew Cass's attention away from the basin. Footsteps. Falco must have heard them at the same time. As Cass reached out for him, he was already moving to the far side of the room. The two of them bent down behind one of the larger basins, pressing their bodies against each other. Cass pulled the tail of her cloak in close and wrapped her arms around Falco to steady herself.

The footsteps grew louder. Cass's heart hammered painfully against her ribs. The light in the room brightened and the footsteps stopped. She held her breath and willed the banging of her heart not to give her away, praying her hair and cloak weren't visible.

Just when she had convinced herself that she was safely hidden, Falco raised his body slightly, as if to peek over the top of the basin. Cass was still entwined with him. She had no choice but to move as he did. A man with a tall, severe-looking forehead and white hair that flowed back from his long face stood in the arched doorway. He held a lantern high, as if he were searching for something. Or someone. Falco's whole body went rigid. Cass ducked back down and pulled Falco with her.

Her shoulder bumped into something hanging over the edge of the basin. Something with fingers. She clamped her hand over her mouth to keep from screaming. Falco's eyes widened in the dark. Cass pointed at the hand as she cowered in her hiding place.

She held her breath again, and Falco moved his face back just enough so that his eyes could find hers. Soft and blue, even in the dark. Then, after what felt like a lifetime, the footsteps started up again, but quieter. Receding.

"It's okay," he whispered finally. "Come on."

"There's a body in this basin," she choked out, unable to pull her eyes away from the pale fingers dangling over the basin's edge. The hand was muscular and hairy, obviously male. "A man."

"Better him than us," Falco said. He was already halfway across the room, heading for the arched doorway. "Come *on*."

Cass didn't need any more convincing. Fighting past the nausea that overwhelmed her, she crept quickly through the rows of basins—wondering if one of them contained Liviana's body, or parts of it. Falco was standing in the doorway. The two of them peeked into the hall. To the left was the room with the broken shutter, and their only escape route. To the right, the faint light of the long-faced man's lantern was barely visible in the distance.

Cass started to ask if they should make a run for it, just as Falco yanked her out into the hallway and turned left. Cass raced behind him, painfully aware of a third set of footsteps pursuing them.

"He's coming," she hissed, fumbling through the darkness as fast as she dared, panic rising like a wave.

"Then hurry," Falco said.

The two of them raced past the table with the dog. Falco vaulted easily through the window and immediately turned back to assist Cass. She made it halfway through, but then got stuck. Her night-gown had snagged on something—the window ledge or the broken shutter. She gave it a furious tug, but it didn't budge.

"I'm caught." Her heart started slam-banging again. *Don't look back.* But of course she did. The long-faced man was striding through the doorway. It would take him only a few paces to get to her. She turned back to Falco, tiny whimpering sounds escaping from her throat.

"Who's there?" the man called out, and the sound of his voice almost stopped her heart completely.

Falco hooked his hands around her elbows and pulled Cass so hard, she thought both of her arms would dislocate. Her body slid through the window with a harsh ripping sound. She was running as soon as her feet hit the cobblestones, tearing through the alley and over to the gondola, which was, thankfully, still bobbing in the dusky water where they'd left it. Falco practically threw Cass in the boat, and as he did, the kitchen knife slipped out of her cloak pocket and landed on the wooden baseboards.

He raised an eyebrow, but went immediately to the platform and began to row, jolting Cass backward into her seat.

She bent down to retrieve the knife, tucking it back in her pocket. "Hurry," she begged, expecting to see the long-faced man appearing from the alley any second. *Soon, bella, it will be your turn.* She saw the bloated corpse from Livi's tomb, the sharp X sliced deep into her once-beautiful skin. Was this man the murderer? Had he sent Cass the note? She got up unsteadily and looked behind them, petrified, as Falco rowed furiously away from the building.

"Is he coming?" Falco asked. For the first time since they'd met in the graveyard, he sounded scared.

"I don't see him," Cass said as Falco navigated the boat down a side canal, putting a row of small dwellings between them and the mysterious building. She held her breath until the gondola was out of the Grand Canal and back into the open lagoon.

"I—I don't understand," Cass said. Suddenly, she was freezing. She could hardly keep her teeth from chattering. "That place— What are they *doing* there?"

"I don't know," Falco said. His voice was grim.

"Do you think we should go back?" Cass asked, her stomach twisting at the thought. Still, maybe Livi's body was there. "We can bring members of the guard . . ."

"Are you kidding?" Falco asked, his voice heavy with disbelief. "I don't ever want to see that place again."

Cass looked out over the dark lagoon and willed herself to remain calm. "But we can't just forget about it. All those basins full of . . . parts. They're doing witchcraft there, or worse."

"No one is doing any witchcraft," Falco said. "Those parts probably weren't even human. Probably harvested from dogs, like the one on the table." He didn't sound convinced.

Cass turned back to face Falco, her eyes bright with anger. "What about the bodies in the big basins?" she asked. "They looked human enough to me. Even if our murderer didn't kill them, they could be victims of vampires or demons." A tremor made its way into her voice. "What if Liviana is there? I will not see my friend's body torn apart by monsters." Cass wanted to curl up in her bed, under all of her covers, and drift into dream. No. She wanted to wake up, and find out that that horrible place—the dog, the body, the man with the long face—*was* the dream. For once she was relieved to see the shore of San Domenico in the distance. Falco let go of the oar and put both hands on Cass's shoulders. He didn't say anything for a minute. Beneath her feet, she could feel the coasting gondola slow to a stop and bob gently in the still waters of the lagoon.

"Cass," Falco began slowly, "I don't understand what that place was myself. But there's one thing I do know: there *are* no vampires or demons. Whatever is happening there . . . it's human. Human experimentation. Human madness, perhaps. But human nonetheless."

The word *experimentation* suddenly recalled to Cass the familiar smell from the small basin. Balsam. That's what it was. Her father used to bring the sticky substance home on his clothes. She didn't remember what it was for—an antiseptic or a preservative or something. "They were using balsam," she said shakily. "I smelled it. It—it reminded me of my father." Her voice was still a little shaky. "He dabbled in medicine."

"See," Falco said. "The man we saw was probably a . . . a physician, or a surgeon. Maybe he's doing research in that place."

"But it's still not right," Cass protested, shrugging away from Falco's grasp. "All those organs just sitting out like that. The church would forbid it."

"This isn't Rome, Cass. Venice does what's best for Venice." Falco took the oar and steered the bobbing gondola back on course. "And we can't say anything to anyone without admitting we broke into the place. We'd be arrested. We have to let it go."

"So that's it? Once again, your grand plan is that we do nothing?" Cass waited for Falco to answer, but he was concentrating on his rowing, or at least pretending to. Despite his reassurances, he, too, seemed afraid of the place. For a couple of minutes, she watched the oar move through the water. Cass saw the outline of her aunt's dock coming into focus through the mist, and she couldn't stop a small fist of disappointment from settling in her stomach. "But what about the murderer? Are you just going to forget about him?" ·

Falco steered the boat expertly up to the dock. "I recently ran across a girl who carries a concealed kitchen knife in her cloak," he said, cracking a small smile. "I'm beginning to suspect *she* might be responsible."

Cass flushed. "You can never be too careful."

"You better be careful not to stab yourself in the leg," Falco said, retying the ropes that moored the gondola to the dock. "See. Your aunt will never know it was missing."

He helped Cass from the boat and took her arm as they headed across the lawn toward the villa. Cass's heart raced as her mind sped over all the details of the night so far. The breeze had died down and she felt cozy in Siena's woolen cloak. The sky had gone from ebony to purple, and Cass knew the sun—and the servants—would be up soon.

"What if we tried a different strategy?" she blurted out, surprised at her brazenness. "If we figured out who the girl was . . . Maybe the murderer was one of her patrons, or someone she knew. I—I'm just not ready to give up," she finished, in response to Falco's questioning look. She told herself it was because she wanted to know what happened to Liviana's body, and who had killed the courtesan. And of course, to protect herself.

But deep down, she knew she also wanted another reason to see Falco. She *needed* it.

Falco paused, rubbing the skin under his right eye. "It's not a bad idea," he said. "But we don't even know if she worked out of a house or on her own. There are more women-for-hire in Venice than there are rats."

"You said yourself she looked young, didn't you?" Cass was thinking out loud. "We could visit a house or two. Speak to the women there, and to their patrons perhaps? They might know of her, even if she was a courtesan working for herself. You seem fairly familiar with the . . . industry."

Falco chuckled. "I know of a few places." He paused as the old villa came into view through the mist. "But a lady of your grace and stature, surely you don't want to go anywhere like that."

"A lady of my grace and stature typically doesn't ride in stolen gondolas wearing only her nightgown," she replied, lifting her chin. "I've told you. I'm not like the others."

Falco laughed. "Fair enough. We'll go then. Tomorrow night or soon after."

Depending on his mysterious business dealings, no doubt. Still, Cass felt a quick burst of excitement. "Where should I meet you?" she asked, glancing nervously at the villa. So far she hadn't seen any light or movement, but sunrise had to be just minutes away.

"I'll find you," Falco said. He lifted one of Cass's hands to his lips and kissed it. Then he turned back toward the dock without even saying good-bye.

Cass fought the urge to call out to him. How would he get home? Where did he live? What had they witnessed tonight? But soon he was swallowed by the mist.

She touched the hand he had kissed to her cheek and then her lips. Her stomach felt knotted, and for a second Cass was certain she would never see him again. She waited for the feeling to pass, but it didn't, so she tucked her hands into the pockets of Siena's cloak and headed into the villa.

Her right hand bumped against the small knife's handle, but closed around something else in the pocket. Falco's drawing. The mysterious nude woman. Who was it meant to be? She knew she would never be able to ask him.

As she slipped inside and shut the door, a creak from the back of the house made her jump. One of the servants was awake. Footsteps. Cass wrestled her way out of the cloak, tossing it haphazardly over the side table. Then she raced up the spiral staircase. Shutting her bedroom door with a click, she leaned back against it, catching her breath and counting the beats of her thumping heart.

"A blow to the head,

if sufficiently sharp,

can produce an indentation

in the skull. Results may be blindness,

muteness, violent paroxysms

of the limbs, and amnesia."

—THE BOOK OF THE ETERNAL ROSE

eight

As soon as Cass opened her eyes, the previous night's events came flooding back to her, as though she had awakened into a nightmare. The bodies, the stolen gondola, finding Falco in the graveyard. *Caspita.* Cass had completely forgotten about the drawing and the knife she had left in the pocket of Siena's cloak. What if her lady's maid had found it?

The wall clock ticked in her ear like a second heartbeat. It was still early—she had slept for only a few hours—but there was no time to waste. Slipping a satin robe over her nightgown, Cass thudded down the stairs barefoot and skidded to a stop in front of the little side table. It was empty, except for Luca's letter.

Her eyes flitted around the entrance hall. A plain corridor led to the pantry, the butler's office, and Agnese's personal storage. She could have sworn she had left the cloak right here, just inside the door. Confused, she headed upstairs to the portego.

One of the servants had opened the shutters, and threads of early spring mist hung in the air, the sky a whitish gray. Cass peeked underneath the divans, searching for Siena's cloak and Falco's drawing. As she moved across the smooth tile floor, she found her eyes repeatedly drawn to the replica of *The Last Supper*. She swore Jesus's eyes followed her from corner to corner. Cass liked the work of da Vinci, but had always found the mosaic a bit disturbing.

Passing through the dining area, Cass descended the servants' stairs and strolled casually into the kitchen, as if it were perfectly normal for her to be prancing about all areas of the villa in her sleepwear. The cook and his assistants were hard at work, preparing what looked to be a very elaborate breakfast. Narissa and Siena both loitered around the long countertop, sneaking occasional bites of food as they pretended to help cut fruit and tray pastries. The younger maid's brown woolen cloak hung neatly on the hook by the pantry. Someone must have found it and replaced it. But who? And had they found the drawing?

Narissa puttered around an area covered with breads and cheeses, carefully selecting the best ones to add to a tarnished oval platter that was already overflowing with food. Cass noticed with amusement that the woman seemed to be eating two pieces of cheese for each one that made it onto the platter.

Siena worked at a separate station, slicing the tops off giant red strawberries. Crystalline bowls of grapes, melons, cherries, and pomegranates already sat in a neat row, ready to be transported to the dining room. The knife in Siena's hand looked a lot like the one Cass had been carrying last night.

Cass plucked a grape from the bowl and popped it into her mouth. "Kitchen duty? Are you two being punished?" she asked, backing her way up to the cloak.

"No, Signorina," the cook answered. "They are just helping. Signora Querini told us last night she wanted us to prepare a gala breakfast for the two of you before she left on her trip." His thick forearms moved gracefully as he carved a block of white cheese into the shape of a swan.

Cass had almost forgotten: it was time for her aunt's trip to the salt baths in Abano. Healing tonics or not, Cass found the idea of sharing a bubbling pool with other people distasteful, but she suspected her aunt benefited as much from the social setting as she did from the medicinal ointments and elixirs. Agnese often came back bragging of how she had won a small fortune betting on cards with her oldest friends. Cass had been excited at the idea of having the run of the villa for a few days, but now she felt a pang of loneliness. The place would be much quieter without Agnese ordering everyone around, calling for Cass fifteen times a day just to make sure her niece was exercising proper decorum.

Too quiet, like a tomb.

"How long until breakfast?" Cass reached inside the pocket of the cloak, hoping Siena wouldn't choose that moment to look up. Fortunately, Siena was so focused on her work that she didn't even seem to hear Cass. Unfortunately, the pocket was empty.

"Fifteen minutes or so," Narissa said. "But you may want to find something a bit more presentable to wear."

Cass turned to go back to her room and then stopped. "Speaking of things to wear, I seem to have misplaced one of my cloaks. Have either of you seen a cloak lying around?"

Siena cried out as the blade of her knife sliced through the top of a strawberry and into her hand. The maid stepped back from the fruit table and studied the droplets of blood oozing from the tip of her index finger.

Narissa shook her head at Siena. "Clumsy girl," she said. "You could have spoiled the whole lot of them."

"No, Signorina," Siena answered Cass, her voice wavering slightly. "I never saw it."

"I haven't either," Narissa added. Her clipped tone hinted to Cass exactly what she thought of careless young women tossing their outer garments casually around.

Cass stared at Siena for a moment, but the maid refused to meet her gaze. The girl must have found the cloak and replaced it, and judging from her silence, it looked like she was going to keep Cass's secret. But what had she done with the drawing?

Cass returned to her bedchamber with Siena in tow. After being quickly laced into a simple but proper gown and twisting her hair up under a hat, she returned to the dining room, sliding into her place just next to her aunt at the vast table. Kind of ridiculous, really, to have such a giant table for just the two of them.

"If I didn't know better, I'd think you'd taken a trip to the Abano baths yourself," Aunt Agnese said cheerfully. "What's given you such a rosy glow, hmm?"

Cass eyed her suspiciously. She knew she looked far from her best. She was sure her aunt would have something to say about her simple attire, or about the misbehaving curls of auburn hair that were no doubt working their way out from underneath the brim of her hat. And Agnese never gave compliments freely.

"You're sure you're not having problems with your eyesight?" Cass said lightly.

"My eyes are about the only thing on this old body that haven't decided to stop working." Agnese's voice softened. "You look especially like your mother today."

Cass's eyes went to the portrait of her mother on the wall. Agnese's whole family was up there: Cass's grandparents, her mother, three uncles, and two more aunts who lived in the nunnery on the mainland. But as always, the other paintings all blurred into the background when Cass looked at her mother. They did have the same high cheekbones and wavy auburn hair. Cass quickly glanced away from the portrait, her gaze skimming past the pair of stoic serving boys who leaned against the mahogany credenza. Her eyes landed in her lap, where her fingers were twisting the cloth napkin one of the boys had placed there.

"There, there, dear. Being sorrowful over the dead is like regretting too many slices of cake." Agnese reached out to pat Cass's hand. "What's done is done, and she's in a better place now, of course."

"I know. I just miss her. And my father."

"As do I, dear. As do I." Agnese bowed her head and Cass did the same. She listened to her aunt murmur out a short grace. "But now," Agnese said, "on to happier news."

Cass took a couple of pastries from the silver platter and passed it to her aunt. One of the servants scooped a spoonful of cherries and melon slices onto her plate. Platters of breads and cheeses and bowls of fruit covered the long table. It was enough food for at least six people.

"What happier news?" she asked, straightening up in her high-backed chair.

"The news of your upcoming nuptials, of course."

Cass almost choked on her pastry. She coughed and swallowed

hard. "What?" she asked, feeling her face redden. "But Luca still has quite a bit of school left. It will surely be years . . ."

"I still thought it was time we made the engagement public. The stars are very favorably aligned at the moment," Agnese said, opening her mouth wide around a particularly thick piece of fruit. Cass could almost see the lump of food moving down her wrinkled neck, like a dead mouse in the body of a garden snake.

"But it's no secret," Cass said. "Plenty of people know of my arrangement with Luca." She was thinking of herself and Madalena, and a few other friends.

"Well, I've passed along a letter to Donna Domacetti, so now *everyone* knows." Agnese smiled so widely, her thin lips almost disappeared into her gums.

Above Cass's head, a tarnished candelabra creaked and groaned as it swayed in a gentle circle. For a second, the candle flames blurred before Cass's eyes and she feared she might faint right into her breakfast. So *that's* why Agnese had been flattering her. Her aunt had been talking to Donna Domacetti! The woman was the biggest gossip—and, incidentally, one of the biggest women—in all of Venice. Donna Domacetti's appetite for food was surpassed only by her insatiable hunger for scandalous stories. She lived with Don Domacetti in one of the most luxurious palazzos on the Grand Canal and spent the bulk of each day watching the canals below her. Cass imagined even the lepers had heard the news of her engagement if Donna Domacetti knew.

Cass's thoughts flew to Falco. What if he had somehow heard? Would he still want to help her investigate? Would he even want to speak to her anymore?

"*Mangia*, my dear," Agnese said, smiling through a mouth half full of food. "You need to thicken up so Luca doesn't feel like he's sharing his wedding bed with one of the serving boys."

Cass cringed. She wished the wooden floor would swallow her whole.

After they'd finished breakfast and Agnese was satisfied that her trunks had been packed appropriately, Cass stood by her aunt in the entrance to the villa while Giuseppe and Bortolo heaved each of the leather chests down the lawn and into the gondola. For being ancient—and blind in Bortolo's case—the servants made quick work of loading her aunt's sizable trunks into the boat bound for the mainland.

"Have a safe trip," Cass said, lifting her aunt's veil to kiss each of her pale wrinkled cheeks.

"Try to keep everything up and running while I'm away, dear," Agnese said, the loose skin on her arms jiggling as she folded Cass into a hug. "Sometimes I think the old place would crumble to bits without a strong woman to support it."

Cass was inclined to think the old place would eventually crumble to bits even if the Dogaressa and her ladies moved in, but she didn't feel like teasing. She was surprised to feel a lump welling in her throat. She watched as Agnese and Narissa boarded the boat and floated away from the shore in front of the villa. Giuseppe would take them to Mestre, where they would catch a carriage to the baths at Abano.

Cass waved as the boat moved out of sight. For a second, she flashed back to the last time her parents had pulled away from their dock at the palazzo where Cass had grown up. The same sense of dread gripped her, as if she were suddenly all alone in the world.

Cass turned away and headed back to the villa. A dark

thundercloud rolled in from the shore, casting a shadow over the grounds. Cass thought of the man with the tall forehead, and the terrible basins full of waxen bodies. She remembered the terrifying note signed with the bloody X. Her aunt's morning pronouncement had almost eclipsed those awful visions, but now that she was alone again, the darkness came flooding back.

There won't be any wedding if the murderer finds you.

Determined to shake off her ominous mood, Cass resolved to forget about tombs and corpses and workshops full of strangely organized gore. She spent time lazing about the garden and skimming the newest additions to Agnese's library, which included a printed book by Michel de Montaigne, one of her favorite writers. Over a light dinner of bits of bread and meat, Cass tried to chat with some of the servants, but they all responded awkwardly, as if conversing with her made them terribly uncomfortable. Later, Cass even attempted a bit of needlepoint, muddling her way through half a handkerchief before tossing the cloth down in disgust and heading up to her room.

Cass's journal lay open on her dressing table. A portrait of the Virgin Mary stared down at her from the wall. Cass lowered a veil of black silk over the front of the painting. She wasn't sure if the immaculate mother would consider writing a vain pursuit or not, but it was best to play it safe.

Time seemed to slow down as she stared at the blank parchment, brimming with things to write but unable to form her swirling thoughts into sentences. She was running her finger back and forth through the flame of her oil lamp when a scraping noise made her jump, nearly upsetting the lamp.

Cass glanced out the window, her eyes drawn to the graveyard gates that were shut tight. Everything was still. She wondered if she was losing her mind. As she returned her eyes to the parchment, she heard the noise again—but louder, huge, as though it was coming from right behind her. One long scraping sound followed by lots of little scratches. Like fingernails on stone. Cass was suddenly seized by the idea that Liviana's missing body was here in her bedroom, that it had been here the whole time.

Cass fought the urge to flee. She got up from her desk and moved across the room to the armoire. Pausing for a moment, her hands curled around the cool brass handles. Then she threw open the wooden doors to find all of her clothes undisturbed, dresses folded neatly, hats stacked one atop the other. She ducked down below the shelves to examine the armoire's dark corners. Empty.

"*Idiota*," Cass murmured, before closing the wooden doors with a soft click. The corner of her velvet coverlet caught her eye. It was folded backward, on top of her mattress, exposing a chasm of darkness under her bed. Cass's heart started pounding. Her legs felt weak and unsteady as she tiptoed over to the bed. With one hand on her chest, she bent down and peered into the inky blackness. Slipper was playing with the ribbon that bound the bundle of letters Cass kept hidden there. The stack of folded parchment represented almost all that remained of Cass's mother. Years' worth of letters, sent from various trips abroad. "Silly cat," she said. "You scared me half to death." Slipper looked up and mewed plaintively, his eyes winking in the dark.

As Cass moved back toward her desk, her heartbeat slowing again, a flickering light from outside the window caught her attention. She could see a small golden circle moving slowly through the graveyard. A lantern. Was it Falco?

Cass felt her fear melt away at the idea of seeing him again. She squinted into the darkness. For a minute, she saw nothing. Then he materialized, as if floating out of the dark. Several feet below her, Falco stood on the mossy lawn, shrouded in darkness, except for the bit of light cast from her window. Where had his lantern gone? Probably he had accidentally put it out while fooling around. He pulled his arm back as if to throw something and then stopped in mid-motion when he saw Cass looking down at him.

"Signorina," he called up, giving her a grand theatrical wave. He tossed a smooth stone up in the air and tried to catch it behind his back.

His voice was thick, as though he'd been drinking. Cass held a finger to her lips and then gestured toward the back of the villa. She wondered how long he had been hanging around on the island. Had he seen her aunt leave that afternoon? Did he know she was in the big house alone, with only the servants? Cass's skin tingled.

But she could trust him. She knew it. She could *feel* it.

Cass descended to the lower level of the villa. Water sometimes seeped through cracks in the stone floor after a particularly strong rainstorm. Right now the floor was dry. One whole side of the villa's first floor was used for Agnese's personal storage. Cass couldn't imagine that the old woman's belongings even came close to filling it up, but her aunt always kept the room locked.

As Cass crept past the butler's office, she heard a soft snoring sound from behind the door. Bortolo must have fallen asleep doing the house inventory again. Cass headed into the kitchen. She lit a candle and held it up to the tiny window. Peeking through the thick glass, Cass saw Falco's distorted form just outside the servants' door.

"Cassssssaaaandra." He stretched her name out playfully as he knocked on the door.

At this rate he was going to wake up the whole villa. Cass slipped outside, shutting the door behind her with a firm click. "You need to be quiet," she said, shielding her candle from the night breeze. For a moment, neither of them spoke. Cass tried to slow her breathing. *There's no reason to be nervous.* And yet, for some reason, she couldn't catch her breath.

"My aunt is gone," she blurted out, blushing when she realized how it sounded.

Falco's eyes widened in fake shock. "Well, then perhaps I should ask for a tour of the house." He grinned, clearly relishing Cass's embarrassment. "Can we start with your bedroom?"

"What did you bring me?" she asked quickly, willing the color from her cheeks as she pointed at the large cloth bag slung over Falco's shoulder.

He raised his eyebrows. "A special disguise." He tossed the bag in Cass's direction.

Cass reached out to catch it with one hand, and the candle sputtered out. "Remember. *Silenzio,*" she said, slowly opening the door and allowing Falco to pass into the house in front of her. She followed him into the kitchen.

Her breath caught in her chest as a form materialized from the shadows, lunging at Falco and Cass, knocking them both to the stone floor. There was a metallic clatter and a quick shout. Someone's knee, or maybe elbow, smacked into her breastbone. She gasped, unable to scream. The dark was a shroud, a tomb; she couldn't see her fingers in front of her eyes. All she could hear was an occasional grunt as Falco wrestled with the mysterious figure. Cass threw herself at what she hoped was the attacker. Her fingers closed around a handful of hair. Long, silky, women's hair. It felt suspiciously like . . .

"Siena?" Cass gaped as the moon emerged from a tangle of clouds, illuminating the face of her lady's maid. "What are you *doing*?"

"Protecting you from an intruder." The lady's maid scrambled to her feet and then bent low to pull Cass off the ground with surprising strength. Siena's keen blue eyes looked Cass over from head to toe. "Are you all right?"

"Is this how you always welcome your guests, Cassandra?" Falco said ruefully, rubbing his head. He stood just behind Siena. A steel saucepan lay at his feet. Evidently Siena had clocked him with it. Cass fought back the urge to giggle. So her lady's maid wasn't as docile and frail as Cass had always imagined.

Siena's head snapped around at the sound of Falco's voice. "Who are *you*?"

"This is Falco. He's my . . . friend," Cass said. She closed and bolted the kitchen door.

Siena relit the candle with unsteady hands. She looked back and forth from Cass to the boy. A look of guilt passed across her face. "I'm sorry, Signorina. I thought . . ." She bit her lip. "Well, it's just that today at the marketplace everyone was talking about the kidnapper . . ."

Cass steadied herself against a countertop. "What are you talking about? What kidnapper?"

"One of the servants from Signor Dubois's estate," Siena said. "Feliciana told me. Her name was Sophia. She disappeared right out of her room last night. She didn't leave on her own. All of her belongings are still there."

Cass and Falco exchanged a look. The disappearance was

probably a coincidence, but still. "Did someone call the town guard?" Cass asked.

"Of course. A waste of everybody's time," Siena sniffed. "Showed up half drunk after dinner. Only spent five minutes in Sophia's room. Some of the other girls said Sophia had been ill in the mornings recently, maybe with child." Siena stuttered a little bit over the last words, her eyes flitting to Falco. "They didn't investigate any further. Figured her for a runaway. Said the rettori wouldn't care about a runaway servant."

Falco gave Cass a knowing look. "What did I tell you? If the councilmen won't properly investigate a servant's disappearance from one of the most well-known estates in Venice, they surely won't waste their time on a common prostitute—or, at best, a brand-new courtesan."

"Courtesan?" Siena looked back and forth from Cass to Falco. "Has a courtesan gone missing?"

Before Cass could respond, a plaintive yowl echoed through the drafty kitchen. It seemed to be coming from the direction of the entrance hall.

"Slipper?" Cass turned toward the noise.

"I'll fetch him, Signorina." Siena scooted past Falco and into the corridor that led to the front of the villa.

"We should tell her," Cass whispered, once Siena had disappeared.

"What reason do we have to tell anyone? I'm still wishing you hadn't told *me*."

"She might be able to help," Cass said in a low voice. "When it comes to the goings-on of Venice, the servants know almost as much as the Senate. Maybe more." She craned her neck to peer through the doorway. The dark had seemingly swallowed Siena whole. "And, if we don't tell her, she's going to think you and I are . . ."

Falco smirked. "We couldn't have that now, could we? Lord knows I don't want to give the woman reason to attack me again." He touched the crown of his head gingerly and winced. "But what makes you think we can trust her?"

Cass had to look away when Falco took God's name in vain. How could he do that so casually? Her fingers went to her waist, but she'd already removed her rosary for the night. She'd say a prayer for him later, she decided. "She covered for me last night. She didn't tell Agnese I'd snuck out."

A smile played at Falco's lips. He brushed an unruly lock of Cass's hair back from the left side of her face. "How did you manage to get caught in the first place?" he asked.

"Long story." Cass still hadn't found his nude drawing, and she didn't want to confess to having lost it. She hoped it would turn up before Agnese got back. If the old woman found it, she might keel over on the spot.

Siena returned with Slipper cradled against her chest. "The silly cat managed to get his head caught between two of the posts on the banister again," she explained. "Probably scared himself half to death."

Cass took Slipper into her arms. "Poor thing." She rubbed his neck and he began to purr.

Falco reached out to touch the white spot between Slipper's green eyes. "Mangy beast," he said. He nodded toward Siena. "Tell her what you want to tell her then, Cass."

Cass gave Siena a quick summary of what she and Falco had discovered at the graveyard. The maid's eyes got bigger and bigger as

Cass relayed finding the open crypt door and the body, and then receiving the note. "But Signorina Cass, you might be in danger!"

"That's why we're going to figure out who's responsible," Cass said, with more confidence than she felt.

"Speaking of which . . ." Falco nodded at the costume bag, which Cass had completely forgotten. A silky garment, trimmed with lace and beaded elaborately, had fallen out during the scuffle.

Siena looked down, and even in the flickering light, Cass could see that her pale skin went bright pink. The lady's maid knelt to retrieve the outfit, a low-cut satin chemise. She pressed the clothing into Cass's hands without meeting her eyes.

Cass felt her own face get red. "It's—it's just a costume. We're going to try to locate some of the dead girl's patrons."

"You mean you're going to masquerade as a . . ." The shy maid couldn't choke out the rest.

"Hired woman," Cass confirmed, wondering if it would have been easier just to let Siena believe that she and Falco had met up for a tryst. She wasn't sure which would have been more scandalizing. "I know it's dangerous, but it's more dangerous to do nothing while a madman plots against me. And Falco will be by my side the whole time. Please don't tell my aunt."

Siena didn't say anything for a minute. She looked back and forth from Cass to Falco. Finally, she nodded. And then, to Cass's amazement, her red face lit up with a huge smile. "You'll need me to do your hair, Signorina."

"Hair?" Cass wasn't sure she had heard correctly. "What are you talking about?"

"Your hair and your makeup." Siena reached out to stroke Cass's thick hair. "Otherwise, no one will believe you are anything other than a noblewoman. I'll put the sides in braids, and twist the back into a knot."

Falco nodded approvingly at Siena. "Excellent idea. We want to make sure everyone can see that beautiful face tonight."

Cass thought her skin might turn permanently red if she continued blushing. She led Falco into the portego, lighting a pair of tall red candles so that Falco could see to move about the room. "Wait here," she said firmly. "And don't break anything. Oh, and don't touch the harp. My aunt cares more about that thing than about her own pulse."

In her bedroom, Cass was surprised by how fun Siena seemed to find the whole adventure. Maybe the girl had a wild side after all. Siena pulled Cass's stays extra tight and slid the shiny teal bodice over her head. Black lace highlighted sheer sleeves, and the neckline plunged so low that the tops of Cass's breasts threatened to spill out. The skirt was made of alternating layers of black silk and shimmery turquoise material. Cass tried to adjust the top for better coverage and Siena laughed.

"You're not going to fool anyone if you don't act the part," Siena said. She grabbed an ivory comb and parted Cass's hair. She fashioned it quickly into delicate fishbone braids and wrapped them around the back of Cass's head. "Now makeup!" Siena left Cass in front of the mirror and returned with a small black satchel. From it she produced crystal containers of lip color, eye color, and cheek rouge made from powdered minerals and crushed rose petals.

"Where did you get all this?" Cass asked.

"From Feliciana. She gave me some of her old things when she moved to the Dubois estate."

"So why don't you ever wear it?" Cass closed her eyes as her lady's maid painted her lids with smoky gray color.

"It wouldn't be appropriate for someone like me," Siena said. Now it was her turn to blush. Cass knew she meant it wouldn't be appropriate for someone of her station.

Cass tried to hold her mouth still as Siena started rubbing a glossy red crème on her lips. "But I wouldn't care," she said, through barely parted lips. She could not necessarily say the same of Agnese—but still, Siena was meant to be Cass's companion.

"Maybe not, but it would be foolish of me to masquerade as my sister," Siena said simply. "I am not beautiful like she is."

Cass waited for Siena to finish coloring her lips before responding. "You are beautiful," she said. It was true. Siena's features weren't quite as striking as her older sister's, and sure, her ears were a little big for her face, but she had perfect alabaster skin and shiny flaxen hair. It occurred to Cass that Siena must feel the same way about Feliciana that Cass often felt about Madalena. Like she just didn't measure up.

Siena smiled shyly. "Thank you, Signorina. You are very kind." She placed a glass stopper back on a tiny circular pot. "All finished. Don't look, though. You and your man must be surprised together."

"Siena," Cass cautioned quickly. "He is not my man."

"If he looked at me the way he looks at you, I would not be so quick to denounce him," Siena teased, her eyes brightening in a way that reminded Cass quite a bit of Feliciana. She stepped back from Cass and gave a satisfied nod. "And now—for me. Shall I change into something more revealing as well?"

Cass realized that Siena intended to accompany her. "I—I think it's better if Falco and I go off on our own."

Siena's flawless skin paled. "Unchaperoned? But that's unacceptable. If your aunt found out, she'd run me out of the villa, if she didn't kill me first."

So true. Cass could just hear Agnese shrieking about what Matteo would think. "She won't find out," Cass promised. "She'll be gone for days. And I won't make a very realistic prostitute with a maid-servant in tow." Cass didn't bother to point out that of all the rules she might break that evening, departing with Falco unchaperoned was the very least of them.

Siena agreed reluctantly, but her good mood had vanished. She led Cass back to the portego, to where Falco waited. A slow smile spread over the boy's face.

"Almost perfect," he murmured. He bent down and gave the seam of Cass's dress a yank. Cass yelped. The shiny fabric slit up the side so that a hint of her shapely calf peeped out. "*Now* it's perfect."

Cass glared at him. Siena gasped, then clapped a hand over her mouth. "Please be careful," she begged. "Your aunt would never forgive me . . ."

Falco flashed his dazzling smile at the lady's maid. "Nothing bad will happen to her. You have my word."

Cass bent close to Siena and gave her a quick kiss on the cheek. "Leave the door unlocked for me, will you?"

Cass and Falco descended the stairs to the entrance hall. Siena followed them, clutching a candle in her hand. Cass turned toward the large mirror that hung behind the side table. In the flickering candlelight, her reflection looked filmy and unreal. Ethereal. The skirt filled out her slim hips. The low-cut bodice combined with the extra-tight stays gave her curves she didn't even know were possi-ble. Soft curls of her hair dangled against her long neck, but the bulk of it was swept out of her face by Siena's braids. Cass lifted a hand to her face. Could her cheekbones really be that defined? And her eyes—they had never looked bigger.

A flash of ivory in the lower corner of the mirror caught her eye. Luca's letter, still unopened. She frowned for just an instant. She'd read it tomorrow for certain. Looking up again, she smiled at Falco's reflection.

"Ready?" he asked, cocking an eyebrow.

She responded with a nod. And the girl in the mirror—that beautiful, smoky apparition—nodded too. Cass had never felt more alive. Siena draped Cass's velvet cloak around her shoulders and Falco took her arm. "Where's your lantern?" Cass asked.

Falco stopped just inside the front door. "I've got eyes like a cat," he said. "I usually go without. But you're right. Tonight we should bring one."

Cass thought back to the fuzzy yellow circle she'd seen moving among the gravestones. She had assumed it was Falco, and that he'd drunkenly set it aside somewhere . . . But apparently she'd been wrong. The light had belonged to someone else. A tremor raced through her body, causing her to shiver beneath the warm cloak. A stranger was prowling the shadows of San Domenico Island.

Was he looking for her? If so, what did he want?

And what would he do if he found her?

"Civilized beings regard the
act of intercourse as the highest
expression of romantic love.
One need only observe the
behavior of animals, however,
to realize that the act is
often a form of violence."

—THE BOOK OF THE ETERNAL ROSE

nine

Cass huddled inside the felze as Falco navigated the gondola through canals that grew narrower with each turn. By the light of her lantern, she could just barely make out the dingy buildings packed tightly together, stucco chipping off to reveal crumbling gray bricks beneath. This area was just as seedy as the block in the Castello district where they had found the workshop full of horrors. As far as Cass could tell, it was also every bit as deserted. Above her head, fraying ropes ran across the canal, hung with threadbare chemises and woolen skirts.

She kept thinking back to the light in the graveyard. It could have been anybody, she supposed, a grieving family member or even the chapel caretaker. Still, Cass couldn't shake the feeling that she was being watched. The canal water bubbled and hissed in places. She flinched at every dark misshapen shadow, half convinced the murderer was going to rise up alongside the boat and reach for her. Falco steered around another sharp corner, and Cass exhaled as a row of lanterns cut through the gloom.

A boy sat near the edge of the canal, plucking out a slow,

melodious song on a mahogany lute. Beyond the boy stood a plain three-story building with two pairs of shutters opened wide to the night. Inside each window, a girl about her own age danced to the sound of the lute. They twisted their sinuous bodies, their bodices cut so low, Cass swore she could see the crest of one girl's nipples peeking above the edge of her neckline.

Both girls had their hair fashioned into thick cones atop their heads. It was a popular style, but in the faint light the writhing silhouettes reminded Cass of satyrs. Or devils. Cass watched as a man approached one of the windows. He said something to a girl with dark hair and thick crimson lips. The girl lifted her skirt and ran her hands over her slender hips. Cass tried to look away but couldn't. Now that her eyes had adjusted to the dim light, she could see that the girl was her age—perhaps even younger. The man ran his hand up one of the girl's pale legs and then tossed a coin through the window. Clapping her hands together, the girl hollered something after the man as he started to walk away.

Falco rowed over to the bank of the canal, stopping just short of scraping against the stone retaining wall. He tied the boat to a wooden post and turned to give Cass his lopsided grin. "Ready?"

"Here?" Cass began to shiver, even though the night air was balmy. Securing her cloak tightly around her body, she forced herself to stop staring at the girls in the windows. Beyond the edge of the canal, the system of alleyways brimmed with activity. So many people. Cass was seized by the irrational fear that she might run into someone who knew her.

Falco raised an eyebrow. "This is one of the best spots for . . . ladies," he said. "Unless you have a better idea."

Cass hesitated before stepping to the edge of the gondola, feeling that parading in front of all of those people would be impossible. "I just expected more . . ." She fumbled for the right word. "Discretion."

Falco raised an eyebrow. "What's to be discreet about?" He plucked the lantern from the gondola and let it dangle from his wrist as he held out his hands to help Cass out of the boat. "We're looking for the same thing as everyone else, right? A little fun."

Cass gritted her teeth, already beginning to regret her decision to come. Her ankles threatened to give out as she maneuvered her dangerously tall chopines onto solid ground. As she clung to Falco's arm to prevent pitching right into the fetid canal water, she was acutely aware of a circle of boys staring at her. A sharp whistle sounded from somewhere back in the alley.

Falco stopped. His eyes moved over Cass's body, lingering a little too long for her tastes.

"What?" she asked coldly.

"You should probably leave your cloak," he said.

"Right." Cass fumbled with the clasp of her velvet cloak. She tossed it back into the gondola and then hugged her arms around herself to hide her shaking fingers. Immediately she felt the heat of more eyes. Above the dancing girls, she saw a pair of women hanging out of a window. They wore bright chemises with plunging necklines and had their hair elaborately fashioned. They giggled and waved when they saw Cass looking at them.

Cass forced herself to uncross her arms. Like Siena said, she'd never be able to blend in if she didn't act the part.

"*Fondamenta delle tette*," Falco announced, with a grand flourish. "Street of tits." The women giggled again and blew kisses in Falco's direction.

Cass's blood thudded in her chest and her ears. "Remind me never to come back here," she said, trying to inject her voice with sarcasm. For a wild second she imagined she would jump back into the gondola and row herself away, all the way back to San Domenico. But instead, she turned a slow half circle at the edge of the canal, wrinkling her nose in what she hoped was disdain.

Falco just laughed and squeezed her hand. "Don't worry. You'll relax once we get where we're going."

Falco steered Cass into the dimmer of the two alleyways. A haze of perfume and tobacco smoke hung thick in the air, its overpowering sweetness nearly making her gag. Beneath it lingered other scents, even more unpleasant, of sweat and urine. Bodies moved in all directions, pressing against Cass as she and Falco headed toward the end of the alley. She fought the urge to cry out as she was jostled from side to side by men and women in various states of intoxication. If Falco let go of her hand, the wild crowd would swallow her up.

The music, the people, the bright colors, loud voices, and sharp smells—it made Cass's head pound, and reminded her, for no reason at all, of an exotic-animal exhibit Agnese allowed Feliciana to take her and Siena to when they were twelve. The older maid had promised ferocious lions and tigers, but there had been only a single lion, and all it did was lie prone inside the wheeled cage that held it prisoner. Cass had stood there, a little afraid but mostly just sad. When Feliciana disappeared into an alley with a muscular elephant trainer, Siena had watched from a distance as Cass wriggled her fingers through the bars to pet the poor beast's matted fur.

Something sharp slashed at Cass's left arm and she cried out. Snapping her head around, she searched for her assailant, but the crowded alleyway blurred into a sea of arms and hands all reaching out toward her. She gasped, beginning to panic, struggling against the current of faceless flesh.

"What? What is it?" Falco pulled her from the tangle of sweaty bodies and pressed her up against the side of a small bakery shop.

Cass looked down at the sleeve of her teal chemise. Someone or something had sliced right through the silky fabric. Falco separated the torn material to examine Cass's skin beneath. He lifted her arm to show her the swollen pink line just below her elbow.

"Look, no blood," he said. "You probably just got your sleeve caught on a sword hilt or belt buckle."

Or a knife. Cass searched the crowd again, but no one was paying her any attention. Falco's hand felt hot on her flesh, almost burning. She pulled her arm away, turning to look back at the entrance to the alleyway. It seemed impossibly far away. Unreachable.

Falco traced his finger along one of the delicate fishbone braids that framed her face. "It was just an accident," he said.

Cass felt the blood return to her face. She glanced down at her torn sleeve. The scratch on her arm was already starting to fade. "Sorry," she murmured. "I'm being silly. It just scared me, that's all."

"It's all right," Falco said. His voice was surprisingly gentle. Cass had been certain he would mock her for being a child, a spoiled little aristocrat afraid of her own shadow. "We're almost there," he continued, pointing at a garishly painted yellow building. "It's one of the biggest houses in the area. And the woman in charge knows everyone and anyone who comes through this way. There's a good chance she'll know if any . . . *ladies* have gone missing." The word *ladies* was tinged with sarcasm. "Do you still want to do this?"

Cass stepped back from Falco and smoothed her skirt. "I do," she said, reminding herself that this escapade had been her own idea.

Besides, she probably *had* just gotten herself snagged on someone heading in the opposite direction. A knife or a blade would have cut more than just the fabric of her sleeve. *Caspita*. She had made such a big deal out of nothing. She was getting as bad as Madalena.

Up close, the house was an ugly yellowish green. A man and woman sat just outside the door, their arms and legs intertwined. Cass could see the woman's milk-white shoulder as the man tugged at her bodice. Falco slid past them without so much as a glance. Cass excused herself as she navigated her flowing skirts around the pair. Falco rapped on the door—three quick knocks followed by two slow ones—and the door was opened by a young raven-haired girl in a simple black dress. The girl curtsied and disappeared into the darkness of the house without a word.

Cass glanced questioningly at Falco.

"How did you know the secret knock?" she asked, more than a little afraid of the answer.

"These things are not as secret as you might think," Falco said with a wink. Cass opened her mouth again but Falco pressed a finger to her lips. Heat flooded her body at his sudden touch. "Enough questions."

He led Cass through the entrance hall to the doorway of an airy salon where groups of men sat at wooden tables, drinking from flasks and puffing on clay pipes. As they chatted, women in various stages of undress wandered among them, stopping occasionally to stroke the men on the back of the neck or whisper in their ears.

"Falco!" A tiny blonde woman wearing only her stays and a sheer underdress made her way up to them and leaned in close to kiss Falco on the cheek. Cass saw her lips graze his earlobe as she whispered a secret message to him. Falco grinned and swiped at the lip mark with his sleeve. Was he blushing? That was a first. Cass wondered what sort of thing a woman would have to say to make *him* blush. The prostitute turned her steely blue eyes toward Cass, making no attempt to hide the fact that she was sizing her up. Cass looked away, toward the far wall. Someone had painted a mural of a naked girl with her hair on fire. The blonde sidled off and Cass wasn't sure which upset her more, that Falco was so well known in these parts or that the woman he seemed to prefer resembled Siena rather than herself.

"Friend of yours?" she asked, proud of herself for keeping her voice steady.

"Now, now." Falco raised an eyebrow. "It is not within a courtesan's nature to be jealous."

"I am not jealous," Cass insisted.

"Good. Andriana is just a professional acquaintance of mine," he said.

"Oh, she looked professional all right," Cass replied. She was not sure Falco heard; if so, he pretended not to. He was already pulling her forward. She wobbled in her tall chopines as Falco shooed her into the salon. She grabbed on to the door frame to regain her balance. A pair of soldiers dressed in scarlet military garb and scuffed silver breastplates looked up from a square table in the corner of the room. Cass looked past them, to the far edge of the table where their broadswords leaned. Her eyes traced their way down the steel blades, and she couldn't help but see the dead girl, the strange X sliced into her discolored skin.

"No more drink for that one or she won't be able to perform," one of the soldiers said, raising a glass of golden liquid in Falco's and Cass's direction.

"I find some of them do best after they fall asleep," his companion responded. Both men broke into coarse laughter before draining their glasses and signaling for refills.

Cass realized she had pressed herself so tightly to Falco that she was starting to sweat. Slowly, she pulled away from him so that the fabric of her chemise unstuck itself from his side. Falco flashed her a dazzling smile. "That's a good girl," he said, making Cass feel like she was about four years old. "Wait here for me, okay? I'm going to speak to Signora Marcoletti."

"Wait—" Cass tried to call him back, but Falco had already turned and disappeared up a short flight of stairs.

Alone in the salon, Cass's fear started to take over again. Her eyes flicked around the room: the two soldiers throwing back pewter mugs of ale, a table of sailors betting on a game played with tiny glass stones, a small cluster of peasant boys with hats pulled low to hide their faces. And beyond them, just in front of the fire-girl mural, a clean-shaven man with shoulder-length blond hair sat alone on a divan. As he chatted sporadically with one of the girls, he folded a piece of parchment into smaller and smaller triangles. He looked vaguely familiar, although Cass couldn't place him.

She slouched against the doorway to the salon. Carved angels and devils decorated the molding, their wings and horns digging into her back. Everyone else in the room was sitting, which made her feel gigantic, even leaning against the wall. Cass wished she could remove her chopines, but no one had offered to take them, and she couldn't just leave them lying around in a place like this. Teetering slightly, she made her way across the chipped and broken marble floor. Despite the fact that the clusters of men all seemed engrossed in drinking or gambling, Cass sensed gazes searing into her from whichever direction she didn't happen to be looking. Tucking her hands into the pockets of her dress, she felt the soft fabric of a handkerchief. A lot of good it would do. She wished she had brought along the kitchen knife.

Anchoring herself against a tasseled divan with a giant rip in the upholstery, Cass counted in her head. *One, two, three.* The servant girl excused herself as she squeezed past Cass with another round of drinks for the soldiers. *Seventeen, eighteen, nineteen.* A tall brunette wearing a silky veil and a scandalously sheer dress circled through the room and whispered something to the blond man on the divan in the corner. His face twisted into a grimace and his right hand clenched and unclenched until the girl walked away. Cass realized he was as uncomfortable as she was, and felt a sudden rush of sympathy for him. He had probably been dragged there by one of his friends.

The dark-haired prostitute walked from table to table, stopping to chat with each of the men. *Forty-three, forty-four, forty-five.* One of the peasant boys followed her through the room and up the staircase Falco had taken. Behind him, his friends put their heads close together to laugh and whisper. *Seventy-eight. Seventy-nine*—a heavy hand landed on her lower back. Cass whirled around to tell Falco how rude it was for him to abandon her like that, but it wasn't Falco. It was a swarthy older man with a dark beard and eyes that were black and dead, like a doll's.

"I like the look of you, *bella*," he said, leering at her. He was missing several teeth, and his breath stank of stale alcohol. "Like a horse that hasn't been broken yet."

Cass tried to swallow her revulsion as the man's callused hand made its way up to the bare skin on her back and neck. She forced a smile.

"I have no need to be trained by you," she said, trying to keep her voice from trembling.

"A fighter then, eh?" One of the sailors abandoned his pile of glass stones to make his way over to Cass. He leaned in close to her, his tan speckled face just inches from her own. "My brother and I like a girl with some fight in her."

Cass felt trapped. She could hardly breathe. The air was thick, the sharp scent of ale melding with the overpowering aroma of cheap perfume. She wriggled her way out from between the brothers. "Excuse me," she mumbled, again almost tripping as she clattered off in the direction that Falco had disappeared.

Gripping the handrail so forcefully that her knuckles blanched white, Cass started up toward the darkened second floor of the house. Hooting and laughter from the salon below faded into white noise as she ascended the stairs. She paused on the landing. A long hallway with doors on both sides receded into blackness. She blinked, trying to let her eyes adjust to the gloom. The hall was empty.

Cass's pulse raced. How *dare* Falco leave her by herself. She looked back down the stairs. The dull roar of the salon seemed very far away. She peered up into the darkness, but the air above her was black and still and quiet as the dead. She moved down the dark hallway. "Falco," she called quietly outside the first door. No answer. She tried the knob. Locked. She moved down to the second door. "Falco," she said again, this time slightly louder.

"Not in here," a gruff voice responded.

No one answered when Cass spoke outside the third door. She tried the knob, and it turned beneath her palm. Cass froze in the hallway, seized by the idea that the unlocked door was a bad omen. Someone was waiting for her. Not someone.

Him. The murderer. Cass could sense him behind the door, a body made completely of bone. He would reach out for her with his skeleton fingers and she would be powerless to turn away.

Cass wrenched her hand back, but the door swung open as if it had a mind of its own. The room was dark except for a row of flickering candles along the mantel of a dark fireplace. Curls of smoke wafted upward. The smell of fatty tallow mixed unpleasantly with the sharp aroma of sweat and rosewater. On the floor, two shadows were locked together in an intense struggle. Cass raised a hand to her mouth. She should run away, find someone, find Falco, get help.

Before she could move, the top figure rose up slowly from the mattress and Cass could make out the slender curves of a woman's back. A *naked* woman's back, her skin slick with oil or sweat. The man underneath her relaxed, his hands exploring the woman's curves as she rocked back and forth on top of him.

This was no struggle. Cass knew she should shut the door and flee, but she couldn't. She couldn't take her eyes off the way the silhouettes moved in time with each other, the way their hips brought their bodies impossibly close together with each gyration.

Cass started to feel hot, as though the candles were burning inside her. The figure on the mattress moaned and the woman on top of him laughed, leaning down. Cass was mesmerized by the woman's glistening skin, her loose black hair shaking back and forth.

A door slammed from somewhere down the hallway and Cass gasped. The raven-haired prostitute glanced over her shoulder as

Cass reeled backward. The woman winked. "Want to join us, *bella*?" she asked.

The man beneath her laughed roughly. "Plenty of room for two."

Cass spun around and headed back down the dark hallway, practically sprinting down the stairs to the first floor. She paused at the threshold of the salon, her heart slamming in her chest.

What had she walked in on? The people were having sex, obviously, but Cass had never dreamed it could be so . . . naked. So animal-like. The movement. The noises. All that glistening, sweaty skin. She had heard Madalena talk about sex, but even the older girl had never actually done it, and her stories of what it would be like were nothing like what Cass had seen.

Falco still had not reappeared and the salon had gotten crowded in Cass's absence. She accepted a glass of wine from the servant girl and loitered awkwardly in a corner, sipping her drink slowly. The room went a little hazy, brightly colored clothing and raucous laughter churning together and clouding Cass's thoughts. She grabbed on to the edge of a wooden table to steady herself, accidentally brushing up against one of the soldiers.

"S-sorry," she stammered, trying to back away.

The soldier nudged his friend. "Time for you to pick one. Looks like this one has chosen me." His hand tightened around Cass's wrist. Instinctively, she tried to pull away, but his grip was too tight. For a second she stared down at his thick muscular forearm, her eyes tracing the purple veins snaking beneath his skin.

"There's been a misunderstanding," she started. "I'm not for sale tonight." She twisted her wrist but couldn't break free.

"Why is that?" The soldier leaned in close and Cass recoiled from the pungent smell of liquor on his breath.

"I—" Her lips pressed together and her brain seized up. All she could see was that room, the noises, the sweaty bodies moving together. She couldn't bring herself to look into the soldier's face. She opened her mouth again, but the only noise that came out was a whimper of fear.

The soldier downed his glass of ale and raked his fingertips down the side of her face. "Don't worry. I'll pay a fair price." He pulled a small leather satchel from underneath his breastplate and started counting out coins.

"She's not for sale, because I've already paid for her." The lone blond man stood up from his spot on the corner divan. He had a soft lilting voice, vaguely foreign. His cloak and boots were made of lush velvet, and even the way he walked across the room marked him as a member of the upper class. She pulled free of the soldier as the man moved to her side, her eyes focused down at the bronze skin on the back of his extended hand.

And then she realized who it was. Cristian. Madalena's friend. He had given no indication that he recognized her. The soldier glared at Cristian for a few seconds, probably debating whether Cass was worth fighting over. He fiddled with the hilt of his sword and mumbled something about foreigners under his breath. Eventually he turned his back on the two of them.

Cristian led Cass through the salon back to the entrance hall. "You should probably go," he said. "You don't seem to belong here."

Mannaggia. What if he did recognize her? If he said something to Madalena, Cass would have to face an inquisition. "I'm new," Cass faltered, keeping her head lowered. "I guess I got a little scared."

An unreadable look passed across Cristian's face. He stuffed his right hand deep into the pocket of his cloak and took her hand in his left. Briefly, he touched his lips to the skin above her fingers. His mouth was cold—too cold. The image of a vampire, its fangs wet with blood, flashed briefly into Cass's head.

Cass pulled her hand away quickly. "Thanks for rescuing me," she said, trying to erase the disturbing picture from her mind. "You don't look like you belong here either." Cristian still hadn't admitted to knowing her, but Cass felt certain that he did. She told herself she was just being paranoid.

"It's that obvious, is it?" Cristian said. "This isn't really my kind of place. I'm just here looking out for some friends of mine. Making sure they leave with at least a few coins left in their purses."

Before Cass could respond, Falco reappeared. Cass couldn't help but wonder if he had been behind one of the closed doors upstairs. Once again the naked sweating bodies flashed back, but this time it was Falco being straddled by the little blonde Andriana.

Falco's eyes flickered when he saw Cristian. "This one is actually with me," he said, slipping an arm around Cass's waist.

"Then you might want to keep a closer eye on her." Cristian nodded curtly at Falco and turned back toward the salon.

Looking back over his shoulder, Falco added, "They tell me she's got special skills." He let his hand slide even lower, onto one of Cass's slender hips, as he directed her back out into the night.

Cass pulled away from Falco the second the door shut and they were out of the man's line of vision. "Special skills?" Her voice burned with acid.

Falco grinned. "You mean you don't?" He leaned in close and snaked both his arms around her waist. "I'm going to require a re- fund then." His breath was hot against her neck.

Cass couldn't help it. She saw the room with the candles again, her naked body intertwined with Falco's, the two of them so close together they were practically wearing the same skin. Her whole body went rigid at the thought.

"Oh come on," Falco whispered in her ear. "I was joking. Acting the part."

Cass softened a little bit but still pulled back from his embrace. She couldn't think of him that way when she was angry. She shouldn't think of him that way *at all*. She took a deep breath and tried to regain control of her thoughts. "And acting the part requires you to put your hands all over me? Or is that just an extra benefit?" She didn't know if she was more angry at Falco for treating her like a common prostitute or for leaving her alone in that house full of brutes.

Falco rolled his eyes. "Don't flatter yourself, Cassandra. I prefer my women a little less . . . repressed."

Without thinking, Cass reached out and slapped him. Her palm connected with the side of Falco's face with a satisfying smack. She withdrew her hand immediately, horrified at what she'd done. To her surprise, Falco started laughing.

"That's more like it," he said, his blue eyes lighting up the night. He rubbed the side of his face. "I think that's going to leave a mark."

"I—I'm sorry," Cass said. A red blotch began to form across Falco's cheekbone.

"Don't be. I'm sure I deserved it. If not now, then at sometime in the past." He winked. "Or the future."

Cass bit her lip and dropped her eyes. She had never hit anyone in her whole life. She couldn't believe she had just struck Falco. What was wrong with her? She looked down at her palm. The heat of the slap seemed to be coursing through her hand.

"In any case, we wasted our time," Falco said, still rubbing his jaw. "None of the girls are missing. None of them had even heard of a prostitute or courtesan gone missing."

"So we made no progress at all." As they maneuvered down the alley again, past the dancing girls, Cass envisioned Liviana and the mysterious dead girl in the windows, their decaying corpses trussed up for the night creatures to feed upon. Then she saw herself among them, her arms and legs nailed to the stucco, bare breasts slashed and bleeding. A surge of bile filled her throat, but Cass fought back the urge to vomit. She wrapped her fingers tightly around Falco's arm, as if he were a talisman that could protect her from evil. For all she knew, the murderer was out there in the streets, stalking her like an animal. Watching her every move. Waiting.

"The scalpel is the ideal
implement for slicing flesh,
its blade expressly designed
to penetrate ligament and
muscle with minimal pressure,
even down to the bone."

—THE BOOK OF THE ETERNAL ROSE

S o, princess." Falco glanced sideways at Cass. She realized she was unconsciously pulling him toward the gondola. "Time to return to your satin sheets?"

Part of Cass wanted nothing more than to wake up *in* bed and realize the whole crazy night had just been a dream. But she knew it was real, as real as the fading scratch on her arm. She couldn't give up now. Not after everything she'd already gone through. She wouldn't. "There must be other places we could check." Dark shadows formed and dissolved in the waning light of the lanterns. Cass glanced over her shoulder. The seductive twisting of the window girls was slowing, their energy fading along with the light.

Falco paused at the edge of the canal. "I know of a couple other houses in the area."

Cass was not happy about repeating the experience she'd just had, but if they could find out anything about the murdered girl, they might also learn something about the whereabouts of Liviana's body. She watched the water ebb and flow against the stone retaining wall. Across a narrow bridge, a row of torches illuminated a line of broken-down buildings, their stucco walls stained and peeling from years of water exposure. Heaps of trash lay strewn at the edge of the canal. A shadow moved in one of the piles. A man, hunched down, pawing like an animal.

"Unless, of course, you'd rather give up." Falco's voice was light, but taunting.

"Of course I don't want to give up." Cass tossed her head. "Lead the way."

They turned away from the sanctuary of the bobbing gondola, back toward the dancing girls. The dark-haired girl was now sitting in the window, resting her head against the frame. Falco pulled Cass beyond them, into a second, labyrinthine alley. They passed under a stone archway and stopped in front of a slick marble staircase, half overgrown by a thick web of vines. "Here is your discretion," Falco said. "This place is one of Venice's best-kept secrets."

Cass dragged a hand across the smooth marble as she allowed Falco to lead her up the stairs. She wondered again how Falco knew so much about places like these.

Just as they reached the top of the steps, something rustled behind the vines. Cass tensed up, again wishing she had brought the kitchen knife. A tall boy wearing plain yellow breeches and a leather doublet pushed through the leaves. Cass thought he looked familiar. When he got closer, she saw his doublet was soiled with smears of paint. He was one of the boys from outside Liviana's funeral—one of the boys who had laughed at her when Falco knocked her down. Falco let out a small exclamation of surprise. The other boy shook his head, and then, ignoring Cass, gestured for Falco to step aside and speak with him.

Falco turned to Cass. "Wait for me here, okay?" he said. "I need to speak to Paolo."

Falco and the tall boy—Paolo—descended the marble staircase and stood a few feet from the house. Cass watched them for a moment, but she couldn't make out what they were saying. All she could see were Paolo's arms gesturing back toward the canal, his chin-length black hair swishing as he shook his head repeatedly. Cass frowned. How had Paolo found them, anyway? Had he been following them?

The double doors in front of her were outlined in gold leaf, and each was adorned with a crest featuring a raven holding a dying serpent in its beak. Cass knew she should wait for Falco, but she couldn't help but think she had gone from obeying Agnese's commands to obeying Falco's.

She was still a prisoner, just in a different cage.

With sudden resolve, Cass pushed open the door. She entered into a long open portego, with chairs upholstered in purple velvet and tapestries of cathedrals on the walls. Above her head, a bronze candelabra swayed slightly as the door clicked shut. A basin of rosewater sat on a pedestal in the corner of the room, perfuming the air with a light scent. Cass was momentarily startled by the prettiness of her surroundings—the place reminded her of Madalena's palazzo.

The room was empty except for a pair of older men in thick velvet cloaks and leather boots laced up to their knees. Golden medallions hanging over embroidered vests marked them as government officials. A girl in a pale blue gown with a square neckline and an enormous wheeled farthingale floated through the room. Her sleeves were made of a gossamer fabric, so long and flowy they reminded Cass of wings. A jeweled butterfly hair ornament held her honey-colored braids back from her face, highlighting her impossibly high cheekbones.

Unlike Andriana, this girl didn't touch the men in the room. She simply smiled at them as she passed. After she exited, another girl walked through, this one with wavy hair so blonde it almost looked white. The girl followed the same path as the one before, stopping just long enough to play a short melody on a wooden flute. Cass couldn't believe how ordinary everything felt here. She might as well have been watching Madalena model the newest dresses her father had brought home from his journeys abroad. Cass tugged at her neckline again, adjusting part of her braids so they fell over her shoulders and covered some bare skin.

Just then, a blast of cool night air ruffled Cass's skirts as a tall stranger slipped inside. The doors thudded closed behind him. He wore thick black robes, like a priest, and a black velvet hat pulled low over his eyes.

"*Ciao bella,*" he said, bending into a deep bow. "Are you here for welcoming?"

"I'm—I'm waiting for someone," Cass stammered. She was afraid to ask what "welcoming" involved.

The man nodded. He grabbed her right hand with a flourish and pressed his lips to it. "I thought you looked a little more *undone* than the girls here. Pity. So tall and lovely."

Cass blushed. She lifted her skirts just high enough to expose her chopines. "It's these shoes. I'm really not that tall."

The stranger's eyes lingered on her exposed ankles. "You shouldn't be ashamed. Are you a dancer, perhaps?"

Cass shook her head. Madalena had taken her to a ballet performance at the Palazzo Ducale once. Impossibly thin girls jumping and twirling across the room like weightless fairies. Cass had found the spectacle mesmerizing.

The stranger reached toward her face and Cass felt her muscles contract. His fingertips brushed the lobe of her ear and returned with a golden ducat in his hand. Cass gasped. "Are you a conjurer?" she asked.

"Maximus the Miraculous at your service." The man removed his hat and held it against his chest as he bowed a second time. His black hair stood up in wild spikes and curls. "And you are?"

"Cassandra."

"My favorite name." Maximus closed his fingers around the coin he had pulled from her ear. When he reopened them, his right palm was empty. He made his left hand into a fist and opened it to display three golden coins. "Apparently I'll pay triple for your company this evening." He made a fist again. "Or if you prefer." He held the hand out to Cass. "Kiss it."

"What?" She felt a little drunk, as if the man had cast a spell on her.

"Quickly now or you'll ruin the magic. Kiss my hand."

Cass glanced around. Falco was nowhere to be seen. The two men in the salon were chatting, oblivious to the conjurer's presence. She hurriedly brushed her lips against the strange man's knuckles and a tiny gray songbird emerged from his hand.

Cass gasped. The bird circled around the candelabra, perching delicately between two red candles, its head just inches from the flames. "How did you do it?"

"A conjurer never reveals his secrets," the man said, holding up his index finger. The bird circled the room once before landing on it, beating its wings softly.

The white-blonde girl with the wooden flute reappeared from behind a thick velvet curtain. "Maximus," she said, leaning in to kiss the conjurer on the cheek. "I'm afraid I have bad news for you."

Maximus waved a silk handkerchief over the songbird and it disappeared. "What is it?"

The girl twirled her flute between her palms. "It's Mariabella. She's gone."

Cass felt her heartbeat speed up. So a girl had gone missing . . .

The conjurer nodded. "Last time I was in the city, she mentioned she had attracted a benefactor. I assumed it was only a matter of time . . ." His voice trailed off. "Does she still room with you? Just down from Santa Maria del Mar, as I recall . . ."

The girl laughed. "Your memory is as splendid as your magic. The doorknobs are shaped like suns. You're welcome to go there now, but you'll have no luck finding her. She hasn't come home in days. Signor Dubois has been seen out in public often, but no one has seen Mariabella at his side. The man must be keeping her shackled to his bed."

Joseph Dubois again. He must have been a patron to the girl—to Mariabella.

"Excuse me," she said, trying to keep her voice from trembling. "What does Mariabella look like?"

The girl with the flute looked at Cass as if she were seeing her for the first time. "Who are you?" she asked, her voice edged with hostility.

Cass quickly devised a story about how she had come to the brothel to find a certain woman for her brother, who had fallen in love with her after spending the evening together. "He's returned to his studies abroad," Cass explained, "but I told him I would try to get a message to the beauty who captured his heart last time he was in Venice."

The girl's gaze lingered on Cass's plunging neckline, as if it were factoring in to her calculations about whether or not Cass could be trusted. Behind her, one of the men wearing medallions coughed gently.

"Excuse me," the girl murmured, shaking her pale hair as she glided across the black and white tile floor to where the gentlemen were sitting. Moments later she led the taller of the two behind the velvet curtain, her wooden flute left behind on the divan.

"Mariabella is divine," Maximus said, leaning in toward Cass. "Beautiful and talented. She used to assist me in my act from time to time. I wouldn't be surprised if she was the beauty your brother fell in love with."

"What did—does—she look like?" Cass asked.

Maximus pulled a rose out of thin air. "She has silky dark hair and the most delicious set of lips." He reached out his index finger as though to touch Cass's lips and then seemed to think better of it. "You resemble her, in a way. Except you don't have her birthmark." He traced the shape of a heart in the air.

Cass's blood accelerated in her veins. A heart-shaped birthmark. It had to be the same girl. Mariabella. A maid missing from Joseph Dubois's estate, and now a dead courtesan, one of his chosen companions. Could it possibly be a coincidence? Emotions churned together in her stomach—excitement and wonder and fear. And more excitement. She leaned in to give the conjurer an impulsive peck on the cheek.

The conjurer pressed the rose into her palm. "I think your master is watching us."

Cass glanced up and saw Falco staring at her—no, at them—from the doorway of the portego. Cass hadn't even heard the front doors open.

"I see you've met my beautiful signorina," Falco said, nodding to the conjurer as he snaked his fingers around one of Cass's small wrists.

The conjurer winked at Cass. "Indeed. There's something magical about her, wouldn't you say?"

"You've no idea," Falco said. He pulled her across the room, out of the conjurer's earshot. "Is it safe to leave you alone for a few minutes while I go speak to the owner of the house?"

"No need," Cass said. She couldn't help but smile triumphantly. "I've not only learned the name of the dead girl, but I also know where she lives."

Falco arched an eyebrow. "All that, and you still found the time to bat your eyelashes at some traveling con man? That is impressive."

"I wasn't batting anything," Cass said. "I was appreciating his performance. Come on. I'll fill you in on the way to her place."

As the two passed the conjurer, Falco's grip on her was so tight, she was afraid he was going to leave a bruise. "Good-bye, Maximus," she called behind her. "Thank you for the magic."

Outside the house, Falco kept his hand wrapped around Cass as they headed down the marble staircase. The tall boy in the vest was gone.

"So who's Paolo?" she asked, pausing at the bottom of the steps to catch her breath. The night had definitely taken a turn for the better.

"My roommate," Falco answered shortly.

"Friendly," Cass said, remembering how the boy had looked straight through her.

"Seems to me you have no shortage of admirers," Falco said. And then, abruptly: "You know conjurers are nothing but common criminals, right? I'd check your pockets—I wouldn't be surprised if several coins are missing."

Cass's eyes widened. "I believe I've heard the same about artists. And it almost sounds like . . . But surely it's not in the nature of a patron of a common prostitute to be jealous." One of her ankles wobbled, and Cass had to grab on to Falco's waist to keep from falling over.

Falco pushed her away playfully and then pulled her tightly to his chest. "Funny," he whispered in her ear. "But I doubt there's anything common about you." He shook his dark hair back from his face. "Ready to get serious now?"

"What do you mean, *Master*?" she asked, half reeling from the heat of Falco's breath on her jawbone. A rush of warmth surged through her body.

"You're the one who figured out where our murdered prostitute lived," Falco said. "Lead the way, Signorina *Avogadore*." Falco linked his arm through hers.

"Murdered courtesan," Cass corrected. "It's just as you thought." Cass recounted the conversation with Maximus and the blonde girl. Falco whistled and Cass swelled with pride.

"So," Falco said. "To Santa Maria del Mar we go . . ."

There were only two streets branching away from the little campo that housed the church of Santa Maria del Mar, and Falco and Cass found Mariabella's house—and the signature sun-shaped doorknobs—on the first street they selected. She lived in a small pink building clustered with several others around a tiny courtyard overgrown with weeds. All the houses here looked abandoned to Cass.

She and Falco made their way to the door, carefully avoiding a network of deep cracks in the crumbling stone walkway. The shutters hung askew, revealing dirt-encrusted glass beneath. Cass put her face to the glass but saw only a distorted reflection of herself. Falco knocked on the warped wooden door. No answer. He pulled something small and silver out of his pocket and jiggled it in the lock.

"What's that?" Cass whispered.

"Scalpel."

Cass watched as Falco twisted the flexible blade. The razor-sharp knife reflected the light from the lantern Falco carried. Cass couldn't stop staring at it, not even when she heard a click and the door swung open with a groan. She couldn't help but think of the X carved in Mariabella's chest. "Why do you carry that?" she asked. "Where did you get it?"

"I use it for detail work when I'm painting." Falco wrapped the blade carefully in a bit of fabric and pocketed it.

A musty smell wafted from the open door, almost overpowering Cass. The place was decent-sized, but dingy, with a square living area leading into a single back room with tiny beds and plain wooden wardrobes pushed against two of the walls.

The bed nearest to them was neatly made. Cass ran a hand over the burgundy coverlet and her fingers came back faintly dusty. Clearly, no one had slept here for days. Cass peered inside the wardrobe. A wooden sitar missing several strings stood in one corner. A rainbow of brightly colored dresses lay folded on warped shelves, most of the garments fraying at the wrists and hems.

"I thought courtesans were wealthy," Cass said. The room had a lonely, desolate feel; she could practically smell it.

"It depends on their patrons. Perhaps she had only just tried to find work outside of the house." Falco knelt down and peered under the dusty bed. He pulled out a royal blue silk bag with a yellow braided drawstring. As he turned the bag inside out, strands of pearls and jeweled hairpieces clattered out onto the floor. "Or maybe she was overly fond of trinkets." Falco wrapped a strand of pearls around his hand and held it up in the faint light. Tossing the bag back under the bed, he slipped the pearls into his pocket.

"Falco!" Cass said sharply.

"What? It's not like she's going to miss it."

"It's—it's disrespectful," Cass said. She felt a rush of pity for this dead girl, the girl who'd lived such a small, narrow life and then been cut down so young. Cass thought about how many times she had complained to Mada about her aunt's musty old villa. How the whole place often felt just one good storm short of crumbling to dust. Compared with this room, Agnese's home was like the Palazzo Ducale.

Suddenly, she couldn't wait to leave. The room seemed to be getting smaller by the minute, the walls subtly closing in on her. Living here would be like living inside her armoire. Cass knelt down on the cold stone floor, intending to reorder the jewelry Falco had scattered, and then something caught her eye.

"Hey, look at this," she said. A square bundle only slightly larger than her journal lay half unwrapped, concealed beneath the bed. Cass lifted the bundle and gently folded back the layers of muslin to expose a small portrait. Mariabella must have received the painting not long before she died, or else surely she would have hung it on the wall.

Falco righted the portrait. Cass squinted, but she couldn't make out the figure on the canvas. She brought over the lantern and held it next to the painting.

It was her. Mariabella: the dead girl from Liviana's crypt. Only here she looked happy, her thick hair hanging over bare shoulders, her red lips forming a playful pout. She had one of her arms extended, as if she were reaching out toward the artist. The painting was done in unusual choppy brushstrokes, giving the picture a blurred effect.

Cass thought of the discolored corpse, the ring of bruises around the neck, purple splotches where blood had pooled. She touched a finger to the canvas, almost expecting her hand to pass straight through it into some other land where things were normal and right and Mariabella was still alive.

"A gift from a patron?" Cass asked.

Falco whistled long and slow. "Or a murderer, perhaps. Or both." He pored over the painting, looking for other clues. He pointed to a thin gray squiggle of paint in the lower left corner of the canvas. "Not much of a signature."

Cass bent close to the canvas. "It looks like a *C*, or maybe an *L*."

"That doesn't really narrow things down," Falco said, bounding back to his feet. "There are probably five thousand registered artists in Venice, and who knows how many amateurs."

Cass deflated almost instantly. He was right. Even figuring out Mariabella's identity didn't help them much. And it was absolutely no use in determining what had happened to Liviana's body.

Falco reached out a hand and pulled Cass off the ground. "But as you said," he relented, "at least it's a start." Cass could tell he was trying to make her feel better.

Cass brushed her hands over her skirts to rid them of as much dust as possible. The room was still suffocating her. "I think we've done enough for one night," she said. "Will you take me home?"

"Of course." Falco's voice was surprisingly gentle. He slipped an arm around her shoulders as they turned back toward the door. "Let's get out of here."

They headed back over the arched bridge to Fondamenta delle

Tette, where their gondola was moored. Cass was relieved to see the boat exactly where they had left it. Falco took his place on the gondolier's platform and Cass settled into the felze, slipping off her chopines and wiggling her toes. The night air had developed a sharp edge, and she wrapped her cloak tightly around her. She turned backward in her seat and peered around the edge of the felze to watch Falco steer the gondola back toward the Grand Canal. She could almost envision the structures beneath the skin of his arms and chest and back moving in tandem. She wondered what it would be like to put her hands on him, to feel the rippling of his muscles beneath her fingertips. If only there was someplace else they could go, together. She wondered if Falco lived in a sad little room like Mariabella. She tried to imagine what sort of place he would call home, but all she could see was a dark room, with flickering candles and a mattress on the floor.

"The women in the houses," Cass blurted out, surprised at her brazenness. "Do they do different things?"

Falco stopped rowing long enough to shrug. "Courtesans do many things—sing, play instruments, write poetry. The women in the houses are mostly lovers for hire, though some also work as dance partners or models."

Models. Of course. *That's* why Falco was so well known.

Cass felt her voice get even tighter. "And as lovers for hire, do they do different things?"

Falco laughed. He took his hands off the oar and let the boat coast through the water. "You ask me these questions as if I have a lot of experience with lovers for hire. I have to save for weeks just to pay the modeling fees."

Cass couldn't bring herself to ask what she really wanted to know, whether what she had seen in that room was normal or some aberration. The slick skin, the noises, the wildness of it all. Was that how couples behaved? Would Luca expect that from *her* someday? She turned away from Falco as they approached the Rialto Bridge. Burning steel cressets illuminated both ends of the structure, its middle glistening faintly under the night sky.

"It's so pretty in the moonlight," she said. She had rarely seen it this way.

"Yes, pretty in the moonlight," Falco echoed. Cass felt his eyes burning into her back, as if he were looking only at her when he spoke. The gondola slowed to a stop and Falco tied up the boat directly beneath the bridge. The stone structure blocked out the light and the wind, making Cass feel as if she and Falco were alone in a warm, dark room.

"Here," he said, pulling a flask from his cloak pocket. "Celebratory libations."

"What are we celebrating?" she asked.

"We set out to discover the dead girl's identity," Falco said. "And we did." He pressed the slick metal container into Cass's palm. "I say that's progress."

Cass sniffed the flask warily. The liquid within smelled sharp and sour, almost chemical.

"What is it?" she asked.

"Some witches' brew I found in my master's studio. Go on, try it." He winked. "Unless you're afraid."

Cass put her lips to the flask and tipped it up just enough to let a tiny sip of liquid make its way into her mouth. She held her breath to keep from gagging. Whatever it was, it tasted awful, nothing like the tart sweetness of the burgundy wine to which she was accustomed.

Falco took the flask back and shook it in his hand as if he were weighing it. "You didn't even take a drink, did you?"

"I did so."

Falco shook the container again. "I don't believe you."

Cass leaned in toward him and blew gently in his face. "See? You can smell that ghastly poison on my breath."

Falco sniffed the air. "All I smell is canal water, and a hint of flowers, probably from whatever soap you use on your hair." He put his face very close to Cass's, reached out, and tilted her chin toward him. "Try again."

Her lips were mere inches from his. Cass struggled to exhale. Her chest tightened as the air trickled out of her body. She noticed a V-shaped scar beneath Falco's right eye. She was seized by an irrational urge to touch her lips to the small imperfection. "What about now?" she asked.

Falco brushed a spiral of hair from her freckled cheek and touched his forehead to hers. "One more time?" He closed his eyes. He reached up with one of his hands and cradled the back of her head, pulling her toward him.

He was going to kiss her. She was going to let him. Falco's face blurred in the darkness as he closed the distance between them.

And then . . . it wasn't Falco she was about to kiss. It was Luca. She lunged backward in her seat, causing the gondola to lurch to one side.

Falco's eyes snapped open. "What happened?"

Cass had no idea what to say. "I—I thought I saw something," she stammered out.

Falco glanced around, as if reaffirming that it would be impossible to see anything in the blackness under the bridge. "A vampire?" His voice was thick with sarcasm.

Cass looked away. "Forget it. You wouldn't understand."

"Oh. I think I understand." Falco turned slowly away from Cass. He dragged his fingers across the shiny black wood as he moved toward the back of the boat. "Forgive me, Signorina. I didn't mean to overstep my station."

"No. I—it's not that," Cass said. Her heart was trembling in her chest.

Falco didn't answer. He vaulted over the side of the boat and headed for the steps leading up to the bridge. Cass followed him, struggling to lift her skirts over the gondola's edge. She fumbled her way up the uneven steps, feeling the dampness of the stones seeping through the bottom of her suede shoes. Falco stood in the middle of the bridge, his forearms resting on the railing. He stared down at the water so intently that Cass thought maybe it was his turn to see murderers and poisonous serpents beneath the surface.

But no, Falco didn't deal in superstition.

Cass cleared her throat. Her chest felt as though there was a giant fist around it, squeezing. "Lately I always think I'm doing the wrong thing."

Falco nodded, keeping his eyes locked on the water. His jaw was tight. "You should stop thinking so much. Do what *feels* right."

Cass imagined them tucked back under the bridge, Falco's hand in her hair, his lips finding hers in the dark. She had no doubt that kissing him would have felt right. To her, but not to Luca. Not to Agnese. "How am I supposed to know what feels right?" she asked. "I was never taught to feel—just to obey. It's suffocating. Most of the time I can barely breathe."

"Well, eventually you're going to have to do what's right for you instead of worrying about the rest of the world. Just let go. Trust yourself." Falco turned to her at last. A smile played at his lips. "And if you can barely breathe, it's probably because of those oppressive undergarments you wear."

Cass laughed. She was ridiculously, unexpectedly glad that he was not going to stay angry with her. "You're right. I swear Siena laces them tighter every day. I sometimes wonder if she's punishing me."

For a few seconds, both of them leaned on the railing of the bridge, looking down at the dark canal water. A gondola floated by beneath them. A man and woman reclined against plush pillows, kissing, barely illuminated by the dim light of a lantern. Cass felt her heart speed up again. Her breath felt heavy in her chest. "Take your cloak off," she said quickly.

"Trying to undress me?" Falco asked. He slid out of his cloak and looked questioningly at Cass.

"Hold it up," she ordered. She adjusted his hands so that the cloak shielded her, and fumbled to undo the bindings around her chest. She began to sweat as she unknotted the laces; in the dark, images of Agnese and Luca floated in front of her, their faces cold with disapproval.

"You all right in there?" Falco asked. "You're thrashing about like you're performing a self-exorcism."

Cass emerged a minute later, red faced but triumphant. She waved her ivory-colored stays above her head. "Now," she said, "I can breathe."

Falco plucked the fabric from her hand. He fingered it and feigned surprise. "Good Lord. What is this thing made of?" he asked. "Steel?"

"Whalebone." Cass clasped a hand over her mouth to stifle a yelp as Falco tossed her stays over the edge of the Rialto Bridge.

"Consider yourself liberated," he said. "Do you feel better?"

Cass couldn't respond. She couldn't describe it, the way it felt to be able to inhale and exhale completely, like for once she was using all of her lungs. Her satin chemise curled and folded against her bare chest, giving her the sensation of being both cold and hot at the same time.

Falco touched his forehead to hers again. His nose brushed against the side of her cheek. Cass's heart sped up. But this time, he didn't try to kiss her. He just held her in the dark, his mouth so close to hers that their breath mingled together like mist off the canals.

Across the city, bells rang out. Matins. Falco stiffened. At the water's edge, a gondolier sat up in his boat, rubbing his eyes. He muttered a curse under his breath and lay back down, covering his head with a tattered gray blanket. In the distance, Cass could see a pair of soldiers patrolling the far side of the Grand Canal, their swords reflecting the pale moonlight.

"I have to be somewhere." Falco wrenched away from the railing and began heading to the steps that led back to the canal.

"Again?" Even the tavernas were closed. Cass wondered if Falco and his friends spent time at brothels. Sure he said he couldn't afford it, but what else could he be doing so late? Gambling? Stealing?

"I have some . . . business to attend to," he said, keeping his voice light. But there was a warning edge to it.

Cass ignored it. "Business?" she repeated mockingly as she followed him. "What kind of business can be conducted at this hour?"

Falco turned around and gave Cass a look that chilled her. "Don't ask questions," he said, "and I'll tell you no lies." He took his place on the gondolier's platform without another word.

Cass felt swallowed by the cold as Falco rowed the gondola down the Grand Canal and out into the open lagoon. Wind whipped her hair around her face, making her eyes water. Cass glanced back at him. His eyes were focused straight ahead, straight through her. Cass didn't understand what she had done wrong. Was he angry that she hadn't kissed him? Did he regret that he had even tried?

Cass closed her eyes. She thought about what she would write in her journal when she got home. She wanted to write about Maria-bella. And the couple in the dark room—engaging in a mix of love and savagery. And the conjurer and his tricks. Cass wanted to know how he had done them.

And then there was Falco. Did she dare write about him? About the way she felt when she knew he was going to kiss her, like her heart had grown huge, too big for her chest, like it was seeping out between the laces of her bodice and being pulled in all different directions?

Caspita. What had she started?

The gondola jolted backward as Falco pulled the rope tight. Cass looked up, surprised to find herself back at the villa already. Falco hopped out of the boat and turned to her with an expectant look.

"What are you doing?" she asked. "I thought you had someplace to be." She couldn't keep the hurt from leaching into her voice.

"I'm going to walk you to your door, of course."

"I can walk myself, thank you." Cass clambered over the side of the gondola, her chopines clutched in her left hand. Her cloak snagged on the boat. One of the tall wooden overshoes slipped out of her fingers and landed in the shallow water. *"Mannaggia,"* she muttered, reaching down to retrieve the soggy shoe. She pushed past Falco as she headed across the lawn.

Falco caught up with her easily. "Cassandra, be reasonable. There's a murderer running around."

She didn't answer. She headed around to the back of the villa, doing her best to ignore him as he loped beside her in the manicured grass. He couldn't just freeze her out for the whole boat ride and then pretend everything was fine. Cass tucked her hands into the pockets of her cloak. Her fingers closed around a scrap of fabric—her handkerchief. She remembered Mada's words. *If he keeps it for a little while, then he's yours.*

Did she *want* Falco to like her? Cass wasn't sure.

"*A presto,*" Falco said, with a short bow. "Until very soon."

"All right." Cass bit back the tears that were suddenly pushing at the back of her throat and eyes. If she turned around, even for a second, she knew that she would cry.

But why? What had happened? She didn't know. She let the handkerchief slip from her pocket as she pushed quickly into the house, shutting the door behind her without looking back.

Leaning against the wall of the kitchen, Cass forced herself to breathe. A single tear worked its way down her cheek, and she brushed it roughly from her face. She turned and peered through the thick glass window. Falco was still there. He had picked up her handkerchief. It looked small in his hands. He paused for a moment, glanced in the direction of the back door, and then tucked the cloth square into his pocket. Overwhelmed by the evening's events and her swirling emotions, Cass let her body slide slowly to the floor. This time she couldn't stop the tears from falling.

"Both the teardrop and the
tempest are made of water,
making it the most yielding and
most destructive force on Earth."

—THE BOOK OF THE ETERNAL ROSE

eleven

Liviana's face was everywhere—in mirrors, in shadows, peering up at Cass from her half-empty dinner plate. Pale blue eyes followed Cass's every move—sad, accusatory. *Why haven't you found me yet?*

Cass fled outside to escape a marble sculpture of her dead friend in the portego only to see her small hand reaching through the sandy soil of Agnese's flower garden, her fingers curling like orchid petals.

"Not real," Cass told herself, stumbling across the front lawn until she reached the path that headed toward the shore.

"Cassandra." The wind off the water called to her in Livi's sing-song voice.

Cass put her hands over her ears. She made it to the shoreline, where the sun reflected off the sand, turning the ground beneath her feet a porcelain white. The tide was coming in, and each roll of the surf delivered a giant block of ice. Inside each block was a girl, imprisoned. Cass wanted to turn, to run, but instead she began chiseling away at the ice. The sun began to melt the ice and the cold water ran down Cass's body in frosty rivulets, freezing her from the outside in . . .

Cass sat up in bed, fully dressed. Her skin was clammy, her pillowcase damp with sweat. A copy of Dante's *La Divina Commedia* lay next to her. She must have dozed off while reading. *Not real. Just a dream.* Cass could see from the fading light beyond her window that twilight had come and gone while she'd been napping.

Siena leaned over Cass, her features amorphous in the dim light. "Sorry to wake you, but you have a visitor," she said with a giggle. "Your handsome man."

Falco. It had to be. Cass started to correct Siena—he wasn't hers, per se—but stopped herself. What did that really matter in the grand scheme of a murder investigation?

The dream had clarified things for her. It had been two days since she and Falco had visited the brothel, two days of being haunted by Livi's face—in her dreams, in the shadows that swallowed the villa at night. She needed to find Livi's body, and protect herself from a murderer. Everything else that had crept in between her and Falco—the touching, the looks, the almost-kiss—was irrelevant. This was not a time to be distracted by feelings she didn't understand.

But Cass couldn't keep her stomach from doing flip-flops at the thought of Falco dropping by to see her. Just knowing he was in the villa made the blood go hot in her veins. The past two days had been an agony of waiting and drifting, and wondering when she would see him again, and what they could do next about Mariabella and Livi. She breathed in deeply and then mentally kicked herself for being giddy. Maybe he had come just to return her handkerchief. What would Mada say about that?

Running a hand through her wavy hair, she slid out of bed and tucked her feet into a pair of soft leather shoes. She started toward the bedroom door.

Siena coughed into her fist, moving between Cass and the hallway.

"What are you doing?" Cass asked, trying to slip past her lady's maid. Now that she had decided there could be no feelings between herself and Falco, she wanted to see him immediately to solidify her resolve.

"Why don't you let me put up your hair?" Siena asked. "It's always good to keep a man waiting."

Cass started to refuse. Then she caught a glimpse of herself in the dressing table mirror and almost shrieked. A chunk of her hair had snarled itself into a giant ratty knot and her left cheek was puffy and red from lying on it. Even if she and Falco could only be friends, it didn't mean she should go strolling around the villa looking like some creepy dead thing that had washed up along the edge of the canals.

"Perhaps a bit of waiting would do him good," she said. She settled into the chair in front of her dressing table while Siena brushed the tangles from her hair and fashioned it into a braid. She coiled the braid into a small bun and pinned it up, letting a few loose tendrils hang down in front of Cass's ears.

Then she rubbed some smooth white cream on Cass's reddened cheek. The cream tingled. Cass felt her skin cooling.

"There," Siena said. "Just give it a few moments." Siena went to the armoire and picked out a silver bodice and matching sleeves. She removed the wrinkled blue clothing Cass had on and laced her into gleaming silver.

Cass glanced in the mirror and nodded with satisfaction. Siena was a miracle worker. The maid began tidying up and Cass headed toward the staircase, expecting to find Falco in the kitchen. Instead, he was in the portego, perched on the stool in front of Agnese's harp. Cass smothered a smile at the thought of the tongue-lashing her aunt would give him if she caught him fooling around on her most prized possession.

He had his back to Cass, his face resting against a carved cherub as he absentmindedly plucked various strings. Cass stared, watching the movement of his neck and back and shoulders: pieces of motion that were discrete, yet interconnected. She remembered his words from the graveyard. *The human form, it's a symphony. Tiny interlocking movements that join together in song.*

"It's about time," he said, without turning around.

He turned slowly, then. The blue eyes. The crooked grin. Cass started to greet him, but her voice stuck in her throat. She reached out for the curlicue bottom of the stairway banister, gripping the bronze for a second, reminding herself that there were no feelings. *No. Feelings.* She flicked her eyes back up at him, felt her lips forming a smile independent of any command by her brain.

Falco cocked an eyebrow. "A beautiful woman who doesn't speak. Every man's dream."

"I see you've made yourself comfortable," Cass shot back. "I wasn't expecting you tonight." *Or ever.*

"I'd thought you might have learned that with me, you must expect the unexpected." Falco got up from his seat in front of Agnese's harp, and it was Cass's turn to raise an eyebrow. Falco was wearing a flowing white chemise overlaid with an embroidered black and silver doublet and knee-length breeches. His hair still curled forward toward his face, but it looked sleeker than usual, as if he had attempted to tame it with some kind of paste.

"Why are you dressed like that?" she asked. "Are you going to Mass?" Not likely since Falco professed not to even believe in God. Cass still couldn't quite wrap her mind around some of his bizarre ideas.

"We're going to a party," he said with a dazzling smile.

"We?" Two nights ago, he had practically kicked her out of the gondola; then he had disappeared for days. Now he wanted to take her to a party. Cass wondered if Madalena found Marco as confusing. At least with Luca, what you saw was what you got. Good old reliable Luca. No secrets there. *Caspita.* Cass really ought to read his latest letter. Her fiancé would be expecting a response eventually.

"Joseph Dubois is hosting a ball. I thought we might do a little snooping around." Falco toyed with the embroidery on his silk doublet. "A Dubois affair will be so overrun with guests that as long as we look the part, no one will question our presence. I won't rest until I know you're safe from this chest-slashing murderer, whoever he is."

Falco's concern for her welfare was flattering, and a little suspicious. Still, Cass's heart did a little jumping dance inside her chest. They were going on another adventure. The investigation was still on. Surely they could find something at Palazzo Dubois. The master of the estate was connected to both Mariabella and the missing servant girl, Sophia.

He was also the man Siena's sister now worked for, one of the wealthiest, most powerful foreigners in Venice. Madalena had mentioned the ball once or twice in passing. Cass had gotten an official invitation a couple of weeks back, but Agnese had thrown it away. Ever since Cass became engaged, her aunt had deemed all social functions with men to be "frivolous."

"We're going to sneak you into a party where any number of servants or guests might know me?" Cass could just imagine the scan-
dalized looks if she, the dutiful fiancée of Luca da Peraga, showed up
at a formal event with another man.

Falco took Cass's arm and steered her toward the front door of the
villa. "Don't worry. It's a masquerade ball. No one will recognize
you."

"I don't have a mask," Cass said, glancing around the portego as
though one might magically appear.

"Leave everything to me," Falco said, flashing her a smile.

Crouched down in the courtyard of Dubois's palazzo with her face
pressed against the spiny leaves of a juniper bush, Cass wondered if
leaving everything to Falco had been a wise decision. They still
didn't have masks, and Cass couldn't take her eyes off Feliciana as
the blonde girl paraded about Signor Dubois's portego in dramatic
makeup and a vibrant gold dress. She'd fashioned her hair into mul-
tiple braids and then twisted them around each other into an elaborate cone.

Cass fought the urge to run up the stairs and embrace Feliciana,
to talk to her the way they used to, to inquire about all the latest gossip from the city. Even in servant's garb, Siena's older sister exuded
pure glamour. She might easily have been mistaken for a guest, were
it not for the silver tray of canapés balanced on one of her slender
shoulders.

"There." Falco pointed at a pair of masked dancers who slipped
out a set of glass doors and strolled down the staircase leading from
the ballroom to the garden. He and Cass ducked back behind the

bush as the pair stopped to sit on a marble bench just feet from their hiding spot. Steel cressets mounted on the outer wall of the palazzo burned brightly, bathing the courtyard in dancing light. Cass held her breath, certain she and Falco would be discovered at any moment. A trickle of sweat began to make its way down the back of her neck.

The couple removed their masks and the man bent down to kiss the young woman. Cass pushed the leaves away from her face and crept toward the bench before Falco could stop her.

The lovers were deep in embrace, their faces melding into one in the darkness. Cass felt a pang of envy. She thought of the almost-kiss beneath the Rialto Bridge, of the bright colors that bloomed inside her at Falco's touch. She should have just let go. It could have been their secret.

How many more times would she get an opportunity to have any secrets at all?

She snatched the masks from the bench and tossed the larger one in Falco's direction. Her mask was black and dark purple, adorned with feathers and tiny glittering jewels. A starling, Cass decided. It covered only the top half of her face, leaving her mouth and chin exposed. She hoped it would be sufficient to conceal her identity. She tied the leather string behind her head and positioned the beak over her nose so she could see through the eyeholes.

Falco's mask was made of beige silk and outlined in strips of orange velvet that Cass assumed were supposed to be a lion's mane. The mouth turned upward in a feline grin.

They headed up the marble staircase and into the crowded portego that had been converted into a ballroom for the evening. The room was awash in crystal and gold. A portrait of the Doge, its frame gilded and encrusted with rubies, hung on one of the shorter walls. Next to it hung a picture of Signor Dubois in an even more ornate frame. Behind a long buffet table heaping with glasses of wine and platters of meat pies, pieces of armor and crossed swords were displayed on marble pedestals. At the far side of the portego, nobles and wealthy citizens of Venice danced to a string ensemble or clustered in small groups sharing stories and gossip. The roar of conversation and the clatter of dancing footsteps layered on top of the music almost overwhelmed her.

"Where do you suppose we might find the famous Signor Dubois?" Falco asked.

Cass strained to see through the swirl of gowns and masks. An obese woman in a cream-colored dress stood just inside the doors, a circle of women crowding around her. Donna Domacetti. Cass recognized her behind her swan mask by her sheer size alone. Donna Domacetti's shrill voice cut through the rest of the noise. It sounded like she was telling a story about a tryst between a noted senator and a young courtesan that she had witnessed from her portego window. During the act, apparently the portly senator had gotten a foot tangled up in the leather curtains of the felze, ripping them down and partially exposing himself to a street full of merchants returning home after a long day at the market. Cass cringed as the woman burst into raucous laughter, her cluster of masked admirers tittering and clapping their hands.

"I don't see him yet," Cass said, scanning the throngs of guests.

"So what do we think?" Falco said, steering Cass to the edge of the room where the weapons and armor lay on velvet-covered marble pedestals. "Is he our man?"

Despite being a foreigner, Joseph Dubois had business dealings with many wealthy Venetians, including Madalena's father. "Dubois is very respected . . . ," Cass said doubtfully. "He has friends in the Senate, perhaps even among the Council of Ten. But it is strange that two women from his employ have now gone missing."

"The real question," Falco said as he watched the masked dancers clapping and moving in unison along the dance floor, "is why would *anyone* want to harm a beautiful woman?" His eyes darkened. "I wonder if Mariabella suspected she was in danger. People are usually murdered by someone they know. Someone they trust."

Cass wondered what black memory was playing out in Falco's head, but before she could ask, the sparkle returned to his eyes and he spun her around in a circle. "Well, that's a relief," Cass said when he pulled her back close. "I should feel perfectly safe. I hardly know *you* at all."

"I said *usually*," Falco teased, glancing again at the men and women swirling across the floor of the portego. "Will you be upset if I tell you I don't know how to dance?"

Cass shook her head. "We're here on official business." Cass stared at the back of a dark-haired girl wearing turquoise and purple skirts over a ridiculously wide farthingale. The girl's train and hat were both embellished with peacock feathers. Was it . . . ?

It was. Madalena, half hidden by a jewel-encrusted mask, stood near the buffet table sipping wine from a blown-glass goblet. Across the room, through the chaos of ornately dressed dancing bodies, laughing faces covered in masks, flickering candelabras, and overflowing glasses, her friend had never seemed so distant to Cass.

"I see a friend of mine over by the food," Cass said, turning her back quickly to Madalena. Mada wouldn't be surprised to see Cass in attendance, but she would be shocked if she realized that Cass had come to the ball with Falco.

Suddenly, Cass felt unmoored, like she was floating in a boat that had been left to drift out into the rough waves of the lagoon, oarless and alone. Everything familiar fading farther and farther away.

And then Falco's hand was on her arm. "Come on." He steered Cass toward the other end of the room. "Look. There's our illustrious host now." He pointed toward a tiered marble fountain with sculptures of golden birds perched on each level. Giant silken banners featuring the Dubois family crest—a golden griffin brandishing a flaming sword—flanked both sides of the fountain. Sure enough, a tall, dark-haired man in a warrior mask leaned against the fountain, surveying the scene with a look of approval. The whole room seemed to orbit around him. Signor Dubois. Cass would have recognized him anywhere, mask or no mask.

"I'm going to go and have a chat with him," Falco said. "I'd love to know more about his taste in the fairer sex."

"But you can't just—"

Falco melted into the crowd before she could finish her sentence. He sidled up to the man in the golden robes and warrior mask. Dubois extended his hand to Falco without hesitation. Jeweled rings glimmered on several of the Frenchman's fingers. She watched with amusement while the man's brow furrowed and relaxed as he pretended to know Falco.

Around her, throngs of masked dancers in brightly colored cloaks and dresses twirled across the checkered floor. It was hot, and the air was heavy with the smell of food, sweat, and perfume. Cass began to feel dizzy. Sweat beaded up on her forehead and trickled down toward her eyes. She lifted the feathered headpiece from her face, waving her hand below her chin to get some air moving. If she could just take her mask off for a few moments, let her face breathe.

She looked around for Feliciana and Mada, but didn't see either one of them in the swirling masses. Just as she contemplated removing her mask completely, a man in a painted tribal mask approached Dubois from behind. Cass blinked hard. She had seen the man's shock of white hair before.

It was the long-faced man from the building in Castello, the place with the organs. And bodies.

Cass froze. If she knew what *he* looked like, there was a good chance he could also identify her. She fumbled to retie her mask, but her shaking fingers could make only part of the knot. The man slowed to a stop a few feet from Dubois when he saw Falco. He finished his approach slowly. Falco quickly nodded and excused himself, but Cass could have sworn he and the long-faced man exchanged a glance of recognition.

Falco returned to Cass and pulled her to the corner of the room where things were a little quieter. "Seems our Signor Dubois hasn't seen Mariabella in over a week," he said in a hushed voice. "How low has a man fallen when even his hired women begin to ignore him?"

Cass only half heard what Falco was saying. "That man," she said. "Who is he?"

"What man?" Falco looked around.

Cass frowned behind her mask. "The man in the painted mask who spoke to you and Dubois. You—you know him."

Both Cass and Falco turned back to Dubois. The long-faced man rested an arm on the host's shoulder. The two seemed to be sharing a hidden joke.

"I don't know him," Falco said. "He must be a friend of Dubois."

"Well, *I* know him. It's the man who almost grabbed me. From the Castello district." Her voice trembled. "Dead bodies in tin basins. Does that stir your memory?"

Falco's expression was concealed beneath the lion mask, but his tone was airy. "You must be mistaken. That place was black as pitch. You couldn't have seen anyone clearly."

"I am not mistaken." She pulled away from Falco. The moments just after her dress had snagged on the broken window came back to her in a series of fragmented images. Falco pulling. Looking back at the long-faced man. The white hair. The furrowed lines in his tall forehead. His arms reaching out for her, fingers just inches away from closing around her legs. Cass would never forget him. His image had been imprinted permanently on her mind.

"But you admit yourself you've been jumping at shadows," Falco pointed out, with a half smile that made Cass want to reach out and strangle him. "And even if it is the same man, it's not like he got a good look at us either. There's no way he would recognize us in our masks."

"I could have sworn you two exchanged a look," Cass persisted. She refused to allow Falco to dodge the subject. "Almost as though you had met before."

"Now I *know* you're seeing things that aren't there," he said, sighing. "Let me get you a drink. It'll soothe your nerves." Without waiting for a response, Falco strode off toward a circular table with a rainbow of blown-glass goblets arranged in a pyramid. He grabbed one hastily, nearly knocking over the glass next to it. Apparently Cass wasn't the only one whose nerves needed soothing.

She turned back to the man in the painted tribal mask. He looked harmless enough in the lamplight, but she knew it was the same man. And she knew, too, that Falco was lying about knowing him.

Cass had to know why.

Falco was heading back toward her with a pair of wineglasses, so Cass acted quickly. As a brunette in a sequined mask pulled Dubois away for a dance, Cass sucked in a deep breath and worked her way through the crowd until she reached the long-faced man's side.

"You look familiar," she said, struggling to keep her voice level. "Have we met before?"

"Angelo de Gradi," the man said, raising Cass's right hand to his lips. "The Dubois family physician. And you?"

Cass paused, trying to think up a plausible identity. She cursed at herself for not having planned what to say. Her cheeks reddened as she struggled to reply.

"Ah," Angelo said. "Another of Joseph's ladies. You will forgive me. I thought his tastes ran a little darker, more raven than starling." He reached out to stroke the plum feathers around her eyes, and his heavy hand loosened the half-knotted string. Cass felt the mask start to slip. She pressed her hand against her face to keep it from falling.

"I can't help but think you look familiar too, Signorina . . ." Angelo trailed off, waiting for Cass to offer her name. The lines in his forehead deepened. He twisted his wineglass back and forth in his thick fingers.

The room seemed to be revolving slowly around her. Every

insignificant movement the man made further convinced Cass of his identity. She took a deep breath. It wasn't like Angelo was going to attack her in a room full of Venice's most influential citizens.

"Perhaps you don't have a name?" he asked, in a tone of amusement.

"I do," Cass said, in what she hoped was a flirtatious tone. "But to give it now would spoil the mystery."

Angelo seemed about to reply when a tall man in a black and brown feathered mask with gold-rimmed eyes—a falcon, maybe—shouldered between them.

"Pardon," he said, extending a hand to her. "Would the signorina care to dance?"

"Yes, thank you." Cass held the beak of her mask to her nose as she allowed herself to be pulled away from the physician. The half-dissected dog and bins full of organs flashed in front of her eyes. Cass now knew the long-faced man's identity. But what she didn't know was whether he was involved in Mariabella's murder.

"Enjoying the ball?" the falcon man asked as the two of them moved awkwardly across the tiled floor and attempted to blend in with the rest of the dancers. Cass tied her mask tightly, and felt better once she had double-knotted it at the back of her head. Unlike most of the guests, who had chosen their brightest apparel for the evening, this man wore only black. Even his hair was obscured by a black velvet hat, pulled low.

"Yes." Cass glanced back over her shoulder. Angelo was heading toward the pair of glass doors that led to the courtyard. Falco had disappeared.

"Your heart is pounding," the man commented as he linked arms with Cass and spun her around in a gentle circle. "I can feel the blood rushing beneath your skin."

"I've been doing a lot of dancing," Cass said absentmindedly. The man released her beneath a low-hanging candelabra. As Cass stepped back into the outer line of dancers, she looked up at the scarlet candles. A drip of wax fell onto the back of her hand, and she jumped. The falcon man's right hand twitched on Cass's rib cage as he went to twirl her again. A strand of her hair tangled itself around his fingers, and Cass winced.

"Sorry," he said. "I have trouble with my hand. War injury."

Cass looked up at him and tried to visualize the face behind the onyx beak. She detected a hint of a foreign accent. "You have seen war with the Turks, then? What was it like?"

"Difficult. Uncomfortable. Brutal." The man's hand continued to tremble against her side. "But there was a certain beauty to it."

Cass shivered. "How can war be beautiful?"

The man didn't answer. He stopped dancing. "Who is it that you're hiding from, Cassandra?"

Cass felt, suddenly, as though she'd been encased in ice. "How— how do you know my name?"

The man leaned in so close that the black and brown feathers of his mask brushed against her skin. "I know many things," he said. He drew her to the periphery of the room. There was something theatrical about the way he moved. Cass tried to disentangle her arm from his, but he gripped her more tightly.

Could it be Maximus the Miraculous hiding behind the falcon mask? Had Cass told him her name? She wasn't certain. The build was about right, and the black hat looked familiar. Cass tried to remember the cadence and timbre of the conjurer's voice, but she couldn't. She faltered in her dancing, nearly colliding with the woman in front of her.

"*Faites attention,*" the falcon man said.

Faites attention? Cass had studied enough French to know the words meant "be careful." But who was this man and why was he speaking French to her? The only person Cass knew in France was Luca, her fiancé. "I need to get back to my friend now," Cass said, attempting to sound unconcerned, in control, although her heart was thudding in her ears.

"Your friend," the man said, in a tone of amusement. "I wonder how your fiancé would feel about him."

Before Cass could respond, the man brought her hand to his mouth and kissed it once; then he melted seamlessly back into the crowd of dancers. He went spinning to the other side of the circle in the arms of a tall blonde woman wearing a low-cut gray dress and black feline mask. Cass watched him for a second, feeling as though her heart might explode out of her chest. She didn't understand how the falcon man could possibly know about her engagement.

Then it came to her: Donna Domacetti. Of course.

One thing was clear: she had been recognized. She needed to go, *now.*

Cass searched the crowd for Falco. She spotted him, standing just beyond the drink table, balancing two glasses of champagne in one hand while chatting with Dubois. As Cass made her way over, Dubois threw his head back and slapped Falco on the back as if the two of them were the oldest of friends. Cass wondered what lies Falco had told to the man.

If Falco was such a skilled manipulator, could Cass trust anything he said?

She slid up behind Falco, careful to stay concealed from Dubois's view, and rested one hand on his waist. "We need to go," she said quietly.

"One moment," he said. "There's a small salon across the hall. Why don't I meet you there?"

Cass didn't want to stay in the ballroom for another second. "Fine," she said, pulling away from Falco and heading toward the front of Dubois's palazzo. As soon as she was away from the heat and crush of the crowd, she felt better. Here, it was empty and quiet, and much, much cooler. Her heartbeat began to return to normal.

She wandered through the salon, which resembled a museum more than a living area. Cass stopped in front of a row of Greek sculptures displayed in front of a gorgeous mural of the Acropolis. The Parthenon sat at the crest of the hill, with the lesser temples scattered below. Cass knelt down to read the embossed plaque in front of the sculpture she liked best, a headless female body with a pair of brilliant white wings. *Nike of Samothrace.*

As Cass reached out to touch one of the intricately carved wings, a shadow darkened part of the goddess's marble form. The air grew thick. Cass felt another presence in the room with her. She turned, slowly, purposefully, scanning the room, but the salon was empty. Just sculptures, and a balcony above her that served to display Dubois's collection of Grecian paintings.

"Jumping at shadows again," Cass murmured to herself.

"There you are, my starling." Falco sauntered into the salon. "Talking to yourself?" he asked.

Cass smiled tightly, but didn't answer. She glanced around the room again as she took Falco's arm. She still had the uncomfortable feeling that she was being watched. For a second, her eyes were drawn toward one of the wall-mounted torches, where a yellow ball of fire split momentarily into two flames, and then came back together.

When she looked away from the torch, she saw spots floating across her vision. But one of the spots wasn't floating. It was falling. Cass watched as the spot passed through the balustrade of the balcony and fluttered toward the ground. She held out her hand to catch it.

A single black and brown feather lay on her palm.

"Delirium can arise from various causes:

imbalance of the humors,

ingestion of poison, hectic fever,

and of course madness."

—THE BOOK OF THE ETERNAL ROSE

twelve

A jagged bolt of lightning slashed across the sky.

"We'd better hurry," Falco said. He dropped his lion mask onto the dock in front of Dubois's palazzo.

He and Cass followed the street that ran alongside the Grand Canal. A handful of other masked revelers were out in the night, stumbling along the water's edge in various states of intoxication. Lightning struck again, this time followed by a blast of thunder. Cass looked up. Massive clouds twisted and swirled above their heads.

"Angelo de Gradi," Cass blurted out. "Are you sure the name means nothing to you?"

"Nothing," Falco said firmly.

Cass let Falco lead her along the uneven stones. She wanted to believe him. She really did. But some tiny dark piece inside of her kept bringing her back to the almost-imperceptible glance Falco had exchanged with the physician. Could she have imagined it? She didn't think so. But one thing was certain: if Falco knew de Gradi, he wasn't going to admit it now.

"You vanished there for a while. Did you find out anything of use?" Cass asked.

"Nothing except that Dubois has more friends than anyone I know. And Mariabella could have known any of them."

She frowned, feeling a quick pulse of anxiety. "Did you see the man in the falcon mask?"

"I wouldn't know a falcon mask from a hawk or an eagle," Falco said. "Why?"

"I danced with him. He knew my name. Said strange things to me."

Falco turned to look at Cass. "What did he say?"

Cass couldn't tell Falco what the man had said, how he had insinuated that Luca would be displeased with their relationship. She wished she hadn't mentioned it. "I don't remember his exact words," she said quickly. "You didn't happen to see Maximus there, did you? The conjurer?"

Falco smirked. "I did not. Perhaps he was in the coatroom, making purses disappear."

Fat raindrops splattered across the front of Cass's dress as the skies opened up in a sudden downpour. Cass ducked quickly inside a nearby arched doorway, pressing her body tightly to the stone to protect herself from the drizzle. Falco squeezed into the arch next to her, his longish hair damp and sticking to his face.

"You're wet," she said, instinctively pushing a strand of brown away from his left eye.

"Very observant," he remarked. "I see those private tutors are really paying off." ·

Cass poked him in the side with her elbow. Even half soaked, Falco seemed to be radiating heat. Cass wished another lock of hair would glue itself to his skin so she could touch him again. She felt close to him, yet miles away at the same time. It was as if what she wanted was on the horizon, but kept disappearing like a mirage.

She reminded herself to be careful. Falco might have lied to her. But maybe she'd only imagined the look between him and Angelo. Falco had been just as scared of that macabre collection of bodies as she had.

"It looks like we're stuck here for a while," Cass said, trying not to let her eyes wander down to Falco's chest. His damp chemise was clinging to his body. The drizzle became a deluge, rain pounding the stone street so hard, it drowned out Falco's response.

Cass leaned in close. "What?"

"I said I know someplace nearby we can go. Until the rain stops." Falco's lips were so close to her ear that she felt a puff of warm air with each *p* he spoke.

Cass trembled slightly. She told herself it was from the weather, but she turned to face Falco even though it meant putting the right side of her dress out into the storm. His expression was neutral, but his eyes smiled at her.

"What sort of place?"

"Tommaso's studio. It's just a couple of streets over."

Cass watched the rain come down in sheets. "Tommaso?"

"Vecellio. He's my master."

Cass sucked in a deep breath. Tommaso Vecellio was descended from the same bloodline as Titian, one of the most famous Venetian artists of all time. Titian had died before Cass was born, but his influence lingered in churches and private homes all across Venice. "You apprentice with Vecellio? How come you never told me?"

Falco slicked his wet hair back from his face. "You never asked."

"And it's okay with him if you take me to his studio?"

"He's in Padua," Falco said with a grin. "He won't even know."

Her aunt wouldn't approve—she considered artists to be just a bit above common criminals, and it was highly improper for Cass to be anywhere with Falco alone. Luca would be furious. But she could hardly cling to the side of an archway all night, praying that the rain would stop.

"Let's go," she said. She told herself she was excited because of the opportunity to see the artist's studio, and not because it would give her more time with Falco.

"Follow me." Falco sprinted across an open area, past the front of a crumbling chapel, and Cass wobbled after him. She paused in the rain to kick off her chopines. Her feet sank an inch down into the mud and mire. So her shoes would be ruined. So what? At this rate her whole outfit would be wrecked beyond repair.

She and Falco crossed over an unfamiliar canal and ducked into a hidden alley. The buildings were so close together, Cass could reach out and touch the smooth walls on both sides of her. They offered some protection from the rainstorm, but not enough. Her dress had been heavy when it was completely dry. Now it felt like it was made of lead.

She struggled to stay close to Falco as he navigated the tangled streets; she was afraid that if he disappeared from her sight, she'd be lost in the maze forever. The two started across another nameless bridge. Long spikes of rain stabbed circular wounds into the surface of the murky canal beneath them. Falco paused on the bridge to consider the view. "Water on water. Beautiful," he said.

Cass stopped just long enough to try to see things through Falco's eyes, the artist's perspective, but all she saw was rain. Rain that was seeping through her dress to soak her undergarments. She put her hands on Falco's lower back and pushed. "Keep moving."

Falco ducked back onto a main path and disappeared through a wooden gate that swung open and closed in the breeze. Cass followed. Beyond the gate were a small courtyard and a winding marble staircase. Falco took the stairs two at a time. At the top, a pair of garishly painted Roman columns flanked a red wooden door.

Cass flinched at the sight of the elaborate bronze door knocker. A gargoyle, but the features looked almost human, like the shrunken head of a screaming old woman. It made Cass think of her aunt. She hoped Agnese was enjoying herself in Abano.

Falco pulled a key from the pocket of his cloak. "Here we are."

Cass was shivering, and her legs were beginning to itch from the layers of wet satin sticking to them. Falco pushed open the door, and Cass followed him inside into the warm, dark room. She heard Falco strike flint against a tinderbox, and a single steel lantern winked to life. Cass blinked, struggling to adjust her eyes to the gloom.

Falco moved smoothly across the room, lighting a pair of oil lamps that sat on a ledge by a window. Gradually, the studio came into focus. She and Falco stood in a large open room with a high arched ceiling. Each wall was painted a different color: ivory, sky blue, soft gray, and the last a ghastly green color that looked like what the town boys spewed into the canals after a wild night of drinking. Cass ran a hand down the smooth stucco wall and was surprised to find that flecks of gray paint chipped off beneath her fingers. Surely Tommaso Vecellio, relative of Titian, could afford a place more majestic than this.

Her eyes flicked around the rest of the room, taking in the sparse furnishings. The standard artist trappings were there: a stool, an easel (empty, she noted with dismay), and a plum-colored divan for posing. Beneath the window ledge, a long table filled with bowls of powder and mugs of paintbrushes ran the length of the studio. Blank canvases stretched over wooden struts were stacked beneath the table. The rest of the room was bare except for a three-panel privacy screen, a large tin basin, and an aging old trunk.

Cass crossed the room and sat on the edge of the divan. She sighed with relief as the little couch absorbed the weight of her garments. She stroked the velvet cushion, no doubt luxurious at one time, but now wearing thin in places. "So Vecellio really works here?"

"Yes. Just like I told you." Falco had his head inside the ancient trunk, so his voice sounded muffled. "What's the matter? Were you expecting something a little . . . racier?" He emerged from the trunk holding a scrap of cream-colored silk and lace against his chest.

Cass lifted her hand to her mouth to stifle a giggle. "What is *that*?"

"Model's costume," Falco said innocently. "You can't stay in those wet clothes. You'll end up like your aunt."

"I hardly think a damp dress is going to turn me into an invalid," Cass scoffed. But the wet fabric *was* uncomfortable—she felt weighed down as though by stones.

"Horrible way to go, if you ask me. Your strength withering away over decades. I'd rather be strangled and carved up like Mariabella." He held the silken garment out in Cass's direction and nodded toward the paneled privacy screen. "Go on, then. I won't watch."

She could feel a hot blush spreading on her cheeks as she accepted the costume. It was about one third the size of the outfit she had worn to the brothels. "But it's so small. Surely there must be something"— she stopped herself from saying *more appropriate* and instead said— "warmer?"

Falco gestured toward the trunk with an elaborate flourish. "Be my guest."

Cass dug through mounds of brightly colored silk and lace, tangles of straps and ribbons, but it looked like Falco had selected the least revealing dress of the bunch. She held up the cream-colored outfit. It had a plunging neckline and a row of buttons up the back that would pull the bodice tight to her chest, but the sleeves were long and flowing and the ruffled skirt would cover part of her legs at least. And it would feel good to be in something dry.

"Fine," she said, sliding behind the screen and attacking the laces of her bodice. "But if you tell anyone about this—"

"I'm afraid it wouldn't make for very interesting news in my crowd," Falco said. "Many of us spend our days with unclothed women."

"Excuse me?" Cass had managed to free herself from her bodice. She unhooked her skirt and the farthingale beneath it, letting the wet gown and its underlying cage fall to the floor with a splat. Then she started working on the laces of her stays.

"Tommaso loves to paint nudes."

Cass wondered if Falco had deliberately said the word *nude* just as she slid her damp stays over her head. But no. He couldn't see her. She hurriedly slid the silken costume up over her legs and torso. "I can't imagine how a woman could be comfortable just lying around naked while a bunch of boys gawked at her."

"You should try it. You might like it." Falco's teasing voice sounded very close, as if he were seconds from ducking behind the screen to see what was taking so long.

"Almost finished," she said quickly. She had her arms in the flowing sleeves, and her fingers were struggling to button up the back of the costume. It felt like there were a million little pearls that needed to hook inside a million little slippery silken loops. She managed to do enough to cover up her lower back and then had to quit. She simply couldn't reach the top buttons by herself. "Promise not to laugh."

"I promise not to—" Falco's eyes widened as she emerged from behind the screen, and he almost dropped one of the glasses of wine he was holding. He looked her up and down, murmured something under his breath that she couldn't make out.

The way he was looking at her made Cass feel like the costume was transparent. "Stop staring," she demanded. She crossed her arms and pointed at the wine. "Is one of those for me?"

"My apologies, Signorina." He handed her a glass of crimson liquid without taking his eyes off her. "I always knew you were beautiful, but I think you may have the longest legs of any woman I've ever seen. And your skin—exquisite! Turn around."

Cass wanted to refuse, but felt herself spinning slowly in a circle so that Falco could look at her. She took a sip from her glass and struggled not to cough. The wine, or whatever it was, was bad.

"Magnificent. Let me help with the buttons." Falco set his glass down on the wooden stool. Before Cass could protest, he was behind her, his fingertips on the small of her back. Cass felt a pearl come loose.

She whirled around, sloshing a bit of wine out of her glass as she slapped his hand. "You undid one," she accused.

Falco laughed. "I'm sorry. I didn't mean it." He reached for her but she leaned away. "Come on, I promise I'll behave."

"Why should I trust you?"

Falco moved to Cass's back again and began sliding each pearl through its loop. He leaned in close so that the side of his face brushed against her neck. "Because you want to."

The wineglass trembled in Cass's hand. She tightened her grip and took another drink. Every time Falco touched her, it got a little harder to breathe. She wasn't sure if it was the outfit, or being so close to him. She sipped from her glass nervously. It was empty by the time he reached the last button.

Falco slid the glass from her fingertips. "I'll refill this, and then we'll get you positioned."

"Positioned?" Cass fumbled over the word.

Falco pulled her over to the divan, then left her standing beside it as he strode across the room to a tall armoire hidden in a shadowy corner. "I'm going to paint you, of course."

"Paint me?"

"Are you going to repeat everything I say?" He returned to her and placed a full glass of cloudy brown liquid in her hand. "Sorry. That was the last of the wine. All I've got left is Tommaso's special brew."

Cass made a face, but accepted the glass. "I'd like to see some of your paintings," she said, in an attempt to stall. Part of her had been hoping that Falco would want her to sit for him ever since she met him, but now that it was happening, she felt horribly self-conscious.

Falco smiled. "You want to see if I'm any good before you become my latest victim?"

"No, I just—"

"I'm joking." Falco removed a stack of canvases from underneath the long table. He held them up one at a time. The first one was easily recognizable—Andriana, in an outfit very much like the one Cass was wearing.

Falco hadn't painted her exactly as Cass remembered her, though. She looked older, more worn. Her lips were full of fine lines, making her smile seem forced.

"She looks broken," Cass said.

He ran a hand through his floppy brown hair. "Yes. That's exactly the feeling I got when I first met her. A broken doll masquerading as a favorite toy. It would be easy to paint her as beautiful, what people see from a distance, but I'm trying to capture the most accurate image possible."

Cass nodded, avoiding the intensity of Falco's eyes. She struggled with the same thing in her writing, the idea of describing the world as it truly was. Falco held up a second canvas, an older woman, Agnese's age. But whereas Andriana was hollow, this woman seemed buoyant, joyous. Falco hadn't misportrayed her age; her face and arms ran deep with wrinkles. Her eyelids sagged, and the skin on her neck hung in thin translucent folds. But there was something about the light in her eyes, her posture, that made this woman more beautiful than the blonde prostitute.

"Who is she?" Cass marveled at the contours of the old woman's body, the outline of blood vessels lingering beneath the skin. She thought again of her aunt and felt a pang of loneliness. She hoped Agnese would return from Abano in high spirits as usual. Despite the fact that Cass often wished she was free of Aunt Agnese's influence over her, the villa was starting to feel empty without her.

"I don't know. A Gypsy. She used to sell rugs at the Sunday

market." Falco traced one finger along Cass's exposed collarbone. "Amazing, isn't it? The human body, so frail—yet so efficiently put together. A study in contradictions."

"Yes—amazing," Cass said. She was a little afraid to admit to Falco she'd been trying to express the very same thing in her journal. She didn't want him to tease her about her writing, as Luca had when they were little. "I feel the same way about the whole world sometimes. People seem simultaneously weak and resilient. Life can be cruel—and yet it is full of hope too."

Falco avoided her eyes as he stacked the canvases. "I've seen my share of cruelty," he said. "Much of it at the hands of the so-called righteous. What is it about religion that leads people to unspeakable violence? Wars, executions . . ." His voice trailed off, and Cass felt certain he was somewhere far away in that moment. But like a curtain lowering and lifting, the darkness in him vanished as quickly as it came.

"Now then," Falco started as he tucked the canvases back beneath the long table. "Have I proven myself, Signorina Cassandra? May I paint you?"

Cass looked down at her long legs protruding from the ruffled skirt. She willed back the images of Aunt Agnese and Luca that threatened to overwhelm her. "You're not going to display it, are you?" she asked.

"I thought I'd hang it by the entrance to the Grand Canal. Call it *Signorina Cassandra Caravello in Her Undergarments*. What do you think?"

"Very funny."

"I thought so." Falco dragged the wooden stool and easel to the center of the room. He gestured for Cass to take her place on the divan. "Please." He pulled a pair of lamps close, murmuring something about the insufficient lighting.

"Under normal circumstances," Falco said, "I would ask you to sit during the daytime. It's the only way to get a clear picture. But it isn't often I have the place to myself." He grinned. "And you are certainly not a normal circumstance."

Cass felt herself blushing; she was sure he would have to paint her complexion a mottled red.

"Make yourself comfortable," he said. "Right now it looks as though you're sitting on a pincushion."

Cass tried a new pose and Falco laughed. "Let me," he said, and, reaching out, set about readjusting her. He gently eased her onto her left hip, letting the right leg fall forward in front of her. He pulled part of her hair over her shoulder so it twisted and curled around her neck. Cass sipped her drink nervously, hoping the alcohol might relax her. Each of Falco's touches generated a tiny bolt of lightning inside her. The charge was starting to build up to dangerous levels.

"Are your legs cold?" Falco asked.

Cass managed to choke out a no. Her whole body was racing with heat, and she felt about two touches away from spontaneous combustion. She was seized by a fleeting impulse to run away; at the same time, she wished he would touch her forever. The costume, the posing, the mysterious alcohol that was dissolving her inhibitions. Cass felt wild and alive, even more so than she had the night they went to the brothels. That night she had been someone else, but tonight she was posing as herself, and she loved it.

Falco stepped back to consider his work. "Almost perfect."

"Almost?" Cass pretended to pout.

"I know." Falco rooted around in the armoire and returned with something folded inside his hand. He held it up for Cass to see—a necklace made of shining amethyst. It reminded her of something, but she wasn't sure what. Probably one of Mada's thousand necklaces. That girl had more jewelry than the Doge's entire family.

Cass shivered as Falco clasped the necklace around her throat. The stones felt like ice against her neck.

"All right. How about a demure look? A stretch for you, I know."

Cass widened her eyes and pursed her lips, just slightly. She tilted her head to the left.

Falco shook his head. "You look like you've swallowed a bee. Forget shy. Let's try something that comes a little more naturally. How about disdain?"

Her eyebrows instantly went up. "I am not disdainful!"

"Perfect." He downed the rest of his muddy liquor. His brush began to flow across the canvas.

Cass felt a charge of excitement, but tried her best not to smile. As she held her position, Falco painted in frantic bursts, pausing occasionally to move the lamps or adjust ringlets of her damp hair. Each time he stopped, she would beg to see the progress and he would shake his head and tell her she had to wait.

As time passed, Cass's muscles started to ache and the liquor began to make her sleepy. She fidgeted on the divan. "What do you think happened to Liviana?" she mused. She shook her head, stifling a yawn. "Where could her body have gone?" A sense of guilt and sadness pulsed through her.

Falco dipped a thin brush into a brilliant red spot on his palette. "You seem to have an unhealthy obsession with that girl's corpse, Cass. Why is it so important to you?"

She twisted the delicate stem of her empty glass back and forth in one hand. "She was my friend. Why wouldn't it be important to me?"

She thought about the other missing bodies in her past—those of her parents. Even in death, she was still somehow robbed of those closest to her. Not knowing what had happened to the bodies—it gave her a sense of unease. Of unfinishedness. How do you move on when you have nowhere to direct your grief?

"Merely an observation." He held his paintbrush up in mock surrender. "I wish tonight had been more productive."

"And you didn't see the man that danced with me? Dressed all in black?" Cass was a little disappointed that Falco had not been paying more attention to her. "There was something about him . . ." She shivered. "Even his mask was different. Predatory, almost."

"I didn't see him, but there are only a few craftsmen in town who produce masks of noble quality. Maybe we could go into town tomorrow and ask some questions."

Cass remembered the feather floating down from the second floor on Dubois's palazzo to land on her hand. If only she had kept it instead of flinging it to the ground. "Maybe we can ask some questions about Dottor de Gradi too. Find out what sort of medicine he practices."

The paintbrush slipped from Falco's fingers, falling to the floor and leaving a splotch of red on the gray stone. Falco bent down to retrieve it. "Maybe," he said. "You look tired. Do you need a break?"

"Yes." Cass sat up on the divan, rolling her head around in a circle. "Can I see?"

Falco refilled her glass and then came to sit beside her. "Not yet," he said, rubbing her neck gently.

"Why not?" Closing her eyes, she tilted her head down to make more room for Falco's hands. Again, something deep inside of her whispered that she should run away while she still could. And again, Cass ignored it.

"Because it's not perfect yet." Innocent words, but he said them in a way that was soft and full of longing.

Cass kept her face down, her eyes closed, afraid of what she'd see if she opened them.

Falco brushed her hair back over her shoulders. He traced a finger around the edge of her lips. "But you are," he breathed, low, right near her ear. And then, slowly, he touched his lips to her cheekbone and left them there.

Cass felt torn in two, like the sky split by lightning. One side guilty. One side wanting. She froze, statue-still, as Falco's lips brushed against her earlobe and then moved down and across her jawbone. His mouth hovered in the air, a parchment's width away from hers. Eternities came and went.

Slowly, Cass tilted her lips to meet his.

And then Falco's mouth was on hers, burning hot, but softer than she had imagined. And Cass felt her whole body tense up and then go weak. Blindly, she reached out for one of his hands, lacing their fingers together. She pressed her lips against him, her soul against him, and she felt truly warm for the first time. Like she'd been living her whole life in a block of ice and had finally escaped into the sun.

Falco's other hand moved up to cradle her face. Cass felt her heart beating against her rib cage like a bird trying to wing free. Their mouths moved against each other, and she couldn't believe the heat they were creating. She couldn't believe it was possible to feel the way she did, so completely intertwined with another human being. It felt like they were on a boat, the whole world swaying around them like waves.

And then: a heavy rapping from outside. Instantly, Cass pulled back, her head throbbing a little. Falco swore under his breath. Both of them looked toward the door. A chorus of drunken voices broke through the quiet night.

"Don't move," Falco said. "I'll get rid of them."

Cass flipped her hair in front of her shoulders. She pulled the costume down over her legs, disoriented. "Who is it?"

"Just some of the gang." Falco brushed his lips across Cass's forehead. He nodded toward the canvas. "Don't peek either."

He slid out of the room, shutting the red door behind him, leaving Cass alone where guilt began tugging at her again.

She was engaged to Luca. She was supposed to be looking for Livi's body. What was she doing? With a shaking hand, she touched her lips. The pressure of Falco's mouth on hers came flooding back. Had it really happened?

Her brain felt foggy. Was it the kiss, or the liquor? She tried to push Livi and Luca and the kiss from her mind. She couldn't think about it, wouldn't think about it.

A burst of laughter from outside caught her attention. She crept over and pressed her ear to the door, curious. She caught snatches of conversation.

". . . another pickup . . . well compensated for our troubles."

Pickup of what? Cass squeezed her eyes closed in concentration.

". . . plague . . . perhaps the next couple of nights . . . San Giuda . . ."

"I'm sick of the smell of death . . ."

The smell of death. That was Falco. She was sure of it. The words swirled in her head, along with the effects of the strange liquor.

The knob rattled and Cass jumped back from the door, but no one came in. She wandered around the room, her heartbeat picking up speed. What did it mean? What secrets was Falco hiding? She nearly tripped when she came upon a full-length mirror leaning next to the armoire. A jagged line bifurcated the surface, slightly offsetting the left side of Cass's reflection. She swayed from side to side, watching her body distort as it moved along the jagged crack. Whatever he'd given her to drink, it was making her light-headed, confused.

One of the lamps burned out, startling Cass. She grabbed for the wall to steady herself, but the room rotated slightly and her palm landed on the cold surface of the mirror. Her reflection fragmented into pieces and re-formed, but it wasn't her anymore—it was Livi.

"No," Cass whispered as the dizziness threatened to engulf her. "You are only a dream," she slurred, feeling hot and panicked. Without thinking, she lashed out at the image with her hand. She gasped as pain ran through her palm and a series of lines spiderwebbed out from the initial crack in the mirror. Cass could swear the image was morphing now, divided by all the cracks: it was turning into an older version of herself. Her father appeared behind her, broken and misshapen in the glass fragments. The woman in the mirror was her mother. Blood seeped through the front of her gown. Cass felt a thick wave of nausea rise up inside her. Her mother bent forward, and Cass saw she had a ring of bruises around her neck and an X carved into her chest.

"No," Cass repeated, stumbling backward from the mirror, and her father reached out his arms to catch her. Only now he was Falco.

As Cass watched, Falco's reflection reached up toward the chain of stones around her neck. Cass knew somehow that if he managed to touch the necklace, he would pull it tight. He would twist it again and again until she fell to the studio floor lifeless, another broken doll.

She wrenched away from him. Air. She needed air.

She stumbled toward the door. But Falco got there first, grabbing her hand before she could undo the lock. He backed her up against the red wood, holding her there easily with one forearm pressed across her collarbones.

"Let me go," she insisted, her voice coming out high and small.

Falco traced his fingertips down the side of Cass's face. "But you can't leave now."

His arm pinned her even tighter against the door. It slipped off her clavicles and onto the soft flesh of her neck, causing the smooth stones of the necklace to press against her windpipe. She struggled to breathe.

"You're hurting me," she whispered as the spinning room started to dissolve before her eyes.

"An open wound, if left untreated,

will grow inflamed and exude

a pustulant fluid that carries with

it the odor of the grave."

—THE BOOK OF THE ETERNAL ROSE

thirteen

When Cass awoke, everything was blurry. She sat up slowly, waving one hand in front of her face to dissipate a strange, sharp odor. She was back on the divan, the coverlet pulled just to her waist.

Falco leaned over her, a small jar of white crystals in one hand. "I'm sorry. I didn't mean to scare you," he said. He looked at her with a mixture of curiosity and concern.

Cass stared at the jar. "What is that?"

"Smelling salts." Falco replaced the stopper and set the jar on the floor of the studio. "You fainted."

"Fainted?" Cass struggled to remember what had happened. It came back to her in pieces: the visions in the mirror, trying to escape the studio, Falco pressing her hard against the back of the door.

Cass fought to stand up in the still-spinning room. "I need to go." She didn't know if she'd feel safe back in the villa until her aunt returned, but anything seemed better than being trapped in the studio. At least Siena was back home. And Slipper. Cass felt like she was floating in the open ocean, and only by clinging to something familiar could she possibly save herself from drowning.

"It's safe here." Falco's voice sounded soft, but Cass couldn't shake the menacing image she had seen in the mirror or the harsh way he had pinned her to the wall. "It's my fault," he continued. "I forgot how Tommaso's alcohol affects people not used to drinking it." He rested one hand on her lower back to support her. "You were seeing things, weren't you?"

Cass's throat seized; she was suddenly worried she would begin to cry. "Liviana. My parents. They were in the mirror." It sounded crazy, but she kept talking. "And you. You were going to strangle me." She felt the necklace, cold and heavy, around her throat.

Falco reached slowly toward her. She tried to shrink away from him, but she was too weak. Her heart thudded erratically. He brushed a lock of hair away from her eyes and tucked it behind her ear. "I would never hurt you, Cassandra," he said. "And you can't go out alone in your current condition, in the rain, especially not in that outfit."

Cass looked down at her exposed skin and blushed. She'd forgotten that she was practically naked. A spot of blood on the cream-colored ruffles swam before her eyes.

Falco followed her gaze. "You're bleeding," he said. He opened the fingers of her right hand and rotated it to see her knuckles. Blood encrusted two of them, and her fingers were starting to swell. "Here, let me clean that."

He left her to fetch something from the armoire. She contemplated making a run for it. She could probably make it to the door before him, but she was beginning to calm down, and he was right that going anywhere in her condition wasn't practical *or* safe. Her head started to pound. She rubbed her temples. Maybe it *was* just the alcohol that had made her see those horrible things.

Falco returned with a brown glass bottle and a bowl of water from the tin basin. Holding her hand over the bowl, he poured some reddish-brown fluid across her broken skin. Tears formed in her eyes. Her hand was on fire. She looked down, not wanting him to see her if she cried. She focused on one of his shirt's metallic buttons.

"Sorry. I know it hurts," Falco said. Pieces of brown hair fell forward in front of his eyes as he bent to dip her hand into the bowl of water. The cool temperature partly extinguished the pain.

She could only watch in silence as Falco lifted her hand from the fluid and blotted each of her fingers with the untucked tail of his white linen shirt. "It's going to be sore tomorrow, but it should be clean. With any luck you won't end up with a fever."

Cass nodded. The motion felt strange to her. She closed and opened her hand a few times. She felt like a marionette, as if all of her joints were operating independently of the others. She let her head fall back onto a circular pillow. "I'm so tired," she said. The words seemed to take a long time to move from her brain to her mouth.

Falco's response also sounded distorted, his syllables breaking up and fading into the warm air of the studio. Cass felt her legs lifting up and then coming to rest on the soft velvet of the divan. A thin coverlet landed on her, its silky coolness a welcome contrast against her warm skin. She balled the fabric up in her good hand and curled onto her side. Cass knew she should throw the covers off, get dressed, and go home, but she couldn't move. As she succumbed to her fatigue, Cass thought she felt Falco's lips press against her cheek.

A numbness in her arm roused her from sleep. She tried to shake it to get the blood flowing, but it was trapped under something heavy. She yanked hard and her arm pulled free. Falco groaned. Falco! Cass sat up on the divan. Falco pulled the coverlet over his eyes to block out the light.

The sun was streaming through a high window she hadn't noticed the night before. She bounded off the divan and almost landed on the floor. *Mannaggia.* Why did her head feel like it had been used as a battering ram? "What time is it?" she hissed.

"Judging from the oppressive amount of light, I'd say late morning," Falco mumbled, burying his face in a pillow.

Cass rushed behind the wooden dressing screen and tugged at the neck of the model's costume she had fallen asleep in. "Why didn't you wake me?" she asked. She was shaking too hard to undo all of the tiny buttons. She gave the garment a hard yank, and a handful of pearl buttons hit the floor of the studio. She wriggled the costume down over her hips.

"Probably because I was also asleep," Falco answered, his voice still heavy with fatigue.

Cass grabbed her clothes, slipping her cotton chemise over her head. She skipped her stays altogether, because the only way she was going to get those cinched properly was with help, and she wasn't about to ask Falco. "You slept next to me all night?" She couldn't keep the accusing tone out of her voice.

"Yes. Is that a problem?" Falco asked.

Cass didn't answer. She stepped into her farthingale and pulled her heavy layered skirts up to her waist. They were still damp from last night's rain. She slid her arms into her bodice, twisting her neck as far as possible to try to thread the ribbons that would secure the garment around her chest. She gave up quickly. She'd have to hide her disarray beneath her cloak.

She was furious with herself. She was an engaged woman, and even if she weren't, what she had done was inexcusable. It didn't matter what had or had not happened. Women who were not courtesans did not go spending the night with men. What if people found out? Agnese would never forgive her. Luca would surely leave her. No other man would want her. She'd end up alone, her only choice to enter a convent or become a courtesan herself. *What would Matteo think?* If Cass disgraced the family name, her aunt's nephew might toss both her and Agnese out into the streets. Even the servants might be released to fend for themselves.

But she couldn't explain that to Falco. If he found out about Luca, he'd want nothing to do with her anymore. Cass was certain of it. And if she admitted to being worried about how others viewed her, he'd scoff and call her a caged bird again, tell her she would be better off without the heavy chains of nobility weighing her down. She couldn't win.

She headed over to the mirror and stopped short at the network of cracks and fissures radiating out in a spiderweb pattern from where she'd struck the mirror with her fist. She looked down at her swollen hand. Cass had had no idea she was capable of inflicting such damage. Slipping the collar of her fur-lined cloak around her neck, she fumbled with the clasp. Her bodice slipped down around her waist.

Falco sat on the divan, watching her with amusement. "Need help?" he asked.

Cass imagined Falco methodically threading the satin laces through each eyelet, his hands repeatedly brushing across her back as he worked. "I'm fine," she said curtly, pressing her arms tight to her sides to hold up her bodice.

"I can see that." Falco's brown hair was sticking up in clumps. Cass had to resist the urge to return to the divan to run her fingers through it. She considered her reflection in an unbroken section of the mirror. Her skirts were wrinkled and her bodice twisted crookedly to one side. She looked like a six-year-old who had tried to dress herself. The strand of amethyst stones still hung around her neck. She started to remove it.

"Keep it for now," Falco said, yawning. He leaned back on the divan like he wished he could fall back to sleep. "It looks good on you."

Cass stroked the necklace with her good hand. She flung her velvet cloak over her shoulders and wrapped it around her whole body. There. She looked almost civilized. She'd just have to hide behind her cloak until she got home.

"Do you remember what happened last night?" Falco asked.

"Some of it," Cass admitted. "I remember seeing things that weren't there." The weird flashes in the mirror stayed with her. Hallucinations, maybe, but for some reason they felt like warnings, like pushing them from her mind completely would be a very bad idea. Then a terrible thought hit her. Maybe she had imagined everything, even the kiss. She lifted a hand to her mouth. Her lips pulsed with their own heartbeat. "Did you actually . . . I mean, we didn't really . . . ?"

Falco seemed to read her mind. He grinned. "No, that part really happened."

Cass's cheeks flushed with warmth. He was looking at her as if he wanted to kiss her again, like he'd be content to spend the whole day snuggled on the divan with his arms around her. Again, she fought the urge to tame his unruly hair with her fingers.

"I have to go," she said, heading toward the door. "If the servants realize I'm missing, they'll be frantic." *And they'll tattle on me.*

Falco stretched and rose from the divan. "I can come with you if you like. If you think you'll get lonely on the journey home." His blue eyes glimmered with mischief.

Cass imagined nestling beside Falco beneath the felze while a gondolier rowed them back to San Domenico. It was unlikely she would be able to resist his advances, and her own desires, during the ride across the lagoon. And she couldn't go kissing him during the day. Anyone might see. She shouldn't be kissing him *at all.* She was risking her whole future for this boy she barely knew. She needed to refocus on what was important—Livi. Mariabella. Keeping herself safe.

"I have a better idea," she said. "Why don't you go talk to the mask makers? See if you can find out the identity of the man in the falcon mask. And ask around a bit at the markets—see if you can find out anything about Angelo de Gradi, too."

Falco's relaxed demeanor seemed to cloud over for just a second, but then he smiled lazily and gave her a mock salute. "As you command, Signorina *Avogadore.* I'll come by the villa later tonight and let you know what I found out."

"How about we meet someplace on San Domenico," Cass said. It wasn't smart to have Falco strolling the grounds of Agnese's estate. Just because Siena was going to keep her secret didn't mean the rest of the staff would be as discreet.

Falco didn't question her. "Come by Il Mar e la Spada. I'll even buy you a mug of their finest swill."

"Deal," she said as he leaned in to give her a kiss on the cheek. Her eyes focused on the scar beneath his right eye. "What happened?" she asked, running one finger over the slightly raised edges.

"A friend dared me to dive into the canals when I first came to town. I had no idea how shallow they were." He rubbed at the scar. "Obviously."

Cass smiled. It sounded like something she might have done as a child. She pressed her lips to Falco's just for a second, and then slipped quietly out the door.

The day was uncharacteristically bright, forcing Cass to squint as she made her way down the marble staircase. She wished she had brought along a parasol the previous evening. She could almost feel new freckles sprouting on her cheeks. By the time she got home she'd look like a speckled goose egg.

When she hit the courtyard, she remembered how she had struggled to keep up the night before as they navigated the twisted network of alleyways. She had no idea how to get back to the Grand Canal. She looked up. The sun hovered almost directly above her, useless for determining which direction to travel.

Past the courtyard gate, smooth stucco walls rose three stories on either side of her. She couldn't even see water. She followed the walls, choosing randomly when she came to a fork in the road. The system of alleys seemed to go on forever, growing smaller with each turn. Cass felt like a prisoner, trapped within the Minotaur's labyrinth. Above her, faceless pairs of eyes peered down from random windows. Sweat began to form on the back of her neck. Her breathing accelerated. Just when she was about to lose hope, Cass saw a rickety bridge in the distance. Bridge meant canal, and canal meant it was only a matter of time before a gondolier came by.

As Cass stood at the crest of the wooden bridge, a thick ribbon of clouds passed in front of the sun, tinting everything gray. She fidgeted in her soggy clothes. A cluster of peasant children pushed past her, giggling behind their dusty hands. An older woman in a gray woolen dress and a white bonnet shushed them and glanced coolly at Cass as she shuffled by on the narrow walkway. It was as if the woman knew what she'd done the night before.

But *Cass* wasn't even sure what she'd done. She and Falco had drunk Tommaso's toxic liquor and kissed. That part wasn't foggy at all. But then the weird hallucinations had started, and her memory after that was fragmented, like the mirror. She vaguely recalled lying on the divan, with Falco cleaning her hand, but she didn't remember him curling up beside her. Had they kissed more? Had they done more than kissed? The image of the room at the brothel—the slick skin, the two bodies rocking together—flashed briefly into Cass's mind.

She shook the idea from her head as a sleek black gondola floated by in the water. No. She would remember if anything like *that* had happened. A wizened old gondolier in a colorful outfit nodded to her, and Cass signaled for him to pull over.

"I need to go out to San Domenico Island," Cass said.

The old man started to protest. Cass pulled a shiny silver coin from a small suede pouch. The gondolier looked unimpressed. "I'll pay the return fare too," she added with a sigh, pulling out a second piece of silver.

The man's eyes came to life at the sight of the second coin. He allowed Cass to board and then turned the boat around with a few well-placed strokes of his oar. The gondola began to cruise smoothly through the water. Just as Cass curled up in the felze, a soft drizzle started to fall. That was Venice in spring: brilliant one minute, raining the next. The gondolier muttered something under his breath. Cass watched the streaks of rain cut through the misty air. She fiddled with the necklace Falco had given her as the boat left the Rialto and headed toward the Giudecca.

As the gondola cut between the Giudecca and San Giorgio Maggiore, wind whistled through the slats of the felze, stinging Cass's eyes and skin. She wasn't cold, though. She might never be cold again. Touching her lips, she replayed Falco's kiss in her head, one delicious second at a time. His lips hovering near her face before coming to rest on her cheekbone. The indecision, the terror that gripped her heart as she decided whether to give in. The way she had every reason to turn away and only one reason to turn toward him—because she wanted to, almost more than she had ever wanted anything in her life.

What would have happened if they hadn't been interrupted by the other artists? She reclined against the back of the felze, trying to imagine Falco's weight on top of her, his mouth finding her neck, making its way down to her bare shoulder while she ran her fingers through his messy brown hair. She had no idea if it was all right for a woman to touch a man or if she was just supposed to let him touch her. She knew what Falco would say: Forget about what's appropriate. Do what feels right.

Cass closed her eyes. Kissing him had felt right. So right. But it shouldn't happen again. Couldn't. Luca would probably challenge Falco to a swordfight if he found out, even though neither boy struck her as the sort who had ever handled a weapon.

And so what if she wasn't thrilled at the idea of becoming Luca's bride? That didn't mean she wanted to be disavowed and turned out into the streets. And worse: see the same happen to Agnese and Siena. Even if he wanted to, there was little chance that Falco could take care of her, and no chance at all he could provide for her aunt and a maidservant.

The gondolier tapped his oar against the side of the gondola and Cass realized with surprise that they were pulling up to Agnese's dock. Even more surprising was the fact that another boat was moored there, a wide blue vessel, with seating capacity for four or five people. Cass wondered who had come to the villa in such a luxurious watercraft. Maybe the boat belonged to someone visiting a tomb.

The old man secured the gondola across from the blue boat and happily accepted the double fare. He pocketed the coins and then stared at Cass for a moment, his thin lips peeling back to reveal a mouthful of rotten teeth. Cass realized her cloak had fallen open, exposing her sagging bodice and disheveled dress. She pulled the cloak tight again, but the gondolier continued leering at her as he helped her from the gondola with one of his bony hands.

"*Grazie*," she said, wrenching her hand away from his quickly as she stepped gingerly from the boat. As she hit the edge of the dock, she froze. Giuseppe the gardener knelt on the manicured lawn, pruning the shrubbery that framed the front of the villa. Just because the old man never spoke to her didn't mean he wouldn't speak *about* her to her aunt. If Agnese ever found out she'd spent the night away from the villa, she was as good as dead. Being dishonored and turned into the streets would pale in comparison to the punishment that the old woman would inflict upon her.

Cass's heart began to race. For now, Giuseppe had his back to the dock, but eventually he would have to turn around to clip the other side of the bushes. When he did, he would see Cass immediately, regardless of the path she took. She had no way of making it all the way to the house without being discovered.

There had to be someplace she could hide.

Cass glanced at the blue boat. It bobbed in the water a few feet away from the dock. Staying low, Cass gave the rope a stern tug, but she wasn't strong enough to pull the boat close. Cass lowered herself off the edge of the dock, her chopines landing on a diagonal plank of wood used to reinforce the structure. She wrapped her hands around one of the end pilings, cringing at the slick feel of algae. Just when her cramping fingers threatened to give out and plunge Cass to the water below, she peeped her head up and saw Giuseppe disappearing around the back of the villa.

Heaving a sigh of relief, Cass pulled herself up from the water's edge, struggling to keep her clothing from snagging on the dock's splintered wood.

She cut a wide path around the outside of the villa's property. Half crouched, she sneaked around to the back of the house and rested her ear against the door leading into the kitchen. When she was convinced the room was empty, she slipped quietly inside, closing the door behind her.

Just as Cass leaned against the door to catch her breath, Siena fluttered down the servants' stairs, frantic. "Signorina Cass!" she said, her voice just above a whisper. "Your aunt returned early from Abano and has been asking for you all morning. I didn't know what to tell her, so I said you had gone for a walk along the shore." Siena paced back and forth next to the long countertop. "Of course she was furious at me for letting you go anywhere alone. I was afraid she was going to send me away, so I told her you insisted."

Agnese was back? This was bad. Very bad. Cass unclenched Siena's hands, squeezing one of them gently. "It's okay, Siena. I'll handle my aunt." She didn't know exactly how she was going to accomplish this, but it felt like the right thing to say. "You did well." Guilt surged deep within her. Not only was she lying, but she was forcing others to lie for her as well.

Siena looked about five seconds away from bursting into tears. "When I woke up this morning and you weren't back, I thought maybe something terrible had happened. I thought maybe your Falco was a kidnapper after all."

"He's not a kidnapper." Cass leaned up against the counter, securing her bodice to her sides with her arms. But who was? Dubois? Angelo, the long-faced man? The stranger in the falcon mask? Were all the men of Venice dangerous? Even Falco might have lied to her. Certainly, he was keeping secrets. How quickly she had let that slip from her mind when they had ended up alone together. Cass bit her lip. She wanted to organize her thoughts in her journal, but first she needed to deal with her aunt, as promised. "Come on," she said, dragging Siena behind her as she headed up the stairs to the dining room. "You've got to help me change before my aunt sees me."

"Signorina Cass, wait—" Siena stopped at the end of the long table. Her hand pulled free from Cass's grip.

But Cass couldn't be stopped. Fueled by the excitement of her close call with the gardener, she stampeded through the dining room and into the portego. Too late, she realized her mistake. Her aunt was sitting in a high-backed chair sipping tea from her favorite gold-rimmed ceramic teacup. And she wasn't alone.

"Cassandra! Where have you been?" Agnese's voice was a mixture of anger and concern. "The servants have been chattering about a kidnapper. I had begun to fear someone had spirited you away."

Cass barely heard her aunt's reprimand. She was too busy staring at Agnese's visitor. Sitting between a pair of manservants was an attractive middle-aged man wearing clothes sewn from cloth fine enough to suit the Doge. His dark hair was streaked with hints of silver, and he wore jeweled rings on three fingers. Cass recognized him at once.

It was Joseph Dubois.

"Personal garments are
the greatest expression of one's
standing in society, but the body
is the greatest expression of one's soul.
Both are temporary trappings."

—THE BOOK OF THE ETERNAL ROSE

C ass opened her mouth but couldn't immediately respond. Dubois showed no signs of having spent the previous night dancing and drinking. It was like he'd sprung straight out of her thoughts and onto Agnese's velvet portego chair.

"*Mi-mi dispiace*, Aunt Agnese," Cass finally stammered, inching away from Dubois toward the corridor that led to her room. "I . . . I went for a walk. I guess I lost track of time." Maybe if she stayed far enough away, Agnese wouldn't realize the state of disarray of her dress. Had Dubois somehow recognized her at the ball? Why else would he be here, on San Domenico, in her aunt's portego?

Agnese's mouth dropped open, causing a second chin to form in the loose, doughy skin of her throat. "You speak of *time* as though it were an unruly canine. What you *really* lost track of, Cassandra, were your manners, and meanwhile the entire house has been turned upside down looking for you." The old woman clucked her tongue. "You need always consider how your actions might affect others." She shook her head as if Cass were beyond hope. "And speaking of manners, come and greet Signor Dubois. He's one of the most influential men in all of Venice, you know." Agnese turned a smile on Dubois.

Reluctantly, Cass approached the Frenchman. His servants looked away as Dubois took her hand and kissed it. "My pleasure," he said, his voice smooth as silk. His smile was dazzling, and his teeth were white and straight.

Blushing, Cass dipped into a shallow curtsy, trying to hold her cloak around her soggy skirts. "It's nice to see you, Signore."

Agnese squinted. Her gnarled fingers reached out to pluck a piece of lint from Cass's top skirt. "Why do you look like a drowned chicken?" The old woman leaned in closer. "And what is that on your face? Is it *blood*?"

Blood from her hand. Possibly paint. Who knew? Cass thought quickly. "I went out on the rocks by the shoreline and a burst of surf hit me. I slipped and fell. I guess I must have scratched my face."

Agnese frowned so deeply that her silver eyebrows met in the middle of her face. For a second, Cass could swear she saw something flash across Agnese's face—anger? Concern? But just as quickly, it was gone.

"Siena," Agnese barked. The lady's maid scampered out from the dining room, where she had no doubt been eavesdropping. She stood just inside the doorway, pale and wide eyed like a goat ready for slaughter. "See to my niece immediately," Agnese said.

"Yes, Signora." Siena dipped into a low bow and then headed toward the back of the villa.

Cass followed close behind her, stopping at the threshold of the portego to curtsy once more in Dubois's general direction.

Agnese pursed her lips into a hard line. This look was easy to determine: *We'll talk about your behavior later.*

As she slipped out of the room, she heard Dubois say, "You're smart to take a firm hand with her. I remember too well what it was like to be a headstrong youth. Ah, the feeling of invincibility."

Agnese sighed. "Yes, she gets that from her parents, I'm afraid. They were both wandering spirits."

Cass paused, straining to hear Dubois's response.

She heard the clink of teacup on saucer. "A little wandering is good for the soul. It's just the company one keeps that may be hazardous."

"Indeed," Agnese answered. "Of course young women are like mules: the harder you pull, the harder they resist. No, I think I know just the thing that will help her . . . regain her focus." Her voice faded away as Siena, terrified of getting caught eavesdropping, pulled Cass toward her room.

In her bathroom, Siena brought Cass a bucket of steaming water, and then helped her get out of her damp clothes. Cass ran a soapy cloth over her skin reluctantly. Even though the warm water felt good, she couldn't bring herself to scrub too thoroughly. She could still smell traces of paint and minty soap on her. Falco. She didn't want to wash him away.

After helping Cass into her dressing gown, Siena grabbed a silver-plated hairbrush from the dressing table and began to brush Cass's hair so furiously that it made Cass's eyes water.

"Not so hard," she grumbled. "No need to punish me. I'm sure my aunt has something terrible planned already. Perhaps I'll have to embroider an entire bedcover, or worse, she'll make me start taking violin lessons again." Cass had endured two years of harp and violin lessons with a tutor from the Rialto, but eventually Agnese had realized that her niece was just not musically gifted.

"Now that would be a punishment for us all, Signorina," Siena said with a delicate smile.

Cass would have been offended if the remark weren't so true. Even the house cats used to run and hide when they saw Cass with her violin case.

"Why did she come back early, Siena? Do you know?" Cass asked.

"Something about a storm approaching, I think." Siena tugged the brush through Cass's hair. "I wouldn't worry too much about punishment. She did come home in excellent spirits as usual—and of course, she doesn't know you spent the whole night on the Rialto."

"You won't tell her, will you?" Cass looked pleadingly at Siena in the mirror.

"I won't—if you promise it won't happen again. I don't like lying, and I'm not very good at it." Siena's eyes met hers. "And I worry about you, even when you are with your lover."

"He's not my lover," Cass said quickly. She didn't understand why Siena seemed determined to believe there was something romantic going on between her and Falco. Just because Falco had kissed her didn't mean he would do it again. It was the alcohol. Neither of them had been thinking clearly. Cass attempted to change the subject. "What is Signor Dubois doing here?"

Siena shrugged. "Personal business with your aunt, I imagine." She lifted her chin daintily. "I am not privy to Signora Querini's affairs."

Cass elbowed Siena in the ribs. "*I am not privy to Signora Querini's affairs,*" she mimicked. "Come on, Siena. I know those ears hear everything."

Siena dropped her glance to the floor and Cass immediately felt guilty. She hadn't meant to imply that the girl's ears were too big, only that the servants always seemed to be hovering just out of sight. Siena put the silver hairbrush back on the dressing table and picked up a hair ornament carved from sea coral and adorned with pearls. She began to twist Cass's hair into a tight bun. "If I heard anything, it was *purely accidental,*" she said, shooting Cass's reflection a warning look. "And only as a result of the normal course of my duties."

Cass winked at Siena in the mirror, amazed at the sleek topknot the girl had created. "Fine. What did you *accidentally* hear while you were responsibly completing your duties?"

Siena pinned the pearl ornament around Cass's hair and pursed her lips. She liberated a couple of strands from the bun and nodded as they curled naturally around Cass's face. "I *may* have heard Dubois say he saw you in unsavory company at his masquerade ball last evening."

Cass's heart stopped. So he had recognized her at the ball, after Agnese had expressly forbidden her from attending. Had he seen her with Falco? Angelo? The man in the falcon mask? "Did he say whom he meant?" Cass slipped her arms into her stays and tried not to flinch as Siena pulled them tight.

Siena selected one of Cass's favorite dresses from the armoire, a gorgeous topaz gown with a lace neckline and cream-colored sleeves. "If he did, I didn't hear it."

"Did he say anything else?" Cass's voice sounded muffled as Siena slid the heavy dress over her head.

"He mentioned the matter of Sophia going missing. He told Agnese not to worry—that there's no snatcher on the loose. Dubois believes she ran off with a traveling minstrel or magician," Siena said. "According to him, she was quite taken with a performer at one of his parties."

Cass frowned. It was certainly possible—but was it true? If so, perhaps Mariabella and Sophia's disappearances were unconnected. The thought made Cass feel slightly better. Mariabella might have been strangled by a jealous patron, but that was easier to stomach than a killer on the loose.

Still, there was the note . . . and that terrible building full of bodies . . . And if the maid had run away with a performer, perhaps it had been Maximus, the conjurer who also claimed to have been fond of Mariabella.

Cass sucked in a deep breath and focused on her reflection. The sun had pinkened her cheeks a bit, but thankfully she didn't see any new freckles. "I believe I can safely return to the portego," she said, "and receive my lecture from Aunt Agnese while looking *proper*."

Cass made her way back down the corridor to where her aunt still sat in the portego, sipping tea from a delicate silver cup. Joseph Dubois and his men had left. Cass took the seat Dubois had vacated. "Aunt Agnese," she said, "I am so sorry. I shouldn't have gone to the ball without your permission. And I didn't mean to worry anyone this morning."

To Cass's shock, the old woman reached out and patted her gently on the leg. "I know. I fear I may have overreacted." Agnese's brown eyes gleamed as she smiled a grin so big, it was borderline scary. "You did look frightful, though. Heaven knows what Luca would have thought. Or Matteo," she added.

Cass was so startled by the leniency of her aunt's response, she couldn't think of anything to say. She had been expecting a verbal flogging, at least.

Agnese reached out to pinch the loose fabric under her niece's arms. "This dress has always been one of my favorites, but it hangs on you like a flour sack. Why don't you take Siena and go see Signor Sesti? He can measure you for a new dress since you insist on being so slender. Take Narissa with you too," she added as an afterthought. "I have a couple of errands for her as well."

Cass stared at her aunt, trying to determine what kind of game she was playing. Was she trying to make Cass feel guilty for running amok and embarrassing her in front of Dubois? Or was she really going to reward Cass's transgressions with a dress-fitting at the most glamorous shop in all of Venice?

"Go on," Agnese said, slipping a sealed envelope into Cass's hands. "That's got instructions for the tailor. I requested some fabric from the weaver a few weeks ago. I think you'll be pleasantly surprised by what he has done."

Cass didn't doubt it. Signor Sesti had designed and altered dresses for Madalena that were every bit as elegant as the ones her father routinely brought back from abroad. Cass called for both maidservants and almost dragged them out the door before Agnese had time to change her mind.

At the last second, Cass grabbed the letter from Luca. It had been sitting on the side table for so long that a fine layer of dust covered the red wax seal. She felt a pang of guilt. Her fiancé probably took time out from his diligent studying to write her letters, while Cass spent her evenings running wild with another man. How quickly would he disavow her if he found out she had let Falco kiss her? Cass almost wished she were the kind of girl who could break hearts and dishonor her family just to get what she wanted.

But no, persuading Luca to leave her might solve one problem—but it would cause too many more to count.

Just sitting inside the tailor's shop made Cass feel better. She had always found Madalena's obsession with beautiful things a little silly, but surrounded by silky fabric samples and wooden forms sporting half-finished formal gowns, Cass realized she and her friend weren't so different. She reached out and stroked the train of a rich green velvet dress that hung on the form nearest to where she sat. The fabric was so dark, it almost looked black. The front of the gown plunged low, its neckline emblazoned with a row of sparkling emeralds. The tailor still needed to finish the cuffs and the shimmery silver sleeves, but even as a work in progress this dress would have outshone almost all of the outfits she had seen at Dubois's ball.

Signor Sesti stood behind a wooden counter, accepting a payment from a young woman with her hair twisted up into a high cone shape. As Cass and Siena waited for the dressmaker to finish with his previous customer, Cass pulled out the letter from Luca. Fiddling with the edge of the folded parchment, she went to break the red wax seal and paused. The wax felt lumpy. Cass examined the blob of red more closely. It looked as if someone had sliced through the wax beneath Luca's lily insignia and then later resealed it. Luca must have reopened the letter to add something. As if anything he had to say was that crucial anyway. Reluctantly, she scanned the first few lines of the letter.

My Dearest Cassandra,

Bonjour, ma chérie. I think of you often. I hope you are not growing lonely and bored being stuck in the villa with your aunt. My colleagues drag me out for a meal occasionally, but I spend the majority of my time studying. Are you also concentrating hard on your lessons? I can only imagine how beautiful you've become since I saw you last, and I should hope there aren't too many men trying to court you in my absence. I know that you see the best in people, but remember, most men are not to be trusted.

Cass refolded the letter in disgust. If she had read it on the ride over, she might have tossed it straight into the lagoon. They were engaged, and yet Luca persisted in being threatened by imaginary suitors vying for her. As if she could just break her engagement and run off with some other man.

No matter how much she might want to.

Siena glanced up as the tailor finished his dealings with the young woman. "Wasn't it kind of your aunt to order a new dress for you?"

"It was kind," Cass mused. "And odd." She hoped Agnese's advanced age wasn't causing her to become feebleminded. Her aunt hadn't seemed forgetful or erratic, but this lack of punishment was definitely inconsistent with her usual behavior.

The woman at the counter bid Signor Sesti good-bye and turned toward the door. She wore a low-cut bodice with a belt cinched tightly around her waist. Cass watched her sashay out of the shop, admiring the way her body moved beneath the lush fabric. Cass wondered if she was a courtesan.

Siena handed the envelope from Agnese to Signor Sesti. Cass peeked over the tailor's shoulder as he scanned the note written in her aunt's big spidery handwriting. His face lit up when he read over the promised payment. Cass's eyes widened. Maybe her aunt *was* getting weak minded. The figure was much too large for a single gown.

Signor Sesti hummed to himself as he disappeared into his supply room. He returned with an armful of bolts of vividly colored fabric. "Your aunt had these delivered from Signor Bochino's shop. Once we have settled on the design and cut the fabric, I will send it across town to be embroidered."

"But I don't need anything this extravagant," Cass protested. The brilliant satin had metallic threads sewn within it, making the whole material glimmer when the light caught it just right. Cass had no doubt she would ruin it the first time she wore it.

Signor Sesti continued as if he hadn't heard her. He held a roll of chiffon up to the light. "And this, maybe with tiny pearls. Don't you think it would make a lovely veil?"

Cass felt sick to her stomach. She leaned away from the bolts of fabric as if they might sprout fangs and bite her. Suddenly, it all made sense—the lack of punishment, the trip to the tailor, Agnese's good mood. The old woman hadn't sent her to be fitted for some new pieces to wear about town. Cass was there at Signor Sesti's shop for one reason only: to be measured for her wedding dress.

"Madness weakens the mind and
disease weakens the body,
but nothing destroys the spirit
like the loss of true love."

—THE BOOK OF THE ETERNAL ROSE

fifteen

Before Cass could utter a word, before she could begin to explain to Signor Sesti that there had been a horrible mistake and she was absolutely *not* ready to be fitted for her wedding dress, the tailor disappeared into the back room and the shop door squeaked open again.

Madalena entered, dressed in a pale lavender gown with silver sleeves and an indigo underskirt. The collar of her cloak was dyed dark purple to match. Mink fur, it looked like. Maybe fox. Mada adjusted her layered skirts and kicked off a pair of impossibly tall chopines as she glided across the front of the shop.

Her lady's maid, Eva, scooped up the shoes and set them just inside the door to the shop. "Signorina Madalena," the girl said. "I'll walk down to the market to get the items your father requested. I'll return in thirty minutes?"

"That's fine." Madalena dismissed the girl with a wave of her fingers.

Cass had never been so relieved to see her friend. "Mada," she exclaimed. "There's been a mistake—surely you're the one getting fitted for your wedding dress? An alteration, perhaps?"

Madalena's heart-shaped mouth widened into a grin. "My dress has been finished for weeks." She freed a tendril of her hair that had caught itself beneath the scooping neckline of her gown. "No, your aunt sent her dotty old handmaid to my palazzo with a message that I was to meet you here to share this *special moment*." She giggled.

Cass worried she might throw up.

Signor Sesti returned from the back room with a measuring ribbon and the two main fabrics Agnese had selected. Mada reached out to touch the bronze satin, fingering the metallic strands woven within the dyed fibers.

"I love this one, don't you?" Mada chirped.

Cass couldn't answer. She couldn't breathe; she had a desperate urge to undo her stays, as she had done with Falco on the bridge.

Feeling as though she were in a dream, she allowed the tailor to lead her over to a small fitting room in the corner of the shop, while Mada trailed behind them. Even when Siena helped remove her skirts and bodice, Cass still felt as though she were being squeezed from all sides.

The tailor motioned for Cass to step up onto a raised platform in front of the mirror. For the first time, she felt almost naked in her long chemise. It didn't usually bother her, but her body felt different now; her skin burned with secrets. *Falco. The studio. His mouth on hers.* Signor Sesti began draping and pinning fabric around her.

"Why didn't you tell me you had set a date for your wedding?" Mada asked. Cass could tell she was struggling not to seem hurt.

"I *haven't* set a date for my wedding," Cass insisted. "You know it will take months for this dress to be made." She immediately felt the sharp stick of a pin in her left hip.

"Signorina. You will need to stand still," the tailor said, humming under his breath.

"I don't even know when Luca's returning to Venice," Cass went on. The words comforted her immediately. Of course—just because she was being fitted for her dress didn't mean she would be married any sooner. Did it?

Siena cleared her throat. She'd been so quiet since Madalena arrived that Cass had almost forgotten she was there. "I believe I saw Signor da Peraga at the market yesterday," she said. "Did his letter not say he was returning to Venice?"

"You must be mistaken, Siena," Cass said. "Luca would have come directly to the villa if he were back in town."

Madalena ignored Siena and went to stand beside Cass. She watched the tailor as he worked, wrapping circles of the glimmering bronze fabric around Cass's slender frame. "Agnese must have arranged a date *for* you, or she wouldn't have scheduled a fitting." Mada pursed her lips as the tailor wrapped a ribbon around Cass's waist and marked it with a piece of chalk. "You really ought to think about putting on a little weight before you get married. I'm sure Luca would prefer you a bit more filled out."

Cass frowned. She hadn't been eating that much lately. Who could think of food? She had too much on her mind: the murder, the missing body. *Kissing a stranger.*

Mada pulled a jeweled hair clip from the back of her head, and her shiny brown braids tumbled around her face. "I have to say—I *don't* see why you couldn't wait until after my wedding to begin planning your own." This time, the hurt in her voice was evident.

"Madalena, I swear. I am as surprised as you are about all of this.

I don't know what Aunt Agnese was thinking." But she did know. Agnese might not have caught Cass on the Rialto, but she knew that her niece was misbehaving. What better way to force Cass back into line than threaten to move up the wedding?

Cass shook her head and the tailor muttered under his breath. "Sorry," she said while he fashioned a high collar around her neck made of starched lace. Then to Mada: "If it were up to me, I would have waited a year or more to even think about any planning. I wish I could postpone the wedding indefinitely. I just don't *feel* ready. Sometimes I wish . . ."

Cass hesitated. She decided that Signor Sesti, as a tailor for both nobles and wealthy courtesans, was no stranger to gossip. Chances were that nothing she could say would make the old man's stoic face so much as twitch.

"What?" Mada prompted her.

"I wish I were a man," Cass burst out. "Or a courtesan, even. At least then I'd have some control over my own life."

"A courtesan?" Mada's voice sharpened to a screech. "You must be joking. They're no better than common whores. Today I passed the Rialto Bridge only to see some courtesan's stays dangling from a mooring post. I can only imagine how they got there."

Cass turned bright red. She had assumed her stays had ended up in the canal, not looped around a post for the whole world to see.

Mada took her embarrassment for surprise. "Yes, that's right. There's a little more to being a courtesan than control. Honestly, Cass, you should feel lucky that you won't have to wait an eternity to start your married life like me." She sighed dramatically.

"But what about love?" Cass blurted out, her mind returning to the kiss she had shared with Falco. A warmth bloomed inside her and spread throughout her limbs. How could a feeling so powerful be wrong?

Madalena again misinterpreted her. "I'm sure Luca loves you," she said. "And if not, he'll grow to, over time." She raised an eyebrow. "Or are you worried about the *love* that happens on the wedding night?"

Cass reddened again. She hadn't even let her mind go there, what it would be like to lie with Luca, skin to skin. They had only even kissed once, and that was because he had demanded it and Cass had been curious to know what it felt like. They'd been sitting on a bench in Agnese's garden. It had happened about three years ago, just before Luca left to study abroad. Back then, Agnese had more energy and used to tend the plants herself. The whole place had been ablaze with marigolds and roses.

"I'm going to kiss you now," Luca had announced, pressing her firmly back against a wooden trellis. She didn't even have time to close her eyes. She just watched as his pale skin came closer and closer. As he touched his cool lips to hers, all Cass could think about was the splinter digging into her shoulder blade; all she could see were the rose blossoms, blurring like red fire against the backdrop of the setting sun.

"You two will figure it out," Mada continued breezily. "I can hardly wait for my night with Marco." She winked at Cass. "I may *not* wait."

Cass couldn't help but laugh at that. She felt a rush of affection for her friend.

Signor Sesti stepped back. "What do you think?" he asked.

Cass looked up at her reflection in the mirror. The tailor had wrapped her in yards of brilliant bronze satin. He held up a smaller bolt of velvet brocade that was embossed with green flower patterns. "We'll use this for the bodice and sleeves. Do you like it?"

"It's beautiful," Cass admitted. The girl in the reflection looked like a stranger. The design really was gorgeous. The tailor had a fine eye for which colors complemented each other, and the green and bronze mixture worked well with her auburn hair.

A young boy appeared, dressed in plain leggings and a sleeveless leather doublet. He looked down at the ground as he mumbled something about problems with the latest shipment. The tailor excused himself and followed the boy through the door leading to the back of the shop.

"You really do look lovely," Madalena said, walking a slow circle around Cass as she spoke. "This dress will be almost as gorgeous as the last collection that Father brought home." She emphasized the *almost* very slightly.

Cass suppressed a smile. Madalena had always been competitive. Maybe that was why she and Cass got along so well. Cass didn't have much interest in competing, especially not about who had the shinier hair or the finer dresses. In those areas, Mada would always win. "I'm sure your wedding will be the event of the entire season," she said. "At least it's not being planned by a half-blind old lady whose favorite word is *frivolous*."

"I don't think you're being fair." Madalena pretended to chastise Cass. "I'm sure your aunt's favorite words are *proper* and *decorum*. *Frivolous* is at best a distant third."

The two girls giggled, and Mada launched into a story about her latest wedding preparations. "You wouldn't believe the gifts that are pouring in from Father's business associates: silver platters, a

Brunelleschi painting, even an antique Roman bust of Nero that was discovered while digging a well. I don't know where we'll put everything." Madalena tossed some of her sleek fishbone braids back over her shoulders. "And the wedding feast! Boiled head of veal stuffed with capers and truffles, roast porcupine seasoned with cinnamon and cloves, and a whole arrangement of pies and pastries for dessert. And did I tell you a friend of my father's has imported wine and cheeses from France?" Madalena gushed. "My reception will be the talk of the city."

"Your father's friend," Cass said, striving to sound casual. "Do you mean Joseph Dubois?" Despite the story that Dubois had given to her aunt, she thought it highly odd that a servant from his estate had disappeared just a few days after his favorite courtesan had turned up dead.

Mada made a face like she'd just smelled something rancid. "Joseph Dubois? No. His parties are better known for their *ladies* than for their food, if you know what I mean. I was actually in attendance at his masquerade ball last night. You know that man had the audacity to hang a painting of himself right next to his portrait of the Doge? I daresay his was a bit larger too," she added. "Still, it was a good time. You should have come."

"Well, you know how my aunt feels about parties," Cass said, averting her eyes so that Mada wouldn't be able to read the lie there.

"Frivolous!" Mada declared, and Cass couldn't help bursting into laughter. Even Siena chimed in.

"I was referring to Father's friend Cristian," Mada said when she had recomposed herself. "You met him at my palazzo, remember?" Mada squeezed in next to Cass so that she could see her own reflection. She adjusted the strand of lilac pearls hanging tight around her throat and then pinched one of her dark braids between the thumb and forefinger of her gloved hand. "Do you think I should lighten my hair for the ceremony?"

Cass shook her head. "I think your hair is perfect just as it is. Besides, all the girls have taken to lightening their hair. You'll stand out more if you keep it dark."

Mada smiled at herself in the mirror, evidently pleased at the idea of standing out. Turning to face Cass, Mada ran her hands over the pinned fabric. She adjusted the draping neckline so that the top half of Cass's breasts peeked out. "Luca is going to faint when he sees you in this dress. Poor thing will spend the entire ceremony and reception counting the minutes until Siena strips you out of it for him."

Cass flinched as the bell above the shop door jangled, announcing the arrival of another patron. Balmy street air rushed into the fitting area as a masculine voice called out, "*Bongiorno*. Anyone here?" It was Marco, Mada's fiancé.

"We're in here," Madalena called. "You can come in. She's decent."

Cass touched a hand to her face. Her skin felt warm. Suddenly, the pinned fabric felt heavy and confining. She didn't want anyone else to see her like this.

Too late.

Marco slipped into the fitting room and whistled long and low as he let the door close behind him. "Signorina Cassandra, you look stunning," he said, shaking his wavy brown hair back from his face. "I swear if I weren't already betrothed, I might ask for your hand right this second."

Madalena gave him a dark look, and he pretended to see her for the first time. "Only joking, my goddess," he said, moving to stand behind her. He swept her dark braids to one side and pressed his lips to her exposed neck.

Signor Sesti coughed as he returned from the back room, and Marco pulled his mouth away from Mada's skin.

"*Mi dispiace*, Signore." Marco straightened the golden medallion that hung around his neck. He gestured to his wife-to-be. "But can you blame me?"

"Marco." Madalena swatted at him, pretending to be angry. But it was as though his presence had made a flame come to life inside of her; she was glowing, radiating happiness and desire.

For the first time, Cass understood what it was like to burn in such a manner. But all of her burning was for Falco, the boy she'd never be allowed to marry, not for Luca, her fiancé. Cass closed her eyes momentarily, remembering the surge of emotion that had coursed through her when Falco had first touched his lips to hers. She remembered the way her body had trembled, the way she felt as if she were emerging from a cold, dark tunnel into the light of day for the first time. Luca would never make her feel that way. Ever.

Why did life have to be so unfair?

Madalena and Marco left the shop to meet Cristian, who was joining them for the evening meal. Signor Sesti unpinned and unwound the fabric from Cass's body, jotting down some rough notes on a piece of parchment as he worked. Siena sat quietly on the bench at the back of the fitting area, watching the tailor as he transformed Cass from a princess back into a normal girl. Cass tried to engage her several times in conversation, but Siena just sat, nodding mutely.

"Are you all right, Siena?" Cass asked, her own spirits rising as the yards of glamorous fabric disappeared. "You're even quieter than usual."

"I was just wondering if I will be accompanying you to Signor da Peraga's estate, or if I will remain with your aunt." Siena began to help Cass get dressed once the tailor had finished removing his pins.

No wonder the girl looked as though she'd swallowed a frog. She was afraid she'd be left behind to molder at Agnese's estate.

"Of course you'll come with me," Cass said. "I'm sure Luca would be delighted to have you as part of the staff." Cass watched in the mirror as her lady's maid expertly threaded and tightened the laces of her bodice. "And we both know I'd be lost without you."

"But perhaps Signor da Peraga has a different lady's maid in mind for you?" Siena's pale reflection blushed scarlet. She nibbled at the edge of a fingernail.

Cass wondered what had put such thoughts in the girl's head. "Nonsense. You'll be joining me at Luca's and that's final." Even as she said it, she felt a twinge of anxiety. Was she really going to marry Luca? And was she now responsible for Siena's future as well as her own?

Later that night, as Cass prepared to meet up with Falco, images assailed her: Falco crashing into her on the day of Liviana's funeral. How he had helped her steer the gondola the first night they had traversed the lagoon together. Tommaso's studio, Falco's eyes drinking in every inch of her body, his hands gentle as he arranged her on the divan. And the kiss. The kiss. Her lips pulsed at the memory.

Madalena was marrying Marco, the man of her dreams, while Cass was denied love, prohibited from finding and pursuing it. If she didn't marry Luca, not only would she disappoint her aunt, but she might very well end up homeless and impoverished. *What would*

Matteo think? Cass hated it that her choices had all been stolen away from her by a boy she'd never even met.

Cass knelt before the gilded crucifix hanging in her prayer alcove. She folded her hands and prayed to St. Anthony of Padua. Her mother used to pray to him when she had lost things. Cass was feeling a little lost herself.

Slipper appeared from the darkness of the armoire and rubbed up against her. Cass managed to smile. She held the cat against her chest, feeling the vibration of his purring against her skin.

Falco's words whispered in her ear. *Stop worrying about the rest of the world. Do what feels right. Let go.*

Cass stood up and blotted her face, which was wet, on her sleeve. She looked at the clock on her bedroom wall. It was time to meet Falco at Il Mar e la Spada. She glanced at her reflection in the mirror, wanting to look absolutely radiant for their meeting, wanting to feel Falco's lips on hers one last time.

Her future might have already been decided, but she was still in control of her present.

"To strangle a person by hand
requires both superior strength and great
determination. The thick cartilage
of the throat must be completely
constricted until suffocation occurs."

—THE BOOK OF THE ETERNAL ROSE

sixteen

Cass moved quickly through the night, guided by the wavering light of her lantern and the certainty that she was doing the right thing. She couldn't believe how at ease she'd become with sneaking around in the dark. She slipped out of the villa, fleeing across the mossy lawn until she reached the path that ran along the shoreline. Sharp stones pressed through the soles of her flat shoes, making her wince. Cass sensed someone following her and whirled around just in time to watch the shadowy form of an emaciated black cat launch itself into a patch of high grass.

Cass held up her lantern as she approached the village. The tight cluster of buildings looked almost deserted, dark except for a faint glow coming from the taverna. Cass's heart propelled her forward. She knew that if she could lay eyes on Falco, everything wrong in her heart would fix itself. Falco didn't believe in fate, but Cass did. She felt as if the forces of the universe were guiding her safely through the night to the man who held all of the answers.

She took a deep breath and opened the door to the taverna, not knowing what she'd do if Falco wasn't there.

The place was warm and dark, reeking of sweat and sour ale. Despite the late hour, the taverna was crowded, and every man seemed to look up as the door swung shut behind her. A rumble of startled disbelief went through the crowd—the taverna was not a place for a woman, especially so late at night. Cass hoped the dim lamplight prevented her from being recognized by any of the villagers.

But then her heart leapt in her chest. He was here, just as he had promised he would be.

Falco sat with three other boys at a table on the far side of the bar. He hadn't yet looked up. Cass couldn't stop herself from breaking into a beaming smile. Just the curl of his dark brown hair against the worn collar of his shirt made her heart thud. Falco's roommate, Paolo, glanced at her with a knowing smirk. He leaned in to whisper something to Falco.

Falco looked up. His whole body seemed to relax when he saw Cass. Bounding off his chair, he weaved his way through the crowded taverna to where she stood just inside the door. "My lovely starling," he said. He cast a glance back at his friends. "Maybe we should talk outside."

Cass and Falco stepped out into the cool night. As the taverna door creaked shut, Falco immediately pulled her close, wrapping his arms around her. Cass rested her chin on his shoulder, breathing in the scent of paint and soap.

There were so many things she wanted to ask him: had he missed her, as she had missed him? Had he been thinking about her? Had he been thinking of their kiss? Her lips were just inches from the skin of his neck.

Instead, she moved back, just slightly, so she could look Falco in the eye, and said, "Did you discover anything today?"

"Nothing about de Gradi," Falco said. "I did find an artisan who believes he made the falcon mask, but he said the purchaser didn't leave a name or address. The man insisted on picking up the item himself since he lived just across the canal." ·

"Where is the shop?" she asked.

"South of San Giovanni," Falco said. "There is a string of palazzos just across the water. Perhaps we can go there?"

They weren't likely to stumble across the masked man just out wandering the streets of the city, and Cass wasn't even sure she would recognize him; she had seen nothing but the hardness of his eyes. All she'd had was a *feeling* about him—that something was off, dangerous. She remembered how he'd spoken of the beauty of war.

But it meant a long gondola ride with Falco, and with the threat of her wedding looming closer and closer, she was willing to go just about anywhere with him.

Before she could agree, the door to the taverna creaked and Falco moved away from her. She whirled around.

Paolo's dark eyes gleamed with amusement. "Signorina. It appears we have a mutual friend," he said. "You should join us."

"This isn't really the place for a lady," Falco said. His voice was light, but contained a bit of an edge.

"Something tells me you can protect her, Falco." Paolo held open the door of the taverna. "I insist. What harm can one drink do?"

Falco arched an eyebrow at his roommate. "Fine. One drink. Then Signorina Cassandra and I have some plans of our own."

"I can only imagine." The tall boy's eyes glittered like black glass. "I take it I shouldn't expect you home tonight then."

Heat surged through Cass's cheeks. She prayed that no one could see her blushing in the dim light. She followed Falco and Paolo back into the dim taverna, and over to a table where two other boys sat swilling some sort of alcohol out of tarnished pewter mugs. Paolo pulled a chair over and situated it next to Falco, who glanced over at her with an apologetic expression as she settled awkwardly into her seat.

"So this is what's been taking up so much of your time." Paolo held up his lantern so he could see Cass better. "A bit skinny, but otherwise not bad. How do you afford her?"

The other boys laughed. Cass stared down at the tabletop, her cheeks burning again. She concentrated on the seams in the knotty wood.

Falco folded his hand around hers, lacing their fingers together. "This is Signorina Cassandra. Cass, you've met Paolo. And this is Nicolas and Etienne." He gestured to the other men, and then turned back to his roommate. "Cass is a friend of mine, so it might be best to keep your attempts at humor to yourself."

"A friend, huh?" Paolo's eyes narrowed. "Well, there's no accounting for her taste. How did you two meet?"

Cass half listened as Falco spun a tale about doing her portrait as a present for her aunt. All she could focus on was the feel of his hand on hers. His fingertips, pressing tiny indents in her flesh. Cass heard a roaring in her head, felt a rushing, as if all of her body's blood was making its way into that hand.

The conversation flowed quickly between the boys—they obviously knew one another well, and chattered easily back and forth. Falco had finished his story and they were now discussing an essay, something Paolo had read and then passed on to the rest of the group.

"Paolo is the learned one of us," Falco explained. "His master is a scholar as well as a painter, so he is always getting his hands on literature from abroad." He winked at Cass. "He is not nearly so dumb as his jokes—and his looks—would suggest."

"True," Paolo said good-naturedly. "And I find I gravitate to the French." He drained his mug and signaled the barkeep for a refill. "Last week I was reading an essay by Michel de Montaigne."

"Not more of this." Nicolas, a stocky blond with the beginnings of a beard, rolled his eyes. "Why do you two always feel the need to impress the ladies with your knowledge of all things dull?" He turned to Etienne and began to discuss his favorite card games and the best places to go gambling.

The barkeep grabbed Paolo's empty glass and slammed down a mug of a sour-smelling liquid with a thin coating of foam on the top. Cass assumed it was ale. He raised his eyebrows at Cass. "Anything for you?" he asked with a grunt.

Cass started to refuse but Falco cut in. "She'll have the same as the rest of us." He produced a coin from his purse and handed it to the barkeep.

Paolo waited for Cass to get her drink before continuing. "De Montaigne. He described marriage as much like a cage full of birds, where the unmarried struggle to get in and the married struggle to get out. Do you agree, Signorina?"

Cass struggled to swallow a mouthful of the sour ale, then set her goblet down on the warped tabletop and met Paolo's challenging gaze. "As you know, there is no conversation more boring than one in which everybody agrees," she said, firing back some of de Montaigne's exact words. "Personally I have no desire to force my way into the cage of marriage." Cass took another long drink of ale. It tasted better the second time.

Paolo's dark eyes widened. "The lady also reads de Montaigne. Impressive."

Falco squeezed her hand. She cast a glance sideways to see that he was looking at her with a mix of surprise and admiration. She wondered what Agnese would do if she found out Cass was using her tutoring to impress boys at the local taverna. The thought made her laugh out loud. "Well, was it not de Montaigne himself who said, 'There is no desire more natural than the desire for knowledge'?" Cass drained her goblet and smiled triumphantly.

Paolo broke into a grin—the first time Cass had seen him smile. "Learned and lovely," he said. "I see now why you've been spending time with her, Falco. Just because she cannot be your bride doesn't mean she cannot be your muse."

Cass's good mood faded instantly. Even in the dingy taverna, the reality was obvious to everyone. She and Falco could never be together.

"Let's get out of here, my lovely muse," Falco said, as if sensing that Paolo's words had upset her. He pulled her chair back for her, and she stood and adjusted her skirts. Cass bid the other artists good night and let Falco lead her to the door.

"Falco." Paolo's sharp voice cut through the hazy darkness.

Falco turned around. "Yes?"

"I trust she knows little of your line of work?"

Cass felt Falco's body tense up momentarily, and then relax. "We've spoken briefly about the work I do for Tommaso, if that's what you mean."

Paolo stared at Falco without speaking. Nicolas and Etienne looked up as well. Cass could have sworn they were having an entire conversation without words.

"Let's go." Falco broke the spell by turning away. He pulled Cass through the door and out into the night.

"What was that about?" she asked, shivering in the damp air.

Falco put an arm around her and pulled her close. "Who knows," he said. "Paolo feels the need to make himself a pain to everybody. I just let him pretend he's in charge." Falco led Cass behind the bakery where a small *batèla* was tied. "Are you ready for our next adventure?" he asked, untying the ropes of the wooden rowboat as though he stole boats every night of his life. "Skulking about the outskirts of a few wealthy palazzos should be child's play compared with some of the work we've done."

Cass tried to smile but found she couldn't. Paolo's words kept running through her mind . . . *She cannot be your bride . . . she cannot be your bride . . .*

She let Falco help her into the small rowboat and went through the motions of adjusting her skirts and settling herself against the side of the batèla as if she were sleepwalking. Falco pushed the boat away from the dock as he hopped over the side. He manned a set of warped wooden oars, their hinges crusted over with dirt and rust.

She cannot be your bride. The words cut her like a scalpel. She looked up, unable to meet Falco's eyes. A handful of stars glimmered through the haze. "What are we doing?" Cass asked. Her voice sounded broken, like a stranger was speaking through her.

The oars made a groaning sound with each stroke, so Falco had to pause to answer her. "We're going to the Rialto. I thought that's what we agreed."

Cass looked at him. Of course they were going to the Rialto. Was he being evasive on purpose? "Not now. I mean us. What are *we* doing?"

"We're trying to find a murderer before he finds us."

"And that's it. That's all?" Cass waited for him to confirm what she was afraid of, that she was his partner in the investigation, but nothing more.

Falco didn't answer at first. He steered the boat between the Giudecca and San Giorgio Maggiore. "I'm not sure what you mean, Cass," he said slowly.

Cass stared out at the choppy water. It was her turn to go mute. She had thought seeing Falco tonight would fix everything, but she felt more confused than ever.

They continued toward the Rialto in silence. When they floated past the church of San Giovanni, Falco pointed out the block where the mask maker had his shop. Cass recognized a few of the palazzos across the canal. Most were owned by senators or wealthy merchants. In fact, they weren't far from Madalena's house. The streets and canals in the area were dead quiet; everyone was tucked into bed by this late hour. Only the yowl of an occasional cat disturbed the silence.

Cass didn't know what she and Falco were looking for, but whatever it was, they weren't going to find it rowing around wealthy neighborhoods in the dark. "This is pointless," she said. "The man with the falcon mask could live in any of these palazzos, or none at all. Besides, we don't even know if he has anything to do with this mess."

Falco shook his dark hair back from his face. "I was worried this would be a dead end, but I . . ." He trailed off.

"You what?" Cass asked.

Falco rubbed at the scar under his eye. "I wanted to see you," he said. "I wanted to spend time with you."

Cass looked away from him. Again, she felt like someone was stabbing her between her ribs. "Maybe that's pointless too," she said. Their boat floated past a gondola. Two forms were visible in the moonlight. A man and woman lay intertwined on the base of the boat. Bare skin, gentle rocking.

Falco followed her eyes. "You know that I care about you, Cass."

"But it doesn't mean anything." Cass tried to keep her voice from trembling. "Because it can't lead to anything more."

Falco set aside the oars and turned her face toward his. "You're wrong. It means everything. You mean everything." He held her chin between his thumbs and forefingers. "Why do my feelings have to lead anywhere at all? Why can't we just be here, now, in this moment?"

His touch made shivers dance up and down her back. Maybe Falco was right. Why did she care so much about the future? Maybe she should just be thankful that they could be together here, right now.

"Why can't you just be who you are?" Falco asked, his lips moving toward hers.

Because I don't know who that is anymore. "You're changing me," she whispered. "I see everything differently now."

Cass didn't fight it when Falco leaned in and kissed her. She didn't resist as he tipped her gently backward and laid her down on the wooden bottom of the batèla. *Just be who you are.* Easy to say, but so difficult to do. Falco unfolded a blanket over her. "So you don't get cold," he said.

"What's going to keep you warm?" Cass asked softly, reaching up to tousle his hair.

Falco laughed. "Trust me, I'm plenty warm."

"Prove it," Cass said, pulling him down to her level.

She pressed her lips to his, surprised at her own bravery, emboldened by the way his body responded to hers. They fell back deeper into the boat, its creaky wooden sides offering privacy in the already-dark night. He kissed her harder, his tongue exploring her lips and mouth in soft circles. The small boat rocked underneath her, swaying with the gentle current of the canal. The weight of his chest pressed down on her rib cage, her hip bones pressed against his, even through the many layers of garments she wore. She felt a rush of warmth, a heat that made her forget everything else that had been bothering her. It was like she had slipped outside of her skin, and that only her soul, her essence, lay in the boat with Falco.

As Falco traced her hairline with his lips, he reached behind her back and loosened the ties of her bodice. He stroked the bare skin of her upper back. Cass couldn't believe how warm his hands felt. She let her own hands wander beneath the hem of his shirt. Her fingers traced his muscles—first the stomach and then the chest. His pounding heartbeat accelerated as they kissed. Her own blood raced through her veins, trying to keep up. Again Cass thought of the way the body was a single thing, yet was made up of so many different parts all working together. She could barely believe this was happening. She felt like a stranger, a wild, impulsive stranger.

"Cassandra," Falco murmured. He reached up and twisted all her hair into one of his hands, pulling it slightly as he held it behind her head. His lips made their way across her cheek and her jaw and her brow bone. His other hand caressed her left leg through her cotton stocking. His fingers followed the repeating diamond pattern embossed into her leather garter and then stroked the soft skin just above it.

Cass felt transported by his touch, his soft voice, and the mist rising off the canals. Everything felt otherworldly. It was a dream or a hallucination. Any moment now she'd wake up tucked beneath her covers with Slipper snuggled against her chest.

Just let go.

The batèla floated beneath a bridge. A man shrouded in darkness hung over its edge, leering at her. Cass sat up suddenly, wrapping the rough blanket up around her shoulders. She looked back toward the bridge. No one was there.

"What's wrong?" Falco asked.

"I thought I saw someone. Hanging over the bridge. Watching."

"Probably just some deviant. Not lucky enough to have the company of a beautiful woman." Falco moved to kiss Cass again.

But fear was drumming through her. It sharpened her focus, and made reality come slamming back. Cass put her hand out. "Wait. We have to stop, to slow down."

Falco sighed. "You're right," he said, running both hands through his hair. "Sometimes I think—well, I fear that you shouldn't trust me."

"Why?" Cass asked. Holding her lantern high in the air, she looked back toward the bridge again, but it was still deserted.

"Because I don't trust myself around you." Falco's voice turned soft again. He ran the knuckles of his right hand down the side of her face. "Who knows what I might do?"

Cass blushed. "Who knows what I might *let* you do?" The words just slipped out, but she didn't want to take them back. She didn't want to hide any longer.

Falco pulled her close to him, positioning her back against his chest. He wrapped his arms around her slender waist and leaned his chin on her left shoulder, his jawbone against her cheek. "Your beauty lights up the darkest night," he said. "I could paint an entire chapel just for you. Maybe I will someday."

Cass imagined herself in the future, standing in a church filled with Falco's art. She could almost see the nude figures frolicking in meadows and pools of brilliant blue water. The forms might be beautiful or not, but they would be real, so real they would come alive and dance off the walls of the church to sit in the pews and stare at her.

And then she saw Luca walking down the aisle, in his wedding outfit. She squeezed her eyes shut, as if she might stave off the waves of guilt that threatened to drown her every time she thought of her fiancé.

"What is it, Cass?" Falco asked. "What just happened?"

Cass realized she was holding her breath. She exhaled slowly. "There's something I need to tell you," she said.

Falco twisted her around to face him. He tucked a lock of hair behind her ear. "You can tell me anything, Cassandra."

"I'm, I have, when I was young, my parents—" She couldn't figure out how to tell him the truth: that she was Luca's, even though she didn't want to be, that she and Falco could never be together the way they wanted. "I'm engaged," she finally blurted out, feeling simultaneously terrified and relieved. "My fiancé is away, studying in France."

Falco nodded. "Of course you are. You're a beautiful woman from a noble family. I'd be shocked to find out that your aunt hadn't secured your future." He looked at her expectantly as if he were waiting to hear more.

"So you aren't angry with me?" Cass buried her shaking hands in the fold of her skirts. How could he not be furious? She had lied to him. Well, practically. She had let him kiss her, even though she couldn't be his bride. She had even kissed him back.

Falco smiled at her through the dark. "Is that what's been worrying you? No, starling. I'm not angry." He pulled her body close to his again, burying his face in her hair. "You smell amazing," he said. "Like roses and butterflies and cool spring mornings." He held her hand up to his mouth, his fingers untying one of her lacy cuffs.

Cass's relief started to fade as Falco's lips found the bare skin of her wrist. "Wait a minute." She pulled away. "*Why* aren't you angry with me? You and I, we kissed, we might have—" Cass couldn't bring herself to finish the sentence. Exactly how far would she have let things go if she hadn't been ripped from her moment of fantasy by the stranger on the bridge? When he had loosened her bodice and reached beneath her chemise to stroke the skin of her upper back, all she had wanted was for him to loosen the rest of the laces. She definitely hadn't been thinking about telling him to stop.

Falco's eyes gleamed in the night. "Go on. We might have what?"

Coldness filled Cass's whole body. She reached out and pushed Falco away from her. "I think I understand." She pulled the lace on her cuff tight so that her wrist disappeared beneath the fabric. "All you wanted was a sordid little tryst? You were just going to keep going until I stopped you? That is so—so . . ." She struggled to find the correct words, but the cold fury that filled her made it difficult to speak.

"Improper?" Falco said. "Fun?"

"Fun?" Cass had half a mind to push Falco out of the boat and right into the murky water of the canal. She reached behind her back and made a futile attempt to retighten her bodice. "You're disgusting," she spat out.

"Would you like help with that?" Falco reached toward her.

"Don't touch me." Cass gave up on the bodice. She wrapped herself tightly in the woolen blanket.

Falco laughed aloud. "You're the one with the fiancé, and I'm disgusting?" He shook his head. "Women."

"You're disgusting because it doesn't bother you to have an affair with an almost-married woman." Cass felt tears pushing at the back of her eyes. That was all he wanted from her: fun. "You could be thrown in prison for that. Executed, even!"

Falco leaned in toward Cass. She stiffened, but didn't pull back. "I know you want this as much as I do," he said. "You aren't going to report me. And even if you did, I'm inclined to think a night with you might well be worth imprisonment."

Cass looked away from him, fighting the urge to soften. He was just trying to flatter her to get what he wanted.

Falco's voice turned gentle. "I wish we could have more. I wish I could lie next to you every night. I wish I could parade you around on my arm in the daylight," he said. "But if we can't be together like that, then why can't we be together like this?" He moved to kiss her again.

A part of her wanted to let him, really wanted to, but she was still offended by his thinking she'd be so willing to have a tryst with him and then marry Luca as if no one would ever be the wiser. "Don't," she said, leaning against the side of the boat. She stared into the night, seeing nothing. No movement. No lanterns. It was as if Cass and Falco were the only two people in the world.

Now it was his turn to look offended. "It can't be wrong if we both feel the same way."

Cass didn't know how she felt; that was the problem. She could feel Falco's eyes burning into the back of her neck, and resisted the desire to turn and meet his gaze. She skimmed her fingers over the water. She wondered exactly how she had found herself in this place. They passed a palazzo where yellow fire from a pair of cressets still lingered, long after a party had broken up. Cass saw her reflection ripple across the water. She hardly recognized the girl that looked up at her. Her face was thinner, paler, almost a stranger.

Then the flames flickered and the reflection shifted slightly. Cass realized she *was* staring down at a stranger. The girl's head floated to the surface of the canal, ringlets of dark hair writhing like serpents, vacant eyes staring up at Cass almost accusingly. Cass screamed as the girl's swollen torso surfaced, her neck encircled with bruises, her chest marred by a bloody X.

"Leprosy rots the body piecemeal,
beginning with the nose, ears, and lips,
endowing the afflicted with the
appearance of a leering skull."

—THE BOOK OF THE ETERNAL ROSE

Falco pulled her away from the water. She turned in toward him, hiding her face in his chemise. She was heaving, gasping for breath.

"It's okay." He cradled her with one arm.

Cass felt the boat come to life and move awkwardly through the water. Falco must be rowing one-handed. She looked up. "What are you doing? Pull over. Here."

"What?" Falco released her to man the oars with both hands. The old boat creaked and groaned its way through the canal water, until the grotesque floating body disappeared in its wake.

"I need to get out." Cass felt bile rising in her throat. She needed to get off the water immediately. She wanted to hurl herself from the boat, get lost deep within the winding streets of the Rialto, run until the floating body disappeared from her mind.

Falco rowed to the edge of the canal and moored the boat. Cass clambered over the side without waiting for his help. Grabbing her lantern, she took off down the closest street with Falco right behind her. Cass had no idea where she was going. All she knew was that she had to put as much distance between herself and that floating dead girl as she could.

She turned into an alley and leaned up against a crumbling brick building, her breath catching in the back of her throat. Falco caught up to her. "Where are you going, Cass?"

She shook her head. "I don't know." In the distance, she saw the glimmer of armor. Moonlight reflecting off a breastplate. Soldiers. She grabbed Falco's hand and started pulling him toward the soldiers. "Come on. We can tell them what we found."

Falco gripped her arm. "What did I tell you about the soldiers? They're corrupt. And besides, nothing has changed since the night we found Mariabella."

"Are you crazy? Everything has changed." Cass stared into Falco's flashing eyes, almost unable to believe he was the man she'd been kissing just moments before. "There's a deranged killer running loose in Venice. Everyone might be in danger."

"Yes, and you're still out alone at night, with an artist. A peasant. What's your aunt going to think? How's that going to look, Cassandra?"

"I don't care," Cass said. Another line from Michel de Montaigne's writings echoed in her head. *A person of honor chooses to lose his honor rather than his conscience.* It was true. Cass would not let her crimes with Falco shame her even further. She had done wrong, but she was prepared to accept her punishment. If she got disavowed, or worse, she could handle it. But she could no longer turn her back on a pair of young girls who had been murdered.

She twisted her arm sharply to break his hold and went running off in the direction of the soldiers. She heard Falco's boots thudding behind her.

"Cass, please," he called.

Cass ignored him. Maybe he was afraid of the town guard, but she wasn't. The soldiers had turned a corner and Cass couldn't see them anymore. She thrust herself deep into the twisted alleys, listening for the sound of their rough voices, their boots tromping in matched cadence against the stone streets. She glanced back over her shoulder. The area behind her was deserted. Either she had lost Falco or he had left her. And the soldiers were nowhere in sight.

Just as she was about to give up, she heard gravelly voices coming from a narrow alleyway on her right. Cass plunged into the dark opening and skidded immediately to a stop. Two hunched-over figures were rooting through a pile of trash. Even in the dark, Cass could make out the telltale lesions on their long, spindly arms. Lepers. They weren't supposed to be out in the streets. The fingers of her left hand reached down toward her rosary, cradling the rosewood crucifix as if it would protect her.

One of the lepers looked up at her from beneath his hooded robe. Circles of flesh were missing from his left cheek and the bridge of his nose. In the faint light, his eyes looked black as coal, as if he were not just diseased but also possessed. His toothless mouth twisted into a grimace as he reached out to Cass with a hand that had only three fingers.

"Hungry," he said, his voice so low and distorted that she almost didn't understand.

Digging into her suede pouch, fighting feelings of terror and revulsion, she tossed a couple of coins at the men and watched as the one retrieved the money with his clawlike hand. The second leper didn't even look up.

Cass retreated from the alley. Back on the main street, she turned a slow circle, looking, listening for any sign of the soldiers. All she saw were heaps of trash and the shadowy outlines of buildings. A trickle of sweat made its way from her hairline to her right eye. Cass wiped at it with her sleeve. No luck. She peeked down the next alley. It was black as pitch, even with her lantern. Cass glanced down and saw that the beeswax candle had more than half melted away. Soon she would be walking the streets of Venice in complete darkness. Alone.

How long had the dead girl been in the water? she wondered. Was there a murderer stalking the streets nearby? Cass gave up on finding the soldiers. Someone else would likely report the body at sunrise, if not sooner. It was time for her to find her way back to the Grand Canal so she could get home.

Squinting between two ramshackle private residences, Cass saw the telltale reflection of moonlight on water. A canal, just a block away. She turned and walked parallel to the canal until it bled into a larger one. She followed the large canal and eventually came upon the Grand Canal once more. She headed back toward the boat, hoping Falco hadn't deserted her completely. Eventually she saw the blue batèla, bobbing at the edge of the water. It was empty.

Cass scanned both sides of the canal looking for Falco. Tall palazzos loomed like fortresses; sculptures of angels and lions hovered protectively over their entrances. Part of her just wanted to leave him. He was used to running about in the middle of the night. He'd be able to find his way home without her. Cass wasn't even sure where he lived. She had assumed he stayed somewhere out on San Domenico, but maybe he just went there to meet his friends at Il Mar e la Spada. There were so many tavernas on the Rialto. She wondered why the group of artists preferred such an isolated little place.

In front of her, Cass thought she saw a flash of light. She headed toward it, crossing over a narrow bridge. Another flicker, almost imperceptible. It came from a partially obscured path running between two palazzos. Cass began to walk faster.

"Falco?" she called softly, her voice echoing off the stone. She'd spend a few minutes looking for him, she decided. For one, rowing the old batèla by herself would be difficult. And maybe she could persuade him to tell her why he was so adamant about avoiding the town guard. Falco had seen much more of the soldiers, of Venice, than she had. Maybe he had a reasonable explanation.

The path twisted past a block of shops and storefronts and bled into a small campo. Weeds pushed their way through the cracked tiles beneath her feet. A life-sized statue lay on its side in the middle of the square. Even with one missing arm, Cass recognized San Giuda from his staff and the tongue of fire sculpted behind his head. A lantern sat next to the fallen statue. No doubt this was the flickering light Cass had seen reflecting off the palazzos.

Across the clearing, a crumbling stone chapel was nestled between a decrepit apothecary and a long brick building that looked to be a monastery. Wind or water damage had whittled the cross on the chapel's roof almost down to a T.

Cass heard voices coming from the side of the chapel. She gripped her lantern tightly again, prepared to use it as a weapon if needed. Pressing her back against the front wall of the building, Cass peeked around the side. The first thing she saw was a wrought-iron fence cordoning off what looked to be a small graveyard at the back of the church.

The second thing she saw was Falco.

The third thing she saw made her blood congeal in her veins. It was Angelo de Gradi, Dubois's doctor, the man from the workshop of horrors. He and Falco appeared to be arguing. Falco was gesturing wildly; Cass caught only snatches of their words.

"What is that place . . . we had a deal . . ." That was Falco. Cass's heart dropped. So she hadn't just imagined that Falco and Angelo knew each other.

"Go home . . . won't want to be here when they . . . tomorrow night . . ." The physician sounded angry.

"Fine . . . then I'm finished."

Falco. *Finished with what?*

Angelo's response was swallowed up by a gust of wind.

Footsteps thudded on stone, and Cass raced to the far side of the church. She hid her body and her lantern among the dense shrubbery growing between the chapel and adjoining monastery and watched as both Falco and Angelo disappeared into the dark passageway.

Cass tried to piece things together in her head. Angelo had told Falco not to be there when something happened. When they what? Found the body? Had Angelo killed the girl in the water? Had Falco? If so, why hadn't either of them had the good sense to hide her like they had hidden Mariabella? And what was going to happen tomorrow night? Was that when the body would be officially discovered? None of it made sense. The only thing for certain was that Cass could no longer deny Falco's connection to Angelo and his macabre collection of human remains.

The dying lantern still flickered at San Giuda's feet. Cass made her way back across the campo and down the path. She peered out from between the two palazzos. Angelo was nowhere to be seen. Falco stood by the blue batèla, looking lost. Cass started back across the small bridge. Falco glanced up and saw her before she got halfway. As he approached her, she was reminded of how they had stood in the middle of the Rialto Bridge just a few days ago, and how close she had felt to him then. That was when Falco had given her the speech about letting go. A fine bit of advice that had turned out to be.

The wind whipped Falco's dark hair back from his face. His eyes were wild. "How could you just run off like that? I was frantic. I looked for you everywhere."

"Did you?" The words came out harsher than intended. "Because when I saw you, you didn't appear to be searching for me at all. You were arguing. With Angelo de Gradi."

Falco recoiled as if he'd been slapped. The blood drained from his face.

"Angelo," Cass continued. "The man you swore on several occasions that you didn't know." Her voice started to break. She was dangerously near to tears. *Please let him have an excuse,* she thought. *Please let him make everything all right.*

"I can explain," Falco said, his jaw hardening. "I'm sorry. I did lie. I do know Dottor de Gradi." Falco took a deep breath. "Angelo. In fact . . . I work for him."

"Doing what?" she asked, trying to keep the tremor from her voice.

"I can't tell you."

Cass felt a surge of anger. She wanted to grab Falco and shake him. She was giving him a chance to set things right. "That's your idea of an explanation?"

"I promise you, he has nothing to do with Mariabella, or with that . . ." His eyes flicked momentarily to the canal water.

"And I'm supposed to take your word for it?" Cass said icily. "So what was the good doctor doing at a chapel so late? Seeking counsel? A late-night confessional perhaps?"

"Apparently, he lost two patients today," Falco said. "A pair of siblings to the plague. He was tending to the family, who happen to live in this area. I imagine the poor mother needed something to help her sleep."

"How benevolent," Cass said, her voice rife with skepticism. "But it doesn't explain how you ended up arguing with him."

Falco raked a hand through his hair. "Why can't you just trust me? There's more . . . There are things I can't explain to you. Things that have nothing to do with either of us. Things that it might actually be dangerous for you to know. Maybe I'm trying to protect you."

Cass squeezed her hands into fists. Of course. Falco just wanted to give her a slick smile and a few soft words so that she'd nod obediently and stop questioning him. Like a pet. "Things you can't explain? Like the dead bodies popping up around Venice? And always when you're nearby?"

Falco paled again. "You know I would never hurt anyone."

"I don't know that," she said, her voice dropping to a whisper. "I don't know anything about you. And what I *do* know, who can say if it's real or a lie?" The volatile emotions, the secrets, the way he had pressed her up against the wall of Tommaso's studio. Cass was no longer sure what he was capable of.

She couldn't stand to look at him for another second. She turned away and hurried back across the little bridge, toward the mysterious stone chapel, away from the spot where their borrowed batèla was moored.

"Where are you going?" Falco yelled after her.

"I can't tell you," she said, enjoying the feel of throwing his own words back at him. The truth was, she couldn't tell him because she honestly had no idea. "Don't follow me. I don't want you near me."

She ran back through the dark passageway, ducking between a small bakery and a blacksmith shop. She heard Falco calling her name. She pressed herself tight against the stone wall. She couldn't face him. He had been lying to her from the beginning. He was working for Angelo. Angelo, the man who dissected dogs for fun and collected human body parts in neatly arranged tin basins. Cass put a hand to her lips; this time when she thought of Falco's kiss, it made her sick. Had Falco also kissed Mariabella and the girl in the water?

Had he planned to kill her too?

Falco ran past the small space where she was hiding. Fortunately, he didn't see her. "Cassandra," he called. She heard him repeating her name as he moved farther down the dark passageway. As his footsteps faded, emotions flooded through Cass, almost overwhelming her. She leaned back against the rough stucco wall, letting her body slide down it until she rested on the ground. Grief and guilt and fear coursed through her, bringing with them a wave of sadness.

The smiles, the kisses, the soft words. Lies, all of it. But what about how she had felt for him—how she *still* felt? She had meant the things she said and did. She *still* meant them. Cass had never felt so lost. For the first time since she had bumped into him outside Liviana's funeral, Cass admitted to herself that she might have fallen in love with a murderer.

"The major piazzas are full of
charlatans peddling rabbit piss
as healing tonic. True tonic comes
from recombinations of the four
humors themselves, and often
by adding a tincture of wild herbs."

—THE BOOK OF THE ETERNAL ROSE

eighteen

The rain came early the next morning as Cass and Siena met Madalena and Eva outside the east entrance of the Basilica di Santa Maria Gloriosa dei Frari, one of the city's largest places of worship. The campo outside the Frari was teeming with nobles and high-ranking citizens dressed in their finest silks, but Mada was easy to find. Her farthingale, encased in yards of emerald silk, was so wide, it could have sheltered several children from the droplets of rain that were just beginning to fall. She was pressed up against the church's red brick exterior, trying to shelter herself from the weather under a tiny stone overhang. Eva opened a leather umbrella and held it in front of Mada.

In the absence of the sun, the church's stained-glass windows looked like three dark circles above her head. Cass leaned against the bricks for support as she exchanged a greeting with her friend. She didn't know how she'd be able to stay awake, let alone focus.

After she had run from Falco and lost herself in the twisted streets, it had taken almost an hour until she had found a sleeping fisherman along the Grand Canal whom she could bribe to take her back to San Domenico. By the time she had sneaked back into her room, it was only a couple of hours until sunrise and Cass hadn't been able to sleep. She had pulled out her journal, intending to list all the evidence she could think of that Falco wasn't involved in the killings, but her pages had remained blank.

Today her lush church gown weighed her down, and she felt as if she could barely stay on her feet. Her feet, her knees, all of her joints pulsed with pain. Was this what her aunt went through every day? Later she would ask Cook if he could fix her a tonic, something to soothe her.

A bell rang twice and the wooden doors of the Frari swung open.

"Come on." Madalena removed the hood of her cloak and adjusted her green veil so that it covered all of her hair. She folded herself into the line of people heading toward the yawning black hole that led into the church. *Like a mouth*, Cass thought, *swallowing the people whole.*

"I'm so glad your aunt let you attend Mass with me today," Mada whispered. She wrapped her gloved hand around Cass's arm and pulled her along. Madalena led her to a pew several rows from the back. They settled in behind a pair of noblewomen whose elaborate coiffed hairdos were fashioned so high off their heads that Cass could see only part of the altar. Behind them, the lady's maids found a spot with the rest of the servants.

"You know why she did," Cass said bitterly. "She wanted me to be seen after her big announcement that Luca and I would be married soon. Three different people congratulated me on the short walk here."

"Who?"

Cass shrugged. "No idea."

A pair of choirboys in white robes with golden sashes made their way down the center aisle. They closed the wooden doors. The bell tolled again and the crowd grew quiet. Everyone stood as the priest appeared and took his place on the raised pedestal just to the right of the wooden altar. A golden crucifix dangled around his neck, and his black robes were trimmed with thick swatches of maroon velvet. Behind him, gray daylight filtered through a wall of arched windows above a giant painting by Titian: *Assumption and Consecration of the Virgin*. Cass had always liked the painting, which showed Mary being raised to heaven by God.

"You know Titian is buried here?" Mada whispered. She relayed this fact every single time Cass attended church with her.

Cass played along. "Really?" She couldn't help but think of Falco. She touched the amethyst necklace that he had given her, which she was wearing beneath her bodice. She had grabbed the loop of purple stones at the last minute, slipping it around her neck but tucking it out of sight. She'd told herself she only wore it because she meant to return it to Falco the next time their paths crossed.

But now her certainty from last night that Falco was a murderer began to dissipate. He *couldn't* be a murderer. He couldn't. Maybe he was painting something for the creepy physician. A special canvas that his master was insisting he keep a secret. She had to find him again and force him to be honest with her. She was sure he had an explanation for what she had seen and heard.

"*Signore, pietà.*" Madalena recited the words along with the rest of the congregation. Cass sighed. Everyone else was apologizing to God for their sins, and here she was dreaming up some new ones.

Cass took a seat on the cushioned bench and tried to focus as the priest began the first reading. It was something about honesty. Fitting.

Madalena leaned in close. She was never one to pay attention during the readings, which Cass agreed often droned on far too long. "Did you see the handbills?" she whispered.

Cass shook her head. The official Venetian notices distributed around the city tended not to make it all the way out to San Domenico Island.

"A girl's body was found in the Grand Canal this morning. A maid, I think. Sliced to ribbons." Mada made a slashing motion against her chest for emphasis. "There's a reward offered to anyone who knows anything."

Cass felt as though her blood had suddenly frozen in her veins. She thought of the bloated torso rising from the waters of the canal, the savage circle of bruises around the girl's throat, the bloody X carved into her chest. A maid, Mada had said. Cass was willing to bet anything it was the missing servant, Sophia, who had disappeared from Joseph Dubois's estate. "How horrible," she managed to choke out. "Do they know the girl's identity?"

Madalena frowned. "I don't know. My wedding is just a few days away and all anyone can talk about is some servant's mutilated corpse. It's a bad omen, don't you think?"

Cass didn't even wonder at Mada's self-absorption today. She herself was too distracted. Bodies, threatening notes, masked strangers, frightening visions—her life had become a series of ominous portents. Cass wished Falco hadn't burned the anonymous note she had received on the canals. Time after time, Cass felt drawn back to that slip of parchment, as if it contained crucial information.

The priest was preparing to read from the Gospel of Matthew. Men and women all around them were making the shape of the cross on their lips and foreheads. Mada glanced over as Cass crossed herself. The older girl's eyes narrowed to slits, her fingertips coming to rest on the strand of purple stones that was barely visible on one side of Cass's neck. She pulled the entire necklace free so that it hung over Cass's dress.

"Where did you get this?" Mada hissed.

The look in Mada's eyes frightened Cass. "I'm not sure," she lied. "From one of the merchants in Piazza San Marco, I think. Why?"

The older women sitting on the bench in front of them both turned around. One scowled. The other raised a finger to her lips. Mada grabbed Cass's arm and pulled her up from the pew. Quietly, the two girls made their way to the wooden double doors and slipped outside.

A soft drizzle was still falling, but Madalena pulled Cass away from the shelter of the brick church, across the campo. She didn't stop until she reached the edge of the canal, as though what she had to say couldn't be discussed too close to the church itself. Behind them, Siena and Eva had also slipped out of the church and now huddled beneath the stone overhang. Decorum dictated that they use umbrellas to help Cass and Madalena stay dry, but apparently both of the maids could tell that the girls were having a private conversation.

"What's going on?" Cass asked, flipping up the hood of her cloak. "What in the world are we *doing* out here?"

Mada wrapped her own cloak tightly around her. She pinched her lips into a hard line. "That's not your necklace. It's Liviana's."

"What?" Cass was too stunned to say anything else.

Madalena touched the purple stones around Cass's neck again. "She had a set of three just like this. One ruby, one emerald, one amethyst. She was wearing this necklace when she was entombed. I'm sure of it."

Cass thought back to the funeral. She seemed to recall a loop of stones around Livi's neck, but it was probably just a coincidence. Because the only way that Falco could have gotten the necklace from Liviana's body was if he had been inside her tomb before her body disappeared. And that was impossible because that would mean . . .

"You must be mistaken." Cass tried to keep the tremor from her voice.

Mada looked up at the sky and quickly made the sign of the cross over her chest. "I'm not mistaken. I never forget jewelry. Besides, I have the emerald one."

Cass had never seen her friend wearing a necklace like the one Falco gave her, but she always thought Madalena owned more jewelry than she could possibly ever wear. She grasped for an explanation. "If you bought the same one, then they can't be that rare."

Madalena was still staring at her as though she were diseased. "No. I have Livi's *actual* necklace. I always loved it and Liviana never wore it. So once when I was over visiting, I asked her if I could try it on, and then I kept it."

Cass's eyes widened. "You stole it?"

Mada glanced around the campo, but the square was empty. "Keep your voice down." She stared at the stones around Cass's neck. "You really don't remember where you got it?" Mada asked.

Cass managed to shake her head.

Mada shivered. "It's another bad omen. I feel like something terrible is going to happen."

A gust of wind sent a ribbon of cold all the way up Cass's spine. "You're not the one wearing it," she said, struggling to sound as if she were joking. "Maybe it's a bad omen for *me*."

The thought seemed to cheer up her friend. "Maybe," Madalena said. She raised her eyebrows. "Maybe you aren't meant to marry Luca after all."

Her words lingered awkwardly in the air for a moment, before Cass cleared her throat. Tucking the necklace back between layers of fabric, she turned away from the canal. "Tell me more about this body they found. You said she was a servant?"

Madalena seemed relieved when Cass had tucked the necklace out of sight. She nodded. "Marco heard she worked for Joseph Dubois."

So it *was* Sophia, the maid Siena had told them about. "Don't you think it's odd," Cass said suddenly, "that both dead girls were connected with Dubois?"

Madalena gave her a funny look. "What do you mean, both dead girls? Has there been another murder I don't know about?"

Mannaggia. Cass had completely forgotten that Mada didn't know anything about Mariabella. She tried to come up with a plausible explanation. "Siena was gossiping about a murdered courtesan," Cass finished weakly.

Luckily, Mada seemed too distracted by bad omens to realize Cass wasn't being completely truthful. The older girl's eyes followed the movement of a lean black cat as it slunk along the front wall of the church. "I haven't heard anything about that," she said. "You know how servants are. Always making up stories." She waved her hand dismissively. "But Dubois is a good friend of my father's. He may be a pig at times, but I'm sure he's not involved in anything sinister."

Cass wasn't so convinced. The fact that he was linked to both dead girls had to be more than coincidence. And then there was his friendly physician, Angelo, connoisseur of corpses. Come to think of it, the whole masked ball had given her a bad feeling. Cass shivered as she remembered the stranger in the falcon mask. She couldn't tell any of this to Madalena, though. Mada would be dumbfounded just to find out that Cass had been at the ball and hadn't told her. Cass glanced back toward the giant brick church. "Do you think we should go back?"

Madalena shook her head. "Let's head home. I think we've created enough of a disturbance for one day. One missed communion won't kill us, right?" She signaled to Eva and Siena, who were still huddled just outside the church's doors.

Cass and Mada left the campo of the Frari and headed toward the Rialto Bridge with their maidservants trailing behind. The great bridge connected the San Polo district with San Marco, where Madalena lived. As they made their way to Madalena's palazzo, the gray drizzle faded away to sprinkles and then to a foggy mist.

Mada pointed out the inked handbills posted on mooring posts and the sides of buildings. "Look," she said.

Cass stopped to read the inky handwriting on the official notice. Rain was starting to blur the letters, but she could make out the family seal in the bottom right-hand corner: a griffin holding a flaming sword.

REWARD: 50 ducats for specific and credible information regarding the death of Sophia Garzolo.

The note was signed by Joseph Dubois himself.

"No mention of a courtesan," Madalena said. "Probably just a rumor. Besides, if Dubois is so good-hearted as to try to seek justice for a servant, I highly doubt he'd be involved in any scandal involving a courtesan." She said *servant* the same way she might have said *insect*.

Cass had to admit it was strange. Since when did wealthy noblemen offer rewards for missing maids?

The girls made it to the back entrance of Madalena's palazzo. Beyond the bronze gate, tarnished by years of exposure to the elements, Cass could see the courtyard garden and the stone table where she had sat with her friend to discuss wedding plans just a few days ago. It felt like a lifetime had passed since then. Mada rang the bell mounted at the side of the gate and a servant appeared to let them in.

"Do you want to stay for dinner?" Madalena asked.

"I better not. My aunt is expecting me straight home after Mass." Cass hoped Agnese didn't ask too many questions about the day's readings.

"We wouldn't want to upset dear Auntie. She might do something rash like delay your wedding," Madalena teased.

If only it were that easy . . .

Cass bid Mada good-bye and then walked along the Grand Canal with Siena, both girls trying to flag down a gondolier for passage back to San Domenico. Unfortunately, churches all around them had just let out and the gondoliers were busy with short fares. They decided to head down near the Piazza San Marco. The giant square was home to the Palazzo Ducale, and backed up to the lagoon. Plenty of boats usually congregated in the waters just south of the piazza. They might not be able to find a gondola, but Cass thought she should definitely be able to find some kind of watercraft willing to take them home.

The two girls approached the imposing U-shaped building that was home to the Doge of Venice as well as the seat of Venetian government. The Palazzo Ducale was as big as several blocks of private homes, with arched windows on all sides. The perimeter was ringed with a breezeway supported by Gothic columns and elaborate sculptures perched above the entrances. Bricks in various shades of brown and gold glittered in the daylight.

The piazza thrummed with activity. Citizens and nobles on the way home from Mass milled in all directions, stopping to buy a bite of fresh bread from the baker or to check out the latest bracelets and brooches the Gypsies had for sale. Water merchants touted the healing powers of their springwater while booksellers pushed carts filled with the latest printed volumes between the throngs of people.

As Cass headed across the square to the edge of the lagoon, she noticed a small crowd of people, a mix of peasants and nobles, clustered in front of the clock tower. They were all standing in a semicircle, their attention clearly fixated on something.

Cass, thankfully, was tall enough to see over most of the other women. Her eyes narrowed when a skinny man in black robes turned around. It was Maximus the conjurer. He pulled a large pink rose from beneath a square of brightly colored silk. He offered it to an old woman.

Cass tried to remember specific details about the man in the falcon mask. Could it have been the conjurer? She considered his height, his build, the crushed-velvet hat on his head. All of them seemed consistent with the masked stranger from the ball. The conjurer had seemed so sincere when they had spoken at the brothel—but he had clearly known Mariabella. If he had performed at Joseph

Dubois's estate, he could easily have met Sophia as well. Another possible connection between the two dead girls. Cass wasn't sure what to make of it.

Cass ducked down behind the tall feathered hat of the man in front of her so that she could watch the conjurer without being detected. Siena waited patiently at her side.

Maximus spoke a magical incantation over an empty stone box, and a stream of doves poured out when he lifted the lid. The crowd cheered. Silver and bronze coins flew through the air and landed in and around a ceramic bowl at the conjurer's feet. Maximus bowed deeply and thanked the crowd. He closed his hands around one of the doves and then opened them with a flourish, producing a giant brown and black falcon in its place.

Cass froze. The bird's striped feathers were eerily reminiscent of the stranger's mask the night of Dubois's masquerade ball. Could it be just a coincidence? The falcon perched on the conjurer's hand, preening itself. It stretched out its wings, and for an instant Cass saw it like a skeleton instead of a bird, each wing made out of delicate bones not too different from the ones in her own hands.

Maximus noticed Cass in the crowd for the first time. Both conjurer and bird stared at her for a long moment.

"Come on." She stumbled back from the crowd, pulling Siena with her.

Cass and Siena continued across the piazza, passing the Basilica San Marco, the Doge's personal chapel. The building was made of fine marble and almost as big as the Palazzo Ducale, with five sets of arched doorways across the front and five shiny golden cupolas laid out in the shape of a cross. Frescoes depicting biblical scenes decorated the area above each arched threshold. Elaborate friezes and bas-reliefs ran along the terrace and roof. Every square inch of the place was gilded or sculpted or painted. Cass always imagined the great building was what the Garden of Eden would look like if it had been magically turned to stone.

A semicircle of six boys sat directly in front of the basilica, drawing its likeness on pieces of yellow parchment. Cass's heart skipped. She couldn't help but look for Falco. He wasn't there, but she recognized Paolo, Falco's roommate, among the group.

He'd been civil to her last night, but who knew how he might act without Falco around to defend her. "Wait here," Cass told Siena. Then she walked up to the boys and stopped just behind Paolo. "Excuse me," she said. All of the boys turned around. A couple of the younger ones giggled.

Paolo weighted his drawing down with a worn leather canteen. *Probably full of alcohol,* Cass thought. The tall boy hopped to his feet. "Come to talk more about de Montaigne?" he asked with a wink.

Cass looked away. From the corner of her eye she could see Siena staring at her. "I actually was hoping you might give Falco a message for me," she said. "I need him to meet me tonight, at midnight, at the churchyard by my aunt's property."

"Churchyard, eh? Sounds very . . . deserted." Paolo lifted his hat and shook his black hair out of his face. "I don't know. You kept him out late last night." The boy gave Cass a long look. "I'm surprised you made it to Mass this morning. But perhaps you had reason to repent?"

Cass blushed. "It isn't like that," she said. "I just need to talk to him."

A gust of wind blew Paolo's baggy white shirt back against his thin frame. Cass could see the contours of his body beneath the fabric. She realized she was seeing everything differently now. Nothing was whole anymore; every figure, every movement, was the sum of smaller pieces.

"I'll give him the message, but don't be upset if he can't make it," Paolo said. "And by the way—congratulations on your upcoming nuptials." A slow grin spread across his face as Cass froze in place. "Don't worry, Signorina. Falco doesn't mind." Then Paolo tipped his hat and went back to his easel in front of the basilica. The boy next to him poked him on the arm and said something under his breath that Cass couldn't make out.

Cass glanced back at the clock tower as she gestured for Siena. It was almost noon. Falco *would* meet her tonight. She was certain of it. In just twelve hours, she would make him give her the answers that she needed. In just twelve hours, things would begin to make sense again.

"Human beings, having originated

in the Garden, require contact

with nature. Even a palace grows

unwholesome to one who is too

long confined within its walls."

—THE BOOK OF THE ETERNAL ROSE

nineteen

That night, Cass stood at the fence surrounding the graveyard, one hand pressed up against the cool metallic bars. She hadn't been inside it since the time she'd gone looking for Falco and caught him drawing the nude girl. Cass had never found the drawing. Siena had probably burned it to protect her. Cass remembered how upset and embarrassed she'd felt when she'd seen it, her obsession with who the girl was supposed to be. It all seemed insignificant now.

She looked up at the sky. The night was unusually clear, and a smattering of stars shone down on her. Cass wished she knew more about constellations. Certain stars grouped together bestowed luck, and Cass needed all the help she could get.

"Starling."

Cass whirled around. Falco. How had he managed to sneak up on her again? Dressed in all black, he was invisible except for his tanned face, barely lit up by the stars.

"You shouldn't have run off," he said seriously. She saw no hint of his usual grin. "I was worried. I tried to follow you; I wanted to make sure you got home safely. But I lost you in the alleyways."

"I—I was afraid," Cass said.

Falco moved closer to her and Cass did not pull back. "Afraid? Or angry?"

"Confused," Cass said. Falco's body was just inches away from her own.

Falco sighed. "I know what you must think of me," he said. He ran a hand through his hair. "If you can just give me two more days, I promise then I can explain everything."

Cass yanked the circle of amethyst stones from beneath the collar of her dress. "And can you explain this as well?" she asked. Her heart thrummed in her chest. "This belongs around the neck of my dead friend, whose body is conveniently missing."

"You must be mistaken." Falco looked away. "That's costume jewelry. It was in with the rest of Tommaso's junk. He probably bought it from a Gypsy."

"Mistaken. Of course." Her skin felt too tight, like she might burst at any moment. Of course he couldn't explain it. Once again, she had given him a chance to make things right, and once again, he had failed. Cass ripped the necklace from her throat, watching as the chain broke and the stones scattered on the wet ground. She gestured toward Liviana's tomb. "There's a dead girl in there who's not supposed to be, and another girl murdered, and you don't care. You don't care about them, or me." She turned and walked away from him, blinking back tears. "I refuse to be lied to any longer." What an idiot she was.

"Cassandra, wait." Falco ran after her, grabbing her arm just before she reached the edge of Agnese's garden. "I do care. Give me two days. That's all I need. And then I will tell you anything you want to know." He stared at her. "Please. I'm asking you to trust me."

"Why should I?" Cass asked, her voice barely above a whisper. The breeze rustled through the ivy. Cass watched one leaf whip back and forth. "Last night you told me not to trust you, and tonight you tell me I should. What's changed?"

"What's changed is that I . . ." Falco reached for her face, his fingertips caressing her cheekbones. "I'm falling in love with you," he said, brushing a strand of hair back from her eyes. "For the longest time I couldn't see it. I didn't want to see it. So impossible. But I can't deny my feelings any longer. You're more than a muse, Cass. I want you to be more. I want you to be mine."

"But you know—" Cass could barely stutter out a sentence; Falco's words were so unexpected, she could hardly breathe. "But I'm engaged . . ."

"Forget the engagement. Forget what you're supposed to do. What do you want to do, Cass? What do you *need*?"

Cass felt her resolve melting away. His fingertips were ten individual spots of heat on her cool skin. She was tired of being cold. All she had to do was lean in and let the warmth engulf her. She thought of their bodies pressed together in the old batèla, her hands caressing his bare skin as their mouths met over and over.

She realized she was crying. Falco kissed away her tears one at a time. Each time his lips touched her skin, she felt a brightness, like he was making flowers bloom inside of her. "I want to believe you, but it's not that simple. I—"

"It *is* that simple." Falco tilted her face upward and pressed his mouth to hers, gently, then harder. Cass didn't even try to resist. The wind whipped his hair around, and hers, tickling her skin as Falco pressed her against the framework of the trellis that lined the back of her aunt's garden. Falco leaned into her and Cass could feel their hearts beating against each other. This was what a kiss should feel like. This was real.

When Cass broke away from the embrace, she was breathless. "All right," she said, exhaling hard into the darkness. "I'll give you your two days. But from then on I want everything explained. No more lies."

"Thirty-six hours," Falco said solemnly. "That's all I need."

Light flickered in the distance. Cass raised a hand to cut him off. "Did you see that?" She pointed to the graveyard. "It looked like a lantern."

Falco turned to look. "It may have been one of the servants lighting a candle?"

"No, look." Cass stared as the flickering light moved between the shadows. "I have to go. My aunt is already furious with me. No one can find me out of bed at this hour." *With you.*

Falco leaned in to give her one last kiss. "Meet me at the Pillars of Justice. Day after tomorrow, at noon. I promise I'll explain everything then."

"I'll be there." Cass fled from the gardens, to the servants' entrance that would take her safely into the kitchen. Her hands trembled as she fidgeted with the knob. The door was locked fast. Someone must have come along behind her and discovered the door unbolted.

Cass swore under her breath. Why did everything have to be as difficult as possible? She felt her way along the rough stone walls of the villa as she headed around to the front entrance. The lantern light still moved along the graveyard fence where she and Falco had met.

Had someone been spying on them? Spies, secrets—they were everywhere now. Cass almost couldn't fathom the strange turns her life had taken over the past few days.

She didn't even make it back inside the villa before she realized something was terribly wrong. When she turned the corner onto the main lawn, she saw that the whole front of the house was ablaze with light. Through one of the arched windows, she could see into the portego. Nestled on the divan facing directly toward Cass was Aunt Agnese. She had never looked so furious.

Even the graveyard, with its possible vampires and murderers, seemed like a safer choice than going inside to face her aunt. But then Cass saw Agnese start up from the divan and totter over to the portego window, her gray hair peeping out from her white nightcap. The old woman pointed one swollen hand at the glass. Then she disappeared from view, as if she had collapsed.

Cass raced up the stairs and into the portego. Her aunt had fallen into a chair. She was hunched over, trembling slightly. Her cap had fallen to the floor, exposing the coarse gray braid that reached just past her shoulders. "Aunt Agnese," Cass said, kneeling down to retrieve the cap. "Are you all right?"

The commotion brought Narissa and the cook running from the kitchen. They were both wearing cloaks. Cook had a lantern, as if he had been preparing to go outside. Slipper trailed along behind Cook as if he thought the portly man might leak scraps of meat from his pockets. Cass stared at them. What on earth was the whole house doing awake?

"Cassandra," Agnese rasped, one hand clutched over her heart. She seemed on the verge of tears. "Where have you been?" Sliding her nightcap back onto her head, she shooed away a hovering Narissa.

Cass was frightened by Agnese's outburst. Agnese was always very stern, but in a sarcastic sort of way. It was not like her to raise her voice. It was even less like her to cry.

"I went for a walk. I—I was just out by the gardens." Cass tried to look as contrite as possible.

"You know you're not supposed to be running about after dark, especially not now, when the whole city is buzzing about a killer on the loose." Agnese shivered. "If it weren't for your cat waking the whole villa with his incessant meowing, none of us might ever have realized you were missing."

Cass didn't answer. She gave Slipper a look of reprimand. The little traitor! No more chicken broth for him.

Agnese's eyelids fluttered. "Honestly, Cassandra, I know you get this—this recklessness—from your parents, but I don't know how much longer I can handle it."

Cass wished she could melt into the floor. She almost preferred her aunt's cutting sarcasm to this quiet, disappointed tone. "I'm sorry. It won't happen again," she said. "I promise."

Agnese shook her head and the loose folds of skin under her chin wobbled back and forth. "Your promises have proven to be as reliable as Bortolo's aim with the teapot. As of this moment, Narissa is in charge of you. She will go everywhere that you go, which will be nowhere without my express permission. You are turning far too wild."

"But Aunt—"

Agnese held up a hand. "Do I make myself clear?"

"But Siena—" Cass protested.

"Has gotten a bit too close to you, I'm afraid," Agnese said. "Siena can work for me for the time being."

Cass looked past her aunt, at the mosaic of *The Last Supper*. Jesus's dark eyes stared back disapprovingly at her. She turned away, toward Narissa and the cook. Was no one going to speak up on her behalf? Agnese couldn't make her a prisoner in the villa, not now, when Falco had agreed to explain everything to her.

"But . . . but I promised Madalena I would meet with her the day after tomorrow," she said. "I am helping her with her wedding preparations." What was one more lie if it meant getting to see Falco?

But her aunt was too smart to be fooled. "*Madalena* is always welcome here, at the villa. That is all. I'm tired. I'm going back to bed. I suggest you all do the same." Agnese swiveled her head toward the kitchen. "Siena," she barked.

Siena scampered into the portego. Without even glancing at Cass, she knelt down and let Agnese grab hold of her arm. Once the old woman was on her feet, Siena walked her toward her room, a half step at a time. Cass thought she heard her aunt muttering something about what Matteo would think under her breath.

"I believe it's time for bed, Cassandra," Narissa said coldly, in a tone that left no room for negotiation.

Cass allowed Narissa to pilot her, dumbly, toward the back of the villa. The corridor seemed to have shrunk in size. She remembered the conjurer, the doves trapped in the small stone box. Cass felt like the walls of the villa were closing in on her, keeping her prisoner from everything that she loved.

"The water that flows through
the canals is both beautiful
and deadly. Its tranquil surface
belies the toxins beneath—
unpleasant to touch, deadly to imbibe."

—THE BOOK OF THE ETERNAL ROSE

twenty

The following day, Cass still felt as if the villa were suffocating her. Not only was she trapped inside, but she was bored out of her mind—so bored that she sat on the stool and plucked random strings on her aunt's harp for a while until Bortolo reminded her that he was blind and not deaf.

Narissa had followed her around all morning like a stout, balding shadow. When the maid excused herself to fetch a basket of mending, Cass contemplated making a run for it. She imagined flying out the front door and down the steps. Running across the lawn until she hit the sandy shoreline and then swimming her way to the Rialto.

And then what?

That was the problem with running away. You had to have somewhere to go.

A sharp rapping at the front door startled her. She glanced around for Bortolo, but the butler had conveniently disappeared. Probably snuck downstairs for a nap in his office. Cass jumped up from the divan, eager for any distraction.

Narissa descended from the servants' quarters with more speed than anyone her age and size ought to be able to muster. She waved Cass back to her seat. "Young ladies do not answer doors."

Young ladies, Cass thought bitterly, *do not do anything but sit and rot.*

Cass watched as Narissa conversed briefly with a boy wearing wrinkled muslin breeches and a sleeveless leather doublet that was fraying at the seams. Cass sighed. Just a messenger. She settled back into the tasseled cushions of the divan with another sigh as the boy handed Narissa two pieces of parchment and turned away.

Narissa held one of the letters out in her direction. "Signorina," she said. "This came for you."

Another exciting missive from Luca. Cass took the letter reluctantly. Had she ever finished reading Luca's last letter? She didn't think so. She had started it at the tailor's shop and then shoved it back in her cloak pocket, where it most likely still sat. Fiddling with the edge of the folded parchment, Cass ran one finger between the layers to break the lily-imprinted red wax seal. Reluctantly, she scanned the first few lines.

My Dearest Cassandra,
   I hope the weather has been mild so that you've been able
   to wander around the garden. I remember how you used to
   like that. Don't forget to be mindful when going into the city.
   Many people, men especially, aren't who they seem to be.

Cass frowned. No one was who they seemed to be. Madalena had stolen a piece of jewelry from a friend. Falco—who knew what he was getting up to in the middle of the night? Even Agnese might be a stranger for all Cass knew. She had always wondered how her aunt managed to stay single after her husband died so many years ago. If Agnese could do it, why couldn't Cass?

"And the other letter?" Cass watched as Narissa set the other letter on the side table. It was rolled vellum, tied with a red ribbon in addition to being stamped with wax, the kind of announcement one might send for a party.

"It's for your aunt."

"I'll take it to her." Anything to escape from Narissa's hawklike gaze for a few minutes. Besides, if Agnese was in a good mood, maybe Cass could cajole from her some small measure of freedom. How long could she possibly keep Cass locked in the villa? Until the murderer was caught? What if he was never caught? Sooner or later, the old woman would have to relent and at least allow Cass to wander the grounds of the estate.

"Good idea," Narissa said. "The cook should be just about finished with your dinner trays." And then, seeing Cass's look of surprise, "Didn't your aunt tell you she was expecting your company in her chambers?"

No, she absolutely had not.

Dinner started out worse than being a prisoner in the Doge's dungeons. Only the smallest sliver of daylight peeked through Agnese's heavy curtains. The musty room reeked of overpowering perfume and herbal ointments, a combination that practically screamed "old lady." And Agnese's mood definitely matched the dour surroundings.

Agnese's plate of sea bass and butter sauce was balanced on her lap. She struggled to manipulate the silverware with swollen fingers. It was painful for Cass to watch. Her aunt would get a bite of sea bass up to her thin lips only to have it tumble from the fork back onto the plate, or worse, onto the velvet bedspread that covered her legs and waist.

After the third piece of fish hit the covers, Cass pulled her chair in close. "Let me help you," she said. Cass speared a chunk of sea bass on her own fork and held it up to her aunt's mouth.

Agnese accepted the fish reluctantly, but then waved away Cass's next attempt with a dramatic flourish of her hand. "I don't need to be fed," she said. "I may be weak and old, but I have always been remarkably coordinated."

Cass resisted making a comment. She was simply grateful her aunt wasn't speaking to her in the soft, disappointed tone she had used last night.

"Remember that," her aunt continued, going after a green bean slick with butter. "Don't fall into the trap of letting others do everything for you. It's noble to accept help when you need it, lazy to accept it when you don't." Agnese blotted her mouth with a thin linen napkin embroidered with roses and doves.

What about accepting a husband you're not ready for? What is that? "Aunt Agnese," Cass said suddenly. "Why are you in such a hurry for me to marry Signor da Peraga?"

"For all the reasons you imagine, dear." Agnese rested her fork on her plate. "As you know, I was forced to sell your parents' estate to repay their creditors."

Cass nodded solemnly. Apparently, her father had made a few risky investments that had put the family deep in debt. Cass had lost almost every remaining piece of her parents because of this—their artwork, their furniture, even their clothing. It was almost like her mother and father had never existed at all.

"My husband's nephew Matteo will be coming of age soon,"

Agnese continued. "Because he is the legal heir to the estate, this property will become his. He hasn't decided if he wants to move here or sell the villa. Either way, he'll eventually start his own family, and although I'll probably be allowed to stay on, given my advanced age, there may not always be a place for you."

"But why Luca?" Cass persisted.

Agnese reached out and patted Cass on the hand. "Your parents loved the da Peragas," she said. "It was always their wish that you two would marry one day. Luca is a good man. Proper. Kind. I will never worry about you, knowing that you are entrusted to him. No matter what anyone has said of me"—here she brandished her fork again—"I have always held to my promises, and I intend to do so until I die."

"But what about what you said?" Cass persisted. "What about not letting people do things for me? What if I want to be entrusted to myself?"

Agnese speared another bean. "I'm sorry, dear, but that's simply not how it's done. I did not invent the rules for us women, and they are not mine to alter. Besides, complete freedom . . . it's an ideal. An impossibility. Haven't you read enough of my books to have learned a thing or two about the world?"

An impossibility. The words hit her like stones thrown from a rooftop. Maybe Cass did want the impossible. Love. Freedom. Maybe she was striving for things that no one could have.

Agnese set her plate to the side and split the red wax seal of the vellum Cass had given her. She skimmed the letter and a smile broke out over her wrinkled face. "How would you like to go to Donna Domacetti's for tea? She has invited you to call on her this afternoon.

It may be only a small taste of freedom, but you'll likely receive an overlarge helping of cake."

Normally Cass would have dreaded sitting about Palazzo Domacetti, listening to that fat old crone cackle and gossip. Cass was still upset that the woman had done such a thorough job of informing all of Venice of her engagement to Luca. But today just the thought of getting some fresh air made it seem worth it. Besides, the Domacettis lived right on the Grand Canal. Maybe Cass would run into Falco or one of his friends. She wanted desperately to let him know she wouldn't be able to meet him at the Pillars of Justice.

"I'd love to," she said, a little too eagerly.

Agnese's eyes narrowed. "Yes, I suppose you would. Well, you might as well begin making friends with Donna Domacetti's circle. They will be your companions very soon."

Cass tried to keep a straight face. The thought of marrying Luca was bad enough. Was she expected to transform into a boring, petty gossip as well?

At least Donna Domacetti knew everything about everyone. She'd probably go on at length about the murders if Cass prompted her.

Cass excitedly informed Giuseppe and Narissa of her outing, and the old gardener made record time preparing the gondola for travel. Even Giuseppe looked different to her now. Cass was fascinated by his gnarled hands, at the way his bones curled like claws around the long flexible oar. As Cass watched him steer their boat around a larger flat-bottomed vessel, she thought of the traffic jam in the Grand Canal, and the threatening note she had received. She had been so preoccupied, she had not thought of the note in days. But now, once again, she wondered who could have sent it. Was it merely a warning, or a true threat?

Neither Falco nor Paolo could have known where to find Cass unless they were following her. But someone like Joseph Dubois could afford to pay an entire battalion of men to stalk her if he so desired. Cass thought back to all the times she had felt like she was being watched: on the path to San Domenico village, in the stalled gondola, at Fondamenta delle Tette, in the batèla with Falco. Maybe it hadn't all been her imagination. Dubois was connected to both of the dead women. But if he had killed them, why would he be offering a reward for information about his maid?

Cass chewed on her lower lip. She was missing something, some crucial piece of the puzzle. For one, the motivation. And she didn't understand how she fit in—unless the murderer saw her in the grave-yard. It was the only explanation. Cass had no connection to Signor Dubois or to either of the dead girls.

Giuseppe hollered to a man on the shore, and Cass realized they were approaching Donna Domacetti's palazzo. Cass had not forgotten about looking for a way to leave a message for Falco.

"Will you be accompanying me all the way to the palazzo?" She smiled sweetly at Narissa.

Narissa nodded. "Yes, Signorina. After you're safely received, I plan to continue on to the market."

Safely received. As if Cass might get snatched stepping from the gondola onto the Domacettis' private dock. Maybe she could sneak away for a few minutes after she had tea. The Domacettis lived within walking distance of Piazza San Marco, where she had seen Paolo the other day.

Giuseppe moored the boat in front of the Domacettis' palazzo and helped Cass from the boat.

Don Domacetti was a high-ranking senator, and everything about his home reeked of excessive wealth. The palazzo was twice the size of those on either side and appeared to be freshly painted, its bright white walls a stark contrast to his neighbors' dingy, water-stained exteriors. The arched main door was overlaid with gold leaf and embellished with tiny golden vines and blossoms. Cass knocked twice on an ornate door knocker made of marble and shaped like an angel taking flight. A servant in the brilliant red and black livery of the Domacettis' estate opened the door and ushered Cass into the palazzo.

The servant escorted Cass up the stairs into a vast portego lined with dark wood and accented with red and yellow paint. Cass fought the urge to wince. The whole room, even the ceiling, was adorned with elaborate sculptures of angels and winged horses. There must have been forty little flying creatures in there, each painted more garishly than the next. The walls were deep mahogany, with white marble moldings carved in swirling patterns. A giant square mirror hung at the center of each wall, reflecting the swirls and wings from across the room, magnifying the entire effect.

It was hideous.

The floor of the cavernous portego was made of tiny glass tiles arranged as a replica of Bottacelli's *Birth of Venus*. Cass walked a circuitous route across the room to avoid stepping on the Venus's uncovered left breast.

A trio of women sat clustered in chairs around one end of a long marble table. At the head of the table, Donna Domacetti sat on a plush red divan, the farthingale of her crimson skirts easily filling the seat made for two. Her ample breasts and belly seemed in danger of splitting her ivory bodice. The fabric was pulled so taut, it looked sheer in places. Cass counted at least three chins nestled beneath the woman's dark red lips.

"The future Signora da Peraga, come join us," the obese woman said, gesturing regally with one hand.

The other women watched Cass as she arranged herself in one of the open chairs. One woman was young and fair, the other older and dark. Both stared at her with narrow, competitive eyes. A servant brought Cass a steaming cup of tea and left a shining silver pitcher in the center of the table.

"Allow me to introduce Donna Hortensa Zanotta and Signora Isabetta da Guda." Donna Domacetti gestured to each woman in turn.

Cass had never met either of the women before, but had seen Hortensa occasionally at the Frari when she attended Mass with Madalena. Her husband, Don Zanotta, was an unattractive but powerful man, reputed to be one of the feared Council of Ten, an elite group of Venetian senators that controlled most of the government. Hortensa wore a low-cut emerald dress and a necklace of jagged black stones. She had high cheekbones and wide-set hazel eyes. She would have been beautiful were it not for the cluster of deep smallpox scars on her right cheek. She'd tried unsuccessfully to disguise them with putty and pressed powder. Cass felt a rush of sympathy for the girl. It was rumored that Don Zanotta could be violent when he got angry. Unblemished, Hortensa might have found a younger, kinder husband.

Isabetta was older, closer to Donna Domacetti's age. She wore a high-collared indigo dress with matching starched cuffs and just a hint of scarlet lip stain. Her dark hair was pinned back into a thick coil of braids and mostly obscured by a deep blue veil.

Hortensa gave Cass a curt nod and then turned back to Donna Domacetti. "Have you met him, then? Don Ernesto of Rome? Rumor has it he can be quite a handful."

"As well as a mouthful, no doubt." The fat woman threw her head back and cackled. "Bit of an odd one, though. He likes his women cold."

"I could be cold," Hortensa said. She looked around the group, as if daring anyone to challenge this assertion.

"So your husband tells us." Donna Domacetti cackled again. "But I don't mean cold as in cruel, Hortensa. I mean *physically* cold. Apparently he makes his favorite courtesan bathe in ice water before he lies with her."

"How unusual," the dark-haired woman murmured. Cass had already forgotten her name. Isabella? No, Isabetta. "Does he not have to worry about the cold affecting his . . . size?" Isabetta asked.

Cass almost choked on her tea. Her face turned bright red. This wasn't what she imagined socializing with Donna Domacetti's circle would be like. What if Agnese had come with her? Surely they wouldn't have spoken so crassly in front of her aunt.

Donna Domacetti chuckled. "Careful, ladies. An innocent sits among us."

Cass forced her lips into a small, closed-mouth smile. She wondered what these women would think of her if they knew of her trysts with Falco. Cass thought of the moment they had shared only last night. What might have happened if the world were only her and Falco, if he could have laid her back on one of her aunt's marble benches and kissed her until sunrise?

"It's hard to imagine the niece of Agnese Querini being *too* innocent," Isabetta said. She sipped her tea and then set the pale pink cup back on its saucer, a smear of blood-red lip stain marring the golden rim.

Cass raised an eyebrow at the dark-haired woman. "What does that mean?"

Donna Domacetti rubbed her chins with the back of her hand. "Nothing, my dear. Simply that your aunt is very wise in the ways of the world."

Cass decided she might as well put the hour she would suffer here to good use. "My aunt wondered if there had been any new developments in catching that maid's killer," she said.

"I heard the body was discovered by a priest on his way to service," Hortensa said, crossing herself.

Donna Domacetti waved a hand in front of her face. "Likely strangled by some drunken sailor in the throes of passion."

"I heard she was carved up." Hortensa said this with a dreamy look, like the idea of a mutilated servant was very pleasing.

"Old news, either way," Donna Domacetti said. "Today I heard my lady's maid gossiping about a second servant gone missing from Joseph Dubois's estate. Since when did the comings and goings of servants become a matter of national importance?" she asked, with a sniff.

Cass's heart jumped into her throat. Another servant missing from Joseph Dubois's estate? After the first two deaths linked back to him? It had to be more than just a coincidence. "Do they think she was taken, just like the first?" Cass fiddled with the handle of her teacup.

"Who knows, dear? Dubois is apparently so distraught, he's been unable to speak to the rettori yet. Seems this girl was one of his favorites—blonde, big eyes, one of those maids who struts around in her servants' garb like she's a courtesan." She snorted. "No wonder he's distraught. The French and their women. At least he likes them warm." Donna Domacetti drained her cup of tea and then let out a satisfied belch. "If you ask me, she probably ran off with some performer. Palazzo Dubois is always crawling with them—poets, jugglers, conjurers. I don't know how the signora puts up with the constant noise and drama. Maybe she's also being entertained after hours." The other women snickered.

So. Another favorite of Signor Dubois gone missing. It seemed increasingly likely that Dubois was to blame for the murders, or was at least connected to them in some way. Perhaps after Agnese allowed Cass to leave the villa again, she and Siena could make a visit to Feliciana. If anything shady was going on at Palazzo Dubois, Siena's gorgeous older sister would likely know of it.

The image of her former lady's maid flashed in her head. *Blonde. Big eyes.* No, it couldn't be. Signor Dubois employed dozens of girls. The chance that Feliciana was the girl who had gone missing was slim. Still, Cass felt her blood racing beneath her skin. She remembered the swollen corpse emerging from the waters of the Grand Canal, the ring of bruises around her neck. That couldn't happen to Feliciana. Or to any other woman. It went against God and nature, against everything.

"You look a bit pale, dear. Let me freshen up your tea." Donna Domacetti reached across Cass for the pitcher of tea the servant had left in the middle of the table. Cass stared at the large ring on her middle finger. It was a bright red oval stone set in silver, with a flower engraved in its middle.

Six petals inscribed in a circle, just like the ring Falco had found in Liviana's tomb.

Just like the symbol on the outside of de Gradi's workshop.

Cass nearly knocked over her teacup. "Your ring," she burst out, clumsily catching the cup before more than a drop had spilled. "It's . . . lovely."

"Oh, this? Thank you, dear. I received it as a gift from a local abbot in exchange for some charitable donations I made. I do patronize a good many churches. It's important to keep in touch with the masses, don't you agree?"

Cass faked a smile and looked down at her lap, trying to control the trembling of her hands. She watched Donna Domacetti out of the corner of her eye. She had almost forgotten about the ring Falco had found in Livi's tomb, but she would swear it looked just like the one Donna Domacetti was now wearing. Could she be involved in the murders somehow? The donna was crass, but seemed harmless. Much too self-absorbed to be caught up in any plot that didn't involve eating, gossiping, or ogling attractive men.

Then again, if Cass had learned one thing in the past week, it was that no one was who they seemed to be.

"So rank is Death

that some men can

smell his approach."

—THE BOOK OF THE ETERNAL ROSE

twenty-one

Later that night, Siena burst into Cass's room. She was ghost-pale and shaking. "She's gone," Siena said, dissolving into tears. The marketplace had been buzzing with the news. Feliciana had vanished from the estate of Joseph Dubois.

Cass couldn't keep herself from envisioning Siena's sister, swollen and slashed up, her body rising to the surface of the Grand Canal. She forced the image out of her head. She couldn't think like that.

"Are you certain?" Feliciana always did have a wild streak. Maybe she'd met a sailor or a shopkeeper while running an errand. "Might she have just spent the evening with a . . . gentleman?" Cass asked gently.

"She's been missing for two days," Siena said, her blue eyes wet with tears. "And my sister is no whore."

Cass pulled Siena to a seated position on the bed next to her. The girl was trembling so badly that if she didn't sit, she might collapse at any minute. Cass couldn't imagine how she would feel if she had a sister who had gone missing. But then, her lady's maid was the closest thing she had to a sister. Awkwardly, she wrapped an arm around Siena's shoulders, trying to comfort her.

She headed down the corridor and turned left into the library. Narissa followed her—of course. Cass noticed Agnese's needlework basket sitting on the floor near the marble fireplace. Her aunt had been fond of sewing before her fingers and joints started to swell. Cass didn't really have the patience for needlecraft, but unfortunately she had to endure several hours of it a week. It was only proper, as Agnese was fond of saying. Narissa actually seemed to enjoy sewing.

"You might as well occupy yourself." Cass gestured toward the basket. "I'm going to be writing for a while."

Narissa settled happily into Agnese's favorite chair by the fireplace, cradling the basket of cloth and thread on her lap. Cass sat at the table where she used to have her lessons, drumming her fingers on a likeness of Neptune that was carved into the tabletop. She tapped the point of her quill against the sea god's trident. Feliciana missing. Donna Domacetti wearing a ring with the flower insignia. Falco and Angelo arguing. How was it all connected? And how did it fit in with the disappearance of Liviana's body? The image of the flower within the circle kept tickling the edge of her consciousness. Cass felt like she had seen it somewhere besides the rings and Angelo's workshop. Somewhere a long time ago . . .

A slamming noise from somewhere in the house made her jump. The tip of her quill pierced the skin of her finger, bringing a fat red drop of blood to the surface. She cursed under her breath and pressed her finger to her lips.

"It's just the wind, Signorina," Narissa said. "A loose shutter."

"Could I trouble you for a glass of wine?" Cass asked. Maybe a drink would calm her nerves.

Narissa set her needlepoint on her chair and left the room. A few minutes later, she returned to the library with a goblet of red wine. Cass swished it around, inhaling the sharp fragrance. She took a long drink and then set the goblet down next to a blown-glass lamp.

Opening her journal, she wrote down a series of names: Liviana. Mariabella. Falco. Angelo. Maximus. Sophia. Dubois. Donna Domacetti. And now, Feliciana. And then, after a bit of hesitation, she added *Cassandra.*

How did they all fit together? Livi didn't seem to have connections to any of the others. And none of the people on the list had connections to everyone. Mariabella and Sophia had been murdered and marked with an X. Feliciana was now missing. The men on the list were all suspicious in one way or another, especially Angelo de Gradi and his gruesome assortment of bodies and body parts. He might have met both Mariabella and Sophia through his dealings as Dubois's physician. He might even have treated them. But if he had killed them, why had one ended up in Livi's crypt and one in the middle of the Grand Canal? Why weren't they both tucked neatly into bath basins? Why didn't he want to keep them for his collection?

Falco had promised to tell her what he was doing with Angelo. Maybe that was the missing piece of information she needed. She struggled to remember the snatches of conversation she'd overheard between Falco and the physician at the small chapel by the statue of San Giuda. Angelo had said something about tonight, but Cass hadn't heard enough of the man's words to know if he was referring to the body in the canal or the chapel or something else.

The little church bothered her. She felt like she knew it from somewhere. Cass closed her eyes. She saw the fallen sculpture, the broken-down chapel, the tiny graveyard attached. She had never been there before; she was certain of it. She'd never even walked that area of Venice before. She opened her eyes and blinked hard; the library looked slightly hazy. The wine must have been stronger than she thought; she noticed that she had drained almost all of her glass. At least it wasn't as bad as the muddy wine from Tommaso's studio.

That was it! When the boys had interrupted Cass and Falco's kiss in the studio, she'd overheard one of his friends say something about San Giuda. Something about a pickup. Something about the smell of death. Could it be just a coincidence? Or was something going on at the crumbling chapel?

Narissa had noticed that Cass's glass needed refilling, and had returned to the library with a whole bottle of red wine. Cass was about to decline when she noticed the hungry way the older maid looked at it as she refilled her glass. An idea began to form in Cass's mind.

"Would you like a glass?" Cass tried her best to sound innocent.

Narissa's eyes went as bright as the fire for a moment, but quickly returned to normal. "I shouldn't, Signorina. But thank you."

Cass winked. "Go on. No one will ever know. I'm sure my aunt is asleep by now. What harm is there in having a sip or two?" *Or three or four or five.*

"Well, if you're certain." Narissa glanced quickly around the library as if she thought spies might be hiding behind the bookcases or in the fireplace. Then she poured herself a small glass of the wine and continued her needlework. Her fingers worked the thread quickly.

When the maid's glass was empty, Cass refilled it without saying anything. Narissa didn't even seem to notice, and finished her glass before Cass had had more than three sips of her own. Again Cass refilled it; again Narissa quaffed it down.

After one final glass, Narissa's head began to nod against her chest. Cass felt a rush of triumph. She knew she was taking a huge chance sneaking out of the villa. If she got caught, there would likely be a padlock applied to her bedchamber door. Or worse, Agnese would send for Luca and arrange an immediate betrothal ceremony.

Cass ripped a page out of her journal and scrawled a quick note to Falco.

Dear Falco,

I cannot meet you by the Pillars of Justice. My aunt has been keeping me close to home. I can try to sneak out after everyone is asleep, if you want to meet me in the garden again. Please know that if I do not show up, it's because I'm being watched, and not because I don't want to see you.

She signed it simply with a *C*. There was so much more she could have written, so much more that wanted to pour out of her—love and fear and hope—but she figured these things were best said in person. Especially since Cass had no idea where the servants kept the wax and would have to leave the note unsealed. She would look for Falco in the taverna. If he or his friends weren't there, she'd leave the message with the barkeep and simply hope for the best.

Then, she'd find a way back to the chapel with the fallen San Giuda.

Cass glanced over at Narissa again. The maid was snoring loudly, chin resting on her chest, half-completed needlework in her lap.

Cass stood up soundlessly and moved into the hall. Should she risk heading upstairs for her cloak? She decided to borrow Siena's again. Fastening the woolen garment around her shoulders, Cass tucked her journal into one of the pockets. Grabbing a lantern and tinderbox from one of the long wooden counters, she unlocked the servants' door and opened it slowly, trying her best not to make any noise. If Agnese caught her this time, she was as good as dead.

Cass slipped out of the villa, and into the night.

"The Black Death announces
itself by the appearance of foul,
egg-sized swellings that erupt
on the bodies of its victims,
followed by spreading boils
and hideous discolorations of the skin.
So excruciating is the pain
that death, when it comes, is a mercy."

—THE BOOK OF THE ETERNAL ROSE

twenty-two

Cass made it to the island's tiny village in record time. She had to look for Falco at the taverna and then escape San Domenico before anyone realized she was missing. When she left the villa, she was reasonably certain everyone was asleep, but who knew when a servant might awaken and find Narissa snoozing in the library. Cass felt a little guilty. Narissa was in for a good scolding—and possibly worse—if Cass got caught. Especially if Cass got caught stealing a boat and going all the way to the Rialto by herself.

But she *wouldn't* get caught.

She had spent the walk to town trying to convince herself that she was strong enough to row across the lagoon and then back again. It was doubtful, but she had to try.

The whole mystery was a tangled web, and Cass was hoping that the chapel tucked away in the back streets of the Rialto held the answers that she sought.

Cass ducked into Il Mar e la Spada. She quickly scanned the clusters of men hunched over the battered wooden tables. No Falco. She made her way up to the bar. The barkeep had a silver hoop in his left ear and a black star inked on each of his fingers.

"Help you?" he asked.

Cass tried not to stare at the ring in his ear. "I was wondering if I might leave a message here for Falco. Do you know him?"

He grunted. "Falco da Padova? Tommaso's boy? I know him."

Cass slipped the man the letter she had hurriedly written in the library, and pulled out a silver coin as well, sliding it toward the barkeep. "Is this enough?"

The man smiled a reply as he pocketed the coin and tucked the letter underneath the bar. Cass noticed he was missing several teeth. He turned away from her as a gray-haired man with a patch over one eye hollered for a refill.

"Good-bye, then," she said, making her way back through the crowded taverna and out into the night.

The air felt thick. The moon above was an almost-invisible sliver of light. She was filled with fear and exhilaration, both emotions running through her like blades. The lantern swayed in her trembling fingers. Cass tightened her grip. Having it comforted her, not only because it provided light, but also because it would make a decent weapon, if needed. She remembered the lepers from the Rialto, how she had been ready to swing the lantern if they attacked her.

Behind the bakery, a small fishing vessel and a long wooden gondola bobbed in the brackish water. Cass was surprised to see the gondolier nestled in the bottom of his boat beneath a ratty gray blanket. Maybe she wouldn't have to row herself all the way to the Rialto and back.

She bent down and tapped softly on the edge of the gondola. The boat bobbled back and forth in the water. "*Scusa*," Cass said. The breeze whipped her braids around her face, tendrils of wild hair stinging her cheeks and eyes.

The gondolier muttered something in his sleep. He turned on his side, pulling the threadbare cover up over his head.

Cass leaned over, gripping the edge of the gondola with one hand to keep from tumbling into the murk. Tiny waves lapped against the dock, sending fine sprays of icy water in her direction. She reached out with one hand and nudged the gondolier gently.

Something silver cut through the inky darkness as the man sat up with a start. Cass fell back onto the dock, wincing as the rough wood bit into the flesh of her palm. Her eyes widened. The gondolier was clutching a dagger in his right hand. He looked at her with a mixture of surprise and confusion.

"Signorina! *Caspita*. You scared me halfway to the grave."

"*Mi dispiace*." Cass couldn't pull her eyes away from the blade still clenched in the man's fist. "Please. I—I require safe passage to the Rialto. Will you take me?"

The gondolier slipped the dagger into the pocket of his breeches and narrowed his eyes at her. "At this hour? What for?"

Cass thought quickly. "I need to return home," she said. "My aunt will disown me if she discovers I snuck out of her palazzo." She tried to look desperate. It didn't take much effort on her part. "Please. I will pay you double. You won't find as good an offer in the morning."

The man smiled knowingly. "Let me guess. You were meeting somebody. *Amore*. Say no more." He accepted Cass's fare and assisted her into the gondola.

Cass settled as far back in the felze as possible, wrapping her arms around her middle to conserve heat. The gondolier handed her his woolly gray blanket. The fabric was scratchy against her skin, but Cass was grateful for the extra warmth.

As the boat bobbed and rolled across the vast lagoon, Cass tried once again to untangle the snarl of suspects and clues regarding the pair of grisly murders and Liviana's missing body. But she kept coming back to Falco. Falco in the graveyard. Falco burning the mysterious threatening note. Falco, who knew of the brothel where Mariabella worked. Falco, who was friends with Angelo, and possibly Dubois as well. Falco, who had twice refused to go to the town guard with information about the murders. Cass wanted—no, needed—to believe he was innocent, but how could she ignore so much evidence?

Cass indicated that the gondolier should drop her by the Rialto Bridge.

"Which one is your palazzo?" he asked. "The streets are unsafe. I will take you directly to your dock."

"It's fine," Cass said. "It'll be quieter if I go around to the back on foot. I wouldn't want any of the servants to awaken when you moor your boat." The falsehood rolled off her tongue with almost no thought. Cass couldn't believe how easy lying had become.

The gondolier shrugged and tied his boat beneath the Rialto Bridge. After alighting from the gondola, Cass slipped into the darkened alley between the large palazzos. The buildings were so close together that their overhanging roofs completely obscured the sky above her. She could have reached out and touched both exterior walls if she had wished. Instead, she moved slowly, her lantern clasped tightly in her right hand.

Despite the darkness and the tangled streets, Cass felt certain she'd have no trouble finding the chapel again. Her body seemed to be moving independently from her brain, as if a higher power were guiding her toward her destination. Sure enough, a few minutes later she emerged into the campo where the crumbling statue of San Giuda lay on its side, and the chapel and monastery sidled up against each other. The night was damp and chilly, the air layered with mist. *Now what?* She decided to explore the chapel first.

She headed around the side of the building, figuring it was safer to sneak in through one of the smaller entrances in case the chapel wasn't as deserted as it looked. Just as she put her hand on the wooden door, Cass froze. Behind the chapel, beyond the wrought-iron gate, a small sphere of light winked on and off in the tiny graveyard, almost as if signaling to someone.

Ducking down, Cass made her way along the stone wall of the church, toward the gate and the graveyard waiting behind it.

The gate was propped open, as if a funeral party had recently brought in a body. But that was madness. No one interred bodies in the dead of night.

As Cass made her way beyond the iron fence, the temperature seemed to drop. Her skin prickled with goose bumps. She stole through the graveyard, holding her lantern close to her body for warmth. She tracked the sphere of light as it moved along the row of crypts. As she approached it, she saw a second, dimmer lantern, propped next to the first.

The pair of lights swirled and wavered in the pitch night. Cass felt herself being pulled forward, like a moth to a flame. Perhaps Falco was here, sketching, as he had been that night on San Domenico. Perhaps she had been magically drawn to him. Not magically, divinely. Perhaps God had brought the two of them together. Just because Falco didn't believe didn't mean it wasn't real.

Fate.

Cass was so certain Falco waited for her at the end of the row of crypts that she opened her mouth to call out to him.

And then a horrible scratching sound rent the air. The noise seemed to tunnel deep inside of her. The lantern slipped from her fingers and fell to the wet grass. The flame went out. Instinct gripped Cass, telling her to get as far away from the graveyard as possible. The scraping noise pierced the quiet night again. It sounded like the claws of demons forcing their way inside a crypt to feed on innocent souls.

Go back. Go back. Go back. Cass heard her own voice screaming in her head. But she couldn't move. She was terrified, transfixed.

Then she heard other voices. Whispering. Muffled cursing.

Falco's voice.

For a moment, the graveyard, the cold, the mist—all of it disappeared. Cass felt as if she were hovering outside of her body: she was walking forward, moving mechanically, without thinking. She could no longer feel anything. She didn't even know that she was breathing.

And then she saw him.

The lanterns illuminated Falco's face. His hair was hanging in his eyes, and his forehead was beaded with sweat. He was standing next to a tomb, dragging a heavy, white-wrapped shape across the ground, toward a wooden cart where Paolo and Etienne were waiting. Nicolas was watching, holding a metal hammer, muttering instructions Cass couldn't make out.

Falco stopped, straightened up, and said something indecipherable. Paolo came forward to help him. Nicolas abandoned his hammer and scooped up one of the lanterns.

Suddenly, the cart and Falco's wrapped bundle moved into the faint light.

An arm broke through a fold in the burial shrouds.

White, bloated, its fingers swollen in death. A human arm, connected to a corpse. Falco cradled the dead body against his chest as he wrestled it over to the cart.

A horrible wailing noise pierced the air.

It took Cass a minute to realize the sound was coming from her.

"Once a corpse is removed
from its grave it should be
dissected without delay, its
various parts sliced thin for
examination by the anatomist."

—THE BOOK OF THE ETERNAL ROSE

twenty-three

S he clamped a hand over her mouth, but it was too late.

Falco dropped the body he was holding, whipping around to face her. His eyes went wild.

"Cass!" Her name echoed through the open space.

She reeled backward, terror drumming through her. She had fallen into hell, into a nightmare. She ran, sobbing, choking back more screams. Her foot landed in a soft patch of dirt and her ankle twisted. She stumbled but didn't fall. As she passed through the open gate, she hitched up her dress with both hands and pushed herself to run faster than she ever had before. The wet grass tugged at her ankles. Cass could sense the boys behind her; she could feel them pursuing her.

Twice she tripped and went sprawling across the campo. The cracked marble cut into her hands. She climbed to her feet without looking back, not thinking of anything but home, and light, and safety, and the heavy locks on her doors, which she would bolt now and forever against the man—the madman—she had fallen in love with.

Racing through the dark alley, Cass cursed herself for lying to the gondolier. If she had been truthful—well, more truthful—he might have agreed to ferry her back to San Domenico. Instead, Cass raced along the side of the canal until she found the same fisherman who had taken her home the night she and Falco had discovered Sophia's body in the canal.

Her footsteps had awakened the boy, and he sat up sleepily in his *sandolo*. A slow smile spread across his face as he recognized her.

"Go, go, go." Cass hopped into the boat, emptying her purse in the boy's direction. Silver coins spilled out onto the damp baseboards. Way too much for the fare, but Cass was not worried about the money.

The boy laughed, not understanding the urgency, but he freed his little fishing skiff with a sharp tug on the rope. Grabbing the oar, he turned the boat out into the center of the canal. Cass looked back as they pulled away from the bridge. Falco stood at the water's edge, watching her leave. His hair snapped and twisted in the wind; the faint moonlight distorted his features so that he looked more monstrous than human.

Or maybe he had always looked like that, and Cass had been too blind to see it.

She turned her back on him, sliding down in the boat. She wished she could die, that the bottom of the sandolo would just split open and let the frigid water of the lagoon suck her down to its muddy depths.

Cass barely registered the ride back to San Domenico. When the sandolo pulled close to Agnese's dock, Cass hurled herself over the edge, not even waiting for the boy to anchor the boat. She no longer cared about the cold or water or being caught. She just wanted to get inside and begin forgetting everything she had seen.

Shivering, she slipped through the back door and into the darkened kitchen. The house was quiet. No one else had woken.

Cass made her way upstairs to her room. She pulled her shutters closed with a bang, triple checking the latch to make sure it was secure. Then she went from candle to candle, lighting them all, as though she could burn away the horrible images in her head. She had had enough of the dark.

She writhed inside her torn and soggy dress, yanking at laces and buttons until the garment fell from her body to the floor of her bedroom. Cass stared at the shredded fabric. Destroyed. Like her life. Like everything. She sank into bed, pulling the covers up to her neck. She couldn't stop shaking. Cass fought the urge to vomit. She had fallen in love with a monster. He could have killed her.

She glanced up at the portrait of the Virgin Mary. The woman looked back from her frame without judgment, but also without answers. Tears came, hot and fast. Cass curled onto her side, pressing her chin to her knees. She began to sob. Her insides felt like they were being crushed from all directions. Bones breaking. Her heart, squeezed to dust.

"The Church decrees that bodies

buried in unconsecrated ground

have no hope of ascending to Heaven.

But Heaven is a myth.

Hope lies in the dead themselves.

It is through the study of their

bodies that we may gain

the key to immortality."

—THE BOOK OF THE ETERNAL ROSE

In the morning, thin beams of light filtered through cracks in the shutters. The candles had long ago burned to useless nubs.

As Cass sat up slowly, memories of the previous night assaulted her, one after the next. Horrible scratching sounds. Bodies sprawled on a cart, like disfigured lovers. Falco embracing a corpse. Had it all been a dream? It must have been.

Of course. A bad dream. A terrible, terrible nightmare.

Cass gasped as Slipper bounded up on the bed. "You scared me halfway to the grave," she told the cat. The words niggled at the edge of her consciousness. Had she heard them in her dream?

Slipper mewed softly and Cass reached out to pet his gray and white head. Her hand stung. She pulled it away from the cat. For several seconds she couldn't bring herself to look at it. She listened to her heart slam-bang in her chest. She remembered tumbling to the hard ground of the campo, falling forward onto her palms, sharp edges of stone cutting into her flesh. *Please please please.* Cass willed her skin to be intact. *Please let it all have been a dream.*

Slowly, Cass lifted her hand to her face. Her palm was marred by several long red scratches. Bile rose to the back of her throat. Blanks in her memory filled themselves in rapidly. Cass tricking Narissa. The note for Falco. The trip home with the fisherman. It was real. All of it. *Falco embracing a corpse* ...

Cass fought back tears. Were the artists witches? Satanists? Were they involved with whatever Angelo de Gradi was doing in the old Castello building? Bodies. Body parts. Cass shuddered. Were they simply stealing the dead, or could Falco and his friends be murderers too?

She glanced around the darkened room. The shadowy outlines of her armoire and dressing table reminded her of sentries standing guard. They were solid, sturdy. The whole house was sturdy. Yesterday the villa had been her prison. Today it was her fortress. Surely, she would be safe as long as she remained hidden inside. She had asked Falco to meet her in the garden that very evening. That was one engagement she wouldn't be keeping.

She spent most of the day tucked away in the library, leaving just long enough to pick at her dinner while Agnese watched, frowning. Cass had been finishing up Dante Alghieri's *La Divinia Commedia*, but the scribe's loopy handwriting was giving her a headache. Some of the wealthier nobles turned their noses up at printed books, but Cass thought the invention of the printing press was nothing short of magic. She tossed the hand-copied book down and wandered over to the shelf where her aunt kept her newest printed volumes. She scanned the spines, hoping for a new collection of de Montaigne essays, but she didn't find one. Absentmindedly, she selected a book with a dyed-green leather binding. She snuggled down in the chair by the fireplace with Slipper on her lap.

The book was by a little-known English playwright named

Shakespeare, and the story was about a pair of young lovers kept apart by a family feud. Cass knew love was probably the last thing she should be reading about right now, but she liked the way Shakespeare wrote, with vivid language and long flowing lines. It was more like poetry than story. Cass flipped the pages rapidly, eager to find out what happened to the star-crossed pair. But the book ended only part of the way through the story. She'd have to search the shelf and see if her aunt had purchased the next volume.

Slipper opened his eyes and yawned at Cass as she set the green book on the table next to her chair. "You'll never disappoint me, will you?" Cass murmured, nuzzling her nose against the white spot on Slipper's forehead.

The cat flexed one paw in response, his tiny needlelike claws catching in the fabric of Cass's dress. She petted him while she looked up at the library's elaborately painted ceiling. A local artist had done a mural of a traditional vision of heaven. Flocks of winged angels played in ponds and flower gardens while a bearded God looked directly down on Cass.

"Signorina Cass." Narissa poked her head into the library. "You have a gentleman caller. I told him you were reading, but he was quite adamant."

Cass's throat went dry. Falco. She shook her head. Her hands unconsciously tightened around Slipper, and the cat wriggled in her grasp. "Tell him I'm ill," she croaked out.

Narissa left the library, and a few minutes later Cass heard muffled voices coming from the front of the villa.

She couldn't make out what Narissa was saying, but she did hear that the voices were getting louder, as if Falco were arguing with her.

Cass leapt to her feet. Slipper squirmed out of her arms and landed hard on the floor. Terror and rage pulled at Cass, freezing her to her spot. She couldn't decide whether to hide away or launch herself at Falco and drag him forcefully from the villa. Clearly he was depraved, but was he violent? Were she and Narissa in danger?

Cass's anger won out, and she stalked from the library down the hallway to the portego. She couldn't believe Falco's nerve. He had no right to raise his voice to Narissa. He had no right to be there, to be anywhere, to show his face in public ever again. Not after what Cass had seen. How had he even contrived admittance to the villa? Probably he was dressed up in some stupid costume again. Cass remembered his poorly fitting aristocrat's clothing from the night of the masked ball. He had never told Cass where he got the outfit, but now she knew. The same way he got Liviana's necklace, by stripping it from a rotting corpse. Her stomach churned. Once again she saw Falco cradling that dead body against his chest.

She turned the corner, ready to yank Falco outside and tell him to leave and never come back. But when she hit the threshold to the portego, she froze. The man arguing with Narissa wasn't Falco.

"Hello, Cassandra," the man said. His brown eyes lit up and he smiled.

"Luca," Cass gasped.

"A leech left to batten too
long on the flesh of a diseased
person may gorge itself so fully
on unwholesome blood that it
bursts open, spilling poisons into
the air and sickening others."

–THE BOOK OF THE ETERNAL ROSE

twenty-five

I admit I was hoping for a slightly warmer greeting," Luca said, still smiling. He held something wrapped in paper out toward her. "These are for you."

A bouquet of lilies. Cass accepted the pale pink flowers, still unable to make any words come out of her mouth. She blinked rapidly, as if her fiancé were a mirage that might disappear.

It had been only three years since she had seen him, but her Luca had grown at least six inches in that time. His shoulders had broadened to the point where his ivory brocade doublet fit tightly across his chest. His legs were long and muscular beneath his trunk hose and breeches. Even his hands looked huge compared with the wiry bookish boy she remembered. Just a hint of sandy-colored hair peeked out from beneath his black velvet hat.

Narissa stepped between Cass and Luca. "Like I told you, Signore, Signorina Cassandra isn't feeling well and really shouldn't be disturbed."

Luca didn't respond immediately. He just kept looking at Cass. She felt herself blushing and had no idea why. So he had outgrown his awkward stage. He was still the same old Luca. Wasn't he?

"It's all right, Narissa." Cass placed a hand on Narissa's shoulder.

"This is Signor da Peraga, my fiancé." She managed to say the word without grimacing.

"Your—" Narissa backed away immediately. She dipped into a shallow curtsy. "Oh! I beg your pardon, Signore. I didn't recognize—" She grabbed the cloak out of Luca's outstretched hands.

"It's fine, Narissa," Cass said. "Signor da Peraga will watch over me for a bit if you'd like to take a break. If my aunt is awake, I'm sure she would like to be informed of his arrival." She touched the older woman's shoulder as Narissa turned to leave. "Would you mind putting these in some water?"

"I'll take care of them, Signorina." Narissa disappeared with Luca's cloak and the lilies. Cass led him back to the library. Slipper was stretched out across the chair by the fire.

"Thank you for the flowers." Cass picked up the cat and reclaimed her spot. There was no way she was going to sit with Luca at her study table. She imagined their legs bumping beneath the carved tabletop, their hands just inches apart.

Luca raised an eyebrow at Slipper. "You're welcome." He stood awkwardly beside Cass for a moment before pulling one of the chairs over next to her. He removed his hat and ran a hand through his dark blond hair. "The maid said you were ill. You do look a bit feverish." He pressed one of his hands against her cheek. His skin smelled faintly of pine and citrus. "Perhaps we should call a physician."

Cass fought the urge to shy away from his touch. It was surprisingly gentle. His hair looked so thick and soft. It had always been uncontrollably curly when he was younger, but now he wore it short and straight. She fiddled with one of Slipper's velvety ears. "Really, I'm fine," she said. "I just haven't been sleeping so well."

"I should think not, with your friend's death and now a murderer on the loose. I'm sorry for your loss." Luca rubbed the bridge of his nose.

"Thank you," Cass said. Luca had known Liviana only in passing. One of his friends in Venice must have mentioned the contessa's death. "Why didn't you say that you were coming?" She was trying not to stare at him, but she couldn't help it. The angle of his cheekbones reminded her of one of the Greek statues from Dubois's salon. His skin was sculpture-worthy as well, creamy and alabaster pale, just the hint of a blond beard showing on his cheeks and chin. Almost nothing about him reminded her of the petulant boy who had demanded a kiss from her three years ago.

Luca gave Cass a funny look. He plucked a series of invisible cat hairs from his black velvet breeches. "I'm sure I mentioned it in at least two letters. Did you not receive them?"

Cass reddened again. Her tongue felt knotted in her mouth. "I must have lost track of time." *Santo cielo.* He was going to think she'd become a babbling idiot.

Luca's smile wavered for a moment. He stretched out his long legs and crossed them at the ankles. "No matter. I'm here now. Just in time to protect you."

Cass gestured toward Slipper, who had gone back to sleep on her lap. "Well, as you can see, I'm in grave danger of being mauled, right here in my aunt's library." She regretted the wry tone immediately. It was the kind of thing she would have said to Falco. Luca would probably take offense at her joke.

But he laughed. "He does look rather fierce," he said. Luca picked up the leather-bound volume Cass had been reading. "Shakespeare," he said, twirling the book in his hand. "Quite a tale. Pity how they both die at the end."

"Luca!" Cass gasped. Slipper jumped down from her lap and padded over to the fireplace. "I had only just completed the first quarto. I was looking for the second volume when you arrived."

Luca looked apologetic. "I'm sorry. A classmate was talking about it at university. You can still read it, Cassandra. It's a fine story, if you like that sort of thing. As I recall, you used to be more into sword-fights and sorcerers."

Cass was about to respond when Agnese glided into the library, dressed in a pearl gray dressing gown cinched at the waist with a wide white belt. "Do I hear arguing already? Save it for your marriage, children." Her eyes brightened and her mouth curled upward as if Luca were a roasted bear on a platter, smelling of cloves and cinnamon. "Narissa told me you'd arrived," Agnese continued. "I apologize for my state of disarray, dear. I retired early this evening."

"Signora Querini. You are every bit as lovely as I remember," Luca said, his cheeks reddening slightly as he bowed toward Agnese.

The old woman crowed with delight. "I daresay you are three or four times as lovely as I remember. Whatever herbs and potions you're taking over there in France, can you spare some for an old lady?"

Luca laughed. "No potions, Signora," he said. "Just growing up."

"Aunt Agnese," Cass said quickly, a little embarrassed by her aunt's comments to her fiancé. "Should we fetch some tea? Maybe have Cook fix a plate of *tartine*?"

"Nothing for me, thanks," Luca said. "It's been a long journey and I just wanted to pay you a visit before I settle in at my parents' palazzo. I'm in desperate need of a restful night's sleep."

"How is your mother?" Agnese asked.

Luca swallowed hard. "Not well, I'm afraid. She's been staying at our estate on the mainland. The doctors say it's best for her to avoid the stress of the city."

"Well, we can't send you home to an empty house. How dreary! I insist you stay here," Agnese said. "Besides, it's been too long since we had a handsome man about the house."

Cass almost laughed out loud at her aunt's flirty tone. What had gotten into the old woman? Then she cringed at the thought of her and Luca under the same roof. She was hoping to avoid him as much as possible until he returned to school in France, where he belonged.

"Well, if you really don't mind." Luca fumbled over his words. "My parents' place is a bit run-down since I've been away for so long."

"It's settled. The servants will get you set up in the spare bedroom between Cassandra and myself." Agnese tucked an unruly strand of coarse hair back under her nightcap. "Until then, I'll let you two catch up on your own."

Slipper bounded after the old lady, chasing a loose thread that dangled from the bottom of her dressing gown. Cass burst into giggles the moment her aunt left the room. "I daresay," she began, mimicking Agnese's voice, "that she was flirting with you."

"I'm certain she was just being friendly," Luca said. But he smiled broadly at Cass.

"What are you doing here, anyway?" Cass asked.

Luca's smile vanished. "I thought you'd be happy to see me," he said. "And your aunt wanted to plan a betrothal ceremony. Didn't she tell you?"

Instantly, Cass's good mood dissipated. A betrothal ceremony? Once she had undergone the official ritual, there would be no going back on her marriage. She would belong to Luca da Peraga. Like his fur-lined cloak or the feather in his hat, Cass would be just one more pretty thing for Luca to call his own. No more studying. No more adventures. She would become, as Falco said, a caged bird, beating its wings against the bars of its prison.

"No, she didn't tell me," Cass said hoarsely, trying to push Falco from her mind. His sparkling eyes. The crooked smile. The tiny jagged scar under his right eye.

"We can talk about it more tomorrow," Luca said kindly, perhaps mistaking her dread for nervousness. "I'll be out running some errands in the morning, but I'll see you at dinner?"

Cass nodded. A pair of servants came for Luca with armfuls of bed linens and towels. Cass fled the library in front of them. She didn't want to watch Luca settle in to the bedroom next to her. She didn't want to think about what it meant for the two of them, and for her future.

The next day, Cass sat at her dressing table, staring at herself in the mirror. Wide-set green eyes, slightly puffy. Thick curtain of auburn hair. Full lips, turned down ever so slightly. She couldn't believe her reflection. She looked almost normal. Where was the evidence that her heart was broken, that things would never be right again?

She traced her fingers along the carved pattern in the ceramic oil lamp that sat on the corner of the table. Her mother had brought it home from the market one day, certain that Cass would love the etched floral design and vivid colors. She stared at the scarlet petals, red paint trickling outside of the carved lines like blood on bone. A yellow flame flickered from the lamp's elongated spout. Light. Love.

Cass contemplated lashing out with her arm, pushing the lamp from her dressing table, watching it shatter into pieces on the stone floor of her bedroom.

She should be delighted that Luca was back. She should be dressing in her fanciest dresses and demanding the most elaborate hairdos in order to impress him. Instead, she was avoiding him . . . which was difficult, since he was staying just on the other side of the wall.

It wasn't even proper, a man living on the same floor as the women, but otherwise, he would have to sleep in a tiny chamber on the third floor with the servants, and that would never do. Cass had assumed he would stay only the night and then return to his family palazzo in the city, but her fiancé had suggested that Cass and Agnese needed a man in the house, at least until the murderer was caught. They wouldn't be safe on their own, especially not at night. Agnese was only too happy to oblige. Cass swore she heard Luca's boots clunking up and down the hallway several times a day, as if he were a guard patrolling.

Even Slipper was miserable. The gray and white cat sat in a muff on the windowsill, mewing plaintively. Cass knelt down next to him, her eyes following his gaze through the glass. A pair of starlings chased each other across the side lawn. Slipper's eyes darted left and right to follow their path. Beyond the birds, the graveyard gate was closed, the chain wrapped loosely through the bars.

Now that she had seen Falco cradle a dead woman in his arms, she doubted that she'd ever be able to set foot in a graveyard again.

Cass shuddered as she thought of the workshop, the basins, the lifeless hand dangling from the larger tub. Had Liviana ended up there? She must have. It was the only thing that made sense.

Folding her knees to her chest, Cass was suddenly grateful her stomach was empty. She forced the image of a young and playful Liviana into her brain. She wouldn't think of her friend sliced into pieces. That wasn't how she wanted to remember her.

Later that day, it was Siena who came to remove her dinner tray. Perhaps Agnese thought a visit from the younger maid might lure Cass out of seclusion. "He's gone," Siena said. "Signor da Peraga. He said he won't be home for several hours, if you want to come out."

"I'm not hiding from Luca," Cass said acidly. She was back at her dressing table, trying again to compose a letter to Falco. The floor next to her was littered with failed attempts.

Siena raised an eyebrow at the mound of crumpled parchment. "Of course not, Signorina." She paused just before reaching the door.

She spoke without turning around. "I beg your pardon, Signorina, but maybe you should count your blessings, instead of focusing on what you have lost." The softness of her voice couldn't conceal the fact that her words were a reproach.

"It's not your place to comment on my blessings," Cass said sharply. "It's not your place to comment on anything at all."

Now Siena turned back to her. "*Mi dispiace*," she said. She smiled a tight-lipped smile. "I have spoken out of turn." She curtsied quickly and then left.

Cass wanted to scream. She wanted to throw something. She was ashamed of how she had spoken to Siena—the poor girl's sister was still missing, after all—but she repressed the guilt under a thick layer of anger, stifling and quick, which rose in her like a tide of mud.

She threw herself on her bed and sobbed—partly from shame, partly from grief, partly from anger. This was it. She would never leave her room again. She would die here, an old maid, her flesh picked apart by spiders.

For three days, she holed up in her room. Narissa brought her meals, each time offering to dress her, but for the most part Cass refused both clothing and food.

On the fourth day after Luca's arrival, instead of Narissa's gentle knock, Cass's bedroom door was flung wide open without warning. Cass drew the covers over her head and pretended to be asleep.

"There you are." Cass was surprised to hear Madalena's voice. A second later, Mada yanked the covers from her head. "Oh, dear. Looks like we've got some work to do." Madalena went to the armoire and began flipping through Cass's dresses. She pulled out the topaz one Cass had worn to the tailor's shop the previous week. With the dress draped over one arm, Madalena tossed Cass her cream-colored stays.

"What are you doing here?" Cass asked, reaching out to catch the stays.

Madalena gave Cass a dazzling smile. "Saving you. And your marriage, too, from the looks of it." She turned around. "Slip that on. I'll help you with the rest."

Cass knew she should get up, that it was rude to loll around in bed when her friend had made the trip out to San Domenico just to see her. But the thought of putting on a full outfit, doing her hair, and sitting around in the portego making idle chitchat was positively excruciating.

"I'm so tired, Mada," she said. "Can't we just catch up here in my room? I'm sure the cook would fix you a breakfast tray as well."

Mada wrinkled up her nose. "Since when have you turned into an invalid? Aren't you going crazy cooped up in here?" She pointed at Slipper, who was scratching at the closed bedroom door. "Even the cat wants to escape."

Cass gathered her covers around her. "Not me. I was thinking I might stay in here forever."

"Not a chance. Have you forgotten my wedding is tomorrow? I won't allow you to show up in your nightgown." Madalena pulled the top cover from the bed with a vicious yank. "Besides, old Agnese threatened to send for the head physician if I couldn't bring you out of seclusion."

Cass groaned. Dottor Orsin was a brutish man who would fill her full of toxic-tasting herbal cocktails and watch with sadistic delight as leeches sucked the blood from her body.

"Fine. You win." Cass stripped out of her nightgown and slid her arms into the stays. At least it would feel good to have fresh clothes on.

"Agnese wins, but doesn't she always?" Mada said, her fingers crisscrossing the laces at Cass's back. "Now what is this about exactly? You hate Luca?"

"I don't hate him," Cass said, lifting her arms so that Madalena could pull the laces tight. "I just don't love him."

"I see." Madalena slipped the topaz dress over Cass's head. "I saw him getting into a gondola the evening of your fitting. Marco and I were meeting Cristian for dinner. Old Luca has gotten quite handsome over the past three years, hasn't he? Are you not attracted to him at all?"

"I—well, no. I do find him attractive . . ." Just saying that made her feel uncomfortable, but she wasn't sure why. She adjusted her skirts around her slim hips. "Wait a minute. You saw him in the city? Over a week ago?"

"I tried to get his attention, but he seemed to be in a hurry," Mada said.

Cass thought back to the day of her fitting. Siena had mentioned seeing Luca at the market, but Cass had assumed she was mistaken. Why would Luca lie about his arrival in Venice? It didn't make sense. Unless he had busied himself preparing for the wedding . . . She cringed.

Madalena fussed with the bodice of Cass's dress. "And the reason you are not interested is . . . ?"

Cass stared at her reflection. The golden dress brought out the red in her hair. "The thing is—" She paused for a moment. Maybe she should just tell the truth, or an abridged version anyway. Mada would understand that she had fallen for someone else. It was very dramatic, and Mada lived for drama. Cass took a deep breath. "The thing is, I met a boy."

Once Cass started talking, the whole story just poured out of her. Falco, running into him again, spending time with him on the Rialto and in Tommaso's studio. The conflicting feelings of desire and guilt and hopelessness. She told Madalena about everything except the murders, and seeing Falco and his friends stealing bodies.

To Cass's surprise, Madalena listened to her whole story without interrupting once or getting distracted by juicy details like what kind of outfit Cass wore to the masked ball or which direction Falco's smile tilted. Cass let all of her hopes and heartbreak and guilt spew forth like a venom that had been killing her from the inside.

Afterward, Mada was silent for a moment. Then she took Cass's hand in her own. Cass stared down at the beautiful golden rings Mada wore on her middle three fingers—one diamond, one sapphire, one emerald. "I'm surprised at you," Mada said.

Cass lowered her head. Had she been foolish to think Mada might understand? "I figured you would be."

Mada squeezed her hand. "No, silly. I'm surprised you let yourself fall for Falco in the first place." She looked at Cass with wide, affectionate eyes. "It's scary to give part of yourself to someone else. I know what it's like to be terrified of pain. Of loss."

"What do you mean?" Cass was startled; she was sure her friend was going to lecture her for her indiscretion.

"When my mother died, my father nearly went insane with grief." Madalena toyed with the golden crucifix hanging from her belt. "And even though I was only ten years old, I couldn't imagine ever letting myself love someone like that. Setting myself up for all that pain."

"But Marco—" Cass started.

"I didn't love him from the beginning," Mada said. "He was kind and handsome, but I still found reasons not to like him. His hands were rough. He sometimes smelled of ship parts—of tallow and burning coal." She shrugged. "But as you can see, he won me over."

Cass bunched up her eyebrows. "So you're saying I'll grow to love Luca?"

Mada grinned. "I would. Did you see the muscles on that man? Toting all those heavy legal tomes around must be working in his favor."

Cass smiled. She wasn't sure if she believed Madalena, that loving Luca was just a matter of letting down her guard, but either way her friend had made her feel better.

"Anyway," Mada added, a mischievous gleam in her eye. "Think of whatever happened with this artist boy as . . . practice." She winked.

Cass blushed. "You're shameless, you know that?"

Madalena ran her perfectly filed nails through Cass's thick hair. Her hand snagged halfway through it. "And *you're* a mess. Your hair looks like a bird's nest. Let me fix it."

"Fine," Cass said, laughing. "Just for you."

"And to keep Dottor Orsin away." Mada smiled.

Cass sat at her dressing table as Mada ripped through her snarled hair with a silver-plated hairbrush, then twisted Cass's hair back into a painfully tight topknot and pinned it with a pearl hair ornament. She flipped open the top of the heart-shaped jewelry casket where Cass's brooches, bracelets, and necklaces lay all jumbled together. She untangled a heart-shaped jade pendant from the snarled mass. She fastened it around Cass's neck. "Perfect. Are you ready to show yourself?"

The jade pendant felt cold against Cass's breastbone. "Is Luca here?"

"Gone, I promise," Mada said. "Some mysterious errands. Probably buying you flowers and fancy jewelry."

Cass cringed. The last thing she wanted was for Luca to try to win her affection with presents. "I hope not."

Mada glanced at the tangled ball of necklaces and bracelets. "Like I said before, you could use some new pieces. Ask for pearls. A girl can never have too many strands of pearls."

As usual, Madalena's mere presence had brightened Cass's mood. There was still an ache deep inside her when she thought of Falco, but it wasn't the stabbing pain of the previous days. Maybe time would continue to dull the sharpness in her stomach, transform it into a smooth stone—heavy, but bearable.

For the first time in days, Cass let herself think about Luca. His shy smile, his light brown eyes, the warmth with which they regarded her. Could she be with him and not yearn for Falco? Cass didn't think so, but she didn't know everything. Maybe Mada was right. Maybe it was pointless to fight the natural order of things. Maybe she *would* learn to love Luca.

"If there be no obvious injury to
the body, the cause of death may be
difficult to determine. The internal
organs are so precisely attuned to
each other that even the slightest
damage to one may produce a general
disturbance that causes the entire
organism to cease functioning."

—THE BOOK OF THE ETERNAL ROSE

twenty-six

Madalena stayed long enough to eat dinner and escort Cass on a walk around the grounds. After Mada left, Cass wandered through the middle of the garden aimlessly twirling a parasol, journal clutched under one arm, thinking about everything her friend had said. Agnese appeared to have relaxed the ban on Cass leaving the villa after the days she spent isolated in her room. In general, the whole villa just seemed happy to see her out of her room. Except for Luca—he was still gone on his mysterious errands.

The plants were arranged in semicircles: rosebushes in the very center, lilies and marigolds in the middle, and a ring of edible herbs on the outside. The arched trellis, providing partial shade for a pair of stone benches, stood at the back of the garden beyond all of the flowers. When the rosebushes grew heavy with blossoms, Giuseppe would take pride in stringing roses through the wooden slats.

The roses were just beginning to bud, but the marigolds were in full bloom: pale yellow, bright gold, fiery orange. Each plant blossomed bigger and bolder, trying to outdo the rest. An uprooted stem of the golden flowers lay among the mostly naked branches of

Agnese's rosebushes. These marigolds were drying out, withering away, as the rosebuds waited to be born. Life juxtaposed with death. One thing ending, another beginning.

It made Cass think of Falco and the way he had talked about how life and death were interconnected, how one could not exist without the other. The image of Falco cradling a corpse flashed in her head. Again and again, she had asked herself the same question: Could there be some *reason* he and his friends were stealing bodies? Some greater good that Cass didn't understand?

No. Even if Falco didn't believe in heaven, the people he had stolen from their graves most likely did. Falco had robbed souls of their chance for eternal life. And if he was involved with whatever Angelo de Gradi was doing . . . Cass didn't even want to think about that.

Cass wondered, not for the first time, if someone had buried her parents' bodies. The thought of her mother and father being forbidden from entering heaven was almost unbearable. What happened to souls denied their afterlife? Did they wander the earth as spirits? Cass felt her throat clench. She wished her mother could be with her. She desperately needed her guidance. Cass closed her eyes and willed her mother to speak to her, to tell her what she should do.

But when Cass opened her eyes, no mystical signs glimmered before her. Only the sun hung low in the darkening sky. Her mother couldn't help her.

Reaching down, she yanked the dying marigold from its spot among the roses, crushing the petals in her hand. She turned away from the trellis. The memory of her kiss with Falco hovered too close to the surface. She tried to lock it deep within her, to bury it. Mada had said it wasn't about forgetting, just about accepting the way things had to be. Cass needed to forget, though. If she couldn't have Falco, she wanted to forget that he ever existed.

As though in response to her thoughts, Luca appeared from around the side of the villa. It was so like him not to use the servants' door. Cass hadn't seen her fiancé in days and had almost gone back to thinking of him as the awkward, bookish boy who left Venice to study in France. Now she was forced to acknowledge his transformation once again. Watching as the wind ruffled his thick blondish hair and blew his cloak back from his broad shoulders, Cass couldn't deny that her fiancé had become incredibly handsome. The thought made her feel awkward and twisty inside, as if merely finding Luca attractive was a betrayal of Falco.

Falco. The boy she could never see again.

"Hello, Cass." The words fell stiltedly from Luca's lips. Cass had never heard him call her by her nickname before. He stopped several feet from her, probably waiting to see if she would bolt out of the garden and into the graveyard rather than be close to him. Cass smiled in response. She gathered her skirts and sat on one of two stone benches near the garden's center.

Luca approached her. He walked stiffly, as if he were still getting accustomed to his long arms and legs. "Sometimes I think we use more water in a day for our gardens than peasant families use for a month's worth of cooking and washing."

Cass looked up at him. "Is there a water shortage I don't know about?" She hoped he couldn't tell she'd been crying.

"No." Just the faintest French accent colored the single word. Luca reached out to examine the beginning bud of a ruby-colored rose. The bloom snapped off in his hand. He twisted it around in his fingers. "I remember when you were a child. You used to have a nickname for all the flowers. You called the marigolds 'fireflies,' I recall, and lilies were 'ladies' purses.'"

"I can't believe you remember that," Cass said. "You hardly even played out here with me."

"Remember how I used to hide things for you?"

Cass remembered. Before they were engaged, Luca would bring her little treasures, things he found when he was out wandering around. Once it was a string of green ceramic beads. Another time he left her a smooth stone shaped like a heart. He used to mark the hiding places with lilies stolen from Agnese's own plants. Cass had forgotten about the game until Luca mentioned it.

"I liked that game," Cass said. "I was sad when you got older and stop playing it. You practically quit talking to me."

"I got nervous around you after our arrangement became official," Luca said. "I used to watch you sometimes, though."

"That's kind of creepy, don't you think?" Cass raised an eyebrow, and couldn't help but crack a small smile.

"You stopped being just a little girl." A red flush crept across Luca's high cheekbones. "I wasn't very good at talking to women. I'm still not."

His shyness surprised her. Luca, the man, was proving to be so different from the boy she remembered. She thought of what Mada had said about growing to love somebody. She looked down at her hands and said haltingly, "My behavior has been inexcusable these last few days, so I won't try to excuse it. I can only imagine what you must think of me."

Luca finally dared to sit on the bench across from Cass. "It's all right," he said, still twirling the rosebud in his big hands. "I guess your aunt sprang it on you, announcing our engagement so suddenly." He smiled, but Cass could tell it was forced. Hurt still lingered in his eyes. "You know, most girls wouldn't mind being Signora da Peraga."

"I know," Cass said. She could think of nothing else to say.

Luca said, this time with a warm smile, "But you are different from most girls, aren't you, Cassandra?"

Her hands tightened around her journal. Somehow Luca managed to see something good in her, even where there was nothing good to see. And yet, his words reminded her of Falco's.

"I'd prefer it if the idea of our engagement didn't make you miserable," Luca continued. "Does it?" he asked softly. "Make you miserable?"

A few days ago, all Cass had wanted was to escape from her obligation to marry, and now she felt Luca loosening the band around her neck, unlocking the door to her cage. But Cass couldn't tell him the truth. She had already hurt Falco. She wouldn't hurt Luca and Agnese too. Being with Luca made sense. Being with Falco was madness.

"I hate seeing you so sad," Luca said after a pause. "I hate to think I may be the cause of your unhappiness."

Cass hovered on the brink of tears again. "It's not you. I've just been feeling . . . alone." She swallowed. "Contessa Liviana's death got me thinking a lot about my parents." This was not a complete lie.

Luca leaned forward on his elbows. "I understand," he said softly. "It's been years, but I still feel my father's death as if it happened yesterday. And I never told you this, but I lost a younger sister back when I was just a child myself. Diana. I think about her every day."

He ducked his head, like the memory was physically weighing him down. "There's no crime in still grieving your parents. You don't ever have to get over them."

Sympathy bloomed inside Cass. Even though she was grieving Falco more than she was her parents, it was comforting that Luca understood her for once. "I didn't even know you had a sister."

Luca looked up. His pale eyes darkened. "She's—she would be a year younger than you. She died the summer before our parents introduced us. My mother can't even bring herself to speak of her."

"I'm so sorry," Cass said. She reached out to squeeze Luca's hand. "Was it fevers? Or the plague?" The Black Death, as Venetians often called the plague, had decimated the population.

"They called it a drowning," Luca said abruptly.

Called it? Cass started. "But you think otherwise?"

"Let's just say my family is riddled with bad luck. Between Diana dying young and my father succumbing to the plague, my mother has gone half mad with grief." Luca blinked, as though the sun were too bright for his eyes. "I wish I could do more for her," he said, slipping his hand from Cass's. He rubbed at a small scuff on one of his leather boots.

As he stood, a single red petal fell from his black velvet cloak. "I'm glad you came out of your room. I hope to see you at supper." Luca unfastened the cloak from around his neck and handed it to her. "Here. It's getting dark. You might get cold."

Cass accepted the cloak and draped it across her front like a blanket. A square of white cotton fell out of the pocket and she reached down and picked it up. Luca's handkerchief. Her fingers stroked the embroidered initials—LdP. She thought back to her conversation with Madalena about dropping handkerchiefs. It seemed like the exchange had happened in another lifetime. She tucked the square of fabric back into the pocket of his cloak.

Luca smiled. "Thanks," he said. "I manage to lose more of those than you can imagine." He turned back toward the house.

The air turned cool as the stars came out, but Luca's cloak kept Cass surprisingly warm. A blurry face appeared at one of the windows. Cass recognized Agnese's favorite white cap. Cass gave her aunt a hesitant wave and the face vanished. Cass wondered if everyone had been worrying about her. She remembered the cautious way Luca had approached her, as if she were a wild horse that might spook and run off.

She ripped a blank page from her journal and started a letter to Falco.

I was wrong about who you are; I cannot possibly love a man such as you, nor can I see you again. It is not fair to either of us. Please do not try to see me or communicate with me in any way.

Cass knew that if she had the letter delivered to Falco, he would honor her wishes. Sighing, she tucked the piece of parchment inside the back cover of her journal. She couldn't send it. Not yet, anyway.

Cass slipped inside the back door, where the cook was busy assembling cream-filled pastries in an otherwise empty kitchen. He wiped his hands on his apron and bowed in Cass's direction. "Tell me the truth. It was my chicken broth that cured you, right?"

Cass laughed. "It must have been. Both Slipper and I enjoyed it."

The cook gave her a severe look. "That little beast should be eating scraps." But then he winked to show Cass he was joking.

When Cass entered the dining area, Agnese and Luca both beamed so brightly that for once the drafty, cavelike room seemed filled with heat and light. A pair of dinner servants stood at the far end of the table in their blue and silver uniforms.

"I'll be right back," Cass said. She hung Luca's cloak over the back of a chair in the portego and then went to her room to put her journal away.

When she returned to the dining room, one of the servants pulled out Cass's chair for her and the other placed an embroidered napkin in her lap. The boys stepped back from the table and stood against the wall, waiting to fetch empty plates or refill wineglasses as needed. Cass smiled hesitantly at her aunt, wondering if a lecture on manners would be forthcoming.

Agnese wore one of her finest gowns, a muted sea-green satin with a strand of dyed pearls to match. Siena had even helped her apply color to her lips and cheeks. Cass hadn't seen her aunt look this vibrant in years. "I knew a visit from Madalena would raise your spirits," Agnese said. She made no comment about Cass's self-imposed seclusion.

In fact, no one commented on Cass's recent behavior. The servants brought each course to the table with their usual polite smiles. Cass's appetite had returned, and she enjoyed a bowl of vegetable stew and a plate of broiled rosemary chicken.

Siena entered the room once, her blue eyes barely lifting to meet Cass's gaze as she hurried past. Cass felt a flash of guilt, and resolved to apologize later for snapping at her. There was still no news of Feliciana, and Cass knew Siena was nearly crazed with worry. No wonder she had told Cass to count her blessings.

Agnese prompted Cass and Luca to talk to each other, but Cass had said almost everything she could think of to say to Luca in the garden earlier. There was not much she could tell him about recent days without incriminating herself or Falco. She cut her chicken into smaller and smaller bits, chewing slowly so that she didn't feel pressured to speak. Luca didn't seem to mind the occasional awkward silences, jumping to fill them with stories about his life abroad.

After the servants cleared the plates, they filled the wineglasses again and served Cass, Agnese, and Luca each a pastry for dessert.

Agnese swallowed half of her pastry in a single bite. "Have you heard anything about the murder?" she asked Luca. "Dreadful, that poor maid floating up in the canal."

Luca had the crumbling dessert halfway to his lips. He placed it neatly back on his plate and rubbed both hands on his napkin. His whole body seemed to tense up. Cass set her fork down. She stared at Luca as she waited for him to speak.

"I have actually heard rumors," he said slowly. "There was some gossip in the city about it. There is talk of a gang roving the cemeteries at night . . ."

The temperature in the room seemed to drop several degrees.

Agnese finished the second half of her pastry and chased it with a big swallow of wine.

"Satanists, if you ask me," Luca added.

Agnese bobbed her head in agreement. "The girl was strangled and then cut up like a chicken, they say. I'm not even sure San Domenico is safe anymore."

"I don't see why everyone is suddenly so concerned," Cass said. Even to her own ears her voice sounded strained. "Venice has always had more than her share of murders."

"Drunken brawls and knife fights," Luca said. He stared back at her. Was it her imagination, or did she see a challenge in his eyes? "But not murders of this kind. And of innocent women."

Cass's throat felt as though she had swallowed a chicken bone. "Why so interested, Luca? Don't you have other, more important duties to which you should attend?" She downed half a glass of wine in one swallow. Her mind flooded with terrible thoughts. Did Luca somehow know about Falco? Had he been spying on her?

"I consider it both my civic and domestic duty," Luca said, smiling tightly. "I want to make sure that my wife-to-be isn't troubled by any . . . *undesirable* company. The women of Venice are one of our most precious resources, after all. I want to be sure they are protected."

Anger flared inside Cass. She couldn't believe she had softened to him earlier—that she had, for a second, even thought she could be *happy* with him. "The women of Venice are far more capable than most men realize," she snapped. If the room got any colder, Cass would have to ask one of the servants to bring her a cloak.

Agnese cleared her throat to speak, but to Cass's amazement Luca cut her off. It was like he'd completely forgotten her aunt was at the table with them. His voice rose and his face reddened again, but this time not from embarrassment. "I am well aware that many women believe themselves to be stronger than they are. They might believe, for example, that it is a fully rational thing to go gallivanting around the city alone at night. They believe that they are playing a game— they have no idea how high the stakes really are."

Cass had never seen Luca show this much emotion, and it was both fascinating and frightening. A chill zipped up her spine. Was he *threatening* her? She forced herself to maintain eye contact. "You are not my husband yet," she said softly, but with force. "And I do not have to listen to you."

Luca's fork fell to the table with a clatter. "Then you are a sillier girl than I thought," he burst out. "And I would urge you to be more careful. Where *have* you been spending your time, Cassandra?"

"One might ask the same question of you," she said. Both Siena and Madalena had claimed to have seen him on the Rialto. They couldn't both be mistaken. Her eyes narrowed. "How long have you really been in Venice, Luca? You told me you had just arrived, but you were seen in the city more than a week ago! How do you explain *that*?"

"All I have done since arriving in Venice is attend to your safety." Luca flung his balled-up napkin onto his untouched dessert plate. "What you don't know *can* hurt you, Cass." He pushed his chair back abruptly from the table.

For a second, no one said a word. The outburst had startled even Agnese into silence. Cass was sure that the servants were taking in every word.

Luca seemed suddenly to remember that there were others in the room. He passed a hand through his hair. "I apologize," he said stiffly. "I don't know why I got so upset." He brushed a few crumbs from his clothing as he stood. "If you will both excuse me, I have some reading I must complete."

Cass turned to her aunt the second Luca disappeared into the portego. "What on earth do you suppose that was about?" she asked.

"It appears that during his time in France, your fiancé developed a bit of a temper," Agnese said mildly, as though Luca's outburst were perfectly normal. She blotted her mouth with her napkin and signaled a servant to bring her a second pastry. "Let's just hope he saves some of that passion for your wedding night."

Cass folded her napkin and put it on the table. She felt nauseated. She replayed the conversation with Luca again and again. He hadn't even denied returning to Venice early. It was true—he'd been in town for at least a week, maybe more. Why had he lied to her? She thought of how she had seen, for just one second, his face contorted with rage as he warned her to be more careful. It was a side of Luca she had never seen—almost as though for just one second, he had slipped on a mask.

Or perhaps he had slipped out of a mask. Maybe, in that moment, he had let drop the image of the ever-composed, always righteous Luca.

It was more than just jealousy or overprotectiveness. Luca was hiding something. Cass was certain of it.

"From death we gain
knowledge of life, and
from this knowledge we
may one day vanquish death."

—THE BOOK OF THE ETERNAL ROSE

twenty-seven

Luca remained holed up in his quarters after supper. Cass retreated to her own room and readied herself for bed. After Narissa helped her from her dress, Cass slipped into a nightgown and stood in front of her mirror. She unpinned each of her braids, letting her thick auburn hair slowly untwist on its own. Cass shook her head and what remained of her braids came loose. She grabbed her hairbrush and brushed until her hair gleamed. The repetitive motion soothed her. Luca had always felt like a constant. Predictable. In the time Cass had known him, both in person and from his letters, he had never been volatile.

He had also never lied to her.

But he didn't deny lying about his return to Venice. Had he been spying on her? Did he know about Mariabella? Did he know about Falco? Was that why he was interested in the group of boys roving the graveyards? Had he seen something? Was that why he had gotten so angry?

Cass thought again of all the times she had felt watched, both on San Domenico and deep within the city. Maybe it wasn't her imagination *or* Signor Dubois. Maybe it was Luca, tracking her movements? But why?

Thwack.

A noise at the window made Cass start. Her heart fluttered in her chest. She moved slowly to the window, both hoping—and hating herself for hoping—that she might see Falco standing on the lawn below, beckoning to her. Maybe it was silly, but Cass still hoped for an explanation of what she had seen. One in which the boy she loved wasn't wicked or depraved.

She pulled open the shutters.

A rock of disappointment settled in her stomach. It wasn't Falco waiting on the grass below. It was Paolo.

He was holding something beneath one arm; with the other arm, he beckoned for her to come down. Fear and curiosity tugged her in different directions. Meeting him, in the dark, alone, was probably a bad idea. But what if Falco had sent him with a message?

Curiosity won out. Cass pointed toward the back door. She slipped out of her bedroom, casting a wary glance in the direction of Luca's room. The door was closed. No light came from beneath it.

Downstairs, Cass wrapped herself in Siena's woolen cloak and unbolted the kitchen door. Paolo and Cass stood facing each other for a moment. The tall boy made an effort to smile, but couldn't manage it. Cass's heart still thrummed in her chest.

"He's not a bad person," Paolo said abruptly. "Sometimes I think that I am, but he isn't." He looked away into the darkness.

"What you do . . . ," Cass croaked out. "What I saw . . ." She focused on the outline of the closest rosebush, its naked branches crooked as a witch's fingers.

"Each man calls barbarism what is not his own practice—"

Cass finished his sentence. "For indeed, it seems we have no other test of truth and reason than the example and pattern of the opinions and customs of the country in which we live." It was another quote from Michel de Montaigne. "Do you really think that applies in this instance?"

Paolo looked up. His dark eyes looked a little sad. "We live in the same place—you, me, Falco. But we live in very different worlds. Surely you understand that?"

Cass didn't know what to say. Paolo went on, a little defensively, "We have reasons. It's not for you to judge us."

He thrust a square parcel, wrapped in rough muslin, into her arms.

"There's a note in there," Paolo said, gesturing at the bundle. "I'm sure he'd rather you hear from him, not me." He bowed slightly, his inky black hair falling forward to obscure part of his face. "*Buona notte*, Signorina Cassandra." With that, he turned away, disappearing into the darkness in just a few long strides.

Cass re-bolted the door. Her heart was still beating hard. She looked down at the wrapped square. It was about two feet by two feet and as thick as her wrist. Lighting a candle, she laid the bundle on the long wobbly table where the servants prepared food for the villa and took their own meals. She held her breath as she tugged at the coarse twine wrapped around the package.

The muslin unfolded in layers, revealing a canvas beneath. A folded scrap of parchment fluttered to the kitchen floor. Cass barely noticed it.

She was too busy staring at the painting.

There she was on the divan in Tommaso's studio. Just a couple of weeks had elapsed between now and then, but already it felt like years, like the dream of a different lifetime. Falco had captured her tiniest quirks on the canvas: the smattering of freckles across her cheeks, the unruly piece of hair behind her left ear that worked its way out of any arrangement. And her smile—Cass almost couldn't believe it was real. She looked radiant, like she was experiencing true happiness for the first time.

She remembered Falco's soft touches as he posed her, how delirious she'd been each time his fingers grazed her skin. She remembered how excited she was at being alone with him, the endless possibilities, the countless dangers. Cass wished she could dive into the painting and go back to that night where she had felt love for the first time.

But she couldn't go back.

She touched the canvas. Liviana's amethyst necklace hung around her neck. A deep sadness pierced her. The purple looked striking against her pale skin, but it was wrong that she had ended up with a necklace Liviana's family had wanted her to take to heaven. That was Cass and Falco: beautiful, yet wrong.

Cass bent down to receive the parchment. She moved closer to the candle and read.

To my lovely starling,

Maybe there are magical words that will make you understand, but if so, I do not know them. Words are your domain. I've always been better with pictures.

I fear you think I am a monster. It's true I've disrupted many graves. The way I see it, the dead are dead. If, after their death, we can learn things from them about the human form—things that will improve the lives of others, things that will increase the sum of human knowledge and the possibilities of art—what harm is that? After death, new life, new beauty. How can that be wrong? My friends and I have made use of some of the bodies as models. Some we sell to surgeons who study them with the hopes of learning something about the frail mechanism of the human body.

I don't know exactly what Dottor de Gradi does in his workshop on the Rialto, and I was as surprised as you were to stumble on it. He couldn't—or wouldn't—tell me if your friend's body ended up there. But he did assure me all of his work is focused solely on extending human life.

I won't lie. I did it for the money as well. Don Loredan is holding a private exhibition in his palazzo tomorrow. The entry fee was quite steep but two of my paintings were accepted. This could be the beginning for me. I could find my own patrons. I could become a real artist, not merely Tommaso's assistant. I could be more than just a peasant.

So yes; a little for money. But mostly I did it for the art.

I don't expect these words to change how you feel. I simply want you not to see me as a monster. I don't want to be a monster. Not anymore. Not after meeting you. I know that we disrupted your dear friend's body, and for that I am deeply regretful. But if we had not done so, if I had not lingered in the San Domenico churchyard after standing guard for my friends, you and I might never have met. Meeting you is one thing I will never regret.

I hope you like the painting. Consider it a wedding

present. How stupid of me to let my heart go. It was a lovely fantasy while it lasted, though, wasn't it?

Yours,
Falco

She looked again at Falco's painting of her—for her. Even though her expression was full of joy, he'd somehow managed to catch a hint of sadness in her form. The hesitance in how she lay there, as though expecting that happiness to vanish at any moment. This must be what Falco meant when he said he had done it for the art. For the first time, Cass understood. This, this truth, was exactly what she wanted to capture in her writing.

She felt like weeping, but she wasn't sure why. She and Falco understood each other, finally. It was the best possible outcome—the *only* possible outcome. But as she refolded a single corner of muslin over the canvas, an overwhelming sense of loss gripped her. This painting, this letter, it was Falco's good-bye. Even if he remained in Venice, he would be gone to her. They would exist side by side, but in parallel worlds that never crossed over.

Cass couldn't believe she had ever thought Falco might be a murderer. What he had done went against the Church, but he did have reasons. Maybe de Montaigne was right. Perhaps Cass had no right to judge what Falco was doing—what he must do—to survive. She had never known, would never know, what it was like to want for money. For anything, really, except for love. Maybe love was to be the one thing that would remain forever out of reach.

The thought was unbearable. Cass sat down at the servants' table and laid her head down against the rough canvas. She tried to feel each individual brushstroke through her cheek. Each stroke was a part of Falco, a tiny piece of the man she loved. She waited for the tears to come. She *willed* them to come, needed them to carry away some of her pain.

But just like at her parents' funeral, when she needed tears the most, they stayed stubbornly, persistently out of reach. Cass sat there in the kitchen, dry eyed, until the candle burned down and darkness overtook her.

"Fainting occurs when
the four humors rush swiftly from the
head and limbs to the area about the heart.
This process is evident in the way the
face grows suddenly pale, as though
drained of its normal essence."

—THE BOOK OF THE ETERNAL ROSE

twenty-eight

Cass woke with a stabbing pain in her neck. Narissa was standing over her. As Cass straightened up, realizing she'd fallen asleep at the kitchen table, Narissa's eyes went immediately to the painting. Too late, Cass tried to cover the canvas. Narissa raised an eyebrow but, thankfully, opted not to do any scolding.

"Betrothal present," Cass said weakly. She rolled her head in slow circles. When she brought a hand to her cheek, she could feel that tiny indents peppered the side of her face where she had slept pressed against Falco's textured brushstrokes.

"I'm sure your future husband will enjoy it," Narissa said wryly. She straightened the empty chair to Cass's left. "Given today's special occasion, your aunt has decided Siena may attend to you. She's probably looking for you in your bedchamber."

Mada's wedding! Cass leapt to her feet. She had promised her friend she would be there for every second of it. Cass had disappointed almost everyone with her recent behavior. She couldn't let Madalena down too.

"*Grazie*, Narissa," Cass said, heading toward the dining area. She turned back just as she reached the doorway. "You won't mention this painting to my aunt, will you?"

"What painting?" Narissa asked. Wrinkles formed at the corners of her eyes and mouth as she smiled.

Cass felt a rush of gratitude for her. Maybe the older maid hadn't completely forgotten what it was like to be young.

It was still early, but Cass knew that Mada would kill her if she was even a minute late. The wedding ceremony would start at ten, and the festivities would run into the night. Cass raced up the stairs and through the long, dark dining room, the tile floor cold under her bare feet. When she hit the threshold to the portego, she pulled up, bracing her arms against the door frame to keep from spilling into the big open room.

Luca sat on a divan facing the *Last Supper* mosaic. Two unfamiliar men in mud-caked boots sat opposite him. Red woolen doublets peeked out from underneath tarnished breastplates. Silver broadswords dangled from their waists. They all stopped speaking when she appeared in the doorway. The two men immediately averted their eyes.

Luca reddened. "Cassandra," he said haltingly, as if it were a struggle to merely form the three syllables of her name.

Cass realized she was standing in the portego in only her nightdress, having left Siena's cloak in the kitchen. "*Molte scuse,*" she said, and darted for her room. Much as she was curious about the men, she had no desire to stand there being gawked at. And she didn't want to give Luca the opportunity to remark on the muslin bundle under her arm.

Cass slipped into her bedroom, shutting the door behind her with a quiet click. Siena's tiny frame was half visible, her head poked deep inside the armoire.

"Siena!" Cass was so glad to see her lady's maid, she could hardly keep from shouting. Then she saw that the girl's eyes were red and puffy. Cass lowered her voice. "Still no word from your sister?"

Siena shook her head. She looked positively stricken, like she might collapse at any moment. Perhaps Agnese had reunited Cass and Siena for both of their benefits. "I'm sorry about what I said to you," Cass began. "I feel awful."

Siena shook her head quickly. "It's all right, Signorina. You were upset. I know what that's like."

The poor girl. Cass had always wanted a sister. She couldn't imagine what Siena must be feeling. "What's going on downstairs? Who are those men?"

Siena emerged from the armoire. "They're from the town guard."

"But why are they here?" Cass demanded. "And why now? This is hardly an appropriate hour for visitors."

Siena ducked back into the armoire. Her voice was muffled. "Apparently, your fiancé returned home late last evening and found a boy sneaking around on the property. He sent for them first thing this morning."

Cass's heart skipped. "Did—did the boy manage to escape?"

Siena gave Cass a doe-eyed look and nodded. "Just. That's why Luca has called in the guard, to keep an eye out for his return. Was it your Falco?"

Cass shook her head. "No." Once again, she didn't bother correcting Siena about her choice of words. She bit her lip to keep back a sigh. She had resolved to stop thinking about Falco, but it was next to impossible. She could almost feel his hands on her, tiny spots of heat that danced across her skin. She wondered why he had sent Paolo in his place. Perhaps he thought Cass would refuse to see him, that she would scream for protection.

Siena pulled out a pale yellow gown. It had matching slashed sleeves that were already laced up. Then she riffled through a pile of lacy accessories and held up a high, stiff white-lace collar and a pair of matching cuffs. "What do you think of this?"

"It's perfect," Cass said. She actually despised the gown. It brought out her freckles and the pink tones of her skin, but she didn't care what she looked like today. Plus, the dress was so bland, Madalena couldn't feel as though Cass was trying to upstage her. Not that Cass had ever believed she could compete in beauty with Madalena.

She thought of the canvas tucked under her arm. Was she really as beautiful as Falco's painting? Or did he see things in her that simply weren't there?

She bent down and slid the bundle under her bed. Then she went to her dressing table and yanked open the top drawer. Her journal lay among a mess of quills and hair ornaments. Cass slipped Falco's letter into the back of the leather-bound book. It was probably the closest thing to a love letter she'd ever receive. She didn't want to lose it.

The note she had begun composing to Falco, in which she told him she never wanted to see him again, was still tucked inside her journal. At least she hadn't sent it. Her own pain was consuming her, but at least she had spared Falco some small measure of additional hurt.

Siena grabbed Cass's best whalebone stays from the bottom

drawer of the armoire. She turned to Cass with the garment in her outstretched hand.

Cass heard the sound of heavy footsteps descending the front stairs. "They're leaving," she said. The wall clock read a quarter past eight. Cass had less than two hours to get ready and get to the church, but she was dying to know what Luca had told the guard. She couldn't bear to wait an additional thirty minutes while Siena laced and buttoned her into the yellow dress. Instead, she tossed on a pale blue dressing gown and rushed out into the hall, ignoring Siena's protestations.

Cass entered the portego just as Luca was shutting the front door. "What was that about?" she asked, keeping her voice light.

Luca pointedly refused to look at her. "Could we discuss this after you get dressed?"

Cass glanced down. Her dressing gown had fallen open. The fabric of her nightdress was thin, but it was far from transparent.

"I just want to know why the guard was here." Cass cinched the belt around her waist, securing her dressing gown around her, more for Luca's sake than her own. "Siena said something about a boy loitering on the property?"

Luca focused on the da Vinci mosaic. He seemed to regain his composure. "The boy claimed to be a messenger but refused to give me a message. He said he had wandered onto the wrong estate by accident."

"What happened to him?" Cass fought to keep a straight face.

"I tried to detain him, but he ran off," Luca said.

Cass arched an eyebrow. "Are you under the impression a simple messenger boy is committing grisly murders?"

"No. I don't think he's the killer, but he was probably up to no good." Luca finally made eye contact with Cass, but it almost seemed like he was looking past her, through her. "That's why I summoned the guard. I'd like to make sure that we have no unpleasant . . . incidents." The way he said it made Cass shiver. "As I've been telling you, Cassandra, you need to be cautious. People are not always what they seem."

Cass lifted her chin and forced herself to sound casual. "I feel very safe here on San Domenico." She added, for good measure, "*Especially* now that you're staying with us."

Luca smiled faintly. "I'm glad to hear it. I thought maybe you were finding my presence burdensome." He flicked his eyes toward the mantel clock. "You should probably get dressed."

Luca was already dressed. He wore black breeches and boots with a wine-colored silk doublet that fit snugly across his broad shoulders. A gold embroidered velvet cape hung from one shoulder. Most of his thick blondish hair was covered by a small-brimmed black velvet hat adorned with a plume of burgundy and white feathers.

"You look nice," Cass said, partially to soften him and partially because it was true.

"So do you," he responded instantly. "I mean, you will—I mean, you do now too, but—"

She turned back toward her room as Luca fumbled over his words. His politeness was sort of charming. So different from the men in the streets who hollered and clapped when women walked by. He probably wouldn't even try to kiss her again unless she specifically told him it was all right. For a brief second, Cass wondered what it would be like to stand on her tiptoes and press her mouth against Luca's pale lips. His beard had grown out some in the past few days. What would it feel like against the smooth skin of her cheek?

Wait. What was she doing? Luca was trying to get Falco's roommate thrown in jail and instead of being angry, Cass was daydreaming about kissing him. She sighed. Everything had gotten so confusing since Luca had moved in.

Back in her room, Cass couldn't keep herself from fidgeting as Siena threaded the silk ties through the eyelets of her stays. The laces would probably end up all upside down and backward, but all Cass could focus on was Falco. She had to see him again, just one last time. She wanted to thank him for the gorgeous painting. She wanted to let him know that Luca had alerted the guard about Paolo. It would be in the artists' best interests if they steered clear of Agnese's estate and the San Domenico graveyard for a while.

She knew where he would be today—at Palazzo Loredan for the art exhibition. Don Loredan lived just a few blocks away from Madalena. Cass decided she would sneak away for a few minutes after Mada's wedding ceremony. It would be easy to get lost in the mob of people as the procession made its way from the Frari to Palazzo Rambaldo for the wedding feast.

Siena fashioned Cass's hair into a tight bun and wrapped a white lace hair ornament around it. Cass grabbed a simple white hat and paused in the doorway of her bedchamber. Turning around, she snatched her journal from the top of her dressing table. Surely Agnese wouldn't object to Cass recording details of the happy day.

Her aunt had put on her finest gown, made of deep purple satin with threads of silver sewn right into the fabric. She wore a lavender veil and just a hint of makeup around her steely gray eyes. Cass could almost see her own mother hovering behind Agnese's wrinkled skin. She had never sensed the resemblance before. Even Narissa looked pretty in a simple green dress, her thinning hair hidden beneath a silky veil. She carried a pair of small rosewood cadenas that contained Cass and Agnese's personal silverware.

"Where's Luca?" she asked as she descended to the entry hall.

"He had an errand to run," Bortolo said. "Probably something to do with the young man he caught skulking about last evening." The old butler was sitting upright on one of the divans with his eyes closed. Cass wondered if he was answering questions in his sleep.

She chewed on her lower lip. Luca could have told her he was going out, but he had been too concerned with shooing her away to finish dressing. *So that he could sneak away undetected.*

"You ladies look lovely, by the way," the butler added with a wink. He stretched his spindly arms above his head.

"Oh, Bortolo," Agnese said. "If only all men were blind. I would never want for admirers." The old woman smiled. "Shall we go?" She offered Cass her arm.

The day was bright and clear. Mada would be pleased. Siena and Narissa helped Agnese down the crumbling front steps and over to the wooden dock. Giuseppe looked especially dapper in his blue and silver uniform, having added a plume of blue feathers to his hat for the occasion. He had even decorated the gondola's prow with a blue and silver banner. "Thank you, Giuseppe," Agnese said. "I may keep you around for a few years yet."

The gardener smiled toothlessly. Cass knew if her aunt had her way, the old man would die within the walls of the villa. Agnese was fiercely devoted to her staff. It must be troubling for her to await Matteo's decision about whether to sell the old estate. The boy was quite young to hold so many futures in his hand.

Agnese stepped carefully over a rotting plank and let Giuseppe assist her into the boat. The others piled in behind her.

Cass and her aunt settled in beneath the felze, safely protected from the sun. Narissa and Siena sat facing them in the middle of the boat. Tiny waves battered the gondola from all sides. Twice, Cass thought for sure that water would splash over and soak the hem of her dress, but Giuseppe proved to be an exceptionally skilled oarsman, navigating the gondola all the way from Agnese's villa to the Grand Canal without allowing any of the water to make its way into the boat.

When they entered the Grand Canal, Cass opened the slats of the felze, and for once her aunt did not admonish her. As the palazzos floated by, each more beautiful than the last, Cass named some of them under her breath. Palazzo di Guda. Palazzo Nicoletti. Palazzo Domacetti. Palazzo Dubois. She shivered in the warm air when she thought of Siena's sister, Feliciana. What had happened to her? Cass wanted to believe she was all right since her body hadn't floated up in a canal, but what if she were lying in a crypt somewhere?

She wouldn't think about it. It was bad luck to be preoccupied by such thoughts on Mada's wedding day. She tried to focus on the activity around her: open-air boats of various sizes packed the canals, crowded with merchants or fishermen, and private gondolas floated serenely between them. As they approached the Frari, Cass could see a huge gathering of people in the campo outside. They formed a semicircle beneath the three circular stained-glass windows above the Frari's main entrance. Just in front of the doors, a priest in black robes and a black skullcap waited, his golden crucifix gleaming in the sun.

Behind the church, residents of the neighborhood peeked out from back doors and windows. A handful of peasant children sat cross-legged at the edge of the canal, watching. All of Venice loved a good wedding, and it was customary for the bride and groom to exchange their vows outside so they could be seen by as many people as possible before proceeding into the church for a traditional Mass. Cass saw many familiar faces: Signor Dubois, Don and Donna Domacetti, Hortensa Zanotta from tea. Even Maximus the conjurer was there, entertaining a trio of peasant children by pulling coins out of their mouths.

Cass, Agnese, Siena, and Narissa joined the group of people awaiting Mada's arrival. Cass quickly found herself trapped within the crowd. She clutched her journal tightly to her side. The moist air intensified the swirling scent of lavender and rosewater perfume. Cass could practically taste the flowers on her tongue. Agnese blotted her face with a handkerchief and grumbled about the heat.

A cheer went up as a gleaming black gondola decorated with giant green and gold silk ribbons and strings of jasmine and orange blossoms approached the dock. Madalena's father sat in the front of the boat and a pair of servants sat in the back. Mada appeared from beneath the felze as the gondola slowed to a stop. She stood up and waved. The crowd roared with applause. A group of barefoot children wrestled their way closer. The gondoliers moored the boat and then assisted Mada's father onto the dock. Next came the servants, who turned to help Madalena.

Mada stood on the dock for a moment, allowing her lady's maid to straighten her skirts and lift the train of her stunning blue dress from the gondola. Mada's satin skirts seemed to change from blue to turquoise to deep indigo in the bright sunlight. It was the color of the open ocean, Cass decided, even though she had never been beyond the nearby Adriatic Sea. The light bounced off the metallic fibers woven into the dress and made it glimmer, just like the sun reflecting off the water.

Mada's dark hair was done up in several braids, half of them twisted into a flower shape on the top of her head, half of them hanging down over her shoulders and back. Her high jeweled tiara reflected the sunbeams, scattering points of light across the campo.

The semicircle of wedding guests split apart, creating a path to the doors of the Frari. Slowly, Mada began to make her way across the square. Children flung fistfuls of rice at her feet.

Marco's gondola pulled up at the dock and the crowd cheered again. Madalena glanced over her shoulder and blew a kiss to her fiancé. He wore long, royal blue velvet robes. Everything was blue: the color of virtue. His dark hair was combed forward. He assisted his parents and his three younger siblings from the gondola before making his way to Mada and taking her arm.

Cass felt two emotions, sharply, at once. She was filled with joy for Madalena and Marco on their special day, but couldn't help thinking that her own wedding day would not be nearly so blissful. And she would not have her parents there as witnesses. With Luca's father deceased and his mother growing weaker, there might not be any parents present at all.

As Mada and Marco took their places below the largest of the stained-glass windows, just in front of the door to the church, and the crowd surged toward her, Cass started to feel faint. It was hot. Her stays were digging into her ribs.

She tried to focus on Madalena, but her friend's image swam before her eyes. How had she never noticed the striking similarity between her best friend and Mariabella? The dark hair, the high cheekbones. Mada looked so much like Mariabella that Cass could almost imagine the ring of bruising around her neck, the X carved in her skin, the blood blooming from her friend's chest.

Calm down. It's not real. But she couldn't shake the impression. She was parched; she needed something to drink. Cass fought her way back through the crowd, away from the building. She let the wedding-goers swirl around her, separating her from Agnese and the maidservants, separating her from Madalena.

A semicircle of people closed around the couple, seeming to swallow them whole. Once again, the mix of smells—sweat and perfume and orange blossoms—overpowered Cass. She couldn't breathe. Breaking free of the throng of people, she stumbled across the campo toward the canal. Several people looked at her inquisitively, no doubt alarmed to see a woman unescorted, but she didn't care. She needed air.

As Cass stood apart from the crowd, a pair of white- and gold-clad altar boys prepared to open the church doors. That meant that Mada and Marco had finished their vows. Everyone would now proceed inside for the remainder of the ceremony and a traditional Catholic service.

The great wooden doors swung open; the entrance into the Frari looked like a dark, gaping mouth. Cass was seized by a sudden fear: if Madalena went inside the church, she would never come back out. Cass had to warn her. Her heart was pounding. She had to warn Mada before it was too late.

The clear day seemed to turn hazy. The brightly colored clothing of the wedding-goers began to blur together. Madalena was at the threshold of the blackness, the diamonds of her tiara burning like white fire. Fire about to engulf her. Cass tried to yell across the open space, but the wind carried away her warning. Mada flipped a quick glance over her shoulder as she gave herself to the blackness.

"No," Cass whispered. It was no longer Madalena in the blue wedding gown. It was Mariabella. Drops of blood fell from her smile.

Cass's mind started blinking like someone was lighting and extinguishing a candle behind her eyes. She wobbled in her chopines. She reached out, toward the wall of the church. Her fingers closed on air. The candle behind her eyes blew out and everything went dark.

"After death, the body cools,
then stiffens, then grows limber
again as putrefaction begins to
dissolve the tissues until the flesh
becomes foul, black slime."

—THE BOOK OF THE ETERNAL ROSE

twenty~nine

ass's eyelids fluttered open. Sharp stone pressed into her back and shoulders. A white blur moved in front of her face. Cass reached toward the blur and it stopped moving. It was a handkerchief. Siena was fanning her. She knelt beside Cass, her face wrinkled with concern.

"Signorina. Are you all right?" Siena wiped beads of sweat from Cass's forehead.

Cass rubbed her eyes. The air smelled sharp, salty. She sat up slowly. "What happened?"

"I saw you run off as the procession started to move inside. You looked like you'd seen a ghost."

"Where's Aunt Agnese?" she asked. Her thoughts felt thick, as though her mind were muffled in a wet blanket.

"Your aunt got swept up in the rest of the crowd. She's inside with everyone else."

Then it came back to her: Madalena. The church doors. The white fire. "Is everyone okay?" she asked.

Siena nodded. "Everyone's fine," she said. "Are you sure you're all right?"

"I'm fine." Cass struggled to her feet, although in reality, she felt dizzy. "I just need a bit of air." Why had she seen the murdered courtesan in Mada's place? It was as if she'd drunk Tommaso's liquor again. She wondered if the combination of stress and sleep deprivation was causing her to lose her mind.

A seagull cawed as it passed overhead. Siena blotted her own face with her handkerchief. A bit of green embroidery in the corner of it caught Cass's eye. It looked vaguely familiar. Cass reached out and snatched the handkerchief away from Siena, who gave a startled yelp.

Just as Cass suspected, the initials stitched in green were LdP. Luca da Peraga.

"Where did you get this?" Cass asked, struggling to keep her voice level.

Siena paled. "I found it in the portego and kept it. It probably fell out of one of his pockets." She inched backward as if she thought Cass might strike her. "He doesn't even know I have it. He—he doesn't know anything," she finished lamely.

Cass remembered the wax on the parchment she had opened at the dressmaker's shop, how it had appeared to have been resealed. Siena. She read the letter, before Cass did.

Cass didn't know what to say. Was Siena in love with Luca? The thought was almost too absurd to believe, but as Siena's blush darkened to almost a plum color, Cass felt certain that it was true.

Cass knew she should be angry, should demand an explanation immediately. But for some reason, the only thought that came into her head was *How can God be so cruel to grow love in such hopeless places?*

Cass glanced up at the Frari's closed doors. She was surprised

Agnese hadn't sent Narissa to find her. "It's okay, Siena," she said. She closed her eyes, and then opened them again.

Siena's mouth fell open. She shook her head. "I'm sorry—I shouldn't have—"

"Forget it." Cass cut her off. She tucked Luca's handkerchief into the bodice of her dress. "Listen, I need a favor."

"Anything," Siena said fervently, and Cass knew she meant it. Cass couldn't believe she had been so wrong about everyone, about Mada's simplicity, about Siena's loyalty, about Luca's predictability. He still had not returned from his errand; he was going to miss the whole ceremony. He must be meeting with the local town guard, or perhaps the rettori. Would they recognize Paolo from his description? Would they put Falco's roommate in jail?

Cass couldn't—wouldn't—let that happen. Not when he had placed himself in danger to a deliver a message on her account.

She needed to warn Falco.

She sucked in a deep breath. She felt steadier on her feet. "There's something I must do. You'll have to make my excuses to Madalena and my aunt and Luca, in case they come looking for me."

"What should I tell them?" Siena asked, her eyes widening.

"I don't know," Cass said. "Figure it out."

Cass scanned the canal. The water was crowded with boats; a gondolier turned toward her the instant she reached out her hand.

Without a word, Siena curtsied and headed toward the church doors.

The gondolier took his time navigating the traffic in the crowded water. Slow-moving flat-bottomed peàtas, laden with burlap sacks of fruits and vegetables, caused bottlenecks in the narrow canals. Cass tapped the heel of her chopine against the base of the boat repeatedly. She watched enviously as fishermen in small crafts easily made their way around the larger peàtas. The sun glinted off piles of shining fish that they would try to sell again the following day.

Cass poked her head out from behind the felze just long enough to ask the gondolier to hurry. On both sides of the canal, barefoot children ran past her boat, laughing, swatting with sticks at the air. Cass swore under her breath. At this rate, the exhibition would be over before she even got there. She asked the gondolier to pull over.

Cass had the payment ready before the boat even reached the canal edge. She dropped a few coins into the man's palm and then leapt from the gondola. Her dress snagged on a crack in the wood. Cass gave it a sharp tug, leaving behind a scrap of pale yellow silk.

Pulling off her chopines, Cass hurried along the water's edge. She edged past groups of peasants, glassblowers, and street performers juggling oranges. She could feel their stares burning into her back. She must look absolutely ridiculous, gasping for breath, pushing her way through the soggy streets in one of her best gowns. Cass didn't care. Her heavy dress dragged along the ground, and pebbles and sticks poked through the thin bottom of her shoes, causing her to wince, but she didn't stop moving until she made it to Don Loredan's palazzo, where the art exhibit was being held.

She slowed down to catch her breath as she ascended the steps leading up to Palazzo Loredan's piano nobile. As she passed into a spacious portego with a vaulted ceiling, she tried to smooth the wrinkles from her skirts, and quickly swiped at her hair to reorder the stray bits. A boy about her own age handed her a quill and asked her to sign a guest book that sat on a marble pedestal. She hesitated a moment and then scribbled her name on the first blank line.

She scanned the crowded room for Falco but didn't see him. Clusters of paintings adorned the vast walls. Artists lingered nearby their work, dressed in their best church clothes, eager to answer questions for potential patrons. Cass quickly passed by the usual cathedrals and portraits and landscapes. They were beautiful in their own way, but there was an idealism about them that didn't resonate with her. The paintings had a false feeling, as if their artists had painted the world the way it should be instead of the way it really was.

Cass picked out Falco's work easily. He had submitted the nude of Andriana with the title *Broken*. For a minute, Cass was transfixed: forgetting that she was supposed to be looking for Falco, she stood in front of his paintings, trying to absorb every tiny detail.

Falco's second painting, *Unfinished*, was of a male body being prepared for burial. Beneath the wisps of white burial shrouds, the man's muscles were clearly defined, the outline of bones apparent in his hands. His skin was speckled with age spots and bruises, the deep purple blemishes reminding Cass of the circles around Mariabella and Sophia's necks.

On the next wall, a painting of a young bride wearing a jeweled tiara made Cass think of Madalena in her gorgeous blue dress. Why had Cass seen the diamonds as fire, as a bad omen? She hoped Madalena wouldn't notice her absence among the large crowd of guests. She had promised to be there for her friend. Once she warned Falco that Luca was on the warpath, she would go immediately to the wedding feast at Palazzo Rambaldo.

Cass paused, frustrated, and looked again for Falco. But the whole room was crawling with artists in black pants and leather vests. Her feet throbbed. In fact, her body ached from head to toe. She felt as though she had aged a hundred years in the past two weeks. For a moment, she wished she could just go back to the way things were—her quiet life on San Domenico.

But she couldn't go back.

Cass pushed past a group of chattering women and stifled a gasp. She was staring straight at Mariabella.

The painting from the young courtesan's room hung on the wall of Signor Loredan's portego. Cass blinked hard, expecting the canvas to morph and change as she inched forward. No, it was the exact same canvas, there was no doubt. Who besides Mariabella's roommate would have had access to her home after she died? Cass supposed that if she and Falco could break in, so could anyone else.

She whirled around, her eyes grazing each of the nearby patrons, looking for a killer. But no one was paying her any attention. She might as well have been invisible.

Cass turned back to the picture. In the light, she noticed fine details she hadn't seen the night she and Falco discovered it: the heart-shaped birthmark on Mariabella's temple, a slight unevenness to the girl's crimson smile.

There were two other paintings hanging beside it, both obviously by the same artist. One of the subjects was dressed in an elegant gown; the other wore a plain black and gold servant's uniform. Like Mariabella, both women were painted in a reclined position, their hands reaching out toward the artist as if to offer themselves to him. Thick hair hung back from their shoulders, exposing their swanlike necks. Was one of these women Sophia? Cass stared at the canvas of the girl in the servant's uniform. She definitely resembled the girl who had floated up in the canal, but was she the missing maid? Cass chewed on her bottom lip. The girl wore black and gold—the livery colors of Palazzo Dubois. Still, Cass had never met Sophia. She couldn't be sure.

Unless . . .

Cass bent close to the small placard that described the artwork. The series was called *The Fallen Ones*. As Cass read the titles, she had to reach out for the wall beneath the canvases to steady herself. Two of the paintings were named simply *M* and *S*. Mariabella. Sophia.

It had to be. Cass felt a momentary flicker of relief that Feliciana's svelte form wasn't represented here.

Two men had shouldered up next to Cass, and were examining *The Fallen Ones* with her. "Do you suppose they're all sisters?" The taller of the two men stroked his brown beard while waiting for his companion to reply.

"Probably just women he's bedding," the shorter man said with a laugh.

The third painting was named *R*. Who was she? An earlier victim? Or an innocent girl who didn't even know she was marked to die? Cass cleared her throat. "*Scusi*," she said, wondering if the two men could hear her heart thrumming in her chest. "Do you know who painted these?"

The taller man bent close to the canvas. "All I can make out is a squiggle. Looks like an L."

"Whatever it is, it's slanting unusually far to the left," the man next to him said. "Maybe the painter is left-handed?"

Cass wondered how many left-handed artists there were in

Venice. Hundreds, at least. Her skin tingled at the idea that the murderer had stood in this very spot earlier in the day. Falco might even have seen him as he arranged his exhibit.

Someone tapped Cass on the shoulder. Her heart leapt into her throat. She spun around, both exhilarated and terrified at the thought of seeing Falco again. But it wasn't Falco who stood behind her.

It was Luca.

"The human body is a book of secrets,
covered in skin and written in blood.
Those who wish to learn its
mysteries must be unafraid to open
it and study its entrails."

—THE BOOK OF THE ETERNAL ROSE

For a second, Cass couldn't speak. Luca was the last person she expected to see. He always spoke of art as if it were a pointless endeavor. Had he followed her there from the Frari? Did he know about Falco? "What—what are you doing here?" she stammered finally.

"I might ask you the same question," Luca said. His eyes flicked beyond her, to the trio of *The Fallen Ones*, and for a moment his expression was shot through with . . . what? Pain? Guilt?

"I wasn't feeling well," Cass said, lifting her chin defiantly. If Luca was going to keep secrets, so would she. "I had to get away from Mada's wedding for a bit."

"Interesting choice of safe haven," Luca replied, keeping his gaze locked on the canvases.

"Do you know the artist?" Cass asked, skipping past all the questions she had already asked herself.

"Do *you* know the artist?" Luca countered. He leaned in close to the nearest canvas—the one called *R*. His whole face contorted for a moment. Cass had the strangest thought that he was going to cry.

She shook her head. She could feel her hair starting to pull loose beneath the white lace in which Siena had wrapped it. Cass could tell he was waiting for her to say more, to explain what she was doing at an art exhibition on the most important day of her best friend's life. Cass looked around once more for Falco; this time she was relieved when she didn't see him. She didn't want him to see her with Luca. The last thing she wanted was to cause him any more pain.

"We should go," Luca said, arranging his face back into a neutral expression. "We have obligations. The wedding party must be heading toward Palazzo Rambaldo by now. If we hurry, we might catch the end of it."

So Luca wasn't going to offer any explanation either. Maybe they deserved each other. He *must* have followed her to the art exhibition. But he couldn't know about Falco—could he? Surely he would have confronted her.

Cass stood frozen in the exhibit hall for a moment, paralyzed with indecision. She wanted to escape from Luca, to search the exhibit and Palazzo Loredan, not just for Falco, but also for clues to the murderer. After all, he had to be here, somewhere. Or if not, surely there was someone who knew the identity of the artist who had painted *The Fallen Ones.* Someone had seen him as he arranged his display. Who knew if their paths would intersect again? If she left now, the killer would slip right through her fingers.

And so would Falco. Cass was still desperate to warn him about the guard coming for Paolo. She was desperate to *see* him. Just one last time, she promised herself. *One last time and then I'll let him go.*

But Luca wasn't budging. And she could hardly tell him about Falco or seeking out the killer. She remembered his outburst at dinner. She would only prove him right about the women of Venice, and herself, if she confessed her recent actions. Cass struggled to think of any plausible reason why she shouldn't follow her fiancé to Madalena's wedding. There was nothing.

After one last glance at the trio of paintings, Cass reluctantly allowed Luca to pull her through the exhibition hall. Was the killer there, hiding in plain sight? Was he masquerading behind handshakes and polite smiles while plotting his next murder? And what about Falco? Was he tucked back in a corner somewhere, watching her from a distance? Cass felt hollow, like a tunnel had been opened at the bottom of her stomach.

Luca pulled Cass through the door of the exhibition hall, and she blinked hard as her eyes adjusted to the sunlight. The wedding procession had opted to parade through the city streets rather than go to Mada's palazzo via gondolas. She could pick out the wedding guests among the normal traffic on the streets by their silken gowns and jubilant expressions. Some of the younger girls were holding hands and laughing as they skipped along the stone streets. The air was still thick with the scent of perfume, and jasmine petals littered the ground. Cass and Luca fell in behind the last few guests as they passed by.

Cass wondered what Siena had told Agnese. Her aunt was sharp and had no doubt seen through whatever tale the maid had concocted. She hoped that the day's festivities would put Agnese in a forgiving mood. If not, Cass might find herself married off to Luca before sunrise.

Luca took Cass's arm as they headed toward Palazzo Rambaldo. She struggled to keep up with him. Her ankles wobbled in her chopines, and she adjusted her stride so that she was taking two small steps for each one of his.

"You missed a lovely ceremony," she said, even though Cass had missed the ceremony herself. Luca's intensity was starting to scare her. Cass tried to keep her voice light. "Madalena's dress is the most amazing blue."

"I'm sorry I didn't make it," Luca said shortly. Then he lapsed back into silence. Cass wondered what he was thinking about. Was his mysterious errand related to his visit to the art exhibition or had he just followed her there? Why had he looked at *The Fallen Ones* with such dismay? Cass wondered if there was any chance Falco would know who had painted the pictures. Maybe he had seen the artist when he dropped off the canvases.

Just thinking of Falco made a sharp pain knife through her chest.

She pushed the pain away. "You hate art, Luca. Why were you at the exhibition? Did you follow me there?" Cass planted her feet on the stone street. She was tired of being led around by men. She would stand there until she got some answers.

Luca turned to look at her. For a long moment he said nothing, his face a strange mix of hard and soft. "Come with me," he said, yanking her forcefully from her position. Cass sensed he was finally going to explain things, to share some of his secrets with her. The two ducked into a nearby alley. The back door to a small house stood open. A peasant girl was emptying chamber pots into the street.

"What is it?" Cass asked breathlessly, trying her best to ignore the fetid stench. The last few wedding guests blurred by them. Behind them, a trio of children in ragged clothing dodged their way through the crowd, pretending to be part of the wedding procession.

Luca licked his lips but didn't speak. Cass suddenly felt uneasy. Her fiancé's grasp was strong. He had pressed her up against the rough stone wall of a neighboring palazzo. Cass tried to pull her hand away. "What?" she repeated, her voice rising slightly in pitch.

The peasant girl disappeared inside the house, slamming the door shut behind her. Luca reached toward Cass's face and she flinched. But he didn't seem to notice. He was in his own world, in the grip of emotions Cass didn't understand. Pain and fear and regret—all of it swirled behind his eyes.

His warm fingers brushed the side of her face. Cass felt hot all over.

"If anything happened to you, I'd never forgive myself," he said, tracing his hand from her cheekbone to her chin.

"Luca," she croaked out, trying to swim up through the haziness of her own confused feelings. "What—"

"Just please stay in the crowd," Luca said. He bent close to her, and for a second Cass thought he was going to kiss her. Instead, he pulled a curling tendril of hair from the corner of her mouth. "Stay with your aunt. Don't go anywhere alone."

"But I don't—"

"Just promise me."

His urgency frightened Cass. She didn't know what he was talking about; had he seen something at the exhibition? "I promise," she said.

"Thank you." Luca brushed his lips across her forehead. Then he took her hand and the two of them headed back to the main street. Cass sucked in a deep breath, and felt the tight whalebone ribbing of her stays press into her skin.

The main doors to Palazzo Rambaldo stood open. A pair of men wearing the distinctive Rambaldo green and gold livery stood guard, making sure that only invited guests were granted access to the inner party and feast.

Servants wandered the piano nobile with trays of wine and tartine. Guests milled around the spacious portego, eating and drinking and laughing. Luca towed Cass through the vast room until he found Agnese, Narissa, and Siena all lingering near a large window.

"I have to talk to a few people," he said abruptly. "Please remember what I said." He vanished into the crowd. Still shaken by Luca's urgent command to her—*don't go anywhere alone*—Cass huddled close to her lady's maid.

Siena pressed her hand to Cass's back just for a second. "I'm glad you're all right," the blonde girl whispered.

Agnese sat on a plush divan, her back to the festivities, looking out over the Grand Canal. Narissa hovered protectively behind her. As Cass stared at her aunt, she wondered if Agnese ever missed her own childhood home.

Cass sank down next to her aunt and the old woman turned blazing eyes on her. Agnese's face was as deeply wrinkled as the purple silk of her dress. "Where have you been?" she demanded.

Cass knew that she had been foolish to hope her aunt would be in a forgiving mood. Agnese hated crowds; she hated being jostled by strangers. "Didn't Siena tell you?" Cass asked breezily, while shooting a meaningful look at Siena. She had no idea what story the girl had told her aunt.

"I told her how you came here to the palazzo early to make sure everything was ready," Siena answered smoothly, with just the slightest flicker in her eyes. "How you wanted everything to be perfect for Signorina Rambaldo."

"Right," Cass said. Guilt pricked at her insides. That was exactly what she *should* have done, but Mada's wedding celebration was the furthest thing from her mind. She had solved the mystery of Liviana's disappearing body, but a killer was still lurking in Venice.

Agnese pursed her lips together but didn't respond. Cass knew her aunt wasn't fooled; then again, she had no proof of Cass's wrongdoing.

Joseph Dubois sauntered into the room with a young girl on his arm—a courtesan, judging by the looks of her. The man brushed a handful of blonde ringlets out of the way to whisper in the girl's ear, and she winked in response. Cass's blood turned to ice. Was this pretty fair-haired girl going to wind up strangled and mutilated, her bloodless body dumped somewhere for an innocent passerby to discover?

Dubois's gaze seared straight through the crowd of wedding guests until it found Cass, as if she'd spoken her thoughts aloud. Cass flinched and looked away.

"Let's go find our spots at the table," Cass said with fake cheerfulness, eager to put distance between herself and the Frenchman. "The servants tell me the feast looks stunning."

Narissa helped Agnese to her feet and the four women headed across the portego. Servants were just beginning to bring out the food: platters of braised peacock and roasted badger stuffed with pears, plates of soft bread, bowls of every type of fruit and cheese imaginable. Cass wondered where Cristian's magical cheese from France had ended up.

Cass and Agnese found their names on pieces of vellum in front of chairs at the far end of the largest table in the portego. Narissa and Siena helped them get settled and then left for the kitchen to go eat with the rest of the servants. At the head of the table, Madalena's father's business associates were admiring the boiled head of veal and making toasts about how they never thought this day would come.

Cass tried to join in the merriment, but she kept thinking back to Luca's words. *Stay with your aunt.* Why was he so worried something might happen to her? Did Luca suspect the murderer was among the guests? And where had he gone? Cass shivered. She scanned the crowded banquet hall, looking for anyone who seemed out of place.

Surprisingly, she didn't see Madalena. Cass frowned. She felt a flicker of anxiety. It wasn't like her friend to miss even five minutes of a party in her honor. Cass thought back to her vision of the white fire outside the church: Mada as Mariabella. Blood dripping from her smile . . .

Cass fiddled nervously with the small piece of vellum bearing her name. She flipped it over and over between her fingers, so quickly she almost didn't notice that someone had scrawled a message on the back. Almost.

With trembling fingers, Cass read the five words someone had written in shaky handwriting on the back of her nameplate. *Do you like surprises, bella?* Cass caught the edge of her wineglass with her elbow. Crimson liquid splattered onto the table and made its way to the edge of the table. Blood dripping, Cass thought as the dark droplets rained onto the stone floor.

"Cassandra! Look at the mess you've made," Agnese scolded.

"Excuse me," Cass mumbled. She pushed away from the table as one of Madalena's servants hurried over to mop up the spilled wine. She hadn't taken even a sip of wine, and still she felt dizzy and disoriented. The sounds of the feast—noise and conversation—

rebounded through the cavernous rooms, filling her head with echoes.

Where was Mada? Where was Luca?

Cass pushed her way out of the portego and turned down a hallway, taking immediate comfort in the cool and quiet. At the end of the hall was a small salon, pale pink, with four cushioned chairs positioned around a small marble table. Cass shut the door behind her. She needed to be alone for a few minutes. She was starting to feel the way she had at the church. The last thing she needed to do was faint again.

One of the servants had decided to use the little room to store wedding gifts, and as Cass leaned against the door, exhaling, she marveled at the mountain of wrapped cartons and boxes. Madalena was fine. She wasn't Mariabella. She was probably off in some dark corner kissing Marco. Those two had never been able to keep their hands off each other. Now that they were officially husband and wife, they had probably decided to kick off their wedding night early. Cass hadn't seen Marco among the revelers either. Of course they were together.

Feeling instantly better, she wandered over to the table and skimmed her fingers over the great jeweled boxes and packages wrapped in brightly colored cloth, trying to guess what they contained. A carved wooden frame peeked out from beneath a giant cylindrical hatbox. A painting. Cass moved the box to see it.

She sucked in a sharp breath. It was a painting of Madalena done in the same small blurry brushstrokes as *The Fallen Ones*. Mada's hair was properly braided and she wasn't reclining like the other girls, but her hand was reaching out toward the artist just as theirs had, as if she were inviting the artist to come closer.

As if she were offering herself up to him.

The whole world seemed to stop as Cass leaned toward the picture. *Please no. Please no. No. Nonononono.*

Yes.

There was that same, wavering initial at the bottom of the frame.

The killer was here.

"The healer and the killer
both rely on the blade:
the physician his scalpel,
the assassin his dagger."

—THE BOOK OF THE ETERNAL ROSE

ass couldn't breathe. The killer was at the wedding, and he was after her best friend. He must be. Cass had to find her, to warn her. She turned to flee the sitting room and nearly bumped into a tall fair-haired man as he ducked through the doorway.

The man wore a black slashed doublet embroidered with silver, and gray velvet trunk hose and breeches. He stopped short when he saw Cass, surprised. "My apologies," he said. "I didn't expect to see anyone in here."

It was Mada's friend Cristian. Cass didn't return his greeting. With a shaking hand, she pointed at the portrait of Madalena. "Do you know who painted this picture?" Her voice was hardly a whisper.

Cristian raised his eyebrows. "Are you not Cassandra Caravello?"

Cass could barely nod. "We've met before. Madalena introduced us."

He inclined his head with a slight smile. "Then do you not recognize the work of your own fiancé?"

"What?" Cass was positive she had heard him wrong.

Cristian traced the carved frame with his left hand. "The painting was a gift from the family of Luca da Peraga."

"No, that's not possible," Cass said. The room had begun to spin. "Luca detests art. He's always considered it a waste of time."

Cristian shrugged one shoulder. "Perhaps your fiancé has secrets that he has not yet revealed?"

"No," Cass repeated instinctively. But slowly the pieces began to fall into place: Luca's erratic behavior, all the mysterious errands, his absence from the wedding this morning. He could have been at Palazzo Loredan dropping off the canvases. Cass knew it was crazy, ludicrous, but still her brain couldn't let go of the idea. Why else would he have been there, at the exhibit? And what was his look of crushing dismay about? Did he suspect Cass might be catching on?

Luca had returned to Venice right about the time of the murders without telling Cass. Since his return, his emotions had raged back and forth between threatening and protective. Was he capable of murder? Cass wasn't sure what anyone was capable of anymore.

But why would Luca want to hurt Madalena?

Cass realized Cristian was staring at her with a look of amusement. "Is it really that shocking to think that your fiancé might have secrets?" Cristian asked. "It's common for men to keep their pastimes private."

Cass was practically shaking. She could only say, "Do you know where Madalena is?"

"I would imagine she's in the portego enjoying the feast," Cristian said. "As you should be." He tilted his head slightly to the left as he stared at her. His brown eyes seared into her skin. "What *are* you doing back here all alone, Cassandra?"

A chill shot through Cass. Something about the way he said her name was so familiar. She was struck by the urge to run, to grab Agnese and Siena and get as far away from the wedding as possible. But she couldn't. She had to find Madalena. Mada seemed to trust Cristian. Maybe he could help. "I think Mada may be in danger," she said.

Cristian's expression changed from one of amusement to one of worry. "Danger?" he repeated. "What possible danger could come to her here?"

Cass was half tempted to tell Cristian everything—about the slashed corpses and the paintings—but she knew there was no time. "She's not in the portego," she said. "I haven't seen her for almost an hour. I have a bad feeling."

Cristian tucked both of his hands deep into the pockets of his black tunic and frowned. "She did tell me she had to meet with some-one between the ceremony and the feast, but I thought surely she'd be back by now. You don't think . . ." His voice trailed off.

Fear gripped Cass. "I don't know," she said, remembering how Luca had vanished as soon as he deposited her into Agnese's care. "Do you know where she went?"

"I have an idea. Come on." Cristian strode out of the sitting room with Cass right at his heels. He pushed through the portego, weaving past small groups of wedding guests who were sipping wine and ad-miring the oil paintings that decorated each wall. He headed down a set of marble stairs to the first floor of the palazzo.

The air was cooler here and smelled musty. Torches were mounted along the main hallway, a few of them lit so that the servants could navigate the dark corridors and fetch supplies for the festivi-ties. The yellow flames cast strange dancing shadows onto the dusty walls. This floor was quiet. Too quiet. Cass couldn't even hear the revelers above her head. If something had happened to Madalena down here, no one would have heard her scream. Cass murmured a prayer under her breath. *Please let Mada be all right.*

Cristian headed around a corner and opened a thick wooden door with a small square pane of glass at eye level. Cass followed him into a dingy storage room. There were no torches lit here. She was almost completely blind as she stumbled through the doorway. She could feel things, though. Water had seeped up through cracks in the stone floor. Dank liquid, black as ink, lapped at her ankles. In that moment, Cass had the silliest, stupidest thought: another dress ruined.

"What is this—?" Cass asked.

"This is where she said she was going," Cristian said, he cuts her off. "She told me she had to meet someone in the wine room. She asked me to make excuses for her, in fact."

Cristian took Cass's hand and led her farther into the darkness. He moved as if he were intimately familiar with his surroundings. Cass remembered that he had supplied a special kind of wine for the wedding feast. He had probably stored it here.

A spiderweb slapped against her cheek and she fought the urge to cry out. The whole place was likely full of cracks and crevasses, where spiders and God knew what else lurked.

Cass's eyes began to adjust to the dim light. Large wooden casks of wine sat on raised pedestals. Crystal pitchers sat next to some of the casks. Cold water dripped from the ceiling above her head. Cass couldn't imagine Madalena ever coming down here by choice. Just the moldy smell of wet stone would have been enough to keep her away.

"Mada?" Cass called out. Her voice echoed through the open space. No answer.

Cristian reached out to touch one of the wooden barrels with his right hand. His fingers twitched as he examined the label.

A low marble table stood against the far wall. Cristian used flint and steel to light a dusty lantern. Strange shadows came to life on the brick walls of the room. The flickering flame illuminated one side of Cristian's face, making it look as if he were wearing a mask.

Cass's heart started pounding. She was positive every step she took was one step closer to something evil.

Cristian gripped her hand again. *"Faites attention,"* he said. "I don't want you to fall."

Cass froze. *Faites attention?* She had forgotten that Cristian was French . . . She was sure she had heard the words before, recently . . .

Cass hoped Cristian hadn't felt her body tense up. She tried to calmly wriggle free of his grasp, but he wouldn't release her. "You're hurting me," she said. "I think we should return to the party and call for others to help."

Cristian pulled Cass deeper into the dark room. "Come on, Cassandra," he said. "It's your turn."

Cass's blood turned to ice. She suddenly realized why the way he said her name seemed so familiar.

Cristian was the man in the falcon mask.

The room started to blur and break apart. "Let go of me." Cass tried to wrench away from him, but he gripped her tighter. She screamed, but the stone swallowed up her voice.

"Do not bother calling for help," Cristian said, allowing his French accent to color his words. "No one can hear you." He gave her arm a vicious twist as he pushed her to the ground.

Cass landed on the wet floor, her ankle folded awkwardly

underneath her. Pain shot through her body and she blinked back tears. He was right. The walls were more than a foot thick. And with the music and festivities in full swing upstairs, the main floor of the palazzo might as well be out on San Domenico Island. She was trapped. Alone.

Cristian advanced on her. "Did you not get my message? I told you that your turn would come." His right hand twitched. He shook it vigorously, clenching and unclenching his fist as he knelt beside Cass.

Images, memories were swirling, colliding in her head: she thought of the crooked letters on the anonymous notes, the sloping signature on the paintings at the exhibition, how the men had commented that the artist might be left-handed. Cristian had probably learned to use his left hand after he hurt his right hand in the war. Cass remembered the man in the falcon mask from Dubois's ball, the way his hand had spasmed and twitched against her.

She remembered, too, what terrible things he had said about the war, and how beautiful it was.

She inched backward on her hands and feet, but Cristian had her backed up against a wall and there was nowhere to go. Cristian produced a dagger from his doublet pocket. Cass's heart seized up. The blade glowed like lightning. She couldn't breathe. She couldn't move. Couldn't focus on anything but that silvery sharp edge . . .

Cristian knelt beside her, methodically tucking his tunic into his breeches to protect it from the mire. He cradled her chin in one hand. Cass could feel each individual finger as he caressed her skin almost lovingly. She squeezed her eyes shut for a second. When she opened them, her vision crystallized. Cass saw each individual thread that made up Cristian's lace cuff. His knuckle creases sharpened into curved knives. There was a pale circle around one of his index fingers, an almost-imperceptible difference in color where he had once worn a ring.

A ring with a flower inscribed in a circle, no doubt.

Tears threatened at the back of her eyes, but Cass forced them down. If she was going to die, she would do it fighting.

She fumbled in the muddy water, her fingers flailing for a loose stone, a piece of glass, for anything she could use as a weapon. Finding nothing sharp or heavy in the sludge that covered the floor, she flung a handful of the dirty liquid at his eyes. Scrambling to her feet, she tried to lunge past him. Cristian grabbed hold of the beaded rosary that hung from her belt and pulled her back like she was weightless, a rag doll. A plaything.

"*Salope*," he cursed at her in French. "You bitch." Pinning her against the wall with one hand, he quickly swiped at his eyes with the other. Then he pressed the tip of the blade loosely to her neck. "It looks like I'll have another model for my paintings," he said. "I wonder what your dear old aunt will think when it arrives at her villa."

"Why?" Fear enveloped Cass like a fog. The cold steel bit against her neck. "Why me?"

Cristian sneered. "Why you?" His voice rose in pitch. "You believed yourself so smart . . . and yet you still don't understand even the simplest things . . ." He tucked a strand of hair back behind Cass's left ear, letting his fingertips linger on her jawbone. "He has gotten everything and I have gotten nothing. It has been that way our whole life. He has taken all that should be mine. It's only fair, isn't it, that I should take some things back?"

Cass tried to press herself farther into the wall. She wished that it would absorb her; she wished she could dissolve into its protection. "What—what are you talking about?" she stammered.

Something flickered behind Cristian's dark eyes. "I see," he said. "Luca never told you about me, did he?" Cristian relaxed his hand, pulling the knife a few inches back from Cass's throat. "My half brother always was ashamed of me, the same way my father was ashamed of my whore of a mother. Not that I could blame him for that."

Cass's mind was spinning. Cristian was Luca's half brother? Had Luca heard about the murders and suspected Cristian was responsible? Was that why he had returned to Venice early?

"Why Mariabella?" Cass asked, trying to quell the fear that was threatening to suffocate her, drag her down. "Why Sophia?"

"Sophia was just a gift," Cristian said, shrugging. "She had started to present Joseph with certain . . . difficulties. That's what happens when you can't keep your skirts down until marriage."

Difficulties. Cass remembered it had been rumored that the maid was pregnant when she disappeared. Cass fought a surge of nausea.

Then Cristian's face changed. His eyes burned; his face contorted with pain. "But Mariabella was different. She claimed to love me, but one man wasn't enough for her. I went mad watching her parade around on Joseph's arm." His voice cracked and wavered, dropping in pitch. "I had to do it. It was the only way. Joseph found out, of course. He finds out everything. He was furious, but it was the only way." Cristian was practically whispering now, as if he were talking to himself instead of Cass. "The only way she could be all mine."

Cass had been so naïve. Falco had been right. Venice was full of more darkness than she had ever imagined. Had Joseph Dubois allowed Cristian to kill both his maid and courtesan? Had he offered protection for Cristian? She realized she was shaking. Cristian was gripping the dagger so tightly that his knuckles had blanched white. The blade hovered just inches from her throat.

"Why did you cut them?" Cass asked, looking up and away from the dagger. "If you loved Mariabella—"

Cristian breathed in deeply, seeming to regain his composure. "Because they were filthy, like my mother, and needed to be marked as such."

"And Madalena?" Cass prompted, her mind cycling frantically, clutching for escape routes, tactics, miracles. "How could you want to harm someone who has been so kind to you?"

Cristian raised an eyebrow. "I have not done anything to Madalena."

"But the painting," Cass protested. "It looked just like *The Fallen Ones*..."

"Ah." Cristian smiled, and somehow it made him look more gruesome. "You have a fine eye for detail. A wedding gift, no more and no less. Partial repayment for the Rambaldo generosity."

Cass felt a flicker of relief. At least Mada was okay. She took in her surroundings. The room was long and dark; the door on the opposite side seemed impossibly far away. She didn't think there was any way she could outmaneuver him. Even if she could somehow get past him, he'd tackle her before she made it halfway to the door. A servant would come down for more wine eventually. Or someone would notice she was missing.

Wouldn't they?

No. She had spent her whole life depending on others. Maybe now was the time for her to start depending on herself.

"Why did you put Mariabella's body in the contessa's crypt?"

Cass forced herself to stare directly at Cristian. He seemed startled by her sudden willingness to meet his gaze, and he withdrew the blade a half inch back from her skin. Cass worked her feet back behind her, trying to regain her footing beneath her heavy skirts so that she could run if the opportunity presented itself. Every tiny movement caused more of the murky water to splash up on her stockings. They were saturated up to her knees now, her skin going clammy beneath the heavy fabric of her dress.

A flash of uncertainty darkened Cristian's features. "I don't know anything about any contessa," he said.

Of course he didn't know about Livi. Cristian had come across the tomb after Falco and his friends had stolen Liviana's body. Cass couldn't believe how narrowly she, Cristian, and the artists had missed each other. If any of them had been just a few minutes earlier or later, they might have all crossed paths in the tiny graveyard that adjoined Agnese's estate.

"Mariabella and I used to meet out on San Domenico quite often," Cristian continued. "Joseph would not have understood our love." His eyes turned to slits. "How do *you* know so much? I hid my Mariabella away so well, I thought no one would ever find her. Except for me. Now I can be with her anytime I want."

Cass wondered if the mysterious lanterns she had seen roaming the graveyard belonged to Cristian. How often did he visit the dead Mariabella? Cass was just about to ask when a more important question came to mind.

"Feliciana," she blurted out. "Did you kill her as well?"

Cristian grinned meanly. He advanced toward Cass until the blade was touching her throat again. Their lips were just inches apart. "Jealous, *bella*?" he asked. "You give me far too much credit. I have not touched Joseph's new little pet, though I have no doubt she needs to be marked like the others." He made an X shape across her bodice with one of his fingers. "Like you."

The dagger was ice against Cass's throat. One wrong move and the tip might pierce her skin and pass all the way through her neck. "You won't get away with this," she gasped, trying to keep the tremor from her voice. "Whatever you think you can do to me. Luca will find you, and hunt you down. He'll know that it was you."

"Oh, I think not," Cristian said, a smile playing at his lips. He clumsily pulled a folded parchment from his tunic pocket with his trembling right hand. He frowned as he held the shaking paper up to his face. *"I was wrong about who you are,"* he recited. *"I cannot possibly love a man such as you, nor can I see you again. It is not fair to either of us. Please do not try to see me or communicate with me in any way."*

Cristian tucked the parchment back into his pocket. "My poor brother. You've seemed so distracted ever since he returned to Venice. It shouldn't be too hard to convince him that you've run off with another man," he said, his tone smug with satisfaction.

"Where did you get that?" Cass demanded. It was the letter she had started to Falco. Cass had tucked it away in her journal just a day ago.

"You really shouldn't leave your personal journal just lying around," Cristian said. "I found it by the entrance to the Frari." He pressed the tip of the blade into her skin. "Illuminating reading. You're lucky it wasn't my brother who found it first."

She must have dropped the journal when she fled from the crowd of wedding guests, just before she fainted by the water's edge. Cass felt the room break apart into darkness . . . Any second now, he would plunge the blade into her neck . . .

"My poor brother," Cristian repeated. "How he bragged about you when our father arranged your engagement. Such betrayal. It will destroy him. You really are a fallen woman, just like the rest, aren't you?"

His body tensed up. The dagger's tip broke through Cass's skin.

A rivulet of blood began to trickle down her neck. The pain was slight, like a pinch or a bee sting, but Cass gasped, half expecting her breath to bubble out through the tiny cut.

"I didn't betray him," Cass squeezed out. She pressed herself back against the stone wall, trying hard not to swallow, not to breathe too hard. She felt a surge of nausea.

"Didn't you?" Cristian withdrew his dagger momentarily and Cass couldn't stop herself from collapsing to the ground. Her legs simply wouldn't hold her. "I seem to recall a second letter tucked inside your journal," he continued. "A rather intimate confessional."

Cass knew it was insane to lament the loss of Falco's note while a madman was brandishing a dagger in front of her. Still, her heart bled a little at the thought of losing the last piece of him she'd ever have.

"Get up," Cristian demanded, yanking her arm.

"I can't," Cass lied. "My ankle. I hurt it when I fell." She bit her lip. The dull pain served to focus her, calm her nerves.

"You have stalled long enough," Cristian said, his silky voice turning rough. "I will have what I rightfully deserve." Grabbing her by her hair, he dragged her across the dank room to the marble table in the corner.

The lace wrapped around her bun came loose and fluttered to the wet floor. She stared at it as it sank below the surface of the mire, as her hair tumbled down around her shoulders in thick waves. Sinking. Dying. Cristian pressed her up against the edge of the table. Marble pressed into her back. He traced the dagger along her neck and collarbone. Silver. Dazzling. Deadly. Cristian's other hand reached up to stroke the soft curls that framed her face.

"So beautiful," he said, burying his face in her auburn mane. He inhaled deeply. "So fragrant. I wish we had more time."

"Luca!" Cass screamed. But her voice was raw, her throat hoarse from terror.

"He'll never hear you," Cristian said, forcing her down, pinning her against the cold marble with his body.

Falco. Cass called out again, this time in her head.

Cristian pulled her hair hard, tilting her chin forward to expose her neck. Cass struggled underneath him. His mouth landed hard on top of hers, his teeth biting into her lower lip.

Blood flowed across her tongue. Cass struck out with her knees and elbows. Her heart battered itself against her rib cage. She screamed, even though she knew no one could hear her. It was no longer the knife she was afraid of.

"You will stop." Cristian pressed a hand hard over her mouth.

Cass clawed at Cristian's face. His dark eyes glowed in the muted light.

She screamed again. She tried to push the dagger away from her neck, but her hands and arms felt heavy. Everything felt heavy. Her legs. Her head. A numbness moved through her. "No," she begged.

Cristian reached around her back with his left hand and fumbled with the top button of her dress. His fingers were too unsteady to pull the button through its loop. He yanked at the fabric, and Cass felt the stiff brocade start to come apart. She wasn't sure if she was even breathing—it felt like her brain was slowing down. It was blocking all but a few sensations. The marble tabletop, which felt like ice against her shoulder blades. The pearl buttons that made little splashing noises as they landed on the wet floor.

Cristian's body crushed down on her chest. "Whore," he repeated. "I only wish my brother could be here to see this." His right hand spasmed and shook as it explored the curves of her body. Cass shuddered with revulsion. She tasted blood again. *Not real. Please let this be a nightmare. Please, please wake up.*

Cristian's knife once again traced its way down the tendons of her neck, threatening to slice through her bodice, her skin, her bones.

"It's your turn, Cassandra," he said, with a fiendish gleam in his eyes. "It's our turn." He let the dagger fall to the table as his mouth found hers, this time gently, then harder. His hands wrapped around her throat. "Good night, bella . . ."

Not like this. I don't want to die like this. Not here. Not now. Cass twisted her head to the side, gasping for air, finding none.

The room started to disappear, the shadows dissolving into mist, the light fading. Cristian looked down at her almost tenderly. For a brief instant, he looked like Luca. Cass hated herself for the thought. Tears welled up in her eyes. Suddenly, inexplicably, Aunt Agnese's face appeared in her mind. What would the old woman think of Cass's death? Would she know how hard Cass had fought?

Cass refused to disappoint her aunt. With a scream, she lunged forward, ramming her forehead into Cristian's face. Luca's half brother recoiled in surprise, but he didn't relinquish his hold on her. Hot liquid spurted from his nose. The smell of blood, coppery and salty, stained the air. He grabbed the dagger. "I'll kill you!" His left arm reared back. The blade headed for her heart. Cass was pinned to the table. She could do nothing but await the impact.

It wasn't the white-hot pain she imagined. The blow felt blunt, more like being punched than stabbed. Cass looked down at her chest. The tip of the dagger had embedded itself in the whalebone ribbing of her stays. She made a sharp sound, almost a laugh, as the dagger fell to its side, the blade bent and useless.

Footsteps sloshed across the wet floor.

Luca? It couldn't be.

But it was.

Her fiancé grabbed Cristian by the shoulders.

"Get off of her!" Luca was shouting as he wrenched Cristian away from Cass. The men went spinning across the dark chamber, arms and legs flailing. Cristian's body slammed into one of the marble pedestals. Luca grabbed him by the throat, forcing him to his knees.

Cass sat up painfully, still dizzy. "Luca," she tried to say, but no noise came out. She gagged. Her throat was burning.

Cristian broke free of Luca's grasp. His face twisted into a look of pure hatred. "Brother," he said, leaping back to his feet. "I was just starting to enjoy myself. We always did have the same taste, didn't we?"

Cristian advanced on Luca, his fists twisting and slashing. Luca lunged at Cristian, throwing his half brother against the brick wall.

Cristian's head snapped forward. He swore, kicking at Luca with the heel of his boot. Luca doubled over in pain, grunting. Cristian tackled him. The two men rolled across the wet floor, slamming hard into the opposite wall. Crystal pitchers fell from pedestals. One of the big casks of wine wobbled dangerously. Cristian managed to pin

Luca to the wet ground. He raised his hand high in the air, a jagged shard of glass pointed down at Luca's throat.

"Cass. Run," Luca said hoarsely.

In an instant, Cass had scrambled from the table.

She grabbed the lantern and flung it at Cristian. It bounced off his back, the flame igniting the hem of his doublet. Luca scrambled to his feet as Cristian beat at the fabric, hopping up and down and cursing loudly. The flames extinguished, Cristian lunged for Luca again, pushing him toward one of the giant casks of wine. Luca's body hit the wooden barrel so hard that it teetered on its edge and came crashing to the ground. It split open, and blood-red wine began pouring into the blackened water.

And then, there were voices. Distant but clear.

Someone had heard them. People were coming.

Cristian must have had the same realization. He shoved Luca out of the way and sprinted for the door.

He stopped, heaving, just before disappearing through the archway. *"A la prochaine,"* he spat out. "This isn't over, brother." Then he disappeared through the dark mouth of the doorway, and was gone in an instant.

"The heart is divided

into four chambers,

two to a side.

When one side fails,

the other must follow,

and the body dies."

—THE BOOK OF THE ETERNAL ROSE

Finally, at last, a flurry of wedding-goers poured into the cellar, some with daggers drawn. Madalena's father was in the lead, and her two uncles followed close behind. Joseph Dubois was part of the crowd; he carried a torch.

"What happened?" Signor Rambaldo's face was pale. "It sounded as if the whole palazzo was crashing down into the canal."

"Did you stop him?" Cass burst out.

"Are you all right, Signorina Caravello?" Madalena's uncle Pietro held out his arms to keep the throng of onlookers from surging forward and surrounding her.

"Please." Cass fought back tears. All she could think was that Cristian was escaping. "He probably went right past you."

"Who?" Signor Dubois smoothed his dark hair. He looked at Cass with a neutral expression, as if he thought she was merely a girl making a fuss to get attention.

"The killer! Cris—"

Luca cut her off. "Cass surprised a thief down here. He snuck in with the guests and was trying to steal wine."

Cass turned to Luca, her mouth falling open. Why was he lying? "No," she said. "No. That's not what happened. I—"

"She thought the thief was going to kill her," Luca continued, wrapping one of his arms around her shoulders. "I think she fell and hit her head. I'll take care of her."

Signor Dubois nodded. His face was stony. A look passed between him and Luca that Cass didn't understand. "I believe the good Dottor de Gradi is in attendance," he said, "should she need to be tended to."

Cass clung to Luca protectively, her fingernails digging crescent moon impressions into the skin of his arm. She glared at Dubois. The man returned her gaze, evenly, as though daring her to accuse him of something. Did Madalena's family know what he was capable of? Did the people of Venice? Dubois knew of the killings, there was no doubt. He had ordered the murder of his pregnant maid Sophia, if Cristian could be believed.

"A thief within these walls. It's unthinkable. And today of all days . . ." Signor Rambaldo shook his head. "Signor da Peraga, if you are certain you don't need our help, I'm going to go check on my daughter. Perhaps Signor Dubois can alert the doctor to Signorina Caravello's condition."

"We'll search the palazzo," Pietro said. "If there is a criminal in our midst, we'll draw him out like the vermin that he is."

Joseph Dubois and Mada's uncles followed Signor Rambaldo up the stone steps. Cass turned to Luca. "Luca, you don't understand. Dubois is working with your brother. Cristian killed one of his maids—"

"You're the one who doesn't understand," Luca said forcefully. "You cannot just go around accusing powerful men of murder."

"But we can't just let them get away with it."

"Cass," Luca said, cupping her face in his hands. "This is larger than just a dead servant. Please. Trust me. There are things, even now, that you do not understand."

"But—"

"Look what almost happened to you. Don't give anyone a reason to try again." His eyes were urgent.

Cass instinctively raised a hand to her throat. She knew, deep down, that Luca was right. She could almost still feel Cristian's hands wrapped around her neck, the burning sensation of her windpipe being crushed beneath his fierce grip.

"Are you all right?" she asked Luca. "You're not injured?"

Luca rubbed at his right side. "A cracked rib, perhaps." He winced. "But I always expected that being your fiancé would come with an element of risk."

Amazingly, Cass managed to smile. "Thank you," she said, feeling heat rise to her cheeks. "For saving me. I don't know what would have happened if—if you hadn't . . ."

Luca looked down at her, his light brown eyes soft with emotion. "That was quick thinking with the lantern. I think you saved me too." He removed her hand from her neck, entwining his fingers in hers. "We make a good team."

Cass felt a rush of warmth. She rested her head against his chest for a moment. His heart thudded quickly beneath the fabric of his tunic. Cass stretched up on her tiptoes and planted a quick kiss on his cheek. "Thank you," she whispered again.

Luca reddened. "Come," he said. "We should see that you're attended to."

He escorted Cass up the stairs to the main level of the palazzo.

The portego, abuzz with whispering and murmuring, went dead silent as the two of them appeared on the landing. Cass caught a glimpse of her reflection in a large mirror hanging just inside the door. Her dress was tattered and soiled, the bloodstained collar hanging at a weird angle. Her thick hair was tangled, her lower lip swollen from where Cristian had bitten her. An angry red welt burned on her skin where she'd been cut.

Someone let out a strangled cry; various people made the sign of the cross. A woman Cass didn't know approached her. "Is she all right?" she asked, bending low to examine the blood on Cass's throat.

Other wedding guests came forward, pressing around her, a storm of hands and voices. The room began to spin. Cass's knees buckled.

"Please, everyone." Luca held up one hand, supporting Cass with his other arm. "Come on, Cass," he said in a low voice. He led her up a second set of stairs. Cass had never seen the palazzo alive with so many people. And yet, she had never felt so alone. A gray-clad servant slipped past her, dark hair knotted on top of her head in a sleek bun.

"*Scusi,*" Luca said. "Please—get us a glass of wine."

"Of course, Signore." The servant curtsied and then returned to the main floor.

Luca pushed Cass toward an open door. "Rest there while I fetch the doctor," he said. "Don't say anything to anyone. Tell them you don't remember what happened."

"No. Not Dottor de Gradi—" Cass tried to protest, but Luca had already disappeared. Maybe it would be all right. Falco seemed to trust him.

Cass wandered dizzily into the plain room and practically

collapsed on a divan situated next to a thick glass window. She raised a hand to her chest, to the area where the dagger had embedded itself in a thin ridge of whalebone. Her heart still raced, just beneath her fingers. *Saved by undergarments,* Cass thought. Suddenly all those days of struggling to breathe beneath the oppressive stays didn't seem so bad.

She inhaled deeply, willing down the desire to cry, or scream. From here, she could see the small courtyard garden. A couple of guests had found their way to the Venus fountain and were now perched on the circle of stones that ringed it. The brilliant sunny day had turned overcast; threads of gray mist hung in the air.

"Your wine, Signorina?"

That voice.

Cass spun around and struggled to her feet. Falco stood in the doorway of the study, dressed in a green and gold servant's uniform. Cass took in the lopsided smile, the hair that curled slightly away from his face. Tears pricked up in her eyes, and Falco began to blur. But he didn't disappear.

She had to restrain herself from running into his arms. Instead, she stood pressed against the window. "How—how did you get in?"

Falco crossed the room to her, pausing just long enough to set a glass of wine down on the desk. "Doors are quite useful, I've found," he said, his eyes sparkling. Then his expression softened into one of concern. When he reached her, his hands skimmed her neck softly. "Are you all right?" he asked.

"Yes," Cass said. "Now."

"When I heard someone had been attacked, I didn't want to believe it was you." He pushed her tangled hair back from her face.

"Then I heard she had fought the attacker off and sent the poor bastard fleeing into the streets." Falco cracked a smile. "I knew it was my starling."

Cass leaned into Falco, allowing him to wrap her in an embrace. She breathed in deeply. As always, Falco smelled like a mixture of paint and minty soap. "How did you find me?"

Falco pulled away and smiled at her. "The whole city's been buzzing about this wedding for weeks," he said. "I paid a servant to let me in. Had to trade away a perfectly good pair of breeches for this outfit, I'll have you know."

Cass had to restrain herself from embracing him again. She wanted to pull him against her. She imagined his soft lips on hers, the way he would weave his fingers in her hair.

But then she thought of Luca, of the way he had looked at her in the wine room, like his whole world would have gone dark if he hadn't gotten to her in time. He had saved her. She stepped back, just slightly, letting a thin cushion of space between herself and Falco.

"I've been worried about you," Cass said. "I came to find you at Signor Loredan's exhibition . . ."

"You were there?" Falco said. "Did you see the—"

"*The Fallen Ones.*" Cass would never forget the trio of pictures. Mariabella and Sophia, both dead. But who was the third woman? Who was *R*?

And how many others had Cristian killed?

"The man who attacked you. Was he the one responsible?" Falco asked. He rubbed at the scar under his right eye.

Cass nodded. "His name is Cristian," she said. "He's deranged, but I don't think he was working alone." She paused, remembering

Luca's warning to keep the real story to herself, and his insistence that there were larger forces at play. But Cass couldn't lie to Falco. "I believe he was working with Signor Joseph Dubois," she said. "They killed the courtesan Mariabella and the maid Sophia." Cass didn't want to think about who else they might have killed. She was desperate to believe Cristian, that he had nothing to do with Feliciana's disappearance. "They tried to kill me," she continued, deciding not to mention that Cristian and her fiancé were related.

"If you're right, you're lucky to be alive," Falco said soberly. "Didn't you say he had ties all the way to the Council of Ten?"

Cass nodded. No wonder Dubois thought he could get away with murder. Again Cass marveled at how naïve she'd been; there was darkness roiling underneath the republic everyone called *La Serenissima*, the most serene.

Falco took both of her hands in his. He lifted her fingers to his lips. "How did you feel after reading my letter?" he asked.

The question was simple, but Cass sensed a thousand others hiding in the subtext. "I—" She glanced toward the doorway and fumbled for a response but could find a hundred, and none. She settled for a question of her own. "Did all the bodies go to Angelo de Gradi? Did Liviana—" Cass couldn't finish.

Falco ran his fingertips down the sides of Cass's face, repeatedly stroking her temples, her cheekbones, her chin. Cass's pain began to fade, as if his mere touch were healing her wounds. "I'm so sorry," he whispered. "I think he kept some and sold others. Maybe she was used for . . . artistic purposes," he faltered. He leaned his forehead against hers. "You're never going to forgive me, are you?"

"I forgive you," she said, fighting the urge to press her lips to his.

She meant it. She couldn't stay mad at him. And even though she didn't understand, she would do her best not to judge. She was far from perfect herself.

Falco exhaled deeply. "That is the best news I have gotten all day," he said. He leaned back, and his face broke out into a wide smile. "And the second-best news is that my paintings did well at the exhibition. A wealthy artisan from the mainland has offered me work. A lot of work."

"Falco, that's amazing!" Cass couldn't resist reaching out to squeeze his hand.

"Life-changing," he said, in a low voice. "Like you. Like us."

Cass opened her mouth to protest, but no words came out. Falco was right. She wouldn't deny that he had reached deep inside of her and unlocked secret places she had never even known existed.

"But the position will mean a lot of travel. Perhaps relocation," he said.

She looked away from him, biting her lip. "You'll be far away."

Falco nodded. "But I might get to see my family again."

"Your family?" Cass had never even thought to ask Falco about his family, whether he had brothers and sisters.

"My mother is a washerwoman and my father a cobbler. My brothers all work at the shop. I have a pair of little sisters in a convent in Verona," he said. "It's been years since I've seen them."

Cass couldn't imagine what it would be like to grow up in such a large family, with so many built-in companions.

"Come away with me, Cassandra," Falco said, his hands coming to rest lightly on her waist. "I can give you a life now. It may not be quite what you're used to, but it will be filled with love."

Before Cass could answer, a servant appeared in the doorway to the study, a glass of wine in her slender hands. Her brow furrowed in confusion when she saw Falco.

"*Scusi*, Signorina," she said. "Your wine . . . ?"

"Just set it down," Cass said sharply, relieved that it was a servant and not Luca who had found them together.

Falco stood. "Think about it," he said to Cass. He pressed his lips to her hand once more and then headed for the hallway. Cass watched him leave. The room seemed to go dim and cold at his exit. The bleak surroundings melded with the hopelessness Cass felt in her heart, which was torn in two opposing directions.

"Water can be a mirror

in which we see our true selves,

yet it forms the haze amidst

which we hide."

—THE BOOK OF THE ETERNAL ROSE

thirty-three

Cass took a deep breath to steady herself, then passed into the arched corridor. She needed to find Luca. She just wanted to go home, to be away from the madness. To think. The celebration raged on beneath her. She could see her fiancé winding his way through the crowd. She met him at the landing of the stairs.

"The doctor is on his way up," Luca said.

Cass shook her head. "Please—I just want to return to the villa. Perhaps Aunt Agnese's physician . . ." She trailed off. She didn't want to see *him* either. Him and his leeches. She just wanted to crawl into her bed and curl up next to Slipper. If she slept for a few hours, or maybe a few years, everything would start to feel normal again.

"You do seem steadier on your feet," Luca said. "Maybe that wine helped soothe your nerves."

Cass thought of the glasses of wine, both abandoned on the desk in the study. It wasn't wine that had soothed her nerves. It was Falco. Just thinking of him made her insides hurt.

"Perhaps." She smiled tightly.

Luca and Cass found Agnese and the servants still in the portego.

Her aunt was pacing back and forth with Narissa at her elbow, doing her best to stabilize the old woman's wobbly gait.

"Cassandra. *Santo cielo.*" Agnese hobbled immediately to Cass's side. She raised her twisted, swollen fingers to Cass's face. "Are you all right? I can barely believe the stories I've been hearing."

Cass was comforted by her aunt's cool touch. "I'm all right. I just want to go home." She had resisted thinking of her aunt's villa on San Domenico as home for as long as she could remember, but now she could think of nowhere else she'd rather be.

Agnese frowned. "This criminal. Was he apprehended?"

"We're not certain," Luca said, looping his arm protectively around Cass's elbow.

Across the room, a flash of dazzling blue caught Cass's eye. Madalena stood next to the head table, a glass of wine in her pale fingertips. Her mouth dropped when she saw Cass, and she turned away from one of her father's friends to begin making her way across the room.

Cass unsnaked her arm from Luca's and hurried toward her best friend. The two girls met in the center of the portego. Madalena threw her arms around Cass's neck, wrapping her in a fierce embrace. "I'm so glad you're all right," Mada said. "I can't believe you got attacked. What were you doing in my father's wine room, anyway?"

"You know me," Cass said, pulling back so that she didn't get blood on Mada's gown. "I have a tendency to wander off and find trouble." She wanted to tell her friend the whole story, but today was Mada's special day. Cass didn't want to disrupt it any more than she already had. "In fact I was searching for you. Where did you disappear to at the beginning of the feast?"

Madalena's brown eyes widened. "I think you're the only one who even noticed I was gone. I was in my bedchamber having Eva redo my hair, because it had gotten mussed on the walk through the streets. But then Marco knocked at the door." Madalena's alabaster skin flushed with joy. "I sent Eva away . . ." Her voice trailed off. She winked at Cass.

Cass raised a hand to her mouth. "You mean you—"

"Do you know how long we waited for this day to come?" Mada grinned. "We simply could *not* wait another moment."

Behind Madalena, Cass saw Donna Domacetti pushing her way through the crowded portego. Cass had no desire to be grilled about her ordeal so that woman could provide all of Venice with the gory details. "So while I was desperately searching for you, you and Marco were in your bed together." Cass laughed. "I hope it was magnificent at least."

Mada leaned close to whisper in Cass's ear. "It was life-changing," she said.

That seemed to be the theme for the day.

Luca, Agnese, and the servants stood at the top of the grand staircase, waiting for Cass and Mada to finish talking. Cass kissed Madalena on the cheek. "That menace Donna Domacetti is approaching from behind you. Distract her for me."

Cass headed down the stairs with the others. Behind her, she heard Donna Domacetti pull Madalena across the room to a table of Venetian socialites. "Now, these are some women you absolutely must get to know," the obese woman lectured. Cass smiled again. Everything was as it should be.

As they exited the palazzo, Luca flagged down a gondolier while

Agnese and the servants formed a protective cocoon around Cass. For the first time in a long time, Cass felt completely engulfed by family. If she ran away with Falco, she would lose all of that. She knew she loved him, but was love reason enough to betray Luca and hurt Agnese?

A sharp rain began to fall as Luca helped the three women into the boat. Cass and Agnese settled in beneath the felze. Droplets splattered against Cass's cheeks, stinging her exposed skin. She turned her face toward the storm. The pain felt cleansing.

Siena huddled close to Cass, deliberately avoiding turning her eyes to Luca for even a second. "I was so worried about you," she said, in a whisper. She looked as pale as Cass had ever seen her.

Cass reached out and squeezed her hand. Siena had her own secrets, but she was a faithful friend. She must have been terrified when she heard that Cass had been attacked. *You need always consider how your actions might affect others.* Cass had thought of Agnese as merely strict, but she was beginning to realize that the old woman's lectures were born of love, and wisdom—not just general grumpiness.

"I should have known if there was trouble that you would find it, Cassandra. You're very like your parents in that way." It was almost as if Agnese had read her mind. Cass watched the raindrops ping against the tiny waves as the gondola left the Grand Canal and entered the lagoon.

Agnese wasn't finished. She turned her attentions to Luca. "And you, Luca da Peraga. If you hope to make Cassandra your bride, you'll have to learn to keep a much tighter rein on her."

Luca's cheeks colored slightly as he shifted in the gondola. "*Mi dispiace*, Signora Querini," he said. "But you speak of your niece as if she's a horse instead of a beautiful young woman." Luca dared to flash Cass a quick half smile.

She smiled back. Luca's willingness to defend her to her aunt made her feel as warm, as comforted, as his heroics in the wine room.

Agnese harrumphed. "If I speak of her as an animal, it is because her antics are positively uncivilized at times." Then her voice softened. "Perhaps I am too hard on you, Cassandra. But please keep in mind that you are all that I have left."

Cass stared down at the bottom of the boat. She often thought about how Agnese was her only true family, but rarely stopped to think that the reverse was also true. "*Mi dispiace,*" Cass said, feeling a swell of relief as the distant shore of San Domenico came into view.

Agnese reached out to squeeze her hand. "Let us just thank God that everything ended as it did."

Except that it wasn't over, and Cass knew it.

The next day, Cass and Luca took a stroll around the tiny island of San Domenico. Cass was surprised to discover that she liked the feel of Luca's arm in hers, the way he guided her around puddles and cracks in the walkway. Women glanced at the two of them as they strolled by, likely envious of Cass. She saw Luca as they must see him: tall, handsome, affectionate. It felt good to be able to be out in public with a man, to be able to laugh and talk without having to worry about who was watching.

They passed in front of Il Mar e la Spada, the little taverna that Falco and his friends liked to frequent. She thought about her nights with Falco: how intense and scary they had been, but how alive she had felt through it all. Would she feel that with Luca? She wasn't sure.

Over time, would she feel something even better? It would be different. Tempered. But maybe that was what Cass needed—someone to complement her impulsive nature, someone who would give her calm and stability.

They made it past all of the buildings to the shoreline. Luca turned to Cass.

"Have you heard of the Order of the Eternal Rose?" he asked, with a sudden urgency in his voice.

Cass looked at him curiously. "No. I don't know what that is."

Rather than explain himself, Luca let out a breath and shook his head. "Never mind. It's nothing. I just . . . I don't know where to start. My behavior since returning to Venice may have seemed strange to you," he said. "I—I wanted the opportunity to explain. A few weeks ago, I received a letter from Cristian. I hadn't heard from him in years. I confess I was hoping he had been killed in the war. He wrote that he had heard of my upcoming nuptials, but warned me that he would see to it that I never received my anticipated happiness." Luca glanced away, squinting in the sunlight reflecting off the lagoon. "I had no doubt he was on the lookout for you. He had taken someone I loved before; he would not hesitate to do it again."

Cass's heart began beating high in her throat. "What do you mean?"

Luca was silent for a few moments, and Cass was worried he would refuse to say any more. But finally, he started speaking again. "My parents used to take my sister and me to Piazza San Marco quite often. Diana used to love the square. She could watch the jugglers and conjurers for hours. She never tired of looking through the jewelry and trinkets that the foreign merchants were hawking."

He exhaled slowly. Cass slipped her fingers inside of his. "My sister was only seven when she died—when Cristian killed her. Her body floated up in a canal; they called it an accident, but I knew better. Diana wouldn't have drowned in a canal. She had learned to swim in a lake near our estate on the mainland. She was unusual. If she had lived, I think the two of you might have become quite good friends."

Cass felt guilt prickling inside of her. Poor Luca. He had endured such sadness. And there was so much about him that she didn't know—that she had never cared to know.

"When I got your aunt's letter about planning the betrothal ceremony, it seemed like perfect timing," Luca continued. "It would give me an excuse to return to Venice and find Cristian before he could find you. I was hoping he was just trying to scare me. When I caught that boy prowling around Agnese's front lawn, I thought that Cristian had sent him as a spy."

Paolo. So Luca had no idea Cass had been running around with Falco. The guilty feelings poked her a little harder. Luca would never know of her affair—as long as her journal remained missing. Cass wondered if Cristian had taken it with him. If he would bide his time and then send the incriminating pages one by one in the days that led up to her wedding. Pain seized her at the thought. She stopped. Breathed. Waited for the sensation to pass.

Luca wrapped an arm around her protectively. Cass inhaled the scent of pine and citrus from his skin and clothing. "Would you like to rest?" he asked. "I know all of this must come as a shock to you."

"No, go on," Cass said, swallowing back the feeling that she might cry. She didn't deserve Luca. He was too good for her.

"When I heard about the murdered servant, I was more convinced than ever that my half brother *was* in Venice. I was terrified he would approach you, that he would try to—" Luca shuddered.

Cass remembered how Cristian had approached her at the brothel, how he had pretended to buy her for the evening. What might have happened if Falco hadn't intervened?

"It wasn't until the art exhibition that I knew for certain. Cristian's signature was in the guest book above your own. One of his paintings reminded me of a woman who occasionally called upon my father. I believe it may have been Cristian's own mother." Luca shook his head. He added, more gently, "I'm sorry if I was ever harsh with you. I wanted to protect you. I should have told you about Cristian. But I thought you might be safer if you remained ignorant. And I also felt—" He stopped abruptly.

"What?" she prompted him. Was that who *R* was—the final *Fallen Ones* portrait? Cass was reeling from the thought of Cristian killing his own mother, but she remembered the hateful way he had called her a whore. Maybe Cristian had seen his mother with a man when he was younger, and something inside of him had snapped.

Luca rubbed his forehead. "Cristian is only my half brother," he said. "He will never have any piece of my estate. That's partly why he hates me. Even so . . . I was worried that if you knew about him, you'd be afraid to marry me."

"Luca." Cass squeezed his hand softly. "I have no right to judge you."

"Well, it isn't like you've seemed too keen on our betrothal anyway," Luca said, staring off into the distance.

Cass stopped. She looked out over the lagoon. The sun was just beginning to set, painting the sky a mix of reds and oranges. Cass remembered wishing she could escape San Domenico. Now the warm colors weaved around her like a blanket. For once, she didn't want to swim away into the sea. "It isn't that," she said slowly. "It just took me by surprise. I wasn't ready."

Luca turned toward her. "What about now, Cassandra?" he asked, touching his hand to her left cheek, his other hand coming to rest on her slender waist. "Are you ready now? I must return to France to study. Come back with me. I can protect you. I will protect you. And I will try—I will do everything I can to make you happy."

Cass didn't know what to say. She stared into Luca's eyes—patient, warm, kind. He would be an excellent husband. An almost-perfect husband. But would he be the perfect husband for her? Cass didn't know.

Just then, something moved in the shadows. Instinctively, Cass tensed up. Her head whipped around as a figure emerged from the taverna behind them.

It was Falco, holding a canvas sack over his shoulder. He froze, watching her and Luca, and Cass saw them as he must: standing close like lovers, their arms intertwined. He was still at a distance, but his stare radiated heat. Not anger, just his own peculiar energy.

Luca did not appear to notice her attention had been distracted. "Will you go with me?" he prompted. "As my wife?"

"I—" Cass looked up into Luca's face. Her fiancé would love her and protect her. He understood pain and loyalty. He would die to keep her safe.

Falco was moving now, walking toward the shoreline. Cass's heart rose into her throat. Her first love. Falco understood her desire to be free from expectations. The man who would support her in living the life she wanted to live.

But what life was that?

Cass stood frozen, unable to decide. Luca was still staring at her expectantly. Falco reached the two of them, raising his blue eyes just long enough to give her a single soft look as he passed by.

As Falco waved an arm to signal a passing fisherman, the sun dipped completely below the horizon. And with the darkness came clarity. The answer had been in front of her the whole time. Cass knew what she must do.

"Just as roses grow

from the decomposed,

so may new life

spring from death."

—THE BOOK OF THE ETERNAL ROSE

thirty-four

Cass sat at Agnese's bedside, the two of them sharing a late supper together, while Luca was attending to business at his family palazzo.

"I daresay you've had a more exciting week than Signorina Rambaldo's," Agnese commented. She raised a forkful of vegetables to her lips.

Cass smiled, pleased at how smoothly her aunt manipulated the utensil. Maybe Agnese was getting stronger. "*Too* exciting," she said. "I'm looking forward to lazing about the villa for a few days. Would you believe me if I said I was even looking forward to next week's studies?" Agnese had arranged for Cass's literature tutor to present a few more lessons.

Agnese's gray eyes sparkled. "No, I would not." She fidgeted beneath her velvet coverlet. "Would you call one of the servants to help lift me up in the bed a bit?"

"I can do it," Cass said. Before her aunt could protest, Cass stood from her chair. She wrapped her hands under her aunt's arms and helped readjust her position. She felt a brief pang as she realized how light her aunt was—like a bird, all hollow bones. Their faces touched briefly, and Cass caught a whiff of rosewater perfume. It reminded her of her mother.

"How's that?" she asked brightly.

"Lovely, dear," her aunt said. "I'm only just beginning to realize how strong you are." She pointed at a white box on her dressing table. "Would you bring me that parcel, please?"

Cass fetched the package from across the room. It was a medium-sized box with a lilac ribbon tied around it. As she went to place it in her aunt's hands, Agnese shook her head with a smile. "It's for you."

"Me? Why?"

Agnese's thin lips curved up into a smile. "I meant it for your birthday, but after the week you've had, I thought you deserved a little present."

Cass untied the lilac ribbon, slipping it into her pocket. Slipper would enjoy playing with it later. She lifted the lid off the box. Nestled beneath the cover was a thick book, bound in soft black leather. Cass folded back the cover. The pages were blank.

"It's a new journal," Agnese said. "As much as you've had to write about lately, I figured you might have run out of pages."

Cass cradled the leather-bound book to her chest. It was the perfect gift. Her aunt didn't even know her old journal had disappeared, yet somehow she had figured out exactly what Cass needed. Maybe that was the magic of family. Maybe the invisible threads that connected Cass to her aunt weren't as frail as she had always imagined. Maybe they were giant ropes that would hold the two of them together in the stormy republic of Venice.

For the first time, Cass didn't think being bound to her aunt would be such a bad thing. She had more to learn from Agnese, about life, love, and the world.

"Thank you," she whispered, surprised to feel tears pressing behind her eyes. "It's perfect." She excused herself quickly and headed back to her bedchamber.

Cass pushed into the room and took a seat at her dressing table. She pulled a quill from her drawer. She lit her oil lamp, letting her fingers trace the flower patterns in the smooth surface. For a moment she sat, staring into space, thinking about all that had happened in just a few short weeks.

There were still so many questions Cass wanted answered: first and foremost, where was Feliciana? If Cristian hadn't harmed her, where was she? Poor Siena wouldn't be whole until her sister returned safely.

And was Feliciana's disappearance connected to the murders? What was the significance of the flower inside the circle? Could it be connected to the Order of the Eternal Rose that Luca had asked her about? She'd seen the symbol on rings worn by Cristian and Donna Domacetti, and on the outside of Angelo de Gradi's gore-filled workshop. Were the three of them involved in something sinister? And if so, how did Joseph Dubois fit in? Cass was certain Dubois was the key to linking everything else together. And what had Luca meant when he implied that the murders were part of something larger?

She sighed, and pushed thoughts of Cristian and conspiracy out of her mind. She felt older, much older, than she had only a month ago. She had done some things in the past few weeks that could be viewed as wrong, hurtful even. But she had lived, and loved, and made the right decision for herself in the end.

Cass thumbed through the pages of the journal, surprised when her finger caught midway through. A loose piece of parchment fell out of the middle of the book. Cass could hardly believe it. It was Falco's sketch—the faceless nude girl he had given to Cass weeks ago. Agnese must have been the one who found the cloak thrown over the side table. The old woman had known about the drawing the whole time.

What if Agnese thought that Cass had posed for the sketch? Her cheeks burned. She stood, preparing to rush back to her aunt's bedchamber and account for the drawing.

But then she stopped. Obviously, Agnese wasn't upset, or she'd have confronted Cass when she first discovered the drawing. She recalled the conversation from Palazzo Domacetti, how the women at tea had insinuated that Agnese hadn't always been stodgy and strict. Cass struggled with the idea of her aunt ever being young and impulsive, but many people had surprised her lately. It only made sense that there was more to Agnese as well.

Cass smiled down at the sketch as she remembered the way Falco had teased her about being embarrassed of her own body. He had seemed so crass back then, before she fell in love with him. Cass touched the drawing to her heart, just for a second. Then she hid it deep within the journal's empty pages. This was one story she would keep to herself. Not everything needed to be explained.

The thought reminded her of something Liviana had said to her once. Before Livi got sick, she and Cass had been playing in Agnese's garden when a funeral party brought a body to be interred in the cemetery. The girls has snuck through the gate and hidden themselves behind a monument, watching as the shrouded body was carried inside a tomb by men wearing black.

"But if they lock the door," Cass had said, "how will his soul get out so it can go to heaven?"

"I don't know," the younger girl had answered. "Maybe souls can walk through walls, like ghosts."

"And will he float up through the sky?" Cass asked. "Or will angels come down and carry him away?"

Liviana had shrugged, but her face remained serene, as if these were questions that simply didn't bother her.

"But don't you want to know how it happens?" Cass persisted, thinking of her own parents, who had died just a few months earlier. Were their bodies trapped somewhere, their spirits unable to ascend?

"Not everything is simple," Liviana had said. "Sometimes things are better off left as mysteries, don't you think?"

Cass didn't think so at the time. Now she wasn't as sure. Maybe she should forget about flowers inscribed in circles and missing bodies and corruption that ran so deep that men got away with murder. Maybe she should focus on enjoying what time she had left with her aunt. Cass didn't know if she could do that, but she knew what she *could* do.

She ripped a single blank page from her new journal.

Dear Luca,

Thank you for understanding, and for being patient. Please know that I care about you, very much. But I cannot give my life to you yet. I am still learning how to live. I am still figuring out who I am.

She looked up from her letter and crumpled it. She tore another page from the book.

Dear Falco,

You changed my life, and you will always be a part of it. But I can't run away with you and abandon the only family I have left. I have learned the hard way that you must take care of the people closest to you, those who need you the most.

Cass sighed. She set that letter aside too. She'd never be able to send it anyway. Falco was gone. She might never see him again.

Cass dipped her quill into the ink and touched it to the first page of the journal. She wrote:

You may study the bodies of the living and the dead for clues about the mechanism of the muscles, the bones, and even the brain, but you can never unravel the mystery of the human heart...

Acknowledgments

Extra-special thanks to Lexa Hillyer and Lauren Oliver for supporting and believing in me even when I had doubts. This has been a Cinderella-like experience, and I'm hoping the clock doesn't strike midnight for a very long time. Also to Jill Santopolo, Julia Johnson, and everyone at Philomel who helped mold this book into something truly deserving of the Philomel brand. Beth Scorzato and Eleanor Herman, thank you for your awesome pitches and your tireless commitment to historical accuracy. Stephen Barbara and the people at Foundry Literary + Media, thanks for your part in making dreams come true and for getting the word out internationally. This book is going to be published in more languages than I will ever know how to speak. How cool is that?

Mom, Paul, Vicky (ahem, alphabetical order, no fighting), thanks for your never-ending support, random edible gifts that kept me from starving, and for not disowning me when I went AWOL from the family for weeks at a time. You guys are right—I do too much. (But I don't see that changing anytime soon.)

More thanks:

To Jennifer Laughran, for good advice and not giving up on me.

To all my awesome critique pals, and to the Blueboarders, some of whom provided more guidance and encouragement than they will probably ever know. Also to Connie, for knowing when to be my cheerleader and when to tell me to suck it up.

To the staff at Kayak's, the best coffee shop in St. Louis, for putting up with all my special orders and for letting me take up the primo table by the bookshelf for insane amounts of hours. (I'm going to bring back the books I "borrowed" eventually, I promise.)

To Kholood Eid, for the amazing author photographs. You rock!

To Raul, Howard, Jeff, and everyone over at the-trades.com, for letting me write reviews and showering me with free books (because, let's face it, part of every writer's job is being a voracious reader).

To Susan Pickering and Dennis Black—you were the best English teachers a girl could hope for, but I'm a little cranky at you both for saying my writing was phenomenal and then telling me I should become a doctor.

Last, but not least, to Adam, for yanking me out of make-believe land and reminding me that the real world can be magical too.

The mysteries and intrigue continue in

THE SECRETS OF THE ETERNAL ROSE

In Florence beauty kills

Belladonna

FIONA PAUL

Turn the page for a look at the next book in
THE SECRETS OF THE ETERNAL ROSE
series

Cass leaned over the side of the Rialto Bridge, the wind lifting her auburn hair away from her face. Wispy clouds swirled low in the sky.

"Cass." The word fluttered on the breeze.

She turned. Falco stood at her side, his square jaw backlit by the sun, his mouth curving into the lopsided smile she loved. "I thought you . . . ?" Cass couldn't finish. *Left.* He had left her, weeks ago.

"I came back for you," he said.

He stroked her face with his hands, one fingertip tracing the smattering of freckles across the bridge of her nose. She wobbled in her chopines and he reached out to steady her, his hand lingering on her arm. The platform overshoes made her taller than Falco, but he didn't seem to notice. Tilting his head toward her, he pulled her body in close to his.

Cass trembled as he closed the gap between them. Their lips met. Hungry. Wanting. Falco's hands wrapped around her waist, caressing her through the layered fabric of her dress. Her body went weak, and she gripped the stone railing of the bridge to keep from pitching over into the water. Her other hand found his hair. She twisted it around her fingers.

"Come with me," he whispered.

Cass didn't even ask where they were going. Falco took her hand and pulled her across the bridge, through the streets. Light became gray. Day became night. His grip tightened around her fingers. Too tight. Cass looked up at him. She gasped. He was falling away in pieces. His hair. His smile. His skin peeling back to reveal teeth and bone.

The street dissolved, and Cass wasn't outside anymore. Dark hallways threaded out in all directions, weblike and impossibly long. She clawed at the damp walls, and the stone chipped away beneath her fingernails, leaving long gouges in the rock. She was being dragged forward, through an arched door. A lantern flickered to life. They were in the wine room. Cass and the man of bone.

Only now he wore a new face: Cristian, her fiancé Luca's half brother. Cristian, the murderer. He started shouting at her, horrible black things about the women he had killed.

A droplet of water fell from above. Cass lay pinned to a low stone table. And Cristian was on top of her, his weight crushing her chest, an icy blade pressed against her throat. She felt death in that pinch of steel, but she was more afraid of the hand that wasn't holding the dagger. The hand that was busy tearing away the fabric of her dress . . .

Cass sat up in bed, her heart banging in her chest, her eyes still shut against the monster from her nightmare. Her nightgown clung to her moist skin.

"Not real," she murmured. She had the dream every couple of

nights. Each time it was a little different, but it always ended the same way.

She opened her eyes. The candle on her washing table had burned down to its nub. Burning tallow all night was expensive, and dangerous, but Cass couldn't bear the dark. Not since Cristian had attacked her. A thin shaft of silvery dawn sliced its way through a crack in her shutters. It was morning, and she was all right. Another night survived.

She tried to put the nightmare out of her mind. She hadn't told anyone exactly what had happened to her the day of Madalena's wedding. Even Luca didn't know that his half brother had more than murder on his mind when he lured Cass down into the wine room.

Her insides twisted like she was a sheet being wrung out to dry. Bile rose in her throat. Resting her head back on her pillow, Cass willed herself to be calm. *Inhale. Exhale. Just breathe.*

Something rough scratched against her cheek. A rolled parchment lay in her tangled bedsheets. The edges were crumbling and the ink was fading in places. It was Falco's letter, the only one she had received since he left Venice. Cass had been reading it last night before she fell asleep. She'd read it a hundred times, knew each word by heart, but she unrolled it again anyway. The words were sweet and soothing. Even in his absence, Falco could make the nightmare fade.

Starling,
*   I haven't stopped thinking of you—I can't. I know that you*
are engaged and want to do right by your family, but you and
I belong together. Call it fate if you like. I prefer to think of
it as the natural order of things. Just as mixing ochre and

sapphire produces the most vibrant green, you and I, when combined, become more alive.

I've stopped doing business with Angelo de Gradi. I've left that life behind. I'm working as an artist-in-residence for a wealthy patron now. The work she has me do is a bit pedestrian, but perhaps it will lead to bigger projects. I meant what I said. One day I will paint whole chapels for you. I spend every waking minute becoming a better artist, a better man. One day I will offer you the life you deserve, the life we both desire.

One day I'll be good enough, or I'll die trying...

Cass glanced at the portrait of the Virgin Mary above her dressing table. She should have lowered the black veil attached to the frame before reviewing her love letter. It wasn't proper to let the Virgin see her swooning over a man who was not her fiancé.

But she could ask for forgiveness later. Cradling the parchment against her chest, she thought about the last time she'd seen Falco. She had been strolling the streets of San Domenico with Luca when she saw Falco flagging down a fisherman for passage. Cass knew he was going away, but she didn't know where. Part of her had wanted to drop her fiancé's hand and run to Falco's side, to escape the tiny island with him.

But she had stayed put, her arm entwined with Luca's, watching Falco's back fade into the setting sun. Following him would have meant abandoning her aunt Agnese and dishonoring the memory of her parents, and Cass just couldn't do it. Besides, she wasn't completely convinced she could trust Falco. Their whole relationship was based on secrets and lies. Even if Falco had stopped stealing dead bodies and selling them to Angelo de Gradi, did that mean he wouldn't turn to crime again the next time he needed more than his art could provide? She didn't know.

But she *did* know Luca might never be enough for her. Cass's heart fluttered in her chest. She felt Falco's lips on hers as if he were there in the room. She remembered their first kiss, in the studio where he apprenticed, the way she felt as if she had lived her whole life inside a frozen shell, melting for the first time at his touch.

She sighed. Luca had been so patient with her the past few weeks, content to enjoy her company at mealtimes and during an occasional stroll along the beach. Just last week he had given her a gift, a gorgeous lily pendant. Cass felt its pressure in the hollow of her throat, the lily's diamond center moving in and out with each of her breaths. Luca would make the perfect husband. He was handsome and kind and smart, a good man, from a well-established Venetian family. And he loved her. He loved her so much, he would die for her; he had proven that already. But Falco was . . . Falco. Just the taste of his name on her lips made Cass a little dizzy.

Her situation was hopeless: betrothed to one man, wildly in love with another.

Heavy footsteps outside her room shattered the reverie. Quickly, Cass slipped the letter under her pillow. She tucked an unruly shock of hair back under her sleeping cap as she hurried to her armoire and grabbed a dressing gown from inside. Securing the belt around her waist, she opened her chamber door a crack and peeked out into the hallway. It was dark, but the corridor was full of strange men dressed in scarlet and gold. Men with swords and clubs tucked into leather sheaths.

Soldiers.

"What's going on here?" Cass asked.

The soldiers turned as one, quickly averting their eyes at her state of undress. "We've orders to search Signor da Peraga's chambers," one of them said stiffly. He wore a gold medallion pinned to his doublet. Cass assumed he was the man in charge.

"*Search* his chambers?" she repeated, incredulous. "For what?"

"Best you step aside, Signorina." The soldier waved her out of the way with one of his filthy leather gloves. "These orders come straight from the Senate."

Cass's handmaid, Siena, appeared at her side, dressed but still half drunk with sleep, her blonde hair stuffed loosely under her bonnet. "Signorina Cass," she whispered. "What's happening?"

"I don't know." Cass followed the soldiers to the room where Luca had been staying. Siena trailed behind her. The two girls stood in the doorway as the men converged upon the bed, tearing the pillows and sheets from it and tossing them to the floor. Finding nothing of interest in the linens, they moved to the worn leather trunk that sat against the wall. Horrified, Cass watched as one of the soldiers flung armfuls of books and clothing over his shoulder.

"Where is Luca?" she asked, her voice rising in pitch. "You've no right to go through his belongings without him present."

"I suggest you go speak to Signor da Peraga yourself," the nearest soldier said. "He's in the *portego* with the rest of the brigade."

Rest of the brigade? Pulling Siena behind her, Cass stormed down the hallway and pushed into the main room of the villa. The shutters were still closed, but the cavernous portego was aglow with torchlight. Agnese's harp and the angel statues that stood on either side of it were casting deformed, wavering shadows across the marble floor. Luca stood near a velvet divan, talking to another group of soldiers.

Cass counted seven of them. They smelled of sweat and ale and ashes. Scarlet and gold blurred before her eyes as the soldiers circled her fiancé like lions preparing to pounce.

"Luca! What's happening?" She pushed her way through the sea of red to Luca's side, her forward momentum almost throwing her into his arms. It had been a while since she had been this close to him, close enough to see how his brown eyes faded to honey at the edges, close enough to smell a hint of cinnamon on his clothing.

"I'm being arrested," he said calmly.

Cass felt as though the ground had opened beneath her feet. "On what charges? Under whose authority?" For a moment, she pressed her face against his broad chest, hiding her skin from the dancing flames of the nearest soldier's torch. The silk of Luca's doublet felt cool against her scorched cheek.

"What is the meaning of all this?"

Cass pulled away at the sound of Narissa's shrill voice. Narissa was Agnese's personal handmaid and the unofficial second-in-command of the villa. The stout, gray-haired woman surveyed the scene with a mix of shock and anger.

A crowd was beginning to gather at the edge of the portego. Siena stood just inside the doorway, her body leaning heavily against the wall as if she might collapse at any moment. She gestured wildly as she murmured to Narissa, but Cass couldn't make out what the women were saying. She felt as though she hadn't yet woken from her dream. Everything was strange and disjointed. Bortolo, Agnese's elderly blind butler, stood behind the handmaids, his grizzled face twisted in confusion. In the other doorway, a trio of serving girls huddled silently together, taking in the scene with wide, frightened eyes.

A large thud made Cass jump. It sounded as if the soldiers were hacking Luca's belongings to pieces with their clubs. With all the noise, Agnese was almost certainly awake now. Cass knew she should go to her aunt's bedside, but she couldn't bring herself to leave Luca.

As Cass watched, Narissa broke away from Siena and strode purposefully toward Luca's chambers, undoubtedly to make sure the soldiers weren't stealing anything or destroying the furniture. Cass knew Agnese would be hobbling her way into the chaos the instant she heard of the transpiring events. Ideally, Narissa could control the soldiers *and* her aunt, who was too weak to deal with something like this. Agnese's latest bout with imbalanced humors had required a large bloodletting, and the doctor had recommended bed rest for a few days.

"On what charges do you arrest my fiancé?" Cass asked again, directing her words to the group. When no one answered, she focused on the nearest soldier. His beard was flecked with gray, and several medallions glimmered on the breast of his doublet. Perhaps he, not the man leading the ransackers, was the leader. "You. Answer me." The soldier looked pityingly at Cass but said nothing.

Cass turned to Luca. "This is madness!"

"They can't tell us the charges." Luca pressed his hands to Cass's shoulders, steadying her. "They probably don't even know. They're just following orders." He touched his lips to her cheek, then angled his mouth toward her ear. "Be strong," he murmured. "And stay away from Signor Dubois."

"Does he have something to do with this?" Cass knew that Luca had been to see Joseph Dubois only yesterday, and every shady dealing in Venice seemed to lead back to the Frenchman. A few weeks ago, he'd ordered Luca's half brother, Cristian, to "dispose" of a maid from his estate. The girl's mutilated body had surfaced in the Grand Canal, and now Siena's sister, Feliciana, another servant at Palazzo Dubois, was missing. Cass prayed to Saint Anthony every night for Feliciana's safe return, but privately she feared the worst.

Luca didn't respond. The remaining soldiers filed into the portego, having apparently completed their search. Between the two groups there must have been close to twenty men. Did the Senate really think it would take so many soldiers to subdue a single man?

"Did you find anything?" The soldier with the graying beard lifted his torch so that the faces of his companions were illuminated.

"Nothing," one of the soldiers barked in reply.

The brigade surrounded Luca and Cass, separating them from the rest of the household. The heat from their torches made the room go blurry. Cass blinked hard, but golden spots floated in the air, melding with the ocean of scarlet fabric, reflecting off medallions and sword hilts. She braced herself with one hand against Luca, trying to keep her knees from folding beneath her.

"Signor da Peraga must come with us now," a soldier said. He detached a coil of rope from his belt and looped it around Luca's wrists, cinching his hands behind his back.

"No!" Cass threw her hands around Luca's neck, pulling him close. She fought back a sob, but a tear escaped, trickling down her cheek before she could brush it away.

"Everything is going to be fine, Cass," Luca said. He leaned down to brush his lips against the tear. "Don't cry."

One of the men took Cass by the shoulders and wrenched her away. She stumbled backward, unmoored. Siena materialized at her side, reaching out, helping her regain her balance. The soldiers engulfed Luca and dragged him toward the stairs.

The front door of the villa slammed, and Cass ran to the window. The sky had gone from silver to blue. The soldiers doused their torches in the water as they forced Luca aboard the sturdy wooden ship. White sails snapped in the breeze as the boat pulled away from the dock. The waxing daylight wasn't enough to see clearly by, but Cass swore Luca turned to look back at her as the ship bobbed out of sight. She touched one hand to the window, her breath condensing on the glass.

Luca was gone.

"Members of the Order must band together to vanquish our enemies. Neither man nor the Church shall be allowed to jeopardize our higher purpose."

—THE BOOK OF THE ETERNAL ROSE

two

Cass heard Narissa's voice before she saw the handmaid helping her aunt down the corridor. "One step at a time. Excellent, Signora. Slow and steady," Narissa said, supporting Agnese as the old woman struggled toward the portego.

"Aunt Agnese!" Cass cried out, wiping at her cheek with her hand. She did not want her aunt to know how terrified she was. "You should be in bed."

"Explain to me," Agnese wheezed, "why those savages thought they could destroy my home." She pointed in the direction of Luca's room. "It looks like the End of Days in there."

"They said they had orders to search Luca's chambers," Cass said. *But search for what?*

"*Orders*," Agnese scoffed. "Don't worry, Cassandra. They'll be taking *new* orders soon." She clutched at her chest, as if the mere act of speaking were taxing. "Narissa, I'd like to return to my room. Bring me wax and parchment. I'll be sending several letters immediately." As she tottered back down the hallway on her handmaid's arm, she added, "And someone put that room back together immediately—there's nothing more debased than an overturned armchair."

Siena touched Cass on the shoulder. "I'll go straighten in there."

A strange protective feeling welled up inside Cass. She didn't want anyone else going through Luca's private things. "I can take care of it," she said quickly. "You go to the market. Keep your ears open. Maybe you'll hear someone talking about the arrest."

Siena curtsied. "Whatever you think is best, Signorina Cass."

Cass had already turned away. She held her breath as she crossed the threshold into Luca's room, afraid of what she might find. The four-poster bed was still standing, but barely. The armoire and washing table were also whole, but overturned. All of Luca's fine clothing had been yanked from the armoire's shelves and dumped in a heap on the floor. Books and stockings were strewn about in front of his trunk.

Cass's cat, Slipper, was pawing at a fur-lined collar that protruded from the mess of clothes. "Shoo," Cass said, bending down in front of the armoire.

Slipper bounded off to explore the tangle of stockings. Cass began to refold Luca's breeches and doublets, placing each piece of clothing back onto the shelves. She caught a whiff of his scent—citrus and cinnamon—from a tailored gray doublet and had to restrain herself from beginning to cry.

She reminded herself that crying would help no one.

Next, she went to work on his chemises. The linen fabric had creases at the chest and shoulders. Luca even folded his underclothes. Cass took her time, matching her folds to the creases, trying to put everything back just as it had been. She told herself that it was all a mistake, that he would soon be home, that he would want his clothes as he had left them.

Slipper had found a scrap of lilac ribbon from somewhere and was parading around the room with the treasure hanging from his teeth. Cass watched him for a moment and then moved to the mess outside of the trunk.

She paired the long stockings as best she could and placed them gently into the back of the trunk. She stacked the books into a pile, scanning each cover as she did so. Most of them were related to law and government—subjects Luca had been studying at university—but one of the leather-bound volumes was the same Shakespeare story that Cass had been reading when he had first returned to Venice several weeks earlier. Luca had never been one for stories, especially love stories. Cass couldn't help but wonder if she had changed him the way that Falco had changed her.

Already, the room was looking better. *If only people, and lives, were as easy to fix,* she thought. What was Luca doing right now? Was he scared? Where had he ended up? Was he being held somewhere clean and well lit, with hot water and fine food, or in a rat-infested, watery prison? She hoped Siena's errands would be speedy. Surely some of the servants at the market would be gossiping about the arrest of a nobleman. Once Cass knew more about the charges, she would go to the Palazzo Ducale and demand to speak on Luca's behalf. While she was there, perhaps she could bribe a guard to let her see her fiancé for a minute or two.

She placed the stack of books into Luca's trunk and rose to her feet. As she headed for the door, her lily pendant came unclasped and slipped down inside her bodice.

Cass fished it out, pausing for a moment to admire its beauty. Four silver flower petals framed a circular diamond in the center. She held the pendant up to the light and watched the way the diamond bent and reflected the daylight, scattering sunbeams across Luca's room.

Slipper abandoned his ribbon and threw his tiny body at one of the dancing streaks of light, colliding instead with the wall.

"Slipper!" Cass said, nearly dropping the necklace. "Are you all right?"

As if he understood her words, the cat walked dazedly in a circle and then licked one paw and rubbed his face before launching himself at another rogue ball of light.

Cass returned her attention to the pendant. As she struggled to work the tiny clasp behind her neck, she thought about the day Luca had given it to her. She'd been in the garden, reading, when he had come around the front of the house, a pale lily cradled in his hands.

"*Grazie*," she'd said when he rested the lily next to her on the bench. Her eyes had flipped back to her book. She didn't mean to ignore him, but she was at a good part in her story.

"Cass." He'd angled his head toward the back of the garden, where roses bloomed in the wooden trellis. Stuck among them was another pale pink lily.

Cass had arched an eyebrow, but then given in and closed her book. She and Luca had played this game when she was younger, both at his family palazzo and at Agnese's. Luca used to hide little presents for her and mark the hiding spots with lilies.

A smile playing across her lips, Cass got up to look at the second pink lily that he had poked into the trellis. Behind the delicate petals, a gold box was tied to the wood. Inside it, this necklace. Cass remembered the soft touch of Luca's hands and the tickle of his breath on her skin as he bent low to work the tiny clasp.

The wall clock chimed, and Cass was shocked to discover that she had been in Luca's room nearly two hours. She slipped down the hallway and knocked quietly at her aunt's door. No answer. She peeked in to find that Agnese was sleeping, her body propped up awkwardly in her bed with several embroidered pillows.

Agnese's health had taken a turn for the worse after Madalena's wedding. Sometimes Cass could hear her coughing well into the night. She watched Agnese's chest rise and fall beneath the fabric of her dressing gown. Her breathing seemed labored, her exhalations shallow and raspy. One gnarled hand, fingers twisted and swollen, dangled off the edge of the bed.

Crossing the room to her aunt's side, Cass knelt down and folded Agnese's arm so that her hand now rested on her lap. The old woman didn't even stir, and Cass couldn't bring herself to disturb her.

As Cass retreated into the hall and closed the door to her aunt's chamber, she saw Siena hurrying down the corridor. They both opened their mouths to speak at the same time, but Siena spoke first. "You have to come quickly, Signorina Cass," she said, her eyes wide.

"What is it?" Cass asked. "What's happened?"

Siena struggled to catch her breath. She tucked her trembling fingers into the folds of her dress. "It's my sister," she said, her voice catching. "I found her."

Look for the final book in this
sensual and thrilling series

Forbidden